Embracing the Mountains

by Suleyman Saglam

Translated from Turkish by Nancy F. Ozturk with Adnan Tonguc
Cover illustration: Iidih Wänhä
Cover design: Deniz Akkol
Layout: Tarkan Togo
Printed at Berdan Matbaası, Istanbul, Turkey

ISBN: 975-6663-56-1

Published by:
Çitlembik Publications
Şeyh Bender Sokak 18/5 Asmalımescit Tünel 80050 Istanbul
Tel: 0 212 292 30 32 / 252 31 63 Fax: 0 212 293 34 66
www.citlembik.com.tr / kitap@citlembik.com.tr

Nettleberry, LLC
44030 123rd Street
Eden, South Dakota 57232
www.nettleberry.com

Embracing the Mountains

by Suleyman Saglam

Translated by
Nancy F. Ozturk
with
Adnan Tonguc

Çitlembik Publications 55

1.
Shadows on the Path

A snake slithered along the bare hillside in the heat of the noon sun, its forked tongue flitting in and out and around its mouth. It was hungry. A mother bird had spotted it and, circling through the air, shrieked in anger and warning as she tried to protect her nest. The bright brown eyes of the snake, shining from behind their slits, were intently fixed upon the nest hanging in one of the bramble bushes. Sensing the danger, the tiny chicks uttered almost inaudible cries of fear. The spikes of the bramble protected the nest, but still the snake slowly approached it, millimeter by millimeter. Its dirty yellow spots and earth-color perfectly camouflaged the snake, which completely ignored the cries of the mother bird.

However, suddenly sensing the presence of the freckle-faced blond boy climbing up the steep hill in the strong heat, the snake changed course before disappearing down the unplastered walls of its stone nest. Oblivious to both the snake and the plight of the bird, the child was intent on finishing the climb and reaching the flats. A flock of starlings resting in the mulberry trees that marked the start of the flats suddenly took flight. The red-breasted birds with their black and white wings swooped through the air as they turned in flight and headed for Droplet Rock.

The flats were so named because their surface was almost entirely covered with large flat stones. The stones had absorbed the heat of the hot sun and as he walked, the boy's bare feet stuck to them for a fraction of a second. The path through the flats was bordered on one side by a rough wall and on the other by oleasters, trees with long silvery leaves and thorny branches. Every now and then an apricot tree would pierce through the low oleasters, its broad green leaves casting a shadow on the path.

The child, licking his parched lips, finally reached the far end of the flats. Here the path was bordered by lush bushes, water elders, and tall mulberry trees. His arrival had disturbed a swarm of dragonflies and as he approached, they rose in a cloud from their perch on the bare branches of the apricot trees, making sweeping arches as they flew across the sky. The child found a shady place from which to watch their transparent wings turning and turning towards the sun. Crouching on his haunches, he ate some of the fallen apricots he had found along the path. When he set off again, he took his time, resting whenever he became weary, trying to avoid the low prickle bushes and stay in the shade that the blackberry and sumac bushes provided. When he finally caught sight of the house at the end of the path, he raised his voice: "Grand-Momma!" Grand-Momma!" he shouted. "It's me! I'm here! Hey, Grand-Momma!"

His grandmother heard his shouts and waited for him in the shade of the house. "Sirri, Sirri. What are you doing out in this heat, child? Oh, my poor baby!"

The prickles were now forgotten as the child raced to his grandmother who met him halfway. She held the child, wet with sweat, to her breast and gave him a hard hug before leading him to the house. She talked as they walked: "My poor baby! My little piece of meat! Who sent you out here at this hour? Look at this heat! If your mother had half a brain, she'd know better! My God, there're snakes out there, and scorpions, too!"

The child kept his head buried in his grandmother's side as they walked. He was very happy to be with her. "Allah is my witness, Grand-Momma, my mother doesn't know I came. She thinks I'm still playing with Yashar. He went home, so I came here. I wanted to see my Auntie."

"Now, you are a little devil! In this heat? You could see your auntie some other time. Just look at this. These feet are roasted! Oh my poor baby!"

They were still talking as they climbed up the two steps into the kiosk, a three-walled room with one open side facing the vineyard. His aunt Fadime was inside, resting on one of the *sedir*, the broad rug-covered benches that rimmed the three walls. Fadime was still wrapped in a sheet from her nap, and now opened her eyes wide with surprise upon seeing her nephew.

"Why, Sirri, is that you? Where did you come from in this heat? Allah! Allah!"

She grabbed hold of the child, fondling his sticky hair. Sitting him down next to her, she picked up his grubby feet and planted them full of kisses. Sirri was happy to be in the midst of this flood of love and to sit on his auntie's lap in the coolness of the thick walls. His grandmother drew a small pail of water from the cistern-well. The water was last winter's snow, packed down into the well and now long-since melted. Brown water fleas swam about in the water, but Sirri paid them no mind as he drank, filtering the fleas through his teeth as best he could. His grandmother caressed the silky strands of his hair and then washed his dirty, scratched feet with the cool water. His grandmother was still muttering her displeasure as she washed and dried his feet.

The child was hungry, so they brought him a plate of new grapes and two of the small flattish bread loaves they had just baked on the iron grille of their outdoor oven. As soon as he had eaten, he took his slingshot out of his pocket and began to play the little man for them as he told them how his older brother, Nuhmemed, had managed to hit and kill a partridge. His grandmother and Aunt Fadime were delighted to listen to the child's talk, and sometimes asked him questions that they knew would keep him talking. He told them all the news he had about his mother, father, brother, about the malaria going around, about the starlings in the mulberry trees, and about the cow that had run away from one vineyard to the next. Time passed quickly and, before they knew it, it was time for the late afternoon prayer. Snake Mountain was now casting its huge shadow across the valley, and the racket made by a flock of partridges resting in the sumac bushes echoed, bouncing off of the great boulders and stones.

The flock of partridges was being led by a huge male, his red beak and colorful breast visible from as far away as the house. As the partridges walked through the tall grasses and shrubs towards the crags higher up, the cry of their male leader fell upon the valley like a clear and narrow waterfall.

Snake Mountain's long shadow passed over the house, the path, and the trees, settling a sheet of coolness with it as it fell. The red starlings again came to rest in the mulberry trees that were thick with finger-long berries. The crickets fell silent. The sun was signaling that it was soon to set, and Sirri also fell silent, as though he were asking for advice. He knew that his mother would be worried and that he had to get home before his father came back from the city. His Aunt Fadime wished he could stay with them, but she, too, realized that he had to go back home.

So Sirri set off, sucking on the large pasha candy his grand-mother had pressed into his hand, holding his slingshot, and pre-tending to be an accomplished hunter. His grandmother and aunt walked him to the beginning of the long path and watched until he was out of sight. The child walked down the now shadowy dirt path until he reached the stone-paved flats. The blackberries, mulberries, and sumac bushes were gone now as he hurried his steps to reach the large elder at the far side of the flats.

Sirri was skipping down the deserted path when he sudden-ly saw a man standing near the elder tree. The man looked strange, probably because he was wearing clothes that seemed very unusual to the child. His trousers were the kind that sol-diers wore, but he had a red shawl-like wrap on his head with tassels hanging on one side. A kind of belt containing bullets spanned his chest. The child was instantly filled with curiosity about the man, but the curiosity soon turned to fear when he saw that the man also had a huge rifle hanging off his shoulder. The fear caused Sirri to hunker down into the bushes so that he could observe the man without being seen himself.

This strange man was facing down the hill, looking through binoculars. Sirri was glad that the man's back was turned to him. The man turned slowly as he looked, first at Enamel Rock, then Threshing Place, and then Shadowy Rock. Maybe he was watching the eagles as they took flight from Filthy Rock or was just looking at the grand appearance of Brave Rock. The child thought the man must be familiar with this place because he knew which way to look.

The man next went through a bag at his side. He was looking for something. The valley was completely quiet and the child held his breath as he lay as still as possible. He watched as the man took out a canteen and drank deeply. The man then grabbed his rifle by its strap and began walking in the direction of Snake Mountain. The child thought that the man walked very fast, as if there were a sail at his back, as he traveled along the goat trail that now lay in deep shadows. Sirri was petrified as he lay under the shrubs watching the man's departure. The man walked all the way to Droplet Rock and then was lost from sight when he entered the oleaster grove.

Nothing could stop Sirri now—no snakes, no thorns, nothing. He ran down the rocky incline as fast as he could. He didn't even register that his feet were scraping against the stones and had started bleeding. In a heartbeat he found himself at the lower road. Sweat pouring off of him, his little heart beating rapidly in his breast, he didn't stop running, even when he got to the dirt road, but ran instead all the way to the house.

Little Mom was the first to see him. Little Mom, the wife of his father's oldest brother, had a broad face with rosy cheeks and a plump body. She was appalled to see the scared expression on the child's face and his bleeding feet.

"Slow down now," she said, "What's happened? What made you run so?"

The child was winded and so spoke in starts:

"I saw a man, a man," he said and continued, "He was holding a rifle and had a red thing around his head."

"What? You saw a man with a rifle? Where? Where was he?"

The child pointed to a spot in the hills.

"I saw him at the Stone Flats. He was under the big elder tree and was looking this way with his binoculars. He had binoculars and he had bullets, too. He went like a sailboat. He went to Droplet Rock and then into the trees. And then I couldn't see him anymore."

"Allah! Allah!" she said. "Who could that have been? Maybe it was Osman, Sariahmed's Osman. Sometimes he carries a shotgun. But what's he doing around here at this hour?"

"I'm not sure," said Sirri. "It might have been Sariahmed's Osman. But he wasn't walking—he was flying!"

Sirri was still so engrossed in what he had seen that he hadn't even realized his feet were bleeding and full of thorns. He tried to describe the man he had seen. Hearing her son's excited voice, Hayriye stepped across the broad stone threshold. Hayriye was a pretty woman with light, freckled skin. She was popular in the neighborhood for she had a big heart and was known far and wide for her courage. She rode a horse with abandon and could fire two guns at a time.

"What's going on? Where have you been? I've been looking all over for you and couldn't find you anywhere."

Sirri was still excited.

"Mommy, I saw a man with a rifle. He had a rifle and binoculars and a lot of bullets and a red cloth on his head. He went up to the Snake."

"A man with a rifle? Who was the man with the rifle?"

Little Mom stared into Sirri's face.

"He's really frightened," she said. "Scared of that man, a man with a gun, at this time of day. It must have been Sariahmed's Osman. Who else would be walking around with a shotgun?"

"Allah! Allah! Why would he be wandering around here during the day? He never comes down from the mountain!"

"I swear to God, Mommy. He was looking at the valley. He was looking with his binoculars across to the other side, looking at Brave Rock and Threshing Place and Net Hill. I hid and watched him. He didn't see me. Then he went up to Droplet Rock."

His mother stepped out of the door and walked towards her son. Their house echoed the basic form of the summer homes of this district. It was simple and functional and suited to the hot and dry Kayseri summers. Since life was mostly spent out-of-doors, the only shelter the family really needed was in the form of shade from the piercing sun. The house consisted of a large, windowless room with an arched ceiling—the *tol*—built on ground level. This room was perfect for storing supplies and equipment and sheltering the family in the rare case of rain or wind. An outside staircase led to the second floor "kiosk," a room with three walls and an open wall facing the roof terrace. Because it received full sunlight, the terrace was used for drying the fruits and vegetables grown in the vineyard. The *seki*, the yard in front of the *tol*, actually constituted the family's main living quarters. The packed clay ground of the yard was kept swept and neat. In addition to the couple of high trees and grape arbors that provided shade, this area also held the family's cook stove, mud brick oven, and water well, along with wood and stone benches for resting. It was here that the daily food was prepared, that the children studied their lessons, and that neighbors chatted over glasses of tea. At some distance from the house were the stables and their yard covered with loose sand to absorb any dirt carried in by animals or muddy boots.

Terraced vineyards and plots stretching along the sloping fields in front of the house were interconnected via a series of dirt-packed stairs. The vegetables were grown on raised plots surrounded by body-width ditches, allowing for easier crop tending and irrigation. The houses in this district had no doors or windows. There were few belongings of any value—the iron grill, the tub for washing laundry, and the pots and pans for cooking—and so there was no need for doors, let alone locks. The animals were considered to be the most valuable property of the folks in these parts. Each family had at least one cow and some also had donkeys or horses. These latter families were considered privileged and better off than the others. It was a disaster for any family if their animals became ill or were stolen.

Hayriye was now intent on hearing for herself what had happened. "Get over here this very minute," she said as she grabbed her youngest son by the arm. "What business did you have going up there in the first place?"

"I went to see Grand-Momma. I wanted to see my Auntie. I was playing with Yashar but he got a thorn in his foot. And it hurt him so he went home. So I went up to see Grand-Momma. Then on my way home, I saw the man under the big elder tree."

Hayriye looked at her son's bleeding feet.

"Your feet are bleeding. The man might have been Sariahmed's Osman. But now get over here. Your father's going to be here any minute. Get in here and let's get you washed up."

Sirri did not hesitate to obey his mother. Resmiye, the *evlat-lik*, a girl from an impoverished family adopted into this family to help out at home in return for the help she herself received from her adopted kin, took Sirri's feet in her hands and started picking out the thorns. She then washed the boy thoroughly with water she had drawn from the well.

Hayriye couldn't make sense of what her son had told her. If it really was Sariahmed's Osman that Sirri had seen, what was that rebel doing in these parts? And at that hour of the day? She drew her son to her knees and started asking him detailed questions. It had to be Osman. Who else would be carrying binoculars and a shotgun?

The sun had turned. Shadows now filled the rocky crevices that sheltered the houses. The augurs of night, the swallows, dipped and dove as they returned to their nests in large flocks.

"What's that outlaw doing in these parts?" muttered Hayriye to herself. "God know there's something good in everything. But what's the good in this?"

She climbed the stairs to the kiosk and took out the family shotgun that was kept in the wooden cupboard built deep into the thick stone walls. She knew what she was doing when she opened the gun and then sighted it. Her expertise was evident as she snapped several bullets into the shotgun's cartridge. She opened the mechanism and then snapped it shut again until she was sure that a bullet had entered the chamber. Then holding the gun over her shoulder, she walked out to the hard clay-packed terrace rooftop. Standing on the edge of the terrace she shouted out to her neighbors that she was about to fire her gun and that they shouldn't be afraid.

"Mother Emine, Big Sister, don't be afraid. Do you hear me? Don't be afraid now. I'm going to shoot off my shotgun," she shouted.

Since her family's house was situated further up the slope, the neighbors had full view of what she was doing. They signaled that they had understood. Hayriye checked the safety before she aimed the gun in the direction of Snake Mountain. Narrowing her eyes, she aimed at Droplet Rock. The sounds of the gun echoed through the mountains and high, splitting sounds erupted as the bullets bounced off the bare rock, sending a cloud of dust into the air. The bullets seemed to embrace the mountains, drawing them nearer to each other and to the people who lived at their feet. The shotgun blasts, echoing repeatedly, gave the neighborhood a feeling of power as the noise wiped away their fear. Hayriye was happy to listen to the commotion she was making. She felt like a tigress, bent on protecting her nest and her young.

The show was over. She took her shotgun back into the kiosk and leaned it against a wall before picking up the now-blackened bullet casings and lining them up on the low stone wall of the terrace. Meanwhile, the neighborhood calm had been jolted into excitement as everyone's curiosity was piqued by the show they had just witnessed.

Aunt Fadime, the nearest neighbor, was first to call out: "Hey girl, what's happening over there? Why'd you shoot off your gun?"

And then Aunt Pembe: "Sister Hayriye, what's going on over there?"

And then all the way from the Threshing Place came Nezahat's call: "Little Mom, hey, are you having problems? Why did you shoot your gun?"

Hayriye shouted back and gave hand signals as best she could. "Sariahmed's Osman is in the neighborhood! Sirri saw him in the vineyards at the rock hill. I shot off the gun to let him know that there are people here. Don't be afraid! Don't be afraid!"

Rather than assuaging their fear, this piece of news caused a blanket of apprehension to spread across the district. Everyone started exchanging news of what he or she knew and had seen. The government had not been able to bring in Sariahmed's Osman. Every so often, the gendarmes—the government soldiers who policed rural areas—would come in force, surround the neighborhood, and then search each and every house. They looked everywhere for Osman, but were never able to find him. The gendarmes would get another search order and begin looking into every single hole in which a deserting soldier might possibly hide, go through every abandoned shelter, and search every single cave, but they still just couldn't manage to find Osman.

The gardens in the backyards of the neighborhood houses were surrounded by thick walls of piled stones. When the soldiers conducted a thorough search, they found built deep into these walls many shelters that had been used by deserters. The gendarmes therefore wrecked though these holes, leaving the walls in a rather forlorn state, with the burrows torn apart and exposed for all to view.

When Aunt Fadime's husband Musa deserted from the army, he spent years living in one of those burrows. That exposed hole would therefore invoke a rush of memories whenever Aunt Fadime passed by. Hayriye herself was afraid of these holes and kept her distance from them, fearing that one of the deserters might just jump out at her if she got too near.

Kemal was Sirri's brother, older by a couple of years. He had a strange head, one that got broader from chin to forehead, hence his nickname, "Kettlehead." That day he had climbed Arpa Mountain to collect goat clover. He had packed the clover into a canvas bag and carried it back to the vineyard. Now home, he understood just by looking at his younger brother that something had gone awry, and so asked his mother what was going on.

"I shot off the shotgun," she said. "Sirri saw Sariahmed's Osman. I shot off the gun so the outlaw would know that we are here and so the neighbors won't be scared.

"Allah, Allah. Where did Sirri see him?"

"Just on top of the hill at the flats. He had gone up to see his Grand-Momma. Can you imagine? In bare feet, and in this heat!" She paused a bit and then turned to Kemal. "Put the clover in the feeding trough," she said, "and then wash up fast. Your father should be home any second now."

Kemal took no heed of the load on his back. "So you shot off the gun, huh?" he said. "I wish I'd been home. Where did you put the casings? Do you really think it was Osman?"

"Well, I don't know for sure whether it was him or not, but Sirri saw a man on the flats with a rifle and binoculars. Who else could it be? Who else carries a rifle and binoculars? Come on, now, Son, stop fiddling around and get moving. Your father'll be here any minute now!"

Kemal stamped and stomped his way to the stairs. The stairs to the upper floor of the house were squeezed between the building's sidewall and two huge rocks formations. They led down to the ground floor yard, and from there to the stables built on even lower ground. Kemal was careful not to step on the eggshells that were scattered at the opening of the snake hole. When a black snake had slithered out of that hole a few weeks earlier, his mother had said that the snake was now the guardian of the house. His father wanted no talk of guard-snakes and so had tried to kill the intruder, but their mother had been firm in her objections. "Killing the snake would bring bad luck on this house," she insisted. Then the snake became so brave it started coming out of its hole to sunbathe in the *seki*. One day Hayriye also decided that she had had enough of the snake and swore: "If you come out of that hole one more time, I implore Allah to deprive you of Mohammad's good favor." Apparently the oath worked, for no one had seen the snake since.

Kemal put the clover in the stone trough, and the fragrance of its bright yellow flowers filled the stable. The children loved to watch their horse Jeylan eat the clover with such pleasure. Now freed of his load, Kemal climbed back up the stairs and stopped when he came next to Sirri.

"So Kid, what have you been up to? Mom says you saw Sariahmed's Osman. Is that right? Where did you see him?" Sirri was happy to fill his brother in on all the details: the path, the elder tree, the soldier pants, the red scarf, and—especially—the binoculars, bullets, and rifle.

"I hid real quiet," he said and then asked: "Do you think he would've cut me up if he'd seen me?"

"Get off it!" was his brother's quick reply. "Why would he want to cut up a kid like you? He probably just wanted to scout out the area. Let's wait and see what Father says," he continued.

15

"Maybe he'll tell the gendarmes and they'll capture him for once and all!"

Actually, Kemal, too, had been frightened to hear that the outlaw was nearby. He washed up with the water brought to him by Resmiye and then sat down next to Sirri on the blanket. The boys were soon joined by their older brother Ahmed, the second born, who had spent the day helping his uncle in the vineyards.

Evening was falling and the sky had changed from blue to a deep purple. The only sound was that of the beating wings of mountain swifts. As the oil lamps were slowly lit one by one, their flitting lights could be seen across the hilltops. Only two families in the area had alcohol lanterns, or "luxury lights," as they were commonly called; Sirri's family had one and the Degirmenci sisters had the other. Lighting the luxury lantern required expertise. It had to be emptied, and cleaned, and then, once lit, pumped and pumped to just the right point to heat up its glass barrel. Hayriye was an expert at this operation. She sat with her boys on the blanket and worked at getting it lit before adjusting its needle by pushing it back and forth several times. Once she had it lit correctly, she hung it from a hook on the wall.

Resmiye was also busy. She was laying out the dinner meal on the blanket. First she put down a large sheet-like cloth and then placed a round low table over the cloth. On the table she placed wooden spoons and soft flat bread that she had just baked on the flat iron grille. The dinner meal was cooked and being kept warm on a corner of the stove.

Scorpions come out at night and if they see a bright light they run to it, in a kind of crazy suicide. It was at this hour that scorpions would emerge from their hiding places in the stone wall that lined the *seki*. Hayriye was vigilant in protecting her family and kept an eye out for any scorpions that would dare come near. She always kept a wooden shoe at her side in the evening. She was a great shot with her shoe and could easily hit any scorpion that happened to run out into the *seki*. As she threw her shoe she would curse her worst possible oath: "Let your lungs scream out their pain!" Hayriye made sure her children did not get off the hairy blanket for scorpions could not walk on its rough surface.

The silence of the evening was broken by the sounds of hoof beats. The group of riders had entered the neighborhood road. The family dog, Yellow, greeted the men with loud barking. Sirri's cousin Tarik was the first to get home, leaving the group at the gate to his father's house.

The group got smaller as each man rode into his own compound and the air was full of loud farewells and the noise of each man's family as he was greeted and helped. It wasn't long before the children's father arrived on his own red horse and the family's eldest son, Nuhmemed, arrived on his donkey. Nuhmemed's donkey was short but strong. The younger boys loved to mock their brother on his donkey as his feet almost dragged on the ground. The poor donkey seemed almost hidden under Nuhmemed's large frame, but still managed to swiftly trot along.

The men first stopped at the sand *seki*, the yard covered with fine sand that would absorb any dirt carried by animals or boots. Nuhmemed easily swung the embroidered carpetbags off the backs of the animals and laid them on the stone seats. The bags were filled with watermelons and honeydews. The children's father, Mehmet Efendi, climbed down from his horse and shook the dust from his suit. He was holding a small bottle of aniseed *raki* wrapped in fine paper. This he carefully handed to his wife.

"I'm going to drink a bit tonight, so you'd best prepare some *meze*."

As he straightened his clothes, the children could spot the pistol he wore tucked into his waistband. They were fascinated by this gun. They knew their father was brave and could protect them no matter what happened. Their father, though, sensed something was amiss.

"Wife, the children are acting strange. What's the matter? Did something happen?"

Hayriye remained expressionless as she broke the news:

"They just got a little scared, that's all."

"Why? What happened? Was it a snake?"

"No, no, nothing like that. What happened is that our Sirri saw Sariahmed's Osman."

17

"He saw Sariahmed's Osman? Come on now!"

"That's what he says, at least. He went up to see his grand-mother and on the way down he saw the outlaw at the top of the hill."

Sirri could no longer hold back his excitement, and with his childish language told his father everything he had done and seen that day.

Mehmet Efendi was now set on allaying his child's fear.

"So, why didn't you catch him? A big boy like you! You weren't scared, were you?"

"No, Daddy, I wasn't scared at all. But he had two belts of bullets. He wore them crossed in front. How could I have caught him?"

"I'm just teasing you, Son. Of course you couldn't catch him. Even the government and all the soldiers can't catch him, so how could you? But one day he will get caught. That's for sure."

Mehmet Efendi realized that his middle son was feeling left out.

"So what did you do today, Kemal? Could you cut the clover? Or did you get carried away seeing Sariahmed's Osman too?"

"No, Daddy, I didn't see anybody. I cut a big bag of clover and put it in the stable."

Mehmet Efendi climbed to the kiosk and took a seat on one of the rug-covered benches lining its walls. "What's that devil doing around these parts?" he asked his wife.

"Whatever, he probably came down to visit the Crazy Sergeant. But he must be up to something. He's an outlaw, after all!"

Resmiye entered the kiosk carrying a tray with the *raki* and the little plates of *meze*, the type of food that traditionally accompanied this drink. Mehmet Efendi cooled off the *raki* with a bit of melted snow water and started to eat his *meze*. Green onions had been finely chopped and mashed with white cheese. And a melon, newly cooled in the underground ice-house, had been cut into pieces. The bread loaves were fresh and hot and there was hot and spicy chemen to spread on the bread.

The kiosk offered a view of the entire valley. Sitting here was like being perched in an eagle's nest. The city, lit up in the midst of the night, could be seen from this vantage point. The oil lights of the other vineyards were like fireflies, their lights flickering through the purple sky. It was at this hour that Mehmet Efendi best loved his vineyard, the peace and the quiet of it.

Mehmet Efendi, the owner of a shoe store on Kayseri's busiest street, was well liked and respected by all. He had been born and raised in one of the small city's poorer neighborhoods and as a young man he had joined one of the country's major political parties with the hope of gaining enough influence to help his district build a school. In time he had worked his way up the party bureaucracy and was elected as a city council member.

As a child he was only able to finish the second grade of an Islamic parochial school before he had to leave school to help his father as a tailor. Both of his father's brothers had died in the long Ottoman wars of the early twentieth century. The first died in a battle near Baghdad, shot in the head by an Arab bullet. The second fought in the Gallipoli War with a division that was victorious in ejecting the English from Turkish soil. From that front this uncle was sent to march to the Allahuekber Mountains to fight against the Russians, but that was the last the family ever heard from him. They never learned if he had died from the cold, from an enemy bullet, or from one of the diseases that swept through the ranks. They only knew that he was just one of the thirty thousand soldiers who never returned from the Russian front. The family responsibilities were great and that was why Mehmet Efendi had to leave school at such an early age to help his father.

By the age of nine he had become an accomplished tailor and opened his first shop. He learned the Arabic script in school, but only learned the Latin script later through his own efforts. He never did learn to write well, however, and this shortcoming plagued him throughout his life. "If I had stayed in school, I might have become a great and influential man," he would say sadly.

Captain Kuddusi Bey, an officer in the Ottoman forces, had acted as the go-between in arranging his marriage to Hayriye,

19

the daughter of a well-to-do family engaged in trade. Because Mehmet Efendi had had an accident that caused him to lose his sight in one eye, her family considered him a good candidate for a son-in-law! Seeing as he would not be conscripted into the army, they figured that any grandchildren born to the match would have the chance of growing up with a father. So they gave their daughter's hand to the poor tailor, never guessing that the Republic would be formed out of the ashes of the Ottoman Empire, and that all the wars would soon cease in the new country.

Now the rest of the world, however, was fighting the horrible and bloody Second World War. Turkey was not yet drawn into this global catastrophe, but everyone was on edge, expecting war to be declared at any moment.

Mehmet Efendi benefited much from his wife's better education, her wide knowledge, and her culture. It was from her that he learned how to tie a tie properly, wear neatly pressed trousers, learn the Latin alphabet, and read a daily newspaper. And his circle of acquaintances and friends increased as well. He and Hayriye formed a good and happy match. They prospered, had children, and were a happy family.

Mehmet Efendi loved his *bag*, his vineyard. The vineyards of Kayseri are built in the foothills of the mountains ringing the valley. To escape the heat of the city the people "migrate" each spring to their vineyards, usually a compound made up of a stone and mud house, stables and sheds, and long fields of grapes. Each of these houses also has vegetable plots and many fruit trees. The houses of the vineyards tend to be clustered together for security, yet still far enough apart to give each family plenty of privacy and "room to stretch." Mehmet Efendi's vineyard was built in the foothills of Snake Mountain, a long and snake-like mountain that throws its cool shadows on the vineyards nestling at its feet and stirs up a cool breeze to blow against the faces of its residents.

The vineyard had belonged to Mehmet Efendi's family for generations and many of the other nearby vineyards were owned by close relatives. He loved this place. He loved the bare and wild view of the mountains and he loved the crisp and clear air. Recently, however, the place had begun to leave a bitter taste in his mouth. Every now and then there would be a raid, with the gendarmes storming into the district and tearing everything apart in their search for Osman. That fugitive living in the hills above them was threatening them all, threatening their serene and secure way of life.

"Wife, I'm thinking that maybe we should leave this place. Our boys are almost grown now and we've spent our whole lives fighting snakes and scorpions. Osman and his gang are trouble and I'm afraid that their trouble is going to find us one day."

Hayriye was sitting next to her husband and turned to stare at him long and hard. "Now you listen to me. You know full well that Osman would never hurt us. We have nothing to fear from him."

"You think I'm afraid of him? Why should I be afraid of him? I've had my share of problems in my life and I've never been scared before, so why should I be scared now? But you know that the house isn't big enough anymore. The boys are growing up. A lot of our friends have moved to Hisarcik. I was thinking that maybe we should buy some land there and build us a better house. They've got roads there, and water, too. We can visit with our neighbors."

"Get off it Mehmet Efendi! Don't be bringing a new set of burdens to lay on my shoulders! What's wrong with this vineyard? And the neighbors we have here? You just stop worrying. Each new day brings new solutions. Allah is great. One day these rebels may just disappear."

Mehmet Efendi felt much better, soothed both by his wife's confident words and by the effects of the *raki*. He agreed with his wife that she had done the right thing in firing off the shotgun. The rebels had to know that the people living here were not just sitting ducks. He took his pistol out of its holster and also shot off several rounds towards the mountain. Upon hearing him, his neighbors all did the same, and the evening air was split with the crash and ring of pistols and shotguns being fired.

Mehmet Efendi was himself fired up, fired up by the excitement, the noise, and the *raki*. He called down to his son

Nuhmemed, ordering him to come and wind up the gramophone and play, "When the Acacias Bloom." Mehmet Efendi loved that folk song and added his own deep voice to the clear voice of the female singer. He thought about his children. He tried to act like a stern disciplinarian with them as he didn't want them to grow up spoiled and soft, but he was a gentle man and loved them dearly.

"Come on, Wife," he said, "you'd better put the food on. The children must be hungry."

The family took their places on the blanket around the low table and spread the large tablecloth over their laps. Each ate with his own spoon from a common large pot of food set in the middle of the table. After the meal the children continued to sit on the blanket, watching the stars and conversing among themselves.

It was time for the children to retire and the beds to be prepared. Nuhmemed was the oldest, so he had a bed of his own. It was a folding camp bed, a bit rickety, but a private bed nonetheless. It was unfolded in a corner of the *seki* with a soft mattress spread over it. The whole bed was then topped with a mosquito net. The legs of the bed were such that it was impossible for scorpions or other nasty bugs to climb up into it. Kemal and Sirri were in awe of the bed and their big brother's right to it. Once the bed had been prepared, he never even let them sit on it (for that might flatten the plumped-up mattress, or so he said). They were full of envy when he would climb onto the soft mattress under the mosquito net.

Resmiye would next prepare the younger boys' beds. A thick blanket was taken out of the deep wooden cupboard recessed into the stone wall and was spread in another corner of the *seki*. Then two small mattresses were plumped up and laid adjacent to one another. Next came fresh sheets and small pillows. The mattresses were topped with thick wool-filled comforters as the air in the hills became quite cool at night. Ahmed's bed was also set up in another corner of the *seki*. Once in their cozy beds, the children would whisper to each other as they watched the stars filling the sky. Their eyes followed the Milky Way before drifting to the empty blue space encircled by the mountains ringing around them. The fragrance of hundreds of different flowers and clover and oats would blend together and they would inhale this sweetness as they drifted off.

The sky that night, too, was filled with stars. A cool breeze licked against the boulders and the vineyards before passing into the valley below. Mehmet Efendi and his wife Hayriye were sitting together in the kiosk when they suddenly saw a large tarantula run past, its form reflected in the light of the luxury lamp. Hayriye picked up her wooden shoe and flung it at the insect. It was a direct hit and the dangerous insect was dead.

"Look at that disgusting thing," said Mehmet Efendi. He had always been afraid of bugs of all kinds and this spider with its sometimes-lethal bite was even more frightening to him. "Let's get rid of it before the children see it."

Hayriye was not moved by any of this. She quietly stood up and began to prepare their bed in the kiosk. Theirs too was a soft mattress on the floor and a single long pillow which they shared, in keeping with the wedding wish bestowed upon them by friends and family—"may you live your lives on one pillow." She turned her back and dressed for bed: ankle-length fine woolen drawers and a long sleeved undershirt. There was nothing left for Mehmet Efendi to do but to follow suit. He checked out the room and made sure the gramophone was covered. After undressing, he hung his suit in the cupboard and placed his gun under his end of the pillow. It was very late and the intensity of the stars had waned. When he turned off the lamp, theirs was the last house in the district to become completely dark. Everyone in the neighborhood was now fast asleep in the overwhelming darkness and silence of the night mountains, broken only occasionally by the snort of a horse in the stable or the far off call of an owl.

Not many hours later smoke began to curl upwards from the cook stoves and chimneys and the air came alive with the crowing of roosters and neighing and stamping of horses. Affluent homes had rich breakfasts: bowls of hot soup, a selection of cheese, olives, and jams, and soft boiled eggs eaten with freshly baked loaves of bread. Poorer families ate their bread loaves with bunches of freshly picked grapes. Those about to set off for the city were busy getting the horses and donkeys ready as they threw the carpetbags over the animals' backs.

Nuhmemed was giving Sirri a piggyback ride around the low hills. Nuhmemed's nose had been broken in a neighborhood soccer match and now tilted slightly to one side giving him a comical yet sweet expression. His forehead was broad and his thick black hair spilled down over it. He was in his last year at the Commercial High School that had just opened a few years earlier. He was proud of the school's uniform cap with its red stripes and proud of the school's modern new building as well.

Mehmet Efendi was still in the kiosk getting ready for work. He sat on one of the benches with his shaving cloth tucked around him as he shaved from a small basin of water while looking in a little mirror perched on one of the back cushions. He was pleased with the results of this morning grooming. He wasted no more time and went down to the *seki*. He spent a few minutes watching his sons play. How he loved them! But still it was best not to spoil them, so he called out, "Hey, don't you boys have anything better to do than make all that noise and disturb the whole neighborhood?"

Mehmet Efendi's left eye had been left sightless by a reckless stone thrown at him by his cousin Chil Agha when they were both nine years old. His family had done everything they could to salvage the eye. They bandaged it with wet bread, they had a holy man blow incense around it, and they even had molten lead poured into a basin over his head to break the evil spirit's power, but nothing had worked. He never regained the sight in that eye.

At least it was a handicap that didn't matter much, he thought. Most people weren't even aware of it, and he cut quite a respectable figure with his wide-brimmed hat, his shoe-brush mustache, his navy blue suit with the vest with its watch pocket, and his highly glossed black shoes. He was well liked by the other shopkeepers in Kayseri. His wife's teaching him to read the Latin alphabet proved to be a tremendous advantage to him and gave him a position not enjoyed by many in his circle.

The family was late in setting off that morning. Nuhmemed had wasted time playing with his brothers and was late in saddling the animals. Now he had to speed up the process before he could lead the horse out into the sand *seki*. His father was on the horse and out of the yard before Nuhmemed could jump on the back of his donkey and get it moving with shouts of "Deh! Choosh!" The poor animal's legs trembled as it hurried to catch up with the faster horse.

As the riders set off they could hear the cries of a flock of partridges coming from Barley Mountain. Nuhmemed's cousin Tarik cupped his hand over his ear trying to hear exactly which boulder the sound was coming from. Nuhmemed was sure that the sound was coming from Sumac Fields and was anxious to go and see for himself, but his father insisted that this was not the time for hunting.

"Son, you can never make a living hunting partridges. If there's something to be done, it's waiting for us at the store. Quit messing around and keep riding."

"I am riding Father. I wasn't thinking of going hunting anyway."

The two young men listened in silence to the call of the partridges. The strong respect they had for their elders meant that they had to do as directed. Tarik's donkey was large, a tall Cypriot breed. It was almost as high as a horse and Nuhmemed felt humiliated because of his own donkey's small size.

The men were now gone and so those who stayed at the vineyard started their daily routines. The breakfast things had to be cleaned up. The mattresses lying in the *seki* had to be picked up, folded into threes, and placed in the deep storage cupboards. The upper *seki* had to be swept clean while the sand in the lower *seki* had to be raked back to an even surface. The children were free to be children. Resmiye told them about the dead tarantula in the kiosk and their first job was to go and have a look. Its head was frightful, even if the insect was obviously very dead. They poured some of the lamp's alcohol over it and then set it on fire, watching its carcass shrivel and disappear. This ceremony didn't last long, however, as their mother saw what they were doing and angrily put out the fire and sent them down to the *seki*. The children went out into the fields to play hide and seek.

The day was extremely hot. Tortoises fought with each other while the crickets filled the air with their chirping. The air was moist and heavy and seemed to sink and stick to the trees. An eagle ascended from the crest of Snake Mountain and floated through the sky, on the lookout for prey.

2.
Echoes of Guns and Birds

I t wasn't yet the season for boiling the grapes into molasses, but Osman had arrived. He used his binoculars to check out every part of the valley. When he saw the cloud of dust at Blacksmith's Writing, he knew that this amount of dust could only be kicked up by a group of mounted gendarmes. It meant that the gendarmes were again trying to find him.

Major Ibrahim Bey was leading the company of mounted gendarmes. With his highly polished boots, his binoculars, and his huge pistol, the major looked very imposing as he sat high on his horse, leading his group of men. Behind him, his mounted troops completely covered the road. The horses didn't seem bothered by the dust they kicked up as they trotted at a brisk pace. The soldiers had short-barreled carbines hung crossways across their chests and cartridges hanging from their sides. Their uniforms were covered with a thick layer of dust as they rode in pursuit of the fugitive.

Major Ibrahim Bey was tall and dark and possessed the piercing eyes of an eagle. His nose was broad with a long hook and his eyes were dark black under his thick and bushy eyebrows. He had sworn to capture Osman. He knew that Sariahmed's Osman had to be hiding somewhere in the Snake Mountain and that he might even be watching him at that very instant. For some reason or other the people in the vineyards and the local villagers seemed intent on protecting him. The major had done everything possible to find Osman. He had searched everywhere and surrounded many places. He had questioned hundreds of people and had had the soles of the feet of some of those same people whipped till they bled, yet in his quest to capture Osman he remained unsuccessful.

From his perch Osman watched the company move along the trail. He knew exactly which roads and paths they would take. These were Osman's mountains. He knew every rock, every crag on Little Snake. He knew every hole and every bush. He knew where the spring poured out of the mountain to flow down to the valleys.

Osman and his gang of vigilantes were originally a group of young volunteers who joined forces to fight against those leading the local uprisings and the invading armies during and in the aftermath of the First World War. They managed to make life difficult for those foreigners, but they didn't stop there. When the gang needed money or supplies, they robbed mail wagons and even a train or two. They also stormed into some villages, taking what they needed. It was these kinds of acts that made them into outlaws.

Their lives changed though with the general amnesty. Most accepted the pardon and returned to the city. Some of the latter managed to blend in with the common folk, while others gained political power and positions of authority.

When Osman was caught and imprisoned, he expected help from his old comrade, Hatem Agha, but instead of coming to his aid, his former partner made sure that Osman was blamed for every single crime that had ever been committed in the province. Twice the Agha had even tried to have Osman killed in prison. Osman managed both times to save himself before later using his quick wit to escape. That's why he now had to hide out in these mountains. His escape had frightened Hatem Agha who tried to do everything he could to get Osman recaptured.

Hatem Agha had become a figure of some importance in the city. He had managed to cleanse his reputation of his rather unsavory past and become as white as Bursa flour. He also managed to become a person of power in the leading party. He was smart and he cultivated the kinds of behavior that made him into a respected personage. He was trusted by the governors, the parliamentarians, the mayors, and the judges and they gave him responsibility over the hapless populace.

The treachery of his former comrade was a heavy blow for Osman to bear. Hatem Agha had the ear of all the officials and managed to poison them against Osman. The common people, though, understood what was going on and they supported Osman, while the government officials supported Hatem Agha. Osman represented a symbol of hope for the little people. When he was in the mountains they felt they had a kind of power on their side. It was in him that they sought their own deliverance.

The world was in the grip of the Second World War and Turkey, too, was engulfed in these horrible global events. The Germans had stormed across Europe and were beating on the Turkish border gate at Edirne. The war had cut Turkey off from the rest of the world and Turkey was suffering from terrible shortages. Kerosene, bread, flour, sugar, and salt were all rationed, these goods now being distributed to the people by their local officials. The people struggled and worked the best they could to make do with what they could grow in their own gardens. In the winter they tried to keep warm in the fierce cold of Kayseri with tiny fires lit in copper braziers.

The people were poverty stricken and lived under the long arms of a strong and powerful government. It was not surprising that they supported and cherished a fugitive like Osman. It was due to the general despair of the people that he managed to remain hidden. He had become a mythic figure and stories about him abounded. Each time the gendarmes were unsuccessful in their attempts to capture him, new stories would spread around the countryside: Osman, they said, had single-handedly fought against a company of soldiers and had sent them running away.

Hatem Agha would lose sleep whenever these stories reached his ears. Of course Hatem Agha, too, kept up his end of the long struggle between the two men. Whenever a robbery or other violent crime occurred in or around the city, he immediately began a whisper campaign that it had been the work of Osman. In this way he tried to get the people to turn against Osman.

The soldiers had begun to climb the path leading along the creek. Osman watched every turn the horses made as they climbed the twisting path. The major's horse was strongheaded. It reared forward and back, twisting and turning with the road and leading the string of horses behind it. Brother-in-law's Creek flowed between two tall cliffs and so the creek bed was dark and deep. Oak trees grew among the boulders on both banks of the creek. Further up the slopes the oak trees were replaced by tall white cedars that seemed to be pointing into the heavens. The creek curved its way through the rocky chasm and the goat path curved with it.

The soldiers had to be very familiar with this place if they were ever to capture Osman. The major himself had the advantage of knowing this place very well. The major knew that Osman had most likely been watching the mounted party since they left the city and that by now he had either gone down to the swamplands or had reached one of the villages in the vicinity. There were houses up and down the valley willing to hide Osman for nights on end. Villagers respected this fugitive and would themselves prepare his mattress on their floors. The major had gotten wind of this several times, but each time he surrounded such a house the villager had managed to hide Osman from their sight or help him escape.

As the soldiers traveled that day, the people came out of their houses to watch their procession. Osman's wife Hurmet, who was currently staying with Osman's niece Semiha and her husband, Blacksmith Mustafa, was among those who watched the soldiers as they climbed up the mountain in search of her husband. Hurmet was a beauty with pale skin, dark eyebrows, and black eyes. Like her husband, she was both a good shot and an expert rider. She had even ridden with him on some of his earlier exploits and had helped him steal flour from a village once when they were hungry. They baked the bread over hot stones before settling down for the night in a little recess in the rocks. She never forgot just how lonely it was in those mountains. And she remembered well the bitter pain that came from watching the valley and the villages below. Osman was her life and she never accepted the fact that those men might one day be able to capture him.

She knew that Osman must be watching these riders this very instant and that made her feel suddenly close to him, and this closeness made her miss him even more. She felt sorry for the soldiers, though, as well, for they would get tired and exhausted as they searched for—but would never find—her husband. Osman was not the kind of man to be captured by lads like this! He sensed danger before it reached him and when in trouble would gallop away on his horse. He had a breast filled with courage. Let the gendarmes look for him as much as they liked—they would never, ever find him!

It was a good thing, she thought, that they had never had children. What kind of life would it be for children to have a father who spent his life roaming the mountains? She and Osman loved his niece Semiha and nephew Sabit as if they were their own children. Osman's horse was being kept at Semiha's and just maybe he would come tonight. Thank God for Semiha, she thought; if it were not for her, what would we do? Such were the thoughts that ran through her head as she watched the gendarmes ride by and into the distance. Once they were out of sight, she went back into the house.

Osman watched the riders from his vantage point in the bushes. Occasionally the noise of a horse neighing or snorting echoed off the boulders and the creekbed was filled with the sounds of hoof beats and cavalry whistles. He knew that the soldiers would stop at the snow water wells to drink and fill their canteens and then take a rest in the deep shade of the Big Snake. Osman believed that it was in this behavior that they made their gravest mistake. If he wanted, at that moment he could easily pick them off one by one. However, he just couldn't bring himself to harm those young boys. The cavalry had reached the well and Ibrahim Bey gave them the order to dismount.

They dismounted in a small clearing that had a deep snow well. All through the winter the shepherds would be sure to pack in as much snow as they possibly could. In the summer the snow would melt into water. It was already late summer and the level had gone down and water had to be drawn from the well. Hot and tired and dusty after their long ride, the soldiers were delighted to find water. They tied their canteens to their rifle straps and lowered them down into the water. They laughed and made noises as they passed the canteens around. Their horses pastured in the grassy meadow while the soldiers lay in the shade for a nap. Just staring up at the majestic Mt. Erciyes, the Argeus of antiquity, just listening to the winding creek, and lying under the tall crags and the hill covered oak and cedar trees, these alone were enough to bring them peace and contentment. They wondered how they could ever find the fugitive in such a place, when there were so many places to hide.

A flock of partridges had come to drink from a hollowed out stone that was full of water, but they flew off when they heard the soldiers and came to rest on top of a nearby crag. The flock's leader, luminous with the sun reflecting off his red head, faced the wind from his perch and gathered his flock around him. The chirping of these red- and black-throated birds merged into a melody that seemed to cheer the landscape. Their song was of hot rocks, wildflowers, white poplars, and fragrant breezes. They chirped back and forth, perhaps communicating the danger that they sensed.

Major Ibrahim eyed the flock sitting on the rock crest. In a sudden flash he picked up his gun and fired. Two hundred birds took flight, as one dropped in a straight line to the ground below. Its red claws opened and closed and red blood began to flow from its red throat. It died. The sound of the major's gun echoed across the rock faces while the air trembled with the beating of birds' wings.

The soldiers ran to retrieve the bird. The fastest runner soon had it in hand and proudly carried it over to the major. As if it were proof of his prowess, the major swung the bird in the air and began to shout: "Osman! Come forward! Wherever you are! Come out and prove you're a man, if you can! Hiding is not bravery! Come out into the open and we'll go at it. Man to man and gun to gun!"

The major's voice echoed across the creeks and the low oaks before stretching up to the mountaintops. The air was filled with his voice as the echoes bounced off one rock face and then another, but there was no answer from Osman. Osman stood at a spot above them, watching and listening to all they did and said. He didn't blame these soldiers. He knew they were acting under command, under command of the governor, and of the general. The governor and the general gave the orders and the soldiers obeyed.

Osman thought, "For God's sakes, man. I could shoot your horse right out from under you this very minute if I wanted. But God knows I have no problem with you."

Osman actually liked the soldiers. One time Sergeant Muharrem had gotten a tip-off. He lay for three days in a rut on the Inecik Road waiting for Osman to pass. On the night of the third day Osman did indeed pass down the road. But when the sergeant heard Osman praying, "Allah! Allah!" from his perch on his horse, the sergeant was either too excited or too sympathetic to open fire.

The sergeant had never reported what happened that night. He simply overlooked it by reporting to his superior that "no incident had occurred." The old saying, "the walls have ears" is very true. In this case it was the trees and the birds that must have had ears for the story of this spread across the city. It reached Osman's ears as well and he even liked the soldiers more from that day on.

Alone at night in the mountains and dark valleys, alone without the sound of another's voice, terribly, horribly alone in the world, Osman would pray. Osman called to Allah for patience and fortitude as he faced Mecca and bowed and knelt and stood in the traditional Islamic form of worship. He had been reciting God's name that day on horseback and he knew that that was why the Sergeant had not shot him. He vowed that day never to shoot at the soldiers. He vowed that it didn't matter whether it was the gendarmes or the police, he would fire for the sole purpose of scaring them away, nothing more. If it hadn't been for Hatem and his lies, he would have given up this life long before. But Hatem had left him with no choice.

The soldiers rested. They ate their rations and drank the cool water. They listened to the far away cry of the partridges and the sounds of the valleys. Finally the major ordered them to remount and ride.

Osman was once again alone in the mountains. With the cavalry gone, the mountain became oppressively silent. It seemed that the partridges were stilled as well, that the eagle would never return to its nest in the crag and that the wind had died down. The creek bottom was filled with a cold and haunting darkness. Osman was torn by an utter loneliness and, worse yet, his shoulder began to ache.

Here in his loneliness he thought again of the trap that Hatem had sprung upon him. That night Osman had escaped; the lad with him, however, had not.

3.
Henna Nights

S everal months earlier Hatem Agha had learned that Osman
would be attending a wedding celebration in a nearby village. Osman had hired a man from that village to raise a flock
of goats and sheep for him. Suvari bought the animals for
Osman in the spring and then pastured them in the thyme
meadows at the feet of Mount Erciyes. When they were grown,
he sold them in a nearby town. Suvari was honest to a "T" and
had won Osman's total trust.

Suvari's mother was one of the tens of thousands of
Circassian refugees who under increasing persecution from the
communist regime had been forced to flee the Soviet Union.
They had flooded into Turkey from its northern border, throw-
ing themselves on the mercy of their Moslem neighbors. The
government had settled many of these refugees around Kayseri,
Suvari's mother among them. It was from his mother that Suvari
had inherited not only his good looks and blue eyes, but his
honesty, cleanliness, and loyalty to house and hearth as well.

Suvari was planning on giving his son Kazim a grand wedding party in the village square. Huge pots of food were to be
put on the fire and several sheep slaughtered and roasted on
spits. Breads were to be baked: the small flat *bazlama* that
resemble thick English muffins, the tortilla-like *shebit*, and the
large sourdough loaves. The entire village populace was invited, many of whom invited their own friends and relatives from

35

neighboring villages. Everyone knew that Osman would be coming and the villagers were overjoyed that he would be joining their celebration. They knew the government forces were searching for him, but he was a hero as far as they were concerned. Legends had grown up around Osman and the villagers believed them all. They believed that he had tremendous courage and that his aim was so good he could shoot a fly in its wing; some said he was even a descendent of the Islamic Saint Hizir, a saint called upon to provide help in the most dire of circumstances.

Some in the village, however, were resentful of Suvari's rather lucrative partnership with Osman. Veli Agha was one of these for he also raised animals and he was jealous of Suvari's success. The excitement of his neighbors over the upcoming wedding made Veli Agha brood even more. Taking his own flock to Kayseri to sell provided him with an opportunity to talk with Hatem Agha. He knew that if he informed Hatem Agha of the imminent visit, the Agha would open his pockets. Hatem Agha had said it himself:

"Listen to me, Veli, you let me know when that devil Osman comes to your village and you'll be a made-man. You name it and it's yours."

And now was his chance. The only problem was that if his neighbors learned he had turned Osman over to the government, they would never let him live in peace in this village. After much contemplation, he finally decided to go ahead and speak with Hatem Agha.

The two met at the springs. Veli had long, thick eyebrows that draped over his small, marble like eyes. His attire consisted of a worn and faded suit, a shirt with a ring of thick dirt around the collar, and a filthy cap perched upon his head. He was very subservient in the presence of Hatem Agha, keeping his jacket buttoned and his hands folded in front of him to show his respect. As is the custom, they first greeted one another and asked after the health of each other's families. Though Veli knew he would be rewarded for providing the information he had, he also knew it would be rude to speak about money at this point. He decided to wait for Hatem Agha to bring it up rather than bringing up the matter himself. But when Hatem didn't fall for the bait, Veli was too excited to hold out any longer:

"Agha, I pray you live a long and healthy life. Have you heard the news? Our village is getting ready to celebrate one of the boy's weddings. There's going to be live music—drums and clarinets. And lots of food—meat and rice."

Hatem Agha paused before finally asking, "And who's getting married?"

"Who else, Agha? Who else but Kazim, the son of Osman's man Suvari. "

"Oh that's all well and good. But tell me now, Veli, who's coming to this wedding? Who's been invited?"

"Lots of people, Agha. Lots of people have been invited. Everybody is invited. Everybody from all the villages around."

"What about Osman? Has Osman been invited? And is he coming? Of course he's coming, isn't he? If Suvari's son is getting married then of course Osman will be there. So tell me now: When exactly is he coming and how exactly will he get there?"

As he said this, he took a pack of expensive Turkish cigarettes out of his pocket and held it out to Veli. Veli very politely removed one of the cigarettes.

"No, no, don't take just one. Take the pack. Where can you find cigarettes like these up in that mountain of yours? I bought this pack for you. Don't be shy now. Take it."

Veli thanked him profusely. "Thank you, Agha. May you always remain healthy. May God never deprive you of anything. Agha, I must tell you though, this situation is a little sticky. If my neighbors ever find out that I told you this, they'll skin me alive. The Circassian is not well liked, but the same thing's not true of Osman. My neighbors will never hand over Osman."

"Allah! Allah! Listen to me, now, who'll ever hear anything about this? Who's going to know we talked today? I'll tell you: I will know. You will know. And Allah will know. That's all. Period. Now don't tell me that you're afraid of Osman? For God's sake, Veli, I'm the one who made a man out of you! Haven't I always wanted what's best for you? And now you come and start whining. Now tell me and tell me fast: When is Osman coming to your village?"

"Agha, nobody's being straight up about when exactly he's supposed to arrive in town. But I want to know something else: Is there an award out for Osman? If there is, I wouldn't hear about it, but you would. Look, Agha, I've come all the way from the village just to talk to you. I came because you would know that."

As he spoke, Veli kept his blood-shot eyes pinned on Hatem Agha, who did not avert his gaze either, but continued looking straight at Veli as he began speaking outright about money. "Listen Son. You know what they say: 'Not all meat can be eaten.' But I'll think of some way to pay you for this favor. For years now you've been saying that you're sick and tired of living in that village. Let's say I bring you to the city and set you up with your own store. You, for instance, could sell rugs or cloth or stuff like that. Your old neighbors would come and shop from you. I've even got a store that's standing empty."

"Oh, Agha, if you did that I would kiss your hands and your feet! But how can I get out of that village alive? You help me, you take me by the hand and show me the way and I'll do anything for you Agha. I'll do anything for you and tell you everything I know."

Hatem Agha knew that he had the situation under control, so he stood up and started to walk around. He began to pace with his hands clutched behind his back. He was silent and deep in thought. "Okay, okay, then, this is how we'll do it. I'll set you up with a store. But before I do, I want to see that Osman brought in. Now, I want you to tell me everything. Do you know the exact day and the time that Osman is coming? Have you heard anything from that Circassian? Quit keeping it under your tongue! Out with it already!"

"Of course there's news, Agha. If there weren't, would I've come all this way? Osman has been invited and is sure to come."

"Okay, good then. But what time will he come? And how will he come?"

Veli evaded the questions and injected his own thoughts on how things should go: "It won't do to have him caught in the village. You'll have to set two traps, one each at both ends of town, because only Allah knows which road he'll take in. Then you can catch him either when he comes or goes. You need to have the gendarmes do the capturing."

"Okay, but the villagers will see the soldiers. Where can we hide that many mounted men? If just one of the villagers sees them, he'll go running to tell and that'll be the end of our trap. Do you think those villagers are so stupid?"

"Look Agha, just listen to me. First give me that store and let me be your slave. Of course I have some brains, too. And my brains will think of a plan that'll work." Veli was so excited about getting his own store that he sort of choked up before he could start talking. He stared at his feet as he talked. It was obvious that he had thought the whole thing through ahead of time.

"Look, Agha, there's a stand of trees a little ways outside the village. You could hide a whole division of soldiers there. The gendarmes should go into the woods at night and leave their horses there. Then they should walk up to the huge rock face just outside the village. Once they're in those rocks, they can't possibly be seen from below. Osman is going to have to come down that road at some point. That's the western end and he'll either travel that way coming or going. So when he does, the gendarmes can just open fire. The only problem is the eastern road and what if Osman decides to both come and go from that end?"

"Yeah! So what would we do then?"

"We'll have gendarmes at that end, too. All the gendarmes will first hide in the rocks on the western end. Then someone can inform them when Osman gets to the village and take half of them to the other end along the back. The soldiers will come at night so nobody will know they're there. Anyway, Osman will have to leave from one end of the village or the other."

Hatem Agha thought about this for a while. "My God, Veli, you do have a head on those shoulders after all! Just listen to you! So we have the horses hide in the woods and the soldiers in the big boulders. If Osman comes from the direction of the Big Snake—and that is most likely where he's going to come from—then they'll be able to pin him good. But it won't matter

39

which way he comes, we'll have him covered at both sides."

"Look, Agha, I've done all I possibly could. Now it's up to you. But whatever you do, for the love of Allah, get me out of the village and into the city. Nobody should get wind that it was me who told you. If my neighbors in the village hear about this, I'll be a goner and that's for sure."

That very same day Hatem Agha took himself off to visit the governor and tell him everything that had happened. The governor, the highest-ranking official in the province and a political appointee from the capital, was delighted with the news. He rubbed his hands together, paced around his office, and appeared very happy. He was especially happy with Hatem Agha, whom he complimented highly. He even walked Hatem Agha to the door. The under-officials realized that something must be up and even they acted with greater respect towards Hatem Agha.

Hatem Agha himself walked with slow and measured deportment through the provincial office building. His large framed body and red face seemed to reflect great propriety and station. As he walked he thought to himself, "My God, these people are all so stupid. Look who they make a governor! Look who they make a mayor! If only they were worth anything! If it weren't for me, these poor swine would be helpless. Let me pull this off and see what they're like then."

* * *

The governor, the local gendarmes commander Major Ibrahim Bey, the police chief, and Hatem Agha were having a meeting. Maps were spread out in front of them as all together they began to work on the details of the plan.

The officials determined that since the wedding was to be celebrated on the following Wednesday, the soldiers should set out on Tuesday night in order to arrive on time. Despite all of the detailed preparations, Hatem Agha was still unsure of how successful the inexperienced soldiers could be. He decided to have one of his own men scout out the eastern entrance to the village. When Osman arrived at the village this same man was to go up to the rocks to tell the soldiers and then bring some of them around, through the back of the village, to the lookout on the east side. Hatem surmised that Osman would be a sitting duck, no matter how he came to the village.

"Don't order him to lay down his arms, or anything like that," Hatem told the governor. "If Osman gets asked anything, he'll find a way to escape. You should open fire as soon as you see him! Let him bite the bullet!"

The governor didn't like this turn. "I can't be responsible for such an act," he insisted. But Hatem refused to accept anything less: "You'll find a way to cover it up," he replied summarily.

So, "without getting any ink wet"—so to speak—the men attending the meeting all signed Osman's death warrant, under the guise of "finding a way to cover it up."

* * *

Osman was on his horse and riding at a brisk pace. It had been several weeks since he had spoken with anyone. He liked the people who lived in Suvari's village and guessed that Suvari had probably gone to a great deal of trouble to make sure the wedding would be perfect. He figured he ought to just stay for the meal and leave that same night. He was the only traveler on this narrow path. His thoroughbred horse moved carefully and gracefully among the rocks and bramble bushes.

The soldiers were so well hidden that Osman never noticed them lying in wait. He wasn't particularly suspicious for he knew that he was popular here. He entered the village in the afternoon on Wednesday. The horse's long mane and tail swept almost to the ground. Extremely beautiful, especially with its Circassian saddle, silver spurs and hand woven blanket, the horse also wore an amulet around its neck to ward against bullets. It was the horse that attracted the most attention from the women and children as Osman and it entered the village.

Osman didn't even have a chance to stretch his numbing legs before the village folk surrounded him. As is the custom, some tried to kiss his hands and others his cheeks and forehead. Suvari rushed to his friend and relieved him of his rifle. The short-barreled carbine was light to the touch and beautifully worked. Osman's pistol, several hand grenades, and his binoculars all hung from his belt. He was armed from head to foot. Repeating over and over again his greetings to the crowd, he made his way to his friend's house. As soon as the musicians spotted Osman, the drummer broke into his most regal rhythm, accompanying Osman with beats of "guhmbede guhm, guhmbede guhm" while the clarinet player blew out a tune for dancing, a swirling and turning melody.

The bridegroom Kazim took the horse to the stables. Osman could easily be spotted in the crowd as he appeared taller than he actually was, probably due to the red turban and high black boots he wore and to his large and very handsome blond mustache. Suvari quickly took Osman up to the house's main room and sat him in the seat of honor. Osman enjoyed talking to the village people. He asked them questions and answered the ones they put to him. They told him that the Germans had moved their armies all the way to the Turkish border and that the English were trying to persuade Turkey to enter the war. President Ismet Inonu, they related, was bent on keeping Turkey out of this war as the country was just beginning to recover from the disasters of the Arab, Balkan, and First World Wars as well as the War of Independence, all fought in the early years of the century. The villagers loved to quote Inonu talking to the English Prime Minister: "I won't let our children be orphaned!" Osman listened to the talk and nodded in unison.

Suvari did everything possible to entertain the guests and make them comfortable. He and his sons and shepherds were constantly darting in and out, serving the guests a variety of food and drinks. They started with a hot beverage that is half milk/half coffee and then moved on to glasses of tea. A round tray, a yard in diameter, was carried in and placed on a wooden ring on the floor, making a low table. On the tray were plates of a creamy spread, honey, thick homemade yogurt, butter, grape molasses, pickles, roasted lamb meat, rice pilaf topped with nuts and raisins, molasses spread, halvah, raisins, walnut meats, dry apricots, and apricot compote. Homemade breads were cut into thick slices. The men sat around the table on their knees and all began to eat. Soon huge platters of bulgur pilaf topped with roasted meat joined the table. The serving bowls and platters were refilled time and time again. As the men ate their fill they left the table and soon others took their places.

The music never stopped and the young people of the village filled the square and the rooftops as they danced. Occasionally one of the villagers would fire his gun into the sky, the sound and the spent bullet marking special celebration for this special day. Everyone talked of Osman, his bravery and his horse. "His horse," they said, "is so smart that it knows when Osman is going to shoot and then goes down on its knees so he can get better aim. And as soon as he shoots, the horse stands up and takes off running again." "His horse knows which direction a bullet is coming from and twists and turns to escape the bullet." The people of the village all wanted to pet the horse and look at its amulet, but Kazim didn't let anyone get near.

And so the wedding party continued. Osman was deep in conversation with the village men. It was the kind of day and the kind of party that would forever remain in memory. The music, the dancing, and the food were all there to celebrate the marriage of Hasibe and Kazim. The henna was made into a hot paste and the women spread it neatly on their fingertips, and brushed a spot in the palm of their hands, leaving cosmetic stains that would last for weeks. The guests ate bowls of candy and trays of nuts and seeds. Under that clear sky the good people of that village enjoyed themselves to the hilt. The village chief performed the legalities of the wedding contract, while the local imam led prayers to honor the couple. Now it was time for the young couple to pay their respects by kissing the hands of all of their elders. After this ceremony, the young couple were sent to their own bedroom, the groom running, holding his new wife by her hand, as his school friends and male relatives all struck him with heavy blows to the back, a kind of test of his "manhood."

While the village was thus celebrating the wedding, there were others engaged in less auspicious activities. The soldiers had taken their positions, and Hatem Agha's most trustworthy man had found a spot from which he could watch the path

43

leading into the valley from Snake Mountain. Bloody Bekir, the foreman at Hatem Agha's farm, was known far and wide for his evil deeds. He had been a member of the original gang and in those outlaw days no one had been able to control him or stop him from committing horrible acts. He had accepted the government's pardon and left the mountains, but had never been able to settle down. The farm laborers were afraid of him and kept out of his way. His body was raw-boned and hard and his face reflected his meanness, with eyebrows that formed a single thick line across his forehead, small, beady eyes, and a mouth that never curled into a smile. His beard grew into a cruel point below his chin. When on the hunt he would sneak up on his prey and descend upon it like a black cloud. He had huge, calloused hands and feet almost as big as baby cradles. He was tough and untouched by bitter cold or by bitter heat or by hunger and thirst. He knew every trick there was to know. And now he was lying completely still among the low oaks, his eyes glued to his binoculars, on the lookout for Osman.

He watched Osman and his horse wend their way down the mountain path and watched them enter the village. He heard the celebrations, the drums, the clarinet, and the sounds of the guns being fired off. Bekir had been ordered to bring some of the soldiers here at nightfall, but he was a clever, cunning, and inordinately greedy person. He reasoned that it would be difficult to find a place in this tiny hole to hide so many others. Right now everyone was busy with the celebration. If anyone saw a single soldier in the neighborhood, the whole village would make sure that Osman was not captured. Bekir, a man who never once in his whole life earned clean money, knew that there was big money riding on this. He thought that this time, however, he should truly *earn* whatever money he was going to get out of this deal. And so he would wipe that swine Osman off the slate of this earth and then get the reward. With the help of Allah he would hit whatever he aimed at; after all, he could slice a thread in two with a bullet.

Bekir fantasized about the money and rubbed his hands together like a loan shark. He was proud of his own wit. "My God, the fools, do they think I'd ever let such an opportunity pass me by?" There was considerable money on the table, and Bekir had every intention of making sure that it was in his pocket by the end of the day. Whoever pleased Hatem Agha this time was sure to be very generously awarded. And Osman himself never went around without money. There must be quite a roll in his pocket, a roll that would be good for the taking. And that money would be enough to form a nest egg, to buy a huge flock of sheep to feed in the Gurun meadows. After all, whatever Hatem Agha was in his parts, good old Bekir was the same in Gurun.

This is what the demon who was bent on killing Osman thought about as he lay under the bushes stroking his Greek carbine, his most valuable possession. He oiled the gun several times and aimed it at various objects along the road, imagining the sound the bullet would make when it hit flesh.

As night wore on, the sounds of the wedding grew fainter and fainter until silence reigned as the drummer and the clarinetist put down their instruments and the guests prepared to take leave. Osman bid farewell to each of the villagers, asking each for forgiveness for any misdeed if he should die before they would meet again. He mounted his horse and the horse flicked its tail and pranced around the square, neighed once or twice, and half reared. Its front hooves beat the air and the silver amulet holder hanging from its broad neck reflected the moonlight.

Osman led the way, followed by the bridegroom's younger brother, Nazim, and both ambled out of the village. The traitor Veli's heart was heavy as he watched them leave. He was afraid that something would happen to the young Nazim, that the young lad might be hit by a stray bullet. He thought to himself, "For God's sake, Nazim, get back here. Come back to the village. You're walking into fire, Nazim. For God's sake, get back here where it's safe." If he thought he could manage without being found out, he would run to the village square and grab Nazim's horse by its reins. His shoulders drooped even more than usual and he broke out in a sweat. He felt a heavy pain in his chest as he wandered around a dark corner of the village.

Nobody asked why Nazim was riding with Osman. They

waved both riders off and sent prayers at their backs. Now music again issued from the drum and the clarinet, and several of the men again shot their guns into the night air. And thus Osman was given a grand send-off from the village.

It was dark and Bekir, lying in his perch, strained his ears to listen to what was happening. From the noise he understood that Osman had set off. He rose from his hiding place and seemed to fly like a crow down into the road where he buried himself under a row of blackberry bushes growing around the bend of the road. His felt cape protected him from the prickles, just as it protected him from the cold and the heat. Wrapped tightly in his cape, Bekir closed his eyes in the dark night, heightening the sensitivity of his other senses. His excitement seemed to spring from the very core of his body. Bloody Bekir was waiting, waiting for his prey.

It was an ill-omened night. The sky was starless and the air unnaturally still. The trees, the rocks, and the bushes along the road all seemed frozen into place. An owl's screeching cry could be heard clearly in the quiet, as it bounced and echoed into every hollow.

Bekir was listening, his ear almost touching the ground. He could tell if there was movement from a distance of a thousand paces and could distinguish how many riders were riding the road. The sound got deeper and then spread and spread, becoming more and more distinct. How could it be possible? There wasn't one rider—but two! Two mounted men were on the road. But who was the second? One had to be Osman, but then who was the other?

He made a snap decision. He would fire twice, not once as he had planned. He didn't care who the second person was. That devil, too, could meet his maker as well. He leveled his gun and held it in position. He opened and closed the safety and then opened and closed it once again. Then he opened it for the last time, put his hand on the trigger, and narrowed his eye as he—the hunter—waited for his prey to come into view. His beady eyes pierced through the darkness; despite the coolness of the night, sweat poured down his forehead. He remained calm and prepared; he knew exactly what he was

46

going to do and how he was going to fire. He waited like a centuries old stone.

Osman's horse moved quietly and swiftly. The two riders conversed as they rode. They talked about whether or not there was any disease in the flocks, about the state of that year's crops, how many young men in the village had been called to the military, and how many girls in the village had come of marriageable age. They rode without fear or apprehension. At one point, Osman asked Nazim about his thoroughbred horse's breed. Nazim then passed Osman so the older man could get a good look at the horse, its rump, legs, mane, and tail. Thus they rode the twisting path to death, the hapless Nazim in front, the fugitive Osman behind.

The owl's cry again sounded in the dark night, and then echoed as it bounced off the rock faces. Someone was watching them in the darkness and that same person was aiming his gun at the bend of the road, waiting for the riders to emerge into view. The gun lay steady in its owner's hands.

It was thus that Azrael, the Angel of Death, lay in wait on that deserted road. Fire suddenly spewed from the gun's barrel. Sparks pierced the darkness and the sudden explosion cut the night's silence. The sound of gunfire bounced in waves from Kizik Hill to Obruk and to Inecikbeli. The second horse to round the bend took flight, bounding off the road, over the blackberry stand, and through the fields beyond. Bekir lost none of his control as he reloaded his weapon. He could see the target in the night. He pulled back on the trigger just as the horse dodged.

The night was again momentarily lit up, and the sound of gunfire again echoed through the mountains. When the bullet found its mark, the rider fell against his horse's neck as the horse galloped out of sight. When the sound of gunfire evaporated, Bekir listened for a while to the sound of the running horse. "I shot both of them," he said to himself.

He wondered at how any horse could move that fast. "Fast as the wind," he thought. If it had been a bird, it never could have flown so fast. "I shot the rider, though," he thought to himself. He knew this for a fact, as well as he knew his own name. But first he had to look at the one on the ground.

47

He stayed for a while in his ambush and smoked a cigarette.

The first to round the bend had not made a single sound before falling under his horse's hoofs. He lay now as he had fallen, his horse standing close to his body. Bekir had his gun loaded and ready to use a third bullet should the fallen rider make the slightest movement. Seeing that the fallen rider made no sound or movement, Bekir rose from his hiding place and walked down to the road, looking like a black mountain wrapped in that stiff felt cape. The horse stood perfectly still over the rider who lay face down in the dirt. Bekir slowly turned the body over. Blood was pouring from a hole in the chest. He had shot him square in the heart. Bekir didn't recognize the victim. Where had he come from? He was so young! Still a lad! Why was this young fellow riding with Osman?

Bekir turned again towards the fields, in the direction of the second rider. He knew he had shot that rider as well. That had to have been Osman. Only Osman could ride a horse like that. The animal had sensed danger and, without even waiting for the command of its rider, had leaped away. Meanwhile, Bekir's bullet had swallowed the distance between his gun and the rider, but the horse had managed to dodge out of range, carrying its mounted companion off with it.

Bekir had expended much energy and time on this job, and now that young thing on the ground had screwed it all up. No one would pay him a cent for killing that rider. Bloody Bekir again walked over to the body and looked at it even more carefully.

"For the sake of Allah, where did you come from, you stupid idiot! You've screwed me up real good, and screwed yourself up even better! You're not worth a penny and now, because of you, Osman has got away. He'll bite the bullet, too, of course. He'll die one day like a slug. But where and how, only Allah knows! If I tell anybody about this, nobody will listen. If I try to explain, nobody will understand. Your time was up, kid. You came, you came here, and you died."

He touched the body lightly with the tip of his boot as he talked and then started hunting around in the pocket of his flea market jacket. He found the dirty rag with the handful of peanuts wrapped up in it and began to snack on the nuts as he walked away from the body lying in the pool of blood. Wrapped in his cape, Bekir felt absolutely no remorse as he walked back towards the mountains, looking very much like a giant ghost in the moonlight.

Nazim's slight figure grew stiff as it lay on the wet road on that dark night. The bats, bad omens themselves, flew off as the devilish Bekir departed, while a swarm of fireflies, their wings silver in the night, began to dart and flit about the body.

* * *

Osman had been shot. The horse had reacted to the gunfire by jumping off the path as they rounded the corner. They were already flying across the flat field when the bullet caught up with them. If the horse had not swerved, the bullet would have hit him square in the back. Instead, he was hit in the shoulder. He would have fallen had he not been able to hold onto his horse's mane. His horse was smart and knew to move as smooth as a pheasant along the goat track, keeping its rider mounted. Blood flowed copiously from its rider as the horse continued to gallop. The horse carried its load lightly and swallowed up the darkness as it ran.

The horse ran until it reached the *seki*. It had carried its burden like a ghost riding through the night, not stopping until it had reached the Crazy Sergeant's vineyard.

The sergeant spotted the horse and its obviously injured rider on the hill. As soon as he made sense of what he was seeing, he began to shout and awaken his wife. They carried Osman into the stone shelter. During the War of Independence, the sergeant had seen a lot of blood and a lot of death as his division chased the invading forces out of Sakarya. He knew what he was doing as he stopped the bleeding. It was a clean shot that had passed just under Osman's collarbone. The bullet left a small hole as it entered the shoulder, but a huge hole as it exited, and had led to a great loss of blood for the victim. The shoulder muscles had been torn apart.

The sergeant sent Osman's nephew, Sabit, to the city to bring Blind Mustafa, a man who made his living applying traditional remedies and wrapping up wounds. Mustafa applied his medicines while Osman lay unconscious, unaware of what was happening. Osman's deeply tanned face took on the pasty shade of death and his strong blond mustache wilted on his cheeks. He was still breathing, though. He was alive.

The Crazy Sergeant and his wife Ayshe cared for Osman as best they could. They cauterized the wound. They wet bread with water, beat it into a pulp, and slowly cooked this mass into a paste before applying it to the wound with gauze. As they worked, Aunt Ayshe continually recited the 256th verse of the second chapter of the Holy Quran: "Then We raised you up after your death that you may give thanks." Their efforts were not in vain. Osman opened his eyes and slowly began to recover.

As soon as he could sit up Osman began sorting out the events of that night. He learned that it was Hatem's Bloody Bekir who had done the shooting. His heart was saddened with the knowledge of young Nazim's death and he was plagued by the memory of the young boy falling from his horse.

The sergeant fed the horse with great piles of hay and clover and the day finally came when they could throw a heavy bag of provisions over its back. The contents of the bag were amazing in those days of such food shortages. They packed in many of the various kinds of breads and cheeses of the region. They added rings of spicy sausages and molasses spread. They sent Osman off just as evening was about to fall. The sergeant and Ayshe gave Osman everything they could lay their hands on and sent their blessings as he rode off.

4.

Hunters on the Path

H is nephew Sabit was Osman's eyes and ears in the city. Sabit was bright, but didn't appear so. He was expert in obtaining reliable information and then passing it on to his uncle. Sabit never asked questions, but he knew who would know what. He would approach that person and only listen to what was being said. He was tall and had bright red cheeks and unruly hair that peeked out from under his hard cap. He looked perfectly harmless. He was respectful of everyone, older and younger, quiet in nature, and seemed to have no opinions of his own. He always obeyed his elders and seemed so shy as to be afraid of his own shadow.

This obedient and respectful demeanor was his most powerful weapon. He could pull the moisture out of a breeze. He was calculating and could put two and two together with just the slightest of clues. Osman never uttered a single word of praise for his nephew, and Sabit never spoke up in defence of his uncle. It was this secret that constituted their real fortune.

Osman would occasionally come down from the mountain and stay with his niece Semiha. At those times, Semiha would bring Osman's wife Hurmet to the house so that the husband and wife might have a brief chance to be with each other.

Now, months later, Osman watched the company of soldiers as they wound their way along the creek bed before turning to begin his own descent down the mountain. He passed through the shadows cast by the Filthy Rock and then rode to the Threshing Place at Suhmbaba. Night had fallen and from his vantage point he checked out the situation at Semiha's house. He could see the *seki* and the family sitting there by the lantern light. There didn't seem to be anything suspicious, so Osman hooted three times with his owl call to make his presence known to those below. The lantern was extinguished, communicating the fact that no strangers were about. Osman glided like a bat down the hill and into the stone shelter.

Osman's arrival brought the house to life. Semiha together with her husband and their children all started to go into a flurry of activity while Hurmet quietly joined her husband in the shelter.

"Welcome home," she said quietly. Actually she wanted to fly into his arms, but she had to restrain her feelings within the house.

The family was sympathetic to the couple's needs and spread a mattress for them in hidden spot among the rocks. Osman finally had the chance to lie on a soft mattress and to reunite with the wife he loved so dearly. The stars that lit up the dome of the sky began to disappear from view. Fragrant breezes licked against the hollows in the rock face as they made their way across the valley. From far away came the rhythmic sound of someone beating on a steel container. Osman embraced his wife. The pain in his shoulder and the pain of loneliness all melted to nothingness as he lay next to his wife. Shortly thereafter they rose from their bed in the rocks and heated water for their bath. They then sat and talked into the wee hours for they knew that before dawn broke, Osman must again climb the hill to hide in the mountains, to hide from the neighbors, the government officials, and from all contact with people.

Preparations for the long and cold Kayseri winter began in mid-summer. Dough was kneaded and rolled into large sheets, cut into fine noodles, then dried and stored in small, white cloth bags. Freshly picked grapes were washed and then carefully spread on clean sheets and put in the sun to dry and become raisins. Fruits were boiled into a smooth mash and spread paper thin on trays, covered with muslin sheeting and left in the sun to dry. These fruit sheets would be used for snacking throughout the winter. Dried mulberries, apricots, and raisins were all stored in clean cloth bags. Eggplants, green beans, and peppers were strung on twine and hung to dry across the eaves of the city houses. Unripe melons, tomatoes, and peppers were pickled and packed into large earthenware pots. White crumbly cheese was mixed with black cumin seeds, packed into earthenware bowls, covered with layers of muslin and stored in underground pits. Potatoes, carrots, and onions were stacked into corners of the shelter.

* * *

That day Nuhmemed did not go to the city with the other men. His father had ordered him to stay home and help his mother gather the dry vines used as fuel for cooking. He had stayed at home, but nonetheless did his best to avoid doing the chores. He was a hunter and he was keen on hunting partridge. He took the shotgun out of the deep cupboard and peered down its barrel. He saw that it was dirty.

His younger brothers gathered around and watched him clean the gun. Once the gun was clean, Nuhmemed cocked the hammer several times and carefully looked down the barrel to check for any more grime.

"Come on, Little Stick Nose," Nuhmemet said to little brother, "today I'll bring home either a rabbit or a partridge. Will that make you happy?"

"Of course it will. But can't I go with you? Please? I promise to be quiet and stay behind you."

Nuhmemed laughed at his brother's childish pleading. "Sorry, Kid, but you're still too young. You gotta grow up a little more and let your bones get stronger. You wait till then and you'll be amazed at the places I take you. But for now, you still can't climb over the boulders."

Just then, their neighbor Mehemmed joined in to the conversation, climbing up to their *seki*, a bunch of grapes in one hand and a small, round loaf of bread in the other.

"Nuhmemet Aghabey, if Kemal goes with you, can I come,

too? Kemal and I'll just wander around. The trouble is, my mom doesn't want me going up to the mountains. She says Sariahmed's Osman's up there."

"Oh for God's sakes Mehemmed! And who is Sariahmed's Osman, after all? If he comes in front of me, I'll know how to take care of him! I'll hold the gun like this: Bammm, bam. If I see him, I'll threaten him with this gun. Once I've got him in front of this gun barrel, there'll be nothing left to do."

Saying this, he held up the shotgun and pretended to aim it straight at Osman. And then, as if wrestling, he acted out getting Osman by the arm and wrestling him down to the ground.

"You know the Japanese sport? Let's say a man is coming at you with a dagger and you feign back to one side and stick out your foot and the man falls on the ground. Then you fall on him and twist his arm till he drops the dagger. It's like that. Who is Osman, that we have to be afraid of him?"

Mehemmed was still not convinced and said with trepidation, "But Aghabey, the guy's got a Martini. And he's a good shot. They say he can even shoot a fly in the wing!"

"Come on, I told you that I would be there, didn't I? I only wish that he would come out and that I'd have the chance to capture him! They put a big reward on his head. If I catch him, I'll be rich!"

This was great fantasy material for the group of boys, who then delved into a conversation about their hopes and dreams.

It was now afternoon and the sun was half hid behind Snake Mountain. The mountain's long shadow fell on the rocks and trees, but the ground was hot and the air still. The clack-clack of tortoises hitting one another could be heard coming from the vineyards while the bee-eater birds cooed from the hills.

Nuhmemet was in his last year of high school and he had grown into a tall and strong young man. He was ready to go hunting. He put some bread and sausage, along with a full canteen of water, into his backpack. Once he had his soldier's boots on his feet and his rifle on his shoulder, he was ready to set out on the path running among the crow-filled trees. The path took him through White House and then up to Brother-in-law's Creek.

The hunting party decided not to go up the Little Poplar Hill as they figured there might be snakes there. The afternoon sun was in the sky and much of the creek lay in shadow. The eastern banks, though, were still in full sunlight and the hot granite boulders along the banks shown like mirrors. The banks were undulant with low bushes, dry thistles, nettles, and goat clover. Eagles glided high above, while the base of the majestic Mount Erciyes seemed swathed in blue tulle. Nuhmemed fired his gun several times, but wasn't able to hit anything. He blamed this on the presence of the children. He said that the boys were making too much noise and scaring off the birds. This, however, didn't stop the children one bit. They jumped from rock to rock. They searched for, and sometimes claimed to have found, wolf dens and fox holes. They hunted under the blackberry bushes, water elders, and the white poplars for rabbits and partridges. The younger children were having a wonderful, exciting time and their voices echoed through the creek bed.

As they were jumping from rock to rock, a large partridge noisily took flight. It shot into the sky like a pigeon and then snapped opened its wings and flew off in a straight line. Nuhmemed didn't react, but waited until he could see it in the gun's sight. Once he had the bird in view he released the trigger. The gun roared like a cannon. A cloud of thick black smoke and the odor of burning gunpowder filled the air. The 'noise bounced against the boulders above and then echoed back to the boys below. The gunshot hit the bird in its neck, back, and head. At first the bird wobbled in flight and then fell, first bouncing against one of the rocks like a plastic ball before falling to earth. The bird was a messy sight, its wings awry, as it lay lifeless on the ground. The children, suddenly transformed into blood-crazed monsters, came running and shouting, ignoring the thorny bushes they rushed through. As they ran they shouted out in praise of Nuhmemed's skills. He, gun in hand, stood riveted in his spot on the rocks, unable to pull his eyes away from his prize. Shouting loudly, the children joined him on the boulders.

Nuhmemed tried to straighten the bird's neck and wings. He stroked its tail as if trying to restore the bird to its original form, but the bird's neck was broken and drooped and bright red blood flowed from its dull red comb. The children finally picked the bird up, lay it on a large flat stone, and then gathered around it. As if the children had not been witness to the event, Nuhmemed elaborated in great detail how the bird had taken flight, how he had found the bird in his gun's sight and then pulled the trigger, and how the bird had subsequently fallen like a bag of yogurt. As he was describing his feat, he reloaded his gun. The children loved listening to the sound the bullets made as they clicked into place. Now was the perfect time for Nuhmemed to light up the cigarette he had pilfered from his father's pack. He acted quite the grown-up as he lit up and then blew the smoke towards the mountains, as if proclaiming that those mountains belonged to him. Now he inhaled again and blew smoke rings to prove his prowess to the younger boys. Next he exhaled the smoke in a long pipe, showing off for his brothers and the mountains.

Actually, the children were not alone. Osman was watching them. He was just fifty yards away, squatting in the bushes, his head swaddled in the dark scarf and his field glasses hanging from a cord around his neck. His rifle leaned against the boulder next to him. Mehemmed was the first to spot Osman.

"Nuhmemed Aghabey, there's somebody over there in the bushes. He's got a gun. My God, it must be Osman!" Even before the words were out of his mouth, the neighbor boy had jumped off his perch and taken off running.

Kemal and Nuhmemed also saw Osman. Kemal was stammering: "Aghabey, Aghabey, it really is Osman. It's Sariahmed's Osman." He rolled off the rock and took off after his friend.

Nuhmemed's heroics evaporated into the thin mountain air. He flung down the cigarette, picked up his catch, and took off after the younger boys. At least he didn't forget the bird he had shot with such difficulty. They ran away without looking back, never minding the rocks, thorns, or prickly bushes they came across along the way. They ran from the rocks to the creek, and then ran for home.

They were exhausted when they finally screwed up the courage to look back up the goat path they had run down. As they looked up the twisting and turning path, they were poised to start running again if they could still make out the figure of Sariahmed's Osman.

They were all talking excitedly as they reached the Licking Stone. The water-filled stone trough was alive with crested grebes splashing in the water. Some dipped their heads into the water and then pulled them back out again, pointing their beaks upwards and holding them in the air for several seconds. The birds dove in and out of the water and then shook their feathers, spraying water in every direction. Their enchanting song ended abruptly when the hunters came into sight and they arose as one and flew off.

The children stopped at the well to catch their breath. They began to settle down once their sweat had cooled off their bodies. Nuhmemed had his eyes pinned on Big Snake. It seemed that they had run down that high mountain in just minutes. He couldn't figure out why they had run from Sariahmed's Osman, so he put the blame on the younger boys with him.

"Come on, Babies, get up and get moving. We're going." The children pulled themselves up. "No telling anybody that we 'got scared and ran,' you hear me? He had his gun in his hand and if he had had the chance he would have blown us away. It's a good thing we ran."

Hayriye heard the boys' excited talk as they approached the house. Mehemmed's mother, Aunt Pembe, and then Aunt Fadime and Little Gramma also heard them. Soon the women were clustering around the young men. They pummeled the boys with questions as they debated the issue among themselves. The boys explained everything: how they had decided to go hunting, how they had climbed up the mountain, how they had shot the partridge, and even how Nuhmemed had smoked the cigarette. Hearing talk of the cigarette, Hayriye gave her son a dirty look from the corner of her eye.

"You little rascal. Just you wait till I tell your father."

Things had just begun to settle down when Tarik joined the circle. "For God's sake! And I thought you were a man!" Tarik continued to tease, "What about all that talk of catching the guy and getting the reward? I thought you were going to block his path or that you were going to set a trap. And then what about that Japanese sport? You had at least forty moves planned. So what happened?"

Nuhmemed had been caught, and caught badly. "Get off it," he countered. "How could I have caught him with two babies to take care of? We ran away and were saved. If you'd been there, you'd have died of fear."

"You flew into a panic the minute you saw Osman and then you ran here."

Were these the kinds of words to be spoken in front of this many women and children?

Nuhmemed had some words for his cousin as well. "So let's go. Right now. Since you're such a man, let's go back and catch the bum. Are you in for it? Are you man enough? Man enough to set off right now this very minute?"

"Do you think he's so stupid as to stay around there once he saw you guys? Anyway, there's nothing you can do with that old junk gun of yours. Let me show you what a real gun looks like! A real gun!"

With that, Tarik motioned for Nuhmemed to follow him to his house. The space that Tarik's family called the kiosk was actually an extension to the *seki*, a roofed area faced by flowerpots and a view over the landscape. The sidewalls were made up of posts, while its roof was of branches. The floor was hard-packed earth. A large heavy cupboard was at the far side of the space while stone benches were in front. Tarik opened the deep cupboard and took out the pieces of a shotgun that were hidden among the sheets and blankets stored there. He opened its cloth wrappings as if performing a very important deed. After its three main pieces were assembled, he locked the barrel into place and then attached the lower stock. He now held in his hands a gorgeous Number 15 shotgun. With great flair Tarik put his eye on the sight and then squinted as he looked around the room.

"That's what I call a gun," he said. "You shoot with this and you make your mark. This'll send gunshot through a mountain. God knows that this gun'll bring down a partridge a hundred meters away. If we get close to Osman with this, we'll catch him for sure."

Saying this, he thrust the gun into Nuhmemed's hand while he continued to brag on and on about his double-barreled gun. The gun really did shine. It had two long, thin barrels and a long channel leading to the sight. Cared for like a baby by the family's great uncle, this Belgian-made gun was rarely taken out of the cupboard. Tarik, though, knew of its hiding place, so he would take the gun out from time to time, play with it for a bit, and then carefully put it back in the cupboard without anyone knowing that the gun had been out.

"If you're going to shoot Osman, then you're going to need this gun to do it. Your gun'll only fire shot thirty meters at the most, and even then it won't penetrate anything."

As he was talking, Tarik removed the bag of bullets from the cupboard and dumped its contents onto the rug. The bullet shell cases were green and red and the gracefully turned bullets themselves were filled with European shot. The two youths picked up the bullets one-by-one—weighing each in his hand, turning each over trying to read the markings—and caressed the fine turning of the metal. Tarik pointed at the shotgun.

"Since you want this so bad, are you up to the both of us catching Osman? We can pretty much guess where he's hiding. Since you saw him today, he's probably going to be spending the night around there. This is our chance to empty our guns into him and finish him off."

Nuhmemed had not expected this proposal and for a second or so didn't know how to reply. It wouldn't be easy to say "No" to Tarik's provocative proposition. Still playing with the bullets, he answered, "Sure, I'm in. But there's no backing down later."

"It's a deal," said Tarik. "So, now here's what we're going to do." Tarik had thought the whole thing out.

That night neither of the young men was able to fall asleep. It was as if they were under Snake Mountain's dark shadow. By the time they finally did succumb to sleep, it was nearly daybreak. Sirri, too, was too scared to sleep that night. Even though he had to pee, he couldn't gather up the courage to walk to the toilet. It was only when the first light broke that he was finally able to bound out of his bed and run to the toilet. He slept soundly after that. Nuhmemed drifted off to sleep sometime after midnight but was awakened by the sound of his young brother's footsteps. He, too, made a dash for the toilet. On his way back to bed, he met his mother who had gotten up to begin to prepare breakfast. He immediately put on his malaria act. Trembling almost violently, he managed to stammer out, "I'm sick, Mama, real sick, and cold. It's the malaria, Mama, the malaria." Hayriye was very worried as she led her son back to his bed and tucked him in. She felt his forehead to see if he had a fever. She told Resmiye to fix a water bottle and to boil some mint and lemon. Nuhmemed tossed from side to side, kicking back his blankets.

The sun seemed to rise late that morning. Mehmed Efendi rose, dressed, and went down to the *seki*. When he heard of his son's early morning illness, he told his wife to let him rest. 'Wake up Ahmed and I'll take him instead."

Nuhmemed had succeeded in using his sickness to stay at the vineyard.

Nuhmemed feigned sleep as he listened for his father to leave. Once he was sure that his father had disappeared down the dirt road and he heard his mother on the upper level putting away the bed coverings, he crept out of his bed, threw on his clothes, grabbed some food off the breakfast table, and skipped out of the vineyard. He could see Tarik standing in his *seki* so he gestured with his gun and pointed in the direction of Barley Mountain.

The morning dew lay in large drops on the grapes, the leaves, and the hay fields. The oak trees shone brightly and thin rays of sun broke through the shadows. A pair of orioles rose in flight from the mulberry tree. The birds flew in great arcs before coming to rest again in the low poplars. The air was alive with birds in flight; bee-eaters tracked wasps and dove after houseflies, their green wings shining in the early morning light.

The young men rested in the shade of the trees along the bend. A sweet breeze broke over Mount Erciyes and reached the boys, caressing their faces and easing their souls. They watched the sun as it rose a sword's length on the horizon. A diaphanous sheet of blue smoke issued from the houses before settling again over the valley. The vineyard laborers had lit fires in their stone hearths and were busy cooking their soup as they prepared for the day's work. The sounds of donkeys braying reached all the way to the place where they sat. And all the way from the valley below them came the smoke of burning wet grasses and the aroma of baking fat and dough. The sounds of the valley were almost masked, though, by the nearer twittering of partridges. Burbling like water, the partridge calls resounded from rock to rock along the ridge.

The fear and excitement felt by the young hunters was a new sensation for them. It was not easy prey they were after this day. They were on the hunt now for an outlaw and their plan was to kill this man. Neither betrayed the fact that fear pressed on his chest like a heavy stone. Each of the young men was obstinate in his determination to prove his courage to the other, and each was planning to kill the man as soon as he was found.

The hunters went around the bend and reached Little Poplars. The sun disappeared as they entered the shade of the grove. The deeply shaded landscape with its thick groves of white poplars, hedges of low bushes, and creek was somehow unnerving. The hunters stood on a rock ledge and looked down into the deepening ravine. They carefully took in everything in sight, letting not the slightest detail miss their observing eyes as they scanned the grove, the bushes, the low oaks and the rock faces glowing in the morning sun. They saw an eagle suddenly swoop down into the oak grove. It was attacking something in that dense wood. They watched it as it rose and then swooped down several more times. Finally, the eagle emerged with a rabbit held tightly in its claws. The poor creature, even as it was carried through the sky, continued to struggle in its attempt to free itself from the eagle's grasp.

Every now and then there would be a loud rushing noise as a flock of partridges took flight up through the trees. The grape starlings, orioles, and blackbirds flew from tree to tree. The youths ignored the snakes that had wrapped themselves along the roots of the trees for they knew that, out of the reach of the sun, the snakes were lethargic and harmless. It was said that "you will live to a thousand if you don't touch a snake." That's what they had heard, so that's what they did.

They walked through the thick trees, the corn cockles, and the low oaks until they reached the northern side of the grove. They were circumspect, though, and didn't immediately walk out into the clearing. They stayed at the edge and looked around. Then at a distant spot that the sun was now hitting, they saw a man-made shelter.

The arched stone shelter had been built at the most favorable spot on the rock face and from it one had an unhampered view of the entire Brother-in-law Creek region. The shelter could only be spotted from above, and was simply impossible to see from a stance below.

Their temples began to pulse and sweat poured out of their bodies. They stayed hidden among the trees as they observed the shelter. They listened carefully but could hear no trace of activity or life. They were almost too scared to breathe.

According to their plan, Tarik would fire first and then Nuhmemed would fire both of his barrels simultaneously. Their rifles were their only source of security. They were almost ready to assume that nobody was in the shelter when the sound of a horse neighing bounced off the rocks. The first sound was long and clear and it was followed by echoes of a thousand neighing horses that bounced off and onto rocks. The whole mountaintop was suddenly filled with the sounds of horses. Before they could even register what was happening, a horse passed them, galloping at lightening speed. Mounted on the horse was a rider leaning onto the horse's back. Horse and rider swiftly passed down the twisting goat path to the valley. The horse's belly seemed almost to be touching the ground as it jumped over rocks and bushes. The hunters were frozen in place; they hadn't even had the time to raise their rifles to their shoulders.

Sariahmed's Osman was oblivious to what had happened as he made his way along the water-washed path. Osman had been in this area for several days. Usually no one came to these parts, but only yesterday the voices of a group of children had echoed through these hills. They had gotten all excited when they shot a partridge with a shotgun packed full of shot. How wonderful to be a child! They were so happy to have shot a partridge, so happy. That's when they spotted him and took off running, screaming as they ran. It was very sad for he would have loved to have been able to talk with those children. The only real medicine for the pain of his loneliness was to be able to see and talk to another person, to share news. But the children had run away. Such was his life: People ran away from him and he ran away from people.

Osman was on his way to the Red Ruins as he wanted to talk with Suvari. Osman's nephew Sabit had learned that it was Bloody Bekir who had done the shooting. During their vigilante days, Osman and Bekir had gone out together on various raid and Osman knew that Bekir would sell his own mother for a few *kurush*. Sabit had also learned that a villager named Veli had been the informer. Veli had guided the soldiers to the village and had helped them set the ambush. Word had gotten out and Veli had gone into hiding. He had sold all of his lands and goods in the village for whatever price he could get and moved his family all the way to the city of Adana. They said he was working in Adana as a *hamal*, carrying goods like a pack animal. Veli had received his punishment for there was no way he could ever return to his hometown. Suvari was a strong man and was dealing as valiantly as he could with his son's death. He had learned that Osman had also been shot and had prayed for his recovery. He knew that after Osman had regained his health, they would be able to take revenge for his son's murder.

After the shooting, the gendarmarie had come to the village and gathered up a number of men whom they tortured with *falaka*, or the beating of the soles of their trussed up feet. The gendarmes questioned, investigated, wrote reports, and drew diagrams. They only pulled out of the village when ordered to do so by their commander, Major Ibrahim Bey. Veli had already left the village by that time. Strangely enough, it had been Veli who had cried so hysterically when Nazim's body was carried back to the village. The whole village had erupted the afternoon they discovered his body lying in the road. The house of marriage celebration suddenly became a house of grieving. The villagers wept and screamed and pulled their hair, but all was in vain. The young man was dead.

As stouthearted as he was, Suvari could not forget the pain of the loss of his son. Now Osman had recovered and was on his way to the village. Nazim's father was aching with the longing to revenge his son's murder.

Osman was mulling all this over in his mind as he and his horse galloped down the hill. His eyes were on the huge mass of Mount Erciyes. The snow that covers the mountain for ten months of the year had now melted, revealing stark rock formations. Erciyes took on a blue hue. It seemed to open its blue arms to the sky as it stood there, a giant opposition to time and change. Everything gets old, but this mountain defies age. Only God knows how many millions of years this rock will continue to stand here challenging time with its peaks in the clouds, its sheer cliffs, its deep valley, and its treacherous glaciers. Osman was planning to finally climb to the very peak of Erciyes one day so he could see for himself if its rock faces were really blue or not. He would climb as far as he could and he would find that blue rock.

Osman was unaware of the young men as he sped past them. The boys themselves were in a state of shock as they stood watching the creek bed and the horse and rider rapidly disappearing along it. Tarik was the first to break the silence.

"It was like he was flying. My God, just look at that. He whizzed by like a bullet."

"It couldn't have been a horse. It was more like a gust of wind. Nobody has ever ridden that fast down these hills before. It was like he was galloping on level ground and the horse's stomach was almost touching the ground."

Nuhmemed's eyes were wide with disbelief as he turned to talk to his cousin.

"Listen, Man. This is not the job for us. If he had known we were here, we would both be goners by this time. He would have shot us both in the blink of an eye."

"Yeah, and it was you that was so keen on catching him. I knew it was going to turn out like this. The gendarmes and the police can't catch him, so how can we?

Nuhmemed was ready to answer. "Now stop trying to squirm out of it! You're all over me now like a pot of olive oil. Wasn't it

64

you who carried on and on about how great your father's rifle is?"

"Anyway, let's just let it go. Forget about it. Let's go up and see what the *tol* looks like."

"And what do we do when we go up there? Let's just get out of here."

"Oh for God's sake, Nuhmemed, you're acting like a real baby, a real yellow baby. The guy's gone. We'll only stay up there for an hour. There's nobody around, so what's there to be scared about? If it's a snake you're so scared of, well, we can shoot a snake."

"Okay, Okay, then, let's go have a look." The boys used the talk to ease their fear and pull themselves together. They walked out of the trees and made their way through the boulders to reach the shelter. Tarik walked in front with his rifle ready. Soon they were at the big rock overlooking the creek. They went through the door of the shelter and stood still as their eyes adjusted to the darkness. There were signs that someone was living here. Hay was piled in a corner and there were food crumbs scattered about, as well as some watermelon rinds and cigarette butts. They spotted a bed made of dry straw in the back corner. The ground gave evidence of horseshoe markings and a man's shoe imprints, but nothing else.

Tarik was really playing the detective now as he picked up the butts trying to see what brand cigarettes they were and then started examining the bed. Light from a tiny window filtered into the shelter, but even with this illumination the place was still very frightening. Nuhmemed had had enough.

"Come on, now, that's enough! You've looked everywhere and you see there's nothing here. Let's get out of here."

Tarik snickered from under his soft mustache. "You're scared, aren't you? Scared, that's what you are. But look at me. I'm not scared. So why should you be? Osman isn't going to eat us. He's not here anyway. You saw him leave."

Nuhmemed tried to hide his anger at Tarik's taunting remarks. They finally left and walked down the path to the valley, following the route Osman had taken a short time before. The day had not yet heated up. The creek bed was still filled with shadows. They were both secretly pleased when they finally set off back for their homes. They jumped over boulders in their way and sang folk songs as they walked. Each felt the lifting of a huge weight. They were lightened by the fact that they had not encountered Osman. They had been screwed down, and now the screw had been loosened. The boys soon got over their anger and each promised never to tell anyone of the events of that day. They went back to their homes as if they were hunters returning from a day of chasing prey. They drank deeply of the snow water they drew from the cistern at Nuhmemed's house and then both stretched out on rugs and fell fast asleep.

5.

A Handful of Flour

When Mehmet Efendi arrived in town, his friends were just opening the security shutters on their storefronts. His adjacent neighbors, Bald Emir and Muhsin Tok, were arranging their window fronts. Both of these neighbors were like walking newspapers. One was a shoemaker and the other a bookseller. The shop directly opposite sold import goods. At that time, it was almost impossible to find imports, but somehow this shop managed to do so. They found and sold refrigerators, radios, and bicycles. The upper floors of that building housed law offices. A very steep set of stairs led to the office of Kayseri's most renowned lawyer of the day, Blind Sacit, and his partner, Ramiz Bey. The lawyers generally came late in the morning and had to push their way up the steep staircase lined with villagers waiting to see them. The villagers carried pots and jars of yogurt, milk, and cheese with them—goods to barter for legal advice. That morning the lawyers' clerk Hasan had not yet opened the office doors.

Mehmed Efendi's other adjacent neighbor was the repairshop of a hadji, an elderly man who had made the pilgrimage—the hadj—to Mecca. Short and fat in stature, Hadji Emmi always came early and kept a lookout for customers. He would come before sunrise, as he believed completely in the saying that "bounty and abundance are for those who work early." He kept a cigarette stuck between his lips and he would turn it one way and then the other as he kept his eye on who was doing business. If you wanted to know who was earning what, you only had to ask the Hadji. A little further down was the city's equivalent of a small department store: "The People's Mercantile Center." When they opened their shutters with great flair, and an equivalent amount of noise, the shopping district seemed to come alive and the trade of the day would officially begin.

Mehmed Efendi's clerk, Saim, had been lured away from cosmopolitan Istanbul with the promise of an ample wage. He dressed nicely, was always clean-shaven, and had a well-groomed appearance. Saim impressed customers because his shirt, tie, and trousers were always spotlessly clean and he spoke with a refined Istanbul accent. His dark eyes shone in the white skin of his face. He was very much the gentleman. He never mixed meals with work hours and when he went to lunch, he did so in an unobtrusive manner. He never complained about anything.

That morning Saim almost sailed into the store. After extending his greetings to his boss, he found a damp rag and started cleaning the storefront windows. He swept the floor and dusted the display shoes on the shelves. In no time at all, he had the shop spotless.

In his office, Mehmed Efendi smoked his Kulup brand cigarette while slurping up a Turkish coffee. He read the government's semi-official daily newspaper, especially all the national news. Today the paper wrote of how Germany was swallowing up all of Europe and described the recent invasion of Czechoslovakia. There were photographs of Germans on motorcycles, on Panzer tanks and wearing steel helmets. The paper said that the Germans were reneging on their words by invading and setting up puppet regimes in all of those places they had promised England that they would not touch.

Kayseri was one of the cities in Turkey that was very affected by the war. Most of the available labor force had been called up to the Army. The economic system had been transformed into a war economy and the city was experiencing extreme shortages. The people were rapidly losing hope as savings were drained and everyone became impoverished. Mehmed Efendi was convinced that things would only get worse. "Seeing as the people are suffering this much even before the war starts here, just imagine what it is going to be like when we do go to war. May Allah protect us!"

The Germans were beating on Turkey's western borders, so the Turkish army had been massed throughout Turkey's European region of Thrace. The Turks were blocking the Germans from moving into the Caucasus, but the Germans were putting pressure on the Turkish president, Ismet Inonu, to let them through. Turkey's leaders had seen their fill of war and their nation on the verge of collapse. They had struggled long and hard to pull together the new Republic of Turkey and they thanked Allah for allowing the country to be saved. Ismet Pascha was using intricate political machinations to protect the country. Using his poor hearing as an excuse, he heard only what he wanted and "misunderstood" that which he didn't want to hear. All the while, he was following world developments very closely.

Ismet Pascha himself told Kashchioglu Omer Efendi that the Germans were sure to attack the Russians at some time or another and that only then would Turkey be safe. He saw that coming and felt that it might happen soon. As Mehmed Efendi read his newspaper he thought, "The strange thing is that nobody in Turkey wants any person or country to stub their toes on a stone." If only the war would end, the country would be able to pull itself together and that would be an ideal time to build that primary school in the old neighborhood. He blamed his own lack of education on the fact that his neighborhood didn't have a school. He didn't want other children to face the same kind of problems. As he was reading his paper, his clerk sold some customers shoes and slippers at the shop's standard low profit margin. If it weren't for the civil servants, there would be no customers. Who among the common folk had money enough to afford a new pair of shoes? Many of the city's people wore clothes that were patched on top of patches and they could only wear underwear made of coarse white calico. Children ran around barefooted. It was only at weddings that the common folk would come to his shop to buy a pair of shoes for the bride.

Mehmed Efendi made his money by selling to civil servants—the people who worked at the airplane factory, the foremen at the cloth factory, and the supervisors in government offices—as they were the only ones with money in their pockets.

Not only did it enjoy a prime location on the city's main commercial street, but the shop's shelves were also filled with the latest style shoes and, with its well-groomed and polite clerk, it attracted the men and women in town who could afford fine quality goods. The common folk only gazed through the shop window, amazed at the order and cleanliness of the display.

An attractive woman wrapped in a checkered, long veil was in a corner of the shop bickering with Saim. The woman was holding a year-old child on her lap. She didn't want the clerk to remove the fancy, red and white shoes from her tiny daughter's feet.

"My husband's a soldier," she said. "I fell in love with these shoes the minute I saw them. Don't tell me these shoes are only for rich babies or for the children of civil servants! Look how nice they look on my baby. I've got thirty kurush in my pocket. My husband's stationed in Edirne and we don't even have much food in the house. If I had known they were this expensive, I would never have come into the shop. I just don't have any more money to give you."

Saim was saddened by this situation, "Look, Ma'am," he said, "what can I do about this? We sell these shoes for 125 kurush. And we invested ninety kurush in them. I can let you have them for a hundred, but I just can't go lower than that. I don't own the shoes. If I did, I would give them to you for free."

Mehmed Efendi heard this exchange. He saw how the young woman's pretty face was now covered with perspiration and how her chestnut brown eyes expressed so much sadness. He saw how tightly she clutched her veil and the shoe on the baby on her lap. He was saddened by all of this. Saim shook his head back and forth in frustration as he tried to pick up the pretty shoes and put them back into their box, but he just couldn't bring himself to pull the shoe out of the mother's hand. The child's face was pale and puckered, but still the mother clutched the shoe, as if asking Mehmed Efendi for help.

"What's happening? What are you saying, Ma'am? Why don't you tell me what's going on?"

"You see, my husband's a soldier. He's stationed in Thrace and there's only me and his mother in the house. She's old and I'm trying to take care of her. We're having a really hard time getting by. When I saw these shoes in the window, I just couldn't stand it, and so I wanted to buy them. I told him that these shoes shouldn't just be for rich babies, for civil servants. One day Allah will smile on us, too. If I had known they were expensive, I never would have set my eyes on them. They look so nice on my baby. I'm thinking that you shouldn't make a profit on these. I've got thirty kurush. I was going to spend it on food, but I'll give it to you instead. I put them on her, now don't make me take them off."

The woman was humiliated as she tugged at a corner of her veil. Perspiration was falling in beads off her face and onto the front of her clothes. She was obviously a woman with pride and she had been wounded sorely by having to beg for shoes for her child. Seeing this, Mehmed Efendi told his clerk, "Give the lady the shoes, Saim. What's a pair of baby shoes to us? Give her the shoes and let her go." Then turning to the woman he told her, "Take these shoes, Ma'am. I relinquish my claim to them. They are now yours. Let your child wear them with a smile! Just pray that this war ends and that all of our soldiers come back to us safe and sound. May Allah protect them!"

The woman's perspiring face now turned a deep shade of red. She was surprised at the generosity of the offer.

"You can apply to the city," he told the woman. "They're passing out a small bit of help to women whose husbands have been called up. There's a meeting two days from now in the city. I'll be there for the meeting. Come then, find me, and I'll help you get on the assistance list."

"May Allah protect you for your kindness! What if they won't let me through the door of the city building?"

"Don't be afraid. They'll let you in. Tell them you're looking for me. Say, 'I've come to see Mehmed Efendi.' They'll find me for you. You go now and enjoy the shoes." As the woman left the store with tired strides, she repeated prayers of gratitude.

There were hundreds of soldiers' wives in the city who faced the same problems. Each day these veiled women would come to the square that served as the flour market and watch silently as the traders sold the flour. A struggle would then ensue whenever one of the sacks was emptied, as the women raced to claim it. Fights for the empty sacks were fierce and sometimes women would even wrestle and grab each other's hair as they pulled at the sack and at each other. Once a woman had claimed an empty sack, she would spread a clean cloth on the ground and then beat the sack with a stick to extract the small amount of flour that clung to the insides of it. She would be happy to get this handful of flour. The saddest days were those when there weren't enough sacks for all of the women to get at least one.

Even though the people were miserable and hungry, the city's mosques and warehouses were stuffed full of wheat. Other warehouses held bags of chickpeas, dried beans, and other foodstuffs. These foods were being saved to feed the soldiers when war finally broke out. The government knew that the soldiers couldn't fight on empty stomachs, so they were saving the food for them. But while this was going on, the soldiers' wives, children, and elderly mothers and fathers were all going hungry. Poor nutrition was leading to the spread of diseases and tuberculosis, malaria, and typhoid were becoming rampant. Flour, rough calico, kerosene, and salt were all rationed and amounts received carefully recorded in identification booklets. The war that was sweeping across the globe had left the young nation of Turkey in a state of hunger and shortages.

Mehmed Efendi had not lost hope. He tried to help all who appealed to him, whether they were neighbors, relatives, people from his old neighborhood, or complete strangers. The winters were especially hard and he did everything possible to find work, money, or food for those who came to his door. But his was just a very small bandage on a very great open wound and there seemed to be no end in sight for overriding poverty and the flour fights.

He would order their lunches—today a plate of roasted mutton—from a nearby restaurant and he and his clerk and son would eat their meal in the basement, out of sight of those who might not be able to find such food themselves. After lunch, he would sit at his moneybox and try to balance the little money coming in with the money going out.

Ahmet had found a corner of the store, out of reach of his father's eye, in which to read his comic and detective books. As luck would have it, a customer always seemed to come into the store just at the most exciting section of the adventure. This time, Saim greeted the large group who entered together.

The people had seen so much war that a rather strange tradition had developed. Boys of fifteen were married off so that at least they could produce some offspring before they were called up to die in battle. This group of customers was organizing such a wedding and they wanted to buy a pair of shoes and slippers for the prospective bride. The girl with her pinched and pale face was barely fourteen and had not fully matured yet. The family bargained long and hard before finally settling on a pair of shoes and slippers. They were just about to leave when the door was filled with the large frame and overriding demeanor of Hatem Agha. He towered above everyone else in the shop and took them all in with his green, probing eyes.

The customers were quick to push their way out of the door and onto the street. Mehmed Efendi rose to greet his new visitor. "Come in, come right in, Hatem Agha. You are very welcome in this shop," he said, gesturing towards the special "guest chair."

Hatem Agha had a florid, round face and white, wiry hair that spilled out of his wide-brimmed hat. "I just dropped in to see how you are, Mehmed Efendi. How are you doing, then?"

The two men went through the long ritual greetings and enquiries as to the health of all family members before Mehmed Efendi ordered his son to bring two Turkish coffees. With Ahmed out of the shop and Saim now busying himself with the shoes, Hatem Agha leaned over and spoke in a loud whisper to Mehmed Efendi.

"Our representative in parliament, Omer Agha, has come to Kayseri. He came on the train last night. The governor sent word, so I went to see him. I don't know if you've met him or not, but he's a good man. We went to the club and ate and drank some and we also talked about you."

73

"That was very nice of you, Agha. And how is Omer Agha? Did he bring any news of any importance?"

"Of course he did. He had a lot to talk about. The biggest issue for the government right now is those Germans bothering us at the border. Thank God we have a smart leader like Ismet Pascha. It's good that we have somebody as experienced as him at the helm in such trying times. Omer Agha says that there are some circles who are putting pressure on Inonu to attack the Russians from our northern borders. The president was very angry at this. If we attack the Russians, we'll end up being chicken feed for the Germans. If we attack the English, we'll get eaten up by the Germans and the Russians. See how far-sighted he is? If there had been anybody else sitting in Ankara, we would go after the Russians and then our children would end up paying for it for another thirty years."

"Yes, Ismet Pascha is a good president."

"He's a man who's had to jump through the hoop of fire. The ordeals that that man has lived through! Thank God we have him as our leader. The people may be hungry, but at least they're not being orphaned."

Now Hatem Agha raised his voice even louder. "If only the people knew his worth. If only they knew!"

Mehmed Efendi agreed with the visitor. "They'll understand sooner or later, but by the time they do, the rabbit may have already fallen off the cliff! Take the railroads, for instance. It's the railroad company that's keeping this country afloat. And look at Kayseri! If we didn't have the state-owned airplane factory and textile mill in Kayseri, the city would be totally destitute."

"You are exactly right, Mehmed Efendi. The Republic did us the biggest favor of all when it opened those factories here. If we didn't have those factories, what would we have? The land's too dry to grow anything and we haven't got any trees to speak off. And if we've got minerals in those hills, nobody's found them yet. That's why everybody that can just leaves this place. Kayseri people are known all over Turkey for being so clever and cunning. Well, we have to be. Our wit is all we have to rely upon."

Hatem Agha picked up the tiny cup of coffee and slurped it up noisily before he started talking again. "Actually, I dropped

74

in today, Mehmed Efendi, because I need some advice. Look, the two of us are like brothers. As you know, I'm not man of great material wealth, but then I've never been one to worry about that kind of thing. The thing that's got me worried is that dog, Osman. He's got me worried and he's got the authorities worried. And he's not just an ordinary worry. No, not him, he's the biggest darn pain-in-the-behind there is. And all these years, nobody's been able to capture him. He just laughs in every-body's face. I wanted to talk to you about this."

Listening to this, Mehmed Efendi remembered the teachings of Islam. "Of course, Agha, of course. We're all brothers. Can flesh be separated from the nail? If one has a problem, then all of us share that problem."

"Only Allah and I know how that Osman has made me suf-fer. He keeps trying to stab me in the back. Not long ago, some-body shot and injured him. Actually, I wish he had been killed. But how in hell am I supposed to know who shot him? Who knows how many people must be out to get him? They killed the kid that was traveling with him. Now he's saying he won't let that blood seep into the ground. The moron! Why in the hell does he put the blame on me? He's left me no peace. I swear to Allah. That Osman is on my mind when I go to bed at night and on it again when I wake up. Don't even try to ask what kind of a problem he is. Every now and then he sends word: he says that my time is up. I am really worried Mehmed Efendi, really worried."

"Patience, Agha, you've got to have patience. Nothing can come from hiding in the mountains. One day he's going to have to understand that. You just have to be patient. You've got to have patience."

"I'm sick and tired of being patient. The government is try-ing to find a solution. They've filled the mountains with gen-darmes and police. There's a soldier behind every stone up there, but even that's not enough. They just can't root him out. Only when the Germans got as far as Edirne did the government decide to put its skirts on fire. What were they doing before that? Now that they've got their behinds in trouble and don't want any more of it, they decide to pardon him! Yeah, that would be just great if that fool knew enough to come out of the mountains. I know that Osman better than anybody else. He's more of a coward than a rabbit and more treacherous than a fox. If only he would accept a pardon and live down here like everybody else!"

"Who said anything about a pardon? Has the government agreed to pardon him? Or are they actually thinking of something else?"

"The government said so. They're top officials and they wouldn't play games with anything like this. I heard the news from Kashchioglu's Omer Efendi. He talked to the Prime Minister and to President Inonu. They said that the Germans were threatening Turkey at the border and so they didn't need some boil festering in the middle of the country. They said that since we can't catch him, we might as well pardon him. 'Let's pardon him and let him settle down wherever he wants,' that's what they said."

Mehmed Efendi slipped into thought before looking up again at Hatem Agha. "That's great. That really is wonderful. If only Osman would accept, then we would be spared from all of these problems. So what are you going to do? The enmity between the two of you goes back a long ways. If he does come down, are you going to be able to settle all your old accounts?"

Hatem Agha stiffened as if hammered with a nail. "What do I have to settle with him? He's an enemy to himself, not to me. On my religion and on all my beliefs, I swear on the sacred Quran sent to us by Allah that if he comes down from that mountain, the two of us will live like brothers. We fell out with each other over nothing actually, but that's another story. He should just smarten up and stop coming after me. Anyway, the two of us have shared a lot in this brief, four-day life we live."

"Whatever the reason behind it, enmity developed between the two of you. You know better than anyone else why that happened. The rest of us are out of the picture and we have always been surprised that the two of you became such enemies. If the government pardons him, then you should find a way to make up with him. Such strife doesn't befit either of you. You're both grown men."

76

"Mehmed Efendi, actually, this job is up to you. You and me, we're nail and flesh. We depend on each other. Something can happen to me today, and to you tomorrow. I can't just go to Osman and tell him that the government has pardoned him and that he needs to come down from the mountain and live in peace and friendship with me. I can't tell him, but somebody has to. Somebody has to make the government trust in him and him in the government. And we can't send just any old body up there to talk to him. We talked about it and we agreed that you are the one and only person for this job. I beg of you, I plead with you, please handle this problem for me."

Hatem Agha choked up as he spoke these final words. Actually, Hatem was hard as nails and could get what he wanted out of almost anybody. He almost never gave in to anybody and never listened to what anybody else had to say. He might appear to be listening; he might appear to be amicable, but everything he did was calculated.

"Look, friend, we're members of the same political party. We are servants of the same neighborhoods. If I stub my toe on a stone, you run to clear the path. If anything should ever happen to you, I would relinquish all my property and goods for you. You know that. We might have had our occasional differences, but praise be to Allah, there are no traces of any of that left. Have I ever gone against the words of our party? We have always worked together to impede those bent on greasing their own palms or to hold our own against those who are so high and mighty with all their education. If we didn't work together, believe you me, they would have turned us into their lackeys. They've read four books in their lives and they think they're soothsayers. If we continue to work together, we'll be able to do much, much more. Listen, I promise you; I will work like a dog to get a school built in your old neighborhood. I swear that on the Quran. Just you wait and see."

"You don't have to swear, Agha. Do you think I don't know you? I know you'd run to help me if I ever needed it. I have no doubt about that whatsoever. But the thing is, I just don't want to get caught up in anything like this. After Osman left jail, he visited us a couple of times and drank our coffee. We have no other shared past. We're not friends and we're not relatives. How could anyone be sure he'd listen to what I have to say? Has the country run out of men? There are lots of men with clout. Find one of them to talk to Osman."

"But there isn't anybody else. If there were, would I come bothering you? If you really don't want to be in on this, then just tell me straight out, and I'll leave you alone. But try to think of someone who could do it, for he has to understand, the government has to understand, and Osman has to understand. Just find me someone who can do that and we'll give the job to him."

Mehmed Efendi sunk into thought. He didn't want to leave Hatem Agha in the lurch. "Agha, you know we are in the same party and I have always supported you on every issue. If it were up to the lawyers and the doctors, neither you nor I would still be in the party. Because of you we held fast and have been able to come to the point we are at today. I don't want to turn you down, but what if this business gets me in trouble?"

Mehmed Efendi's explanation rekindled Hatem Agha's hope. His eyes glistened now as he talked. "Look Mehmed Efendi, my brother, whatever happens, we are in this together. I promise you on my religion and my beliefs, on the honor of my marriage, that nothing is going to happen to you. You're just going to find him and tell him that the government has offered him a pardon. He either accepts, or he doesn't. That's it. You'll be acting as the government's envoy."

"All right, but I need to think this through very carefully. Whatever I say now is meaningless. This situation is like a stick with mud on both ends. What if the government sets a trap for him? I'll let them cut off my head before I'll be a party to such a thing. Let me think about it and I'll send word in a few days time."

Hatem Agha accepted this. Anyway, he knew that Mehmet Efendi was to be called to the governor's office the next day and that some powerful people were going to be talking to him and that these were the kinds of people who could not be turned down or put off.

"All right, then, Mehmed Efendi, you think this over. They told me to explain this all to you. The governor is expecting you tomorrow at ten. Some other leading officials, some MP's, are also going to be there. You need to listen to what they have to say. All good comes from Allah. We've talked a lot, Mehmed Efendi, and I should take my leave now."

He took out his large handkerchief and mopped his brow as he propelled his heavy body to his feet and placed his sweat-faded brimmed hat back on his head. His huge frame cast a long shadow across the shop door as he stepped out into the street, nodding his greetings to acquaintances as he made his way down the avenue.

After having seen his visitor to the door, Mehmed Efendi remained standing in front of the counter. The pardon would be a wonderful thing, if the government was indeed acting straight. The pressure being put on the people would come to an end and everyone would be relieved. Osman could start living like a human being again. But what if they were trying to trick Osman down from the mountain and were really out to get him? If that happened, Mehmed Efendi would be the guilty party. If that were the case, he would be wrapping a fringed shawl of big trouble around his head. Who should he believe and what should he do? He just couldn't see his way out of this quagmire.

The shop filled with customers and the money drawer opened and closed several times. Soon he noticed that the day had started to turn and it was almost time to return to the vineyard. When Mehmed Efendi gave the sign, they started to close up the shop. The items strung in front of the window, the locally made house slippers, baby shoes, and the *pantufla*, the traditional felt slippers, were taken back into the shop and the long, bent pole was used to pull the shop shutters across the shop face. The large padlock was slipped into place. Mehmed Efendi was still busy behind the half-shut shop, gathering the money from the drawer and then spitting on his finger before he counted the takings. He then tied the money into a bundle and placed it in their safe.

Another workday drawn to a close, Mehmed Efendi folded up his newspaper and slipped it into his pocket, the paper's name visible to all. He checked the lights before finally leaving the shop. They formed a small procession as they walked,

79

Mehmed Efendi leading and Saim and Ahmed following at a respectful distance behind. Their walk took them from the base of the old citadel along the ancient walls to the Republic Square and then along the main avenue. They first stopped at a butcher's shop to purchase two kilos of mutton and then filled their carpetbags with a watermelon, tomatoes, eggplant, peppers, and cucumbers. The veins on Ahmed's neck grew thick as his bag grew heavier.

Still walking with their heavy bags, they exchanged greetings with friends they encountered on their way. Tired from carrying his heavy load, Ahmed had trouble keeping up with his father's long strides. They finally reached their city house. It was an old and large house that had once been regarded as a mansion. Mehmed Efendi had purchased the still-beautiful house from his father-in-law.

Like the other houses in Kayseri, the house was ringed with a walled-in courtyard. The courtyard was itself a fortress with its tall walls and entry accessible only through a stout, double winged wooden door locked with an ancient mechanism. Mehmed Efendi took out the seven-inch long iron key to unlock the door, which opened with its customary groans and squeaks. His horse was tied at one corner of the yard and he slapped the flies from her rump as he prepared to saddle her. First came the felt blanket, and then the Circassian saddle.

Mehmed Efendi began to speak to his horse in a soft, soothing voice as he gently stroked her head while sliding the bit into her mouth. The carpetbag—actually two bags joined by a wide strip that fit over the horse's back—was then placed across the its back.

The donkey was also loaded and the men were ready to set off for the vineyard. They rode their animals down the manure-dotted narrow path of a lane that led between the courtyards. The lanes were foul with stench for all the septic pits in the neighborhood had holes opening onto the street. The heat of the summer day had settled deep into the steamy streets, attracting thousands of flies that nipped at the riders' feet as they passed. From their animal-back perch the men could see the dirty children playing on the flat rooftops of the houses in the crowded quarters. Their mothers, heads covered with the traditional cotton scarf, turned their heads out of modesty as the men passed, but still managed to watch the men out of the corners of their eyes.

One by one the men were joined by other riders who were setting off for their own vineyards, so that they soon became a large group of conversing men. The dust cloud could be seen for miles. The sun now setting behind its back, Big Snake's shadow grew longer and longer. Soon the plain was bathed in shadows while the sunbeams still shining on the mountaintop sprinkled the plain with shafts of light that bore into the riders' eyes and made their foreheads bead with sweat. The path through the plain smelled of horse urine and manure as the riders, most sitting sidesaddle, rolled thin cigarettes that they smoked as they conversed. Their conversations reflected the men's patience and tolerance as they talked of their vineyards, the war, and the severe shortages. They all had a strong belief in fate, and so accepted the state of affairs with calm magnanimity. They might appear rough and coarse with their coating of dust and dirt, but they were all men filled with love and hope for the future, and this reflected in their self-confidence and security.

The riders would also pass among groups of men on foot, many carrying packs filled with onions and potatoes, and then new exchanges of greetings and news would begin.

This long trek home was repeated each night of the summer season. The clouds of dusts worked up by the travelers would settle deeply on the vegetable and chickpea fields lining the road. As the Big Snake's shadow fell even further and deeper across the plain, individual men would break off from the group and head down narrow lanes towards their own vineyards, each trying to reach home before utter darkness fell and the threat of highwaymen became real.

As soon as the riders came into sight, Hayriye ran down to help with the bags. Ahmet and Nuhmemed tended the animals. First they curried the horse. After being groomed, the horse spread its two back legs releasing a long stream of yellow urine. Now relaxed, the horse drank the lukewarm water the boys placed before her. Her drinking was a noisy affair, accompanied by much snorting and an occasional neigh.

Mehmed Efendi asked about his son's health before climbing to the *seki*. Bats were floating through the dark sky as Hayriye began to serve the evening meal. The light emanating from a torch reflected across the plain, attracting the fireflies and bats into that direction. Soon the family heard shouts, the beating of tin drums, and an occasional gun being fired. This display was one way for the people, tired from a long day of labor, to demonstrate their strength and prowess in an uncertain world. The people loved to hear a gun being fired and then the sounds of shot as it echoed in and out of the mountainsides.

Mehmed Efendi downed the alcohol in his red glass in one long gulp. He took a bite of the ripe cantaloupe and dunked a piece of the fresh bread into the dry cheese that had been mixed with chopped onions. The combination of alcohol and food set him aright and now he could gaze into the star-lit sky content and at peace.

Nuhmemed tossed and turned in his narrow bed. The neighing of Osman's horse still echoed in his ears and he couldn't forget how the outlaw had passed them like a ghost in the night. Suddenly there was a light in the sky. This bright white light passed from one side of the sky to the other before being lost in the darkness. Kemal was the first to see it.

"There's the searchlight," he shouted. The searchlight swept clean Nuhmemed's thoughts and swept away his sleepiness. He jumped from his bed and sat cross-legged on the ground near his brothers, holding the younger's head in his lap.

Gazing into the sky, Nuhmemed told them what he knew about the searchlights. Now there were two. The first one had been installed in the yard of the airplane factory and now another one had been set up behind the government's textile factory. The long white columns of light searched the sky, on the lookout for any enemy planes. Sometimes the paths of the two lights would cross and sometimes their lights seemed to engage in long dances with one another. The searchlights lit up not only the skies, but the lives of the remote villages as well, as villagers in villages across the plain lit their lanterns to watch as the lights combed the skies.

"German aircraft, German aircraft," they shouted.

"Nuhmemed, did you know that if an enemy plane gets caught in the light, it can't fly anymore?" Ahmed told his older brother. "The light gets in the pilot's eyes and he can't see and the plane crashes."

He was cut off by his brothers curt, "Don't be silly. The searchlight doesn't do anything, it just lets the people on the ground know where the plane is. There are gunners, you see... gunners on top of Ali Mountain and Lifos. When the lights pick up a plane, the gunners will shoot it down."

Some people in Snake's foothills were out twirling gum. A long cord would be smeared with greasy gum resim and then one end set alight. When the slowly burning cord was twirled above the head, sparks would form large arcs in the air, making lighted paths in the darkness. First discovered by just one or two persons, this trick soon caught on as a general form of entertainment. The silence of the night was broken by the sounds of gunfire and tin drums. This was a vast valley party with everyone wide-awake.

Mehmed Efendi sat at the edge of the upper terrace, looking at the lights that flashed across the plain. He shouted out a loud, "Haydahhh," every time he heard a gun fired. He watched the searchlights, the arcs of burning gum and the torches and listened to the beating drums for a while longer. Finally, the searchlights disappeared, just as suddenly and dramatically as they had appeared.

The darkness brought quiet to the plain as the torches and cords were extinguished and the noise of drums and shouting gradually died down. The valley was again alone and deserted. Hayriye called to her husband from her bed, "What would enemy airplanes be doing around here anyway? They're going to fly all the way from the border to here? That's enough, man, come to bed now. We've got to get up early tomorrow."

Mehmed Efendi heeded his wife's words and settled down on the double-layered wool mattresses. The couple gazed at the stars as they embraced each other, drifting off to a warm sleep.

* * *

Of the children, only Sirri had not fallen ill with malaria. But now he was having eye problems. When he awoke in the mornings, his eyes were often crusted shut. His mother would bathe his eyes in a mixture of water and iodine so that he could open them. She did this so gently and expertly that Sirri, grateful to his loving mother, would climb into her arms and smother her with kisses while she stroked his long, blond hair.

The next morning the family arose to their common routine. Resmiye prepared their breakfast soup, a soup made of broth and homemade tomatoe sauce and thickened with the tiny noodles his mother had made and stored the autumn prior. Before eating, the heavy soup was lightened with a splash of sour grape juice.

Mehmed Efendi shaved and put on a clean white shirt and a tie. He carefully brushed his brimmed hat hanging from a nail in the kiosk and smoothed his tiny mustache. He called down to his oldest son to ready the animals while he himself went down to the *seki* to hurriedly down his breakfast.

Nuhmemed was thoughtful as he flung his leg over his short donkey. He hadn't told anyone what had happened the day before. Today seemed to be just another ordinary day, and yesterday's adventure only a dream. He waved to his younger brothers who were still on the *seki*, teasing each other into a pillow fight. He watched as his mother put a stop to the destruction of her pillows and shooed the boys out into the yard.

The ride into town was uneventful, marked only with the shared greetings of the other travelers and the nuisance of having thick dust settle onto their otherwise clean clothing. They again rode to their city home and spat on the long key before twisting the ancient lock open. The animals were tethered and left with ample feed and water before the men set off for the shop.

The shop chores were the same: the iron shutters were noisily swung back; the shop was swept; and the merchandise displayed. Mehmed Efendi had only to sort of straighten up the boxes of shoes before taking his place behind his money drawer, while Nuhmemed and Saim busied themselves with more demanding tasks. The slippers, baby shoes, and *pantufla* were again hung on display outside. One of the shop windows featured their best and most colorful women's shoes and slippers, all the very latest style. The other window was reserved for men's shoewear, glossy leather shoes displayed in a way to make them even more attractive, some pairs straight, others on their sides, and some on little racks. Saim was fast and efficient. He sprinkled the shop's floor with water before giving it a thorough sweeping. He emptied the middle counter and washed every surface before replacing the now-dusted shoes. He took a rag to the windows, making sure that neither had the tiniest smudge. He straightened up the customer's chairs. He set to the task silently and soon had the shop spotlessly clean.

Mehmed Efendi was again engrossed in his *Ulus* newspaper. "Goodness," he thought, "those Germans! What do they think they're doing? They're setting the whole world on fire." Every day they seemed to invade another country. Austria, Czechoslovakia, and France have all been invaded, and Greece and Bulgaria have gone down as well. And now the Germans are at Turkey's borders."

The cool morning air warmed and it was almost noon, but Mehmed Efendi still hadn't received any news. He was patient though, for he knew that he would hear something soon. "Those worms," he thought to himself, "they sit there with all their power. I know they're not going to let me wriggle out of this." He knew he would be fingered for this difficult task.

Just as he was mulling over these thoughts, Hatem's Agha's huge frame cast a shadow across the shop door. The shop was full of customers and they immediately backed out of the way for this imposing visitor. His eyes darted around the shop and then lit on Mehmed Efendi, who had risen to greet him. "Mehmed Efendi, it's time for us to go. I came to fetch you. They're waiting for us right now, so we better go quickly. It wouldn't be right to make men like that wait."

"Come on now, Agha, just sit down for a moment and get your breath. Anyway, we'll go, but let's drink a coffee first."

"This is not the time for drinking coffee. Come on, let's go. We'll have our coffee with the governor. That heathen must have enough in his pocket to buy us a coffee, even though he acts like his money purse is sewn shut. I can't tell you how many times I have feasted him at my house, but never once did he return the favor. Not once. He's not a governor, he's just a ragdoll."

"Don't dwell on it, Agha. If you say it's time to go, then let's go."

6.
Manti Nights

I t had been a very busy day, but finally the shopping district was slowly beginning to clear out. Mehmed Efendi was troubled; at least forty questions were running through his head. He was trying to figure out how he would talk to Osman. He would be utterly ruined if the government didn't keep their word. No one would let them live in this city ever again. But these are the country's leaders, after all, and they did give their solemn promises. Omer Efendi of the Kashchioglu family was not the kind to lie.

The Waterman's Crazy Sergeant was the only one who could set up a meeting with Osman. The sergeant never tried to hide the fact from Mehmed Agha that he was in contact with Osman. So the sergeant had to trust in the plan first. The sergeant knew some things, whether right or wrong. Mehmed Efendi counted the sergeant as both a relative and a friend.

The Crazy Sergeant had suffered much in his life, spending almost all of it fighting in one war after another. He even deserted at one point, but he was counted as an honorable deserter because he deserted the Ottoman forces to join ranks with the freedom fighters. In the battle of Sakarya he had tried to help an injured Greek soldier, but when the Greek drew his weapon the sergeant was forced to kill him. When the war was over, he was convinced that the Turks had relinquished too much in the treaties. His pride was wounded and he lost faith in the authorities. When the weather permitted, he spent most of his time alone in a tiny hut-like house perched on the top of Hero's Ridge. Mad at the world, he found new solace in Osman, whom, he believed, was getting back at the government for all of their wrongdoings.

While caught up in this reverie Mehmed Efendi realized he could hear shutters being pulled shut. "Shut up the shop," he shouted to Nuhmemed and Saim. And so he folded his news-paper and stuck it in his pocket before slowly walking out of the shop while his son affixed the strong lock to the now-closed shutters. He was still deep in thought as they made their typical parade through the shopping district, with Saim leaving them at the corner as they turned into the street to the house. Without turning to look at his son, he spoke to him over his shoulder.

"You know where the Crazy Sergeant's vineyard is, don't you?"

"Of course I do, *Baba*."

"As you should. You're an almost grown man now. And you know their house that looks down from the city side of Hero's Ridge?"

"Yes, *Baba*, I know that too."

"The sergeant will most certainly be at home. How many times did I tell the crazy buzzard to mix a little bit with other people? How many times did I tell him to get closer to other people? But, no, no, he's mad at the world! The rabbit's mad at the mountain and the mountain doesn't even know it. And now we have to work with him."

"Why do we have to have anything to do with him, *Baba*? Does it have something to do with all those people that came to the shop today? Where did you go with them, *Baba*?"

"Son, you have no idea. Trouble has wrapped itself tight around this head of mine. I'm not afraid, but I don't know where this matter is going to take us. Omer Bey brought word from Ankara that the government is going to offer Sariahmed's Osman a pardon. If we end up going to war, the government doesn't need a rebel causing more trouble. They're saying that while their troops are at the western front, they don't need a fes-tering boil erupting at its back. That's why they want to pardon

Osman. They gave me the job of telling this all to Osman. That's all well and good. But what if they're setting a trap? That would be just terrible for us. Now this has fallen from the sky onto our heads."

"Anyway, isn't that what always happens to us? We find out that the government wants us to do something and we rush in blindfolded. They know you, so they found the best person for the job. No one else could handle it. Even if they did find someone else, Osman wouldn't talk to him. If the pardon isn't a lie, then no one can blame you for anything. You will have done a great service. God willing, that's how it will turn out."

"That's exactly what I think, son. But I'm trying my hardest not to make us any enemies. Anyway, they gave their solemn word. Now don't you go telling anybody about this, not even your friends."

"Are you crazy, *Baba*? Who would I tell? Of course I wouldn't tell anybody. I won't even breathe a word of it to our babies at home. Don't worry about that."

The sound of their animals' hooves hitting the cobblestones echoed down the narrow passage lanes. The men were plagued with flies until they could ride out into the wider and cleaner streets. When they reached the city well, they stopped to water their animals. Mehmed Efendi remained seated while his son tugged the animals by their bridals and led them to the stone watering trough.

"Son, you'll turn off the road at Net Hill. You know what to say to the sergeant, right? Tell him, 'My mother's making *manti* and my father has some important things to talk to you about. They're expecting you to come with Aunt Ayshe and they send you both their greetings.' That's what you've got to say. Now, go ahead, and don't let me down."

"Okay, *Baba*, don't worry. I'll tell them just what you said."

"All right, son, but make sure you don't say anything else. Only say exactly what I told you to say. Now let me describe the road one last time. There's a fork at the road at Suhmbaba. You take the road to the right, pass by Brother-in-law Rock, and then come to Hero's Ridge. If you follow the road it'll take you straight to the sergeant's house, but it's a pretty steep climb."

Without waiting for his son's reply, Mehmed Efendi turned the horse onto the road and left in a cloud of dust.

After watering his donkey at the well, Nuhmemed fumbled about in his pocket until he found his pack of Kulup cigarettes. Holding the lit cigarette in one hand, he thrust his leg over his donkey and settled on the animal's back. The animal turned and headed off down the dusty road. The dust was just about to settle when they met another group of riders and another dust cloud formed. The horses snorted and the donkeys brayed occasionally as they picked their way along the manure and urine soaked dirt road. Despite everything, the men of the vineyards were a happy group. It was almost as if they were racing to get home. Many of the men on foot hung their shoes from their shoulders and carried bags stuffed with supplies as they tried to race the horses.

Nuhmemed was busy puffing on his cigarette and enjoying his independence. His thoughts were pleasurable ones as he rode along on this mission. Night was about to fall. Mount Erciyes had cast its huge shadow, leaving the valley in darkness. The sun was now sinking behind Big Snake. Nuhmemed was deep in thought as he pushed his poor donkey on up the hill. The animal's legs trembled as it struggled to climb with its heavy burden up the steep path. Once they got to the flats, though, the animal had an easier time of it.

Nuhmemed turned off the road at Net Hill as his father had ordered and then took the right fork, heading towards Brother-in-law Rock and, finally, Hero's Ridge. Darkness had fallen. Watching the stars in the wide expanse of the sky, Nuhmemed quietly rode along. He felt completely alone, as if there was no other being between this sky and this earth. He let his imagination wander and murmured words to accompany his dreams: "Serpil, Serpil," he sighed. He had been completely entranced by the teacher that time he took the class book in for her sign. She noticed his absent-mindedness and scolded him for it. Nuhmehmed felt abashed and humiliated at her rebuke and had no idea as to how he should respond. From that moment on he tried to shut her out of his thoughts, but to no avail; Serpil Hanim's perfume, her walk, her smile that opens as delicately as a flower bud—he could not get any of these out of his mind. This woman was completely different from any other female he had ever seen in his short life. Her dress was different and so was her speech. Her breath emanated the fragrance of spring.

Serpil Hanim was from Istanbul. Her easy demeanor and smart dress had caused a sensation among the students. She represented a window into a totally different lifestyle. She was unique in every way—her dress, her manners, her fineness, and her clear skin (clear like a swiftly flowing brook, he thought). Nuhmemed was not alone in this affection; the whole class was in love with her. The class was full of young men who were secretly writing romantic poems, those who fantasized about her constantly, and those who sufficed with long, drawn-out sighs.

Their teacher was quite aware of the effect she was having. The attention usually saddened and embarrassed her, but she blamed it on their ignorance. She knew that this is what could happen in a class made up entirely of males, young men who lived in a society almost entirely devoid of contact with girls their own age.

The path was disappearing in the dusk and Nuhmehmed had to strain his eyes in the growing darkness. There was a weak light or two in the area, but these were not enough to ease his sense of loneliness. On the remote road the darkness seemed to extend to the mountaintops ringing the valley, and the starlight that only offered occasional brief glimpses of light only seemed to heighten his feeling of being utterly alone. The sky seemed his only way out. Could it be that the stars offered better worlds and warmer loves than those here on earth?

He was so hungry for affection, for a woman, for love. He felt that unhappiness lurked in the very corners of man's happiness and that man had to struggle to find contentment. Why, he wondered, was this so when there was so much beauty in these rocks and these spare and stark mountains. If people could only see, really see, the beauty around them, maybe they could find happiness in this beauty. If the soft hands of a woman could embrace a man's spirit, then he would be able to lay aside his loneliness, his dejection, and his wickedness.

As he thought about these things, he started to sing a folk song he knew, a guise to help him fill the dark night with some companionship. "Girl, your hair, your hair. Shoulder blades a quiver. Yar, yar, yar aman." His singing didn't last long. That huge rock, Brother-in-law Rock, had risen against the sky. What was it that they said? Oh, yes, that a sacred mystic named Suhmbaba had been buried there. They said he came out of the rock at night, said his prayers, and then went back into the rock. Remembering that was enough to make Nuhmehmed break off singing. He gave his donkey a couple of kicks and then coughed in a loud voice. His eyes grew wider and wider as he neared the giant rock. He wondered what a spectre would be like. Was it naked when it came out of the grave, or was it still wrapped in its shrouds? But his shrouds must have rotted away by now. "Come on, you're scaring yourself," he told himself in a loud voice. He knew that the dead couldn't come back to life. But this wasn't a dead person; it was a phantom. It was a phantom that came out at night, waited to say the early morning prayers, and then went back to the rock. He thought that the rock looked really huge in the dark. In which of its dark corners would a spectre lie? Nuhmemed was now wrapped in fear. He started to fear any tree root he saw and even the sound of the wind. As the donkey neared the rock, Nuhmemed had to resist the urge to jump off its back and run in the opposite direction. Where would he run if he could? Djinns, and the devil, and phantoms can move in a wink of an eye and grab you by the shoulder. An icy hand seemed to clutch his heart. He knew he had to eradicate this fear. He suddenly remembered to pray and shouted out a loud, "Bismillah." Then he rattled off every prayer he had memorized. Whatever prayer came to mind soon rolled off his tongue. With the bats flying around it, that crag really did look as though it were rising up against the sky.

Nuhmemed rode out of the darkness reciting his prayers. Perspiration dripped from his hands and face. He had passed by the rock and now had to face Hero's Ridge. He was too fearful to look back over his shoulder as he continued to pray. Every now and then, he called something to his donkey, just to hear a human voice. Finally he made out a light or two. When he got to the top of the slope, he could hear faint voices floating through the dark. The faint lights got stronger and stronger until he could see bright lights coming from vineyards. The voices and the lights erased his fear and he began to laugh at himself. "For God's sake, kid, you are really something. There are no ghosts, no djinns, no phantoms... So what's there to be so afraid of? Maybe someone saw a swinging branch or a rolling stone and thought it was a ghost. This is how legends spring up. Can the dead ever come back to life? Even the prophet died and left forever." He was surprised at his own fearful reaction.

Nuhmemed's imagination kept spinning as he thought of phantoms, and rocks, and his school. His donkey had found the path and was traveling on its own. The lantern hanging from a branch of the mulberry tree cast a yellow light, turning the huge shadow into a foggy dusk. The Crazy Sergeant had long before heard the approaching visitor. He knew that no one would have just passed by this place and he wondered who was coming to see him. He grabbed his gun and took the rider into its sight. He was expert enough to hit his target, but before he would pull the trigger, he had to make sure who it was that was approaching. He stood in the shadow waiting for the rider to appear.

"Uncle Sergeant, Uncle Sergeant, it's me, Nuhmemed!"

The sergeant recognized the voice and the name. "Kid, Nuhmemed. Is it you, nephew? What are you doing around these parts? Where did you come from? Allah, Allah! Hurry up now and come this way. This way."

Nuhmemed approached the *seki* and rode his donkey into the light. He tied the reins to the nearest apricot tree. "My father sent me. He sends his greetings. Uncle, my father wants to talk to you. They're asking you to come to our house tomorrow. My mother's going to make *manti*. You are invited to our house for dinner tomorrow tonight."

"Allah, Allah. Just come over this way, nephew. Sit down here for a while. Just look at you! So how did this kind of thing come up? What's your father got to talk to me about? Why does he need to talk to me? We would come at any time."

He leaned his shotgun against the wall as he talked. "Girl!

Ayshe! Look who's come? It's Nuhmemed. Nuhmemed! They're inviting us for *manti* tomorrow. And I remember just how good Hayriye's stuffed *manti* is!"

"My father has got something to talk about with you, Uncle. That's why he's expecting you tomorrow."

Aunt Ayshe was folding her apron as she walked out into the *seki*.

"My poor child. My poor baby, Nuhmemed. How did you come all this way in the dark? My God, you've become a grown man. Just look at you! Mashallah! You just sit down here and I'm going to bring you some food. Your uncle dug up the potatoes."

The *seki* looked down over the plain and from here one could see the vineyards lit up across the valley. The lights were a mirage, a mirage of lights in a sea of darkness. If it weren't for the lights blinking from the plain below, one would think this was an altogether different planet.

The sergeant sat down next to the young man and started to converse. "So, tell me, son, what are you studying to be? If only I had been able to study, nephew. If I had studied, there are many things I could have done. Would I ever have ended up like this?"

"What's wrong with the way you are, Uncle? Thanks to Allah, you have a vineyard, and a mountain of your own, and everything you need. And everybody likes you and respects you."

"That's true, but if you only knew what it took to get here. That's why I'm telling you, Boy. Study. Study. Be whatever you want to be. Studying will let you be the handle to any anvil."

While they were talking, his wife brought them tiny loaves of bread baked in the vineyard oven and a bowl of potato stew. The water was cool snow-water from their well and the dessert was a huge platter of newly cut grapes from the vineyard.

The sergeant had never had the opportunity to receive any schooling. Conscripted into the army when still young, soldiering became the only craft he knew, and then after the wars he joined a renegade gang. He had seen much and suffered much during his life. He was plagued by his inability to read and write and that's why he wanted to talk with Nuhmemed. Nuhmemed briefly told him about the political events and how Turkey was trying to stay out of the war.

"War is a horrible thing, Son. When I think about the families that were torn apart and the hearths that iced over because of the wars I saw... So much money wasted, and so many people, people wasted. When I think about the battle against the Greeks when they invaded Sakarya after the First World War, so many young men died, young boys who only had a fluff of mustache. We fought for years and years. And for what? After the war, we got these no-good devils in Ankara sitting on our heads."

"But Uncle, if men like you hadn't fought, what would have happened to the country? We could never be like we are today. It's because of people like you that men of my generation have a chance in life. But you shouldn't be so upset. In time, the right always wins out."

"That may be so, but for what? If I knew how to read and write, I might not feel like this. When I was a soldier, I couldn't even write home. I'd buy one of those ready letters and just press my fingerprint on it. And I wasn't the only one. Most were like me. But now that's all changed and even little babies know how to read and write."

It had gotten late, so Nuhmemed took his leave, bending over from the waist and kissing the back of the old man's hand and then lifting it to his forehead in a sign of respect. He rode back home as fast as he and his donkey could travel. His parents both exhaled a huge sigh of relief when their son rode into the yard. They waited up for him to tend to the donkey and climb into his own narrow bed before finally retiring to theirs.

* * *

The next day, Mehmed Efendi left the shop early to head back to his vineyard. The sergeant was already there, sitting on one of the long benches in the kiosk with a cloth over his knees as he rolled a cigarette.

The group of women was down in the *seki* sitting in a circle around a huge tray, conversing among themselves as they rolled the *manti*. Hayriye had already prepared the stuffing. She had first used an ancient cleaver to chop a large hunk of lean meat into a fine mince. This was a hard job and not all women could do it right. In the large cupboard she kept a special chopping block made out of a tree stump and used it solely for this purpose. The meat had to be chopped into tiny, tiny cubes that looked like minced meat but had a more solid consistency. She chopped with hard and swift strokes, cutting the meat into ever smaller chunks. She knew not to pound it to a paste, because then the manti would end up being pasty as well. The meat was then mixed with finely chopped onion and some chopped parsley and mixed just right. The dough was made of flour, water, and eggs, all kneaded together to the "softness of an earlobe." She rolled the dough out into paper-thin large circles that she cut into long strips, and then into tiny, half-inch squares. Now each woman sat with a pile of the squares, and a small plate of the stuffing in front of her, putting a dab of stuffing in the middle of the tiny square and then carefully folding it into a specially-closed bundle. Just before serving, these tiny bundles would be dropped into boiling water and, once cooked, added to a fresh tomato sauce. The *manti* would be served in wide flat soup bowls with a dollop of thick yogurt and a sprinkling of dried sumac. The old saying was that there should be 40 bundles of *manti* to each spoonful, but everyone knew this was an unobtainable dream and happily settled for eight to ten per spoon.

The fragrance of cooking *manti* wafted up to the men and whetted their appetites. Both knew it was time for them to begin the conversation. "So, Mehmed Agha, tell me now, what's the news around here? What's been happening? I don't go down to the city anymore. If there was a war, I'd join up. That's for sure. Not that I like war. And while we're talking about war, I just remembered something, something I've never told you before. Back then, the government sent word to this district that at least one guard had to be appointed to protect every neighborhood. So me and a bunch of my friends signed up. They gave us each a shotgun and a horse. So one evening, this gang of us entered a Moslem village that we were supposed to be protecting. Well, their food was still on their trays, but there was nobody to be found. There was nobody in the village. The beds were all made up on the floor, but they were all empty. There were dogs and cats in the village, but no people. We all camped out that night and came back the next morning. Still nobody around. One of my buddies sat on the ground and leaned his back against a wall. He was going to have a smoke. And what would you see, but the whole wall caved in! There was a cave down there, a cave like you never saw before. And there were all the people of the village. It was horrible. They had killed them all, every last one of them, babies and all. We think it was those Armenian rebels that did it. Whatever. But I still can't forget about what I saw there.

"The next day the people from another village were packed into a mosque and the mosque was set on fire. Burned them alive. We found the gang that did it. There were fifty of them and a hundred or so of us. We got them cornered down by the valley.

"Allah forbid that we ever see those kind of terrible times again. An uncle of mine told me that when he was fighting in Yemen he and his buddies were so hungry and thirsty that they shot each other just to get a watermelon they found. He fought for a long time in that desert in Yemen. Yes, all the soldiers had a hard time in those years. And the things I've seen. I've seen people hunting through horseshit looking for undigested grains. And people who boiled whatever leather they had to make soup."

"But sergeant, these are not the things I called you here to talk about. Some other important things are happening."

"So hurry up and spill it out then."

"Well, let's walk down to the mulberry tree and talk about it down there, out of reach of anybody's ears. And just you wait. I've got a treat for you down there. The mulberry's full of those long honeyberries.

The men sat on the hard clay ground as they ate the finger-long mulberries. "So, sergeant, this is what's going on. The Germans are at the border and we will probably be at war with them at anytime now. As soon as they are given the nod, they're going to attack us in Thrace. There're two things they want. The first is to open up a road to Syria and the second is to hit the

Russians from the Caucasus. Of course the country can't give them permission to do that, so it looks like we might have to fight to keep them out. The Turkish armies are going to have their backs turned to the country as they fight, so they don't want any problems breaking out at home. That's why they want to end all their fights with vigilantes, smugglers, and the like. They're asking all these people to join with the country rather than fight against it. The other day our MP, Omer Efendi, came from Ankara. He called a meeting at the governor's office and told us that the president himself had told him they want to pardon Osman."

"What?? They want to pardon Osman? Now that's something I will never believe. Just the other day, they had the whole mountain full of soldiers trying to shake him out. If they are so keen on pardoning him, why are they sending their guns after him?"

"Well, I don't know anything about that. This only came about yesterday. I believe that they are serious about this pardon and that's why I wanted to talk to you. They've given me the job of acting as the government's envoy and talking to Osman. They want me to tell Osman about the pardon. And I want you to help me set up a meeting with Osman."

"Oh for God's sake, Mehmed, how in the name of Allah did you get yourself into such a rotten mess? You and me, we're relatives. I wouldn't want you to even scrape your fingernail on a stone. But this world is full of panders and pimps. What if they're tricking you?"

"Well, the people who are making these promises are all men at the very top. They all had a meeting and they chose me to act as their envoy. They told me they wanted me to explain this all to Osman."

The sergeant wasn't yet convinced. "These people have all suckled on raw milk. I have no idea what they said or how they're thinking. There just might be a louse's bite hidden behind this. It's easy to tell this to Osman and convince him to come down from the mountain. But what if they hang him when he does? That'll be stirring up a whole caveful of bats."

"How could such a thing happen? Would such a thing ever

happen? The people who are making this promise are our top leaders. Do you think they can pull the wool over my eyes? All I want from you is to help me meet Osman. I just want to tell him what they have to say and for him to listen. Then it's up to him to accept or not to accept. If he accepts, he can move back down to the city, and if he chooses not to, he can keep on traveling from one mountain top to another."

"Listen cousin. We have always looked out for each other. I have never gone against you and you've never gone against me. If that's the way you think, then so be it. But let me tell you the worst thing that can come out of this. They may bring him out of the mountain, and the government may even kill him, but whatever happens, Hatem Agha is going to have his finger in it. You should know that."

"You're right on that point. The government's not going to lie, but nobody can trust Hatem Agha. And he's one of the people in on it. Do you know what happened yesterday? Ibrikchi's Kadir said the same thing you said. He said to Hatem Agha, right to his face. He just said whatever he was feeling. Let out all his feelings."

"And he was telling the truth. That Hatem cannot be trusted. Hatem Agha will kill Osman the first chance he gets. And then you'll be tainted as well."

"Right, but the thing is, we're not alone. We feel like we should all get together to protect Osman. At this point we've got Kadir, the Habib's Nuh, the Islam's Rifat, Numan's Mehmed Agha, Hadji Kuchuk, the Jenkchi's Jemal, and a whole bunch of others. We all feel that he should always stay with one of us. And if he doesn't want to do that, then he should let the government change his name, give him a new identity, and move him somewhere else. That's what the governor suggests."

"My goodness, Mehmed, it looks like you've been thinking about all the details. And if I were in your shoes, I'd be thinking the same way. And if you want me to set up a meeting, then I will. But let me tell you one last time. You better think this through real good. Real good. It'll take some time anyway before I can set up a meeting."

Once Mehmed Efendi had the sergeant's agreement, he

plowed ahead to set things into motion. They agreed that the sergeant would find Osman and set up the meeting and then use his lantern to signal Mehmed Efendi from Hero's Ridge. "You need to shoot off your gun if you see my signal. Shoot it off so I'll be sure you've seen it."

"Okay, cousin. You're a good man and may Allah protect you. This will be good news for Osman. He doesn't have a life up there, moving through the mountains and doing nothing else but waiting for police or gendarmes to come up and shoot him. No man should have to live like that."

"That's true enough, but what else can he do? I don't like the fact that he's up there either. But they're out to shoot him. It's a pot of filth if he lives in the mountain and a pot of filth if he comes down."

The men walked back to the house and sat cross-legged on the bench cushions. A small bottle of *raki* was resting in a jug of cold snow water. The two cousins wound up the gramophone and listened to foxtrot, a kind of music that neither liked much, as they puffed on cigarettes while waiting for the women to carry in the steaming bowls of *manti*. They spent the rest of the evening drinking and talking of the country, its past, and its future.

7.
Cur Cramps

Just a couple of days later, the entire political situation changed dramatically. The Germans surprised everybody by attacking the Russians, not the Turks. The German artillery began their sudden and deep invasion into the Russian steppe, mercilessly smashing everything they encountered.

Captain Kuddusi Bey paid a visit to Mehmed Efendi. The two men exchanged general news before Mehmed Efendi explained the task to which he had been appointed. He told him of his conversation with the sergeant and how he was waiting for further news. The captain congratulated Mehmed Efendi on everything he had accomplished thus far. The two men then discussed the latest news and turn of events.

Mehmed Efendi was not happy. "We should have supported the Germans and gone with them into the USSR. We could have attacked those Russians in the Caucasus. I can't understand what the President is thinking. We have always suffered at the hands of those Russians and then when we have the chance to get back at them, we end up not taking it. We could have finished the Russians off."

"Yes, we would have finished them off all right," concurred Kuddusi Bey nodding his head. "But let me tell you something. You should be sure of one thing: The Germans have lost this war."

"What are you talking about? The Germans are leading on every front. Look how many countries they've taken. And when they took them, they got everything those countries had. They got their gold, their mines, their money, their factories, their tanks, and their cannons. All of that now belongs to the Germans. What have the Russians got left anyway? The German forces will soon be in Moscow and when they are, nobody will be able to stop them. If we had attacked the Russians from here, we could have taken the Caucasus for ourselves."

"Forget about it. It's a good thing we didn't attack. You just wait and see. Ismet Pasha is a great man. He's got a lot of foresight and is a great statesman. Didn't he keep saying that the Germans would attack the Russians? This has proved him right. Believe you me, this has been a saving grace for Turkey. What are we saved from? From the Germans, that's the main thing. And now the Russians are in no shape to do us any harm either; that's the second thing. And the English will stop hounding us to fight with them; that's the third. But the end of all of this is going to be the utter defeat of the Germans. You'll see."

Mehmed Efendi couldn't make sense of what the captain was saying. "These men are taking city after city, and country after country," he said holding up his *Ulus* newspaper. "Look, look at this newspaper. Every single article is about how the Germans are winning. They're not an easy people to defeat. They're hard-working and smart, too. Let them take over the world and you'll see."

"Mehmed Efendi, there are some things that are hard to see. Once upon a time, Napoleon entered Russia. He got even further than the Germans have. And then what happened? How was he defeated? He was defeated by the mud, by the cold. It's summer now and the ground is still dry. Just let the rainy season begin and that will be the end of the Germans. You'll see. I wager you they will be looking back but unable to turn around and run that way. Right now the German vehicles, tanks, and planes are all working, but when that Russian cold sets in, let's see what those same troops do when they can't find food, clothes, ammunition, gasoline, or kerosene.

"You know what they say: 'The thief who plans on stealing a minaret has to prepare its cover first.' Of course the Germans must have thought this through. Can't they buy bread and gasoline from over there?"

"That would tie the Germans' hands. If that's how they plan to do things, then the Russian partisans just have to get control of the food and the Germans will be gone for. It looks like that's exactly what's happening. The Russians are burning the food supplies, destroying the bridges, and hiding whatever gasoline and kerosene they can get their hands on. And they're dumping the rest. That's why the Germans turned back when they got to Kiev. They were going to utilize the grain stored there, but let's see if Stalin lets them. What I'm trying to say is that the Germans are going to face some hard times, some very hard times. I believe that the day they invaded Russia was the day the Germans lost the war. And this has been very good for Europe, and very, very good for us."

Captain Kaddusi Bey continued with his argument. "What's an army of this size going to eat and drink? With this many tanks and cannons, just how are they going to march? May Allah be beneficent to all of us. Let's just pray that our country manages to stay out of it, and that this time at least our boys, our soldiers, won't be killed and so many of our children won't be left orphaned."

* * *

The Turkish army, though, remained stationed at the border, weapons ready to fire. And the people remained hungry. Women still flocked to the flour market and tussled over the empty sacks, each trying to find a handful of flour to feed her waiting family. Women and children wandered around the city with dark circles under their eyes and loose skin hanging from their frames. Their faces were mirrors of hopelessness and poverty and their bodies writhed with hunger.

In those days, as Mehmed Efendi walked near the grain market he saw a pile of wheat and watched as the seller put a fist-size stone on the scale, claiming it weighed a kilo. Furious, he grabbed the seller by the collar and pulled him off to the city inspectors. The seller tried to squirm out of Mehmed Efendi's grasp while declaring his innocence. The inspectors decided to test his stone and all were amazed to see that the stone really did weigh exactly one kilo. Still, they decided that the seller should not be allowed to make any more sales with his non-standard weight. Mehmed Efendi was still angry when he got back to his shop, angry about how many people in his city were hungry and angry that there was nothing he could do about it.

* * *

Days passed and still there was no word from Osman. Mehmed Efendi's life went on as usual. He traveled to and from his shop to his vineyard every day, spent what time he could with his family, and occasionally spent an evening at the City Club with his friends. No one asked him about Osman.

One evening, as usual, Mehmed Efendi arrived home on his horse and his son on his small donkey. The three younger boys had lined up in the *seki* to greet their father.

Somewhat later, Mehmed Efendi heard noises coming from the stable. The horse seemed to be snorting in an unusual way and there were sounds of it moving about. He called for Nuhmemed to bring a lantern and they went down to investigate. The horse greeted them with teary eyes and neighs of pain. The horse was on its side in its stall, trying to stand. When it did manage to stand, its legs trembled violently, and the horse had to lie down once again. Nuhmemed immediately untied the horse and father and son both struggled to get the horse on its feet. Tears were streaming down the horse's face, its legs trembled and it emitted strange neighing sounds as it jerked its head about. Mehmed Efendi became extremely concerned.

"The horse is in pain. This must be gas cramps. Look how swollen her belly is. Run to Camel Watch and call your Recep Emmi. Hurry up now." As he was talking, he massaged the horse's belly as hard as he could. Mehmed Efendi loved his horse and now he rested his own head against that of his horse, seemingly trying to share the horse's pain.

Nuhmemed did as he was told and shot out of the stable and into the dark night. Recep Emmi's house was at the bottom of

Stone Hill and the young man was determined to run the distance. It wasn't long after that Nuhmemed and Recep Emmi made their way into the yard. Recep immediately made his way through the group of neighbors and relatives who had gathered in the stable and walked to the side of the horse.

He spoke in his most authoritative doctor voice. "Move out of the way now and let me have a look. Hold up the lantern! And put down that chain." He moved his hand expertly and lightly all over the horse's body. It was obvious to all that he knew what he was doing and took pride in his expertise. Recep Emmi was a tiny man with white hair, a huge head, wide forehead, and hands almost as big as camel feet. His beady eyes seemed to be forever moving about in his wrinkled face and with every move the dirty cap perched on his head would bounce up and down. His false teeth didn't quite fit his jaw, making the upper part of his mouth look larger than the lower.

There seemed to be no spot on the horse that Recep did not feel with his huge hands. As he prodded the horse's fatty sides and pinched at its skin he seemed to understand just which organ he was examining. The family members, their uncle and cousin Tarik, all stood back and watched Recep Emmi's every move. The old man grabbed the horse by the nose and looked deeply into its eyes before once again patting its belly. He must have walked around the horse ten times. He asked no questions while he worked. He then stepped back a few paces and gazed at the horse long and hard. "Cur cramps," he said.

The men seemed to respond with one voice. "What? Cur cramps?" Mehmed Efendi seemed to spit out his questions. "What're cur cramps? And how did he get them? And what's going to happen now?

Recep Emmi was calm. "There's a solution to every problem," he said. "Now I want you three young fellows, you Nuhmemed and you Tarik and young Ahmed there, I want you to start bringing us water. You've got to massage that horse's belly with water. You've got to pour the water over the horse real slow like while you rub her belly. She's gotta get rid of that gas in her belly if she's gonna get better. But we need a cramp *chipki*, a *chipki*, that's what we need."

"What? A *chipki?* What's a *chipki?*"

"And you've never heard of no *chipki?* It's sacred, that's what it is. Sacred. It's a holy object you can't touch without praying. A *chipki* is the answer to just about everything that might ail you. Black Ismail's the man that got one. His father was a hodja. I know he'll have one. That's what we need. A cramp *chipki.* And somebody with a pure heart, somebody with a good character has got to whip that horse through the Holiness Cemetery seven times. You'll see then that the horse'll be just fine. But if we don't do it, that horse is going to die of those cur cramps!"

Recep Emmi's cap had slid back over his head. He was deep in thought as he gazed at the horse. He seemed to be sure that he had given the right prescription. Tarik, Ahmed, and Kemal were all busy rubbing the horse's stomach and keeping her on her feet.

Mehmed Efendi was thoughtful as well. "Recep Agha, are you sure that in this modern age we want to use a cramp *chipki?* Isn't there any other medicine we can use? What's this got to do with a *chipki?* Isn't there something we can cook up and feed the horse? I mean, I would feel better if there was a medicine we could give her."

"Mehmed Efendi, do you know what a cramp *chipki* is? As Allah is my witness, it works for just about everything. Anyway, where are you going to find a doctor or medicine on the top of this mountain? You've got to know that it's prayer that moves the earth and sky. And just what are you planning to cook up? This is cur cramps, cur. So we've got to find a cramps *chipki*, and the right prayers gotta be said, and that horse has got to be rode around the Holiness Cemetery seven times. That'll cure it. You'll see the horse'll be just fine when it gets back. That's the way to handle this sickness. Medicine is just no cure for the cur cramps."

Mehmed Efendi was left with no other choice but to shake his head back and forth in disbelief of what he was getting himself into. "All right then, the first thing we've got to do is to get this cramp *chipki* from Black Ismail. Okay, Son, you better get on your donkey and go over to Black Ismail's and see if he can help you out."

This was a perfect opportunity for Tarik to tease his cousin.

"Nuhmemed, don't be scared now if the djinns come after you. But beware of the black goat. If a black goat crosses your path, you're a goner for straight. If you're too afraid, don't go. Let me ride the donkey and you can walk next to us."

Nuhmemed was on his donkey's back and not taking kindly to the provocation. In a low voice he told his cousin, "Just back off. You just stay here and do your chores. You better start carrying the water 'cause there's a lot of water to be hauled up here. No black goats, or djinns, or devils are goings to come after me on the road. It's people like you they go after." So saying, he shouted a loud "deh" to his donkey as they trotted out of the yard, Nuhmemed's feet almost dragging in the dusty path.

In the stable, Recep Emmi, Mehmed Efendi, his brother, and all of the children started rubbing on the horse's belly and massaging its nose and ears. They poured water over the horse as they kneaded its body. The horse was having a hard time staying on its feet, but the group did not allow it to lie down. Recep Emmi again stood back and gazed at the horse before pulling it lightly by its tail.

"Mehmed Efendi, the horse has got to be whipped lightly with that cramp *chipki* and then rode through the Holiness Cemetery seven times while the rider recites the 'Allahuhla.' You'll see. That horse'll be even better than it was before it got sick."

"Recep Emmi, I'm not too sure about this *chipki* business. I do remember my father telling me that when his horse got sick, they used a *chipki* to cure it. But that was in the old days. Today is the age of science and I wish we could find some scientific medicine to use."

"Mehmed Efendi, prayer is the answer to all our problems. Last year the bandager, Bald Mustafa's horse got sick. It had the cur cramps, too. And I cured it with a cramp *chipki* that I also got from Black Ismail. Listen to me now, if that horse of yours doesn't get better after we treat it the way I say, then I'll pull out my mustache, hair by hair. I promise you that."

Mehmed Efendi's brother was looking at the horse with undisclosed pity. He couldn't help but jump into the conversation. "If one of the religious holidays falls on a Friday, then people bring thin branches to the mosque and place them under the pulpit. The prayers said on those holiest of days are thus said on the branches. These prayed-on branches become cures for everything."

Moving the horse around and the constant kneading and massaging began to have an effect. The horse suddenly let out a loud fart. Recep Emmi was delighted by this noisy expelling of gas. He went behind the horse and took a good whiff.

"Just smell this! This is what I call the cur cramps. That's what it is for sure. The horse just can't take a poop. I can tell by the smell. Come on now, horsey, get it out." Recep Emmi again started to knead the horse's belly and worked to get the horse to expel more wind. The first fart had brought the horse notable relief. It was no longer snorting and moving about skittishly. Still it had trouble staying on its feet and seemed to look at the men as if pleading for help.

* * *

When Black Ismail heard someone approaching, he told his son Şerafettin, "There's someone about. Could be a thief, could be trouble. Get the gun and hand it to me." Şerafettin was a huge lad, almost as big as the house's door. He grabbed the old shotgun, a relic from the earlier wars, and hurriedly placed it within his father's reach. They first heard donkey steps and then a familiar voice. "Hey, Ismail Emmi! Şerafettin! It's me, Nuhmemed!"

"That's Nuhmemed's voice. Mehmed Efendi's son. He's no stranger. Come on up here, son. What's about? Is it good news or bad? What are you up to at this hour of the night?"

Nuhmemed strode into the light of their lantern. He was out of breath. "Our horse is sick, Ismail Emmi, our horse. We called Recep Emmi and he says you've got a cramps *chipki* and asks that you give it to us. He says the *chipki* is sacred and will cure the horse of the cramps. I came to get it because our horse is really sick and may even die."

"Allah, Allah. I wonder what happened to that horse. Must have been something she ate. That Recep tells everybody about our *chipki*. I've got nothing against you, but if the government ever found out, we'd be in a whole lot of trouble."

"No, no, Ismail Emmi. You don't have anything like that to worry about from us. We wouldn't ever want you to get in any trouble. We're just not sure that the *chipki* will cure the horse. That's our worry."

Black Ismail's face, hidden in deep shadows by the weak light of the lantern, seemed to grow even darker as he listened to the young man's words. His eyebrows crossed and deep wrinkles formed in his forehead. "The *chipki* is blessed, son. When did a doctor's medicine ever work for us? This cramp *chipki* has cured a lot of people, a lot of poor people, in these parts."

"I guess I never heard of it before, Ismail Emmi."

"There's a lot you haven't heard of yet. So, you're saying the horse's got cramps, huh? And you're saying that Recep Agha asked for the *chipki*, huh? That's a man who understands the *chipki*'s worth."

"Yes, it was Recep Emmi. He asked for the *chipki*."

"Şerafettin, go to the cupboard and take out the *chipki*. Don't touch it without first saying, 'Bismillallah'. Don't ever touch it without first saying the name of Allah. If you don't pray when you've got it in your hands, you'll never understand anything from it. But once you touch it with the name of Allah on your tongue, then you will feel its real power. You've got to keep your spirit pure. You've got to keep Allah in your thoughts and you've got to pray. You've got to keep praying all the while you're striking the animal with the *chipki*. If your spirit is pure, everything will be all right."

Şerafettin handed his father a package wrapped in a green cloth emblazoned with some sacred phrases from the holy Quran. "Now, Nuhmemed my son, say that you will take this in the name of Allah and keep Allah in your mind and heart as you hold it. Think only of good things. Never think of evil, but only of good. Pray and you'll see the strength of the *chipki*."

He opened the covering and pulled out a thin blackberry switch with dry and wrinkled bark. Black Ismail raised the switch to head level and with eyes tightly shut began to recite long prayers. Turning his face towards kible, he was now unaware of this world as he noisily breathed out his prayers. When his prayer was finished, he held the *chipki* towards Nuhmemed. "Pray, my son, pray. Take the name of Allah—Bismillah—and say whatever prayers you know. Keep praying as you walk."

At this point Nuhmemed's only wish was to run away from the overwhelming effect of Black Ismail's fire-branding eyes, his deep voice, and his supplicant hands. In as loud a voice as he could muster, the young man called out Bismillah as he grasped the switch. He held it at some distance from his body, at his chest level. There was nothing special about the *chipki* as far as he could see. It was a long, dry switch. But a fire seemed to light in Nuhmemed's breast and then slowly spread throughout his body. Still holding the switch in this respectful manner, he threw his leg over his donkey and they set off for home. The donkey knew the road. Nuh's eyes were wide open as he kept the *chipki* in his sight in the dark. He recited every prayer he knew. The miracle was yet to happen though.

The switch seemed glued to his hand and he felt a tremendous power flowing into him from the *chipki*. He was happy to feel this power and this happiness made him even more intent on reciting his prayers in an even louder voice. Surprisingly enough, the darkness suddenly seemed to break and he could make out the stonewalls lining the road. This unexpected ability to see further encouraged him. Someone else was now riding the donkey, someone whose eyes glowed in the dark and who felt as powerful as the high mountains surrounding the valley. A tiny seed seemed to have been planted in his chest, a seed that grew and grew until it was as powerful as a mighty plane tree. Nuhmemed felt an overwhelming love, love for his donkey, for the walls, for the stones and trees, for everything he could see. This mysterious power cut through the darkness and showed him the truth. His love for the real world continued to expand and grow. He reached home bathed in the power and light emanating from this love. He was experiencing something between dream and reality.

Tarik was the first to notice the change. "Hey, were you

struck by a djinn or something? Did you see a black goat? Hey, come on, look at me. Is that the cramp *chipki* you're holding?" he said as he went to grab the switch.

Tarik's words broke the spell and Nuhmemed wiped his sweaty palms on the *palana*, the broad donkey saddle. Tarik was holding the *chipki*, turning it this way and that in his hands, trying to find out what was so mysterious about it. "Is this what they call a *chipki*? It's just a dry old stick. And this is going to cure a sickness? Oh sweet baby, just think of that! The only thing this stick is good for is to stir up a fire. This is just another of Recep Emmi's delusions."

He handed the *chipki* over to his father who then took it to Recep Emmi. Recep Emmi accepted the switch with a loud "Bismillah" and immediately began to pray aloud. His voice filled the stable as he held the switch in front of him at breast level. Everyone watched the old man with great curiosity. Acting as if he were alone, Recep Emmi began to pray and exhale as he walked around the horse. He used the switch to touch the horse on her belly, back, haunches, and head. He was performing a ritual that was almost as old as the land itself. Deprived of opportunities for doctors and hospitals, the people of this land had developed their own treatment methods for ailments that plagued them. The cramp *chipki* represented a ray of hope for people to grasp, and a sense of power in their lives.

The animal did appear to be better. The light switching seemed to act as a narcotic. The power passed from the *chipki* to the horse. This was witnessed by all those in the stable.

Nuhmemed had not found an opportunity to speak as he watched the proceedings. The old man's voice was loud: "Bring the saddle. Hurry up there. Now keep switching. Now you've got to take the switch and ride this horse to the Holiness Cemetery and you've got to keep switching her as you lead her through the cemetery seven times." He looked at Nuhmemed as if they shared a secret. "Nuhmemed's going to do this. He knows the *chipki*. He understands its power. The lad's got a pure spirit. His prayers will open the gate and expel the cramps." He was quiet for a few seconds and then began to speak once again. "But remember: The only words you say will

111

be prayers. You will pray as you ride through the cemetery and you will pray when you are on the road. The one who is praying must be clean of heart and soul. I say that Nuh Efendi is the one to do this. But he's got to pray if he's going to see the truth."

Recep Emmi led the horse out of the stable with the bridle. The animal stood quietly, waiting for Nuhmemed to mount. Once seated on the horse's back, Nuhmemed accepted the *chipki* with a prayer and continued to pray. Mehmed Efendi was quite touched. He had never seen his son like this before and couldn't understand what had come over the boy. Still he felt that he should encourage his son further.

"Don't be afraid, son," he said. "Man should never fear the djinns or the devil. I've passed through the Holiness Cemetery many times. There's nothing to be scared of there. Anyway, you're almost a grown man now. I'm counting on you now. Do like Recep Agha says and keep praying. Prayer is a powerful thing."

Nuhmemed did not speak, but moved his lips as he mouthed his prayers. Seeing his cousin like this made Tarik laugh. "He's moving his lips like that out of fear. Fear! He's so scared he's delusional."

These words angered his father who gave him a sharp blow on the shoulder. "You dog! You've got nothing of religion or morals. Don't you see how that boy brought that *chipki* here in the dark? Do you think he could have done that if he was so scared? People believe in the *chipki*; they believe in its power. Because of the *chipki*, the people in these parts don't feel hopeless. The *chipki* opens a path through their helplessness. So what's there to laugh at now, you filthy devil?"

His uncle turned towards Nuhmemed. "Don't be scared now, my lion of a nephew," he said. "Nothing bad can happen as long as you pray. Your spirit is clean and your prayer will find its purpose. And we will send our prayers and our breaths with you from here."

Nuhmemed wanted to be alone with the *chipki*. He wanted to experience its powers once again. Without even mouthing a farewell, he urged the horse out of the yard. He was again holding the switch aloft as he left the group of houses and went out

112

into the dark road. His family stood on the *seki* watching him leave, praying for him and exhaling their prayers behind him.

Nothing happened at first, but slowly Nuhmemed again felt something well up in his chest. The *chipki* was showing its power as the young man's eyes began to glow like coals. It wasn't long before the curtain of darkness again lifted with light, illuminating the road. Nuhmemed could see the trees, the road, and the low walls lining the road. All physical objects seemed to be spread out before him in the light. The light swept away any fear he might have had of the dark or of the trees moving with a soft swooshing noise in the light breeze. The power that was moving from the *chipki* to the young man seemed to be moving to the horse as well, for now the horse seemed to be gaining in power and determination.

Horse and rider rode through the night, passing crossroads leading to other clusters of vineyards until they came to the main road and then to the low walls of the cemetery. The walls, trees, and gravestones all were bathed in a cool light. Nuhmemed sensed an indescribable feeling of security and contentment course through his body. He gave the horse free rein and the horse picked its way along the paths through the graves. Nuhmemed felt as though he, too, had been enlightened, that he had gained some hitherto unknown knowledge of life. He felt happy and free. His spirit was filled with love as he rode through the dark place of death.

The horse and rider kept turning through the cemetery until Nuhmemed lost count of how many times they had ridden the cemetery paths. The horse then left the cemetery of its own accord and started up the vineyard road. Suddenly the animal stopped in its tracks, spread wide its legs, and let out a huge stream of urine and dung. The strong smell and explosive noise brought Nuhmemed out of his trance. He waited patiently on the horse's back while the animal spent long minutes relieving itself with bursts of gas and excreta. While sitting there, the lad felt the power he had experienced gradually dissipate. No matter how he tried to hold on to that indescribable feeling, he felt it slowly drain out of his being. He prayed feverishly, but it was to no avail. There was nothing left to do now but return to the vineyard, and the horse, also anxious to get home, set off at a fast trot. Nuhmemed still held the *chipki* respectfully and continued to pray, but the prayers no longer had the same effect.

They took the shortcut on the narrow lane, kicking up a cloud of dust as they traveled. Nuhmemed kept his eyes fixed on Mount Erciyes' majestic white face as they rode. It was as though he understood for the first time the exquisite beauty of the mountain. The darkness lifted as they rode and red rays of the sunrise soon filled the sky. Cooking fires were being lit in some of the house yards and they even passed a rider leaving early for the city.

The peaks of the Snake were bathed in red and the birds of the valley awoke and came to life, piercing the silence with song. He watched as a flock of partridges swooped down into White House. And then a huge flock of starlings flew over the Girl's House before dropping into Choke Mustafa's mulberry trees at Hero's Rock. They busied themselves by noisily vying for position in the branches and on the ground and their chirping echoed in loud and melodic song against the ridges. Bee-eaters with their red and green wings shot like arrows through the sky intent on their prey. The air was bathed with the fragrance of dittany, thyme, and tortoise clover. Despite his lack of sleep, Nuhmemed was bursting with happiness and was pleased to have the opportunity to watch the world burst into life in the beautiful morning.

From his stance on the terrace Mehmed Efendi watched his son's distant approach with deep relief. He had spent the night there, waiting and watching for his son's return, and scolding himself time and time again for urging Nuhmemed to this difficult task. He broke into prayers of gratitude when he first heard the sounds of hoof beats and then caught sight of his son and horse. "Praise be to Allah, you've come home safe and sound, son," he shouted as he met the lad in the lower *seki*. I was so worried! Are you all right? And what about the horse? Could you go and come without being scared?"

Nuhmemed understood that his father had been very worried so, coughing out the deepest voice he could muster, told his father that all was fine. "And the horse is better, too. She's much better now. Why didn't you go to bed?"

"I sent you to the cemetery, but Allah knows I was very sorry I did! I was very sorry not to have gone myself. But they said it had to be you, and that I wouldn't do. Were you scared out there?"

Nuhmemed was very tired and sleepy after this long night, but his voice still rang with happiness. "No, *Baba*, I wasn't scared. You can't tell who's alive and who's dead out there, but still I wasn't scared. The horse got better. That's the important thing."

Mehmed Efendi didn't understand much of what his son had said. "Well, you got back safe and sound and that's all that interests me. But your face looks pinched and pale. What happened to you out there."

"Nothing happened, *Baba*. It's just lack of sleep. But I will tell you some thing. This Black Ismail's *chipki* taught me something tonight, but I don't know if what I experienced was real or imaginary. But the horse relieved itself and then got better."

"Allah, Allah. Let me have a look at that *chipki*. It sure doesn't look like anything much. Which prayers did you say?"

"I said every one I knew, whichever one came to mind. As long as I prayed, I wasn't scared at all. All I remember is getting close to the cemetery walls and then the horse relieving herself."

Mehmed Efendi examined the *chipki* as he listened to his son talk. It was just a wrinkled up switch. Nothing else. He looked at his son quizzically. "I feel that you're holding back on something. Tell me the truth, now, you didn't get scared, did you?"

"No, *Baba*, I didn't get scared. Really. But this night has taught me a lot. And the morning did, too. Shooting birds. Cutting down trees. Thinking badly about somebody. From now on, that's all over. There's no more of that for me."

"Allah, Allah! What's come over you, son? This night has helped you understand a lot. I can see that now. Good for you, my brave son. But you look really tired. You'd better sleep now and come to yourself."

Mehmed Efendi was very touched by his son's demeanor and words. Resmiye was up and preparing breakfast. Mehmed Efendi decided he, too, should sleep some, so he climbed the

115

uneven stone stairs to the upper level. Nuhmemed had also settled into his bed and into a deep sleep, with his smile still lin-
gering on his sleeping face.

It was almost noon before Mehmed Efendi woke up and
learned that Ahmed had gone into the city to open the shop.
The family spoke in whispers so as not to awaken Nuhmemed.
Mehmed Efendi went down to the stables and stared keenly at
his beloved horse. He embraced its neck and kissed its eyes. He
was overjoyed to see that the horse had completely recovered.
He saddled her up and left for the city.

Kemal and Sirri only sprang to life after their father had ridden out of the yard. They ran around the *seki* for a while before
settling down at their older brother's side. One tried to tickle
him awake while the other pulled at his toes. They had learned
that their brother had left in the dead of night and had only
returned in the morning, yet still they couldn't bring themselves
to let him sleep. Nuhmemed finally awoke and looked affectionately at his younger brothers. He jumped out of bed and
took after Sirri, wrestling him to the ground before lifting him
aloft. Still holding the boy in his arms, he sat on a cushion and
lovingly tousled the boy's blond hair. The young man had visited a strange world and had brought its treasures back with
him. He was very happy and felt extremely blessed. He wanted
to share this happiness with his younger brothers. His brothers
listened in awe as he told them briefly about the events of the
night.

Meanwhile the women of the neighborhood started coming
to the house one by one to learn the news first hand. Sitting in
a circle sipping their Turkish coffees, they all agreed that
Nuhmemed had been very brave to ride the horse through the
cemetery at midnight and decided that he was definitely a person with an unsullied character, otherwise the *chipki* would not
have cured the horse.

Aunt Fadime was very impressed by the events. "Listen, girl,
something very great happened last night. The boy has to be
clean of heart or else those djinns would have struck him dead.
You were all spared and now you have to do something in
return. You should sacrifice an animal."

116

Hayriye didn't agree. "No, it wasn't like that." And then she pretended to spit in a circle, thus driving away any evil spirits nearby. "His efforts were expended for good, not evil. And he prayed the whole time." As the women talked, they snacked on fresh bread and grapes and that afternoon they sat in a circle and made *manti*.

8.
Whistling in the Dark

One evening, after returning from the city, Nuhmemed took the animals to the stable and then sat on the *seki*, watching the stars overhead. He could see the lights of the city stretching off into the distance. Suddenly his eyes spotted something at Hero's Ridge. He saw a light slowly moving from side to side. It paused momentarily and then started up again. It was as if someone were trying to communicate something. Nuh called out to his father, "*Baba, Baba,* there's a light. I think someone is signaling with a lantern."

When he saw the light, Mehmed Efendi realized it was the signal being given by the sergeant. "Signal back, Nuhmemed, right away, now, son. Grab the shotgun and fire twice. Fire it so he'll know we saw his lantern. So, Osman must have come. Osman's there and that's why the sergeant is signaling us."

Nuhmehmed ran for the gun, raised it to the stars, and released the trigger. The noise echoed across the mountains and the valley. The noise echoed back and forth, embracing the mountains and drawing them near. As soon as quiet had been restored, Nuhmemed again pulled the trigger, setting off another volley of noise echoing through the mountains.

It pleased Mehmed Efendi to listen to the echoes. He also climbed up to the terrace to be part of the action. His son was picking up the empty casings. "Okay, they got the message because the lantern is no longer burning. Let's eat our dinner

118

fast and then you saddle the horse. I'm going to go to the Crazy Sergeant's. I pray that this works out okay."

Nuhmehmed convinced his father to take him along on this important visit, but Hayriye had joined them on the terrace and had heard them talking. "Are you crazy, man? There is no way in hell or heaven that I will let you go there on your own. And I won't let the boy go either. What are you going to do with an outlaw like that? Have you gone out of your mind? I am not going to let you go there. In the name of Allah and all of his saints, I don't want you to go. But if you must, then at least take your brother and Tarik with you. If you have to go, you should at least go in a crowd."

Mehmed Efendi ignored everything his wife was saying. He picked up his pistol, loaded it, and slipped it in his shoulder holster. While he was doing that, Hayriye skipped down the steps and out of the yard, wrapping her scarf around her head as she ran. Ignoring the dogs barking around her, she ran into her brother-in-law's *seki*.

"Hey, what's going on Hayriye. A bit ago I heard your shotgun. Why did you shoot it off? Is something wrong?"

"Listen, I need help with your brother. He's planning on going up to Hero's Ridge, to the Crazy Sergeant's, all on his own. In this dark. He says he has to go alone and I say I'm not letting him."

"What in the world is going on at the Crazy Sergeant's that he wants to go up there?"

"He says that he's going to have a meeting with Osman. That the government is going to pardon him. Please, for all our sakes, don't let him go alone. You should go with him. And Tarik, too. It's better if a crowd of you go."

"Now don't be so scared, girl. So they're going to meet tonight, are they? Tarik, listen son, get your donkey ready. You should come, too, and so should Nuhmemed. This is an important task and we shouldn't leave Mehmed all on his own to do it."

So saying he strode to his cupboard and took out his large Smith-Weston pistol. He wiped off its oil and checked its bullets before expertly sliding it into the holster he next strapped around his waist. His wife, son, and sister-in-law all watched him intently.

Hayriye ran back home and helped Nuhmemed with the animals, praying and blowing her prayers as she worked. They saddled the horse together and then strapped the saddle seat on the donkey before walking together up to the family's *seki*. Mehmed Efendi had finished his dinner and lit up his cigarette as he walked down to the lower yard. He saw the fear and excitement mirrored in his younger children's eyes. "Don't be scared now. I'll be back before you know it."

His wife, still praying at his back, suddenly started talking. "Listen, man, you'd better hurry back here. And don't try to play outlaw with no outlaw! It's taken me all kinds of time and energy to raise our son to this point, and now I'm placing him and you into Allah's hands. I want you to return to us in the same condition you left."

The four men began to silently ride along the dark path. His brother led the way with the two young men in the middle and Mehmed Efendi bringing up the rear. Although silent, the two young cousins were both excited and nervous about finally coming face to face with Osman. They whispered together as they rode. The older men were silent, but each prayed when they passed the place of the holy grave at Brother's Rock and each made a silent wish. The older man begged the holy man resting there for a safe ending to that night's events.

A huge shadow fell from the mountain across the already dark road. Tarik's large and stately Cypriot donkey stepped through the shadow with confidence and ease, but Nuhmemed's tiny donkey balked and gave his rider a hard time. By the time Nuh rode out of the shadow, the other riders were well ahead of him. He could see the towering mass of Hero's Ridge in the near distance. When he raised his head, the mountain looked like a dragon rearing above him, a dragon with stars flying around its head.

The riders suddenly heard a sharp whistle coming from behind a low wall lining the path. The sound was very near. Mehmed Efendi drew his gun and peered toward the sound through the dark trying to see the whistler.

"Who's out there? Who whistled? Step forward, whoever you are."

Mehmed Efendi's voice echoed among the rocks, but there was no reply. The men listened keenly. Mehmed Efendi called out once again. "Hey, whistler, whoever you are, stand up and show yourself. It's just us. We're on our way to the Sergeant's."

The young men sat as still as stones on their animals' backs, trying to make some sense of what was happening. There was still no answer. The uncle had also removed his pistol from his holster and both men sat still, aiming in the direction of the sound. "Let's keep going then. They're probably going to meet us. Let's ride as if nothing had happened."

The horses again started to walk down the road and both young men kicked rather vigorously at their animals to make them keep up. They hadn't gone very far when they heard another whistle. They stopped again, listened intently, and looked around, but they could hear or see nothing at all. They again set off, this time even more circumspectly than they had before. Both of the older men were still grasping their pistols that they rested against their saddle horns. The horses moved more slowly along the path, accompanied every five minutes or so by the whistling which sounded sometimes from the right, sometimes from the left of the road. The riders made out long fields of vineyards on their right while the left dropped steeply down the hillside. Below them they could see the lights of Suhmbaba. They finally climbed all the way to the foothills of Hero's Ridge, which stood before them like a fierce dragon, a dragon with stars circling about its head.

Although they never caught sight of him, they knew that the whistler had accompanied them all the way. As they passed through the opening in the ridge, they could see a lantern shining in the Sergeant's *seki*. The lantern spread a huge shadow and they realized they were being observed, while they themselves could not see who was watching them. The whistling had stopped.

The Crazy Sergeant stepped out of the shadow and walked forward to meet the two older men. "Praise be to Allah, I am very happy that you have come. You are very welcome to my house, both of you. Welcome, Uncle, welcome." His greetings were warm as he took hold of the horse's bridles.

"Thanks, cousin, we are happy to be here. Tell me, has your guest arrived?"

"Yes, he has. He's waiting for you inside."

"Do you know what, Sergeant? We were accompanied by whistles all the way up here. We couldn't see who it was. What was that all about? Have you got any idea?"

"Well now, cousin, you shouldn't worry too much about that. Of course they had to know who was coming and how you were coming. That's all. The important thing is that you got here safely. And they saw to that. They communicate by whistling and they passed you from one lookout to the next as you came. Anyway, welcome to my home. Let me tie up your horses for you."

Nuhmemed and Tarik arrived out of the darkness. The Sergeant was highly pleased to see the young men. "Now, just look at my nephews! Welcome lads, welcome. You've honored me. Bring your animals over here. There's a place for you to tie them. And now, if we're all set, we can go in."

The four men walked through the lantern light and entered the Sergeant's three-arched *tol*. A group of men were sitting around on cushions placed next to the walls of the room. The nearest to the door, Şamirli's Mehmed Efendi, sprang to his feet the minute they walked in. He was tall and lanky, wearing traditional dark blue, baggy trousers, a white shirt, and a colorful scarf belted loosely around his waist. Behind his thick and dark lashes his eyes darted about, scrutinizing each man closely, while his face warmed with a genuine smile. He held out his hand, "Welcome friends, welcome."

Sitting next to him was Mehmed Efendi's second cousin, Chil Agha, the cousin who had put out his eye when they were children. Chil Agha had green eyes and a face full of freckles— chil—hence the name. His rather comic appearance belied a tough temperament. He was known for his irascibility. Chitoglu's Mahmud Efendi was also in the room. He was yet another distant cousin. A traditional stiff, egg-shaped cap was perched on the back of his knobby head. His body drew attention as it was out of proportion. He had huge hands and a long thin neck with a bobbing Adam's apple. He would have almost been a comic figure were it not for the sharp intelligence mirrored in his eyes.

Sariahmed's Osman sat on a cushion in the far corner of the room, but he also rose to greet the men. He was armed to the teeth. A thick belt held a pistol in a holster on one side, and a silver sheath with his knife on the other. Heavy bandoliers, full of bullets, crossed his chest. Another band above his belt supported several hand grenades. His rifle was propped up against the wall, within his easy reach. He wore a semi-military kind of outfit, uniform trousers and knee-high leather boots, and a red, fringed scarf around his neck and shoulders.

The men began the evening with the traditional greetings. Mehmed Efendi's older brother, Ahmed, began as he walked around the room, shaking each man's hand and greeting him by name. When he held out his hand to Osman, the younger man bent over to kiss it as a demonstration of respect to his elder, but the uncle quickly withdrew it in a counter-show of respect for the younger man's position.

Mehmed Efendi also exchanged greetings with each man in turn. He and Osman called each other "brother" as they hugged each other. Once the two older men had finished their greetings and everyone had taken their seats once again, the younger men could now kiss each man's hand as they made their way around the room. Kissing hands is a deep demonstration of respect. The young men bent low from the waist, lightly kissed the back of the other's hand, then touching the hand to the forehead. The older person being so honored sometimes kissed the cheeks of the younger, or sometimes just uttered the honorific, "May you live a long life."

Once all were seated, the second part of the greeting could begin. Now each and every man enquired of each other's health and well being. The room began with a bevy of "Mehmed Efendi, how are you? Are you well?" and replies of "Thanks be to Allah, I am, and you, are you well?" "Ahh, and you Osman Agha, are you well?" "Praise be to Allah, I am Uncle. And I am even better now that I have seen you." And finally it was

123

Osman's turn to speak with Mehmed Efendi. "So brother Mehmed, how are you? Are you well? I pray your work is going well. And look at your sons, here. It looks like you've raised them into men."

He stared long and hard at the two younger men as he spoke. He then turned to them. "So, there, nephews, how are you? May Allah be praised, Nuhmemed, you've grown into a man. The mountains and rocks are nothing to you, and you've developed into quite the hunter."

He seemed to be smiling behind his mustache as he talked to the younger men. Without waiting for their response, he next turned to Ahmed Efendi. "Uncle, I am very glad to see you. I sometimes get to talk to Mehmed Efendi at the farm, but I haven't had the opportunity to talk with you for a very long time. Anyway, who's up in the mountains to talk to? You stay up there long enough and you start talking to the birds and wolves. It's not easy to find people to sit down and converse with. When you are up in the mountains long enough, you even forget how to talk to people. And now I am here and have the chance to talk to all of you. It makes me very happy to have this opportunity."

"The same is true for us, too, Osman Agha. Mehmed Efendi and I have long awaited the chance to have a conversation with you. And now the sergeant has been good enough to let us have this opportunity. We are all very grateful to him for this."

The Sergeant broke in to say that he had wanted to set up such a meeting for a long time, but that he had had a hard time finding Osman. "You think it's so easy to send a message to our Osman? Well it isn't. He never stays in one place long enough for us to find him."

Osman interrupted his old friend. "What in the name of Allah are you saying, Sergeant? Living a life like this, I've got to have ten eyes and twenty ears. I can't trust anyone on this earth. Allah protect us all, but life is full of dangers. There can be a trap anywhere, and that trap can lead to death. That's why I always have to take precautions. People don't die from gun shots or beatings, people die from the treachery of those they know as friends. I can't tell a single soul about my whereabouts.

I like and respect each person in this room and I am most grateful to the Sergeant. Chil Agha, Şamirli, Mahmud Efendi... These are all special people, one-of-a-kind. And as for Uncle Ahmed, he's an uncle to all of us; he's our elder. And I count Mehmed Efendi as a brother and believe that whatever he has to say is for the good of all of us."

"Yes, for the good of all of us, for each of us here and for our country, Osman Agha," interceded Mehmed Efendi. "Look, Osman Agha, the Germans are at the border and Turkish soldiers have been posted on every mountain and boulder, waiting to stop them from entering. Any second now the Germans will be attacking us. The people's food has been taken from them and is being stored in mosques and warehouses. How else can we feed that many soldiers? We can't rely on the fact that we have food. The people are out of work, and hungry, and miserable."

"Yes, you're right about that, Mehmed Efendi: Men who murdered for a lousy three kurush are now men of stature. That's what bothers me so much. But there's nothing I can do about it. The rabbit's fallen off the cliff."

"Look, Osman Agha, we know each other; we know each other well. You've been in those mountains long enough now. You and I are very much alike. We grew up in the same neighborhood. What kind of life have you got up there? There's no sleep, no bread, no real food. Your life is just full of climbing from one mountaintop to another. But anyway, I've got good news for you. I'm here to do a good deed."

Osman sat on his knees on the floor cushion. In the low light of the lantern, he seemed very thoughtful as he pulled at his mustache. "So, just what is that 'good deed'? The sergeant told me something about it, but I didn't understand much. Allah knows that I am indeed tired of roaming those mountains."

"See? You think the same way I do. The government's in trouble with those Germans. They want to use Turkey to attack the Caucacus and to get at the petroleum in Mosul."

Şamirli interrupted his words, "They sure are! And the English! They keep putting the pressure on us. 'Hit those Germans,' they tell us. Old Deaf Ismet is playing them both along, letting them both think he's on their side. But nobody knows for sure just how long he can spin them along."

Mehmed Efendi again took up the talk. "That's why I am here, Osman Agha. The government is sure we are going to go to war and they've filled Thrace up with soldiers. When they're fighting on that front, they say they don't want to put down a disturbance somewhere else. That's why Ismet Pascha ordered the Kayseri MP, Omer Efendi, to call a meeting in Kayseri. The government doesn't want any trouble here."

Osman was shifting about nervously. "So, they don't want a disturbance and that's why they send a whole division out after me? The whole mountain is full of their soldiers."

"Look, Osman, they're all gritting their teeth trying to bring you in. They're afraid that if they don't bring you in, the whole situation is only going to grow worse. The government's right on that. All of Kayseri's leading officials were at the meeting and Omer Agha talked at some length. He said that Ismet Pascha himself had given the order. He said that Ismet Pascha said, 'You haven't been able to catch that Osman, so I want you to pardon him.' The Deputy Prime Minister called Omer Agha and talked to him and then Omer Agha called our meeting. They charged me with the responsibility of telling you that they are offering you a pardon. I came to tell you this because I think it would be the best thing for you, and the best thing for the country."

Osman was still thoughtful. "Allah, Allah. So that's how it is, is it? I always did like that Deaf Ismet. No matter what people say, he's a smart man. But he thinks that I'm going to form a gang and organize an uprising against the government? Allah knows that if they let me, I would go myself to fight against the Germans. Nobody should think I'm a pussycat just because I'm hiding in the mountains. If I could live in the city like everybody else, I'd still be in the thick of things. The government seems to have thought this through very well. And thanks be to you and to Allah, Mehmed Efendi. But there's still one snake in the grass that we have to contend with. And you know who that snake is, Mehmed Efendi. That snake Hatem will not let me be. He'll be the first to bite me in the neck. I'm not worried about the government or its soldiers—but the treachery of that snake Hatem? That's another matter. I worry about him and about his treachery."

126

"Osman Agha, Hatem won't be able to do anything. His hands will be tied. Just accept the pardon and come down from the mountains and leave the rest to us. Anyway, you are Hatem's worst nightmare. He's scared to death of you."

"What are you saying, Mehmed Efendi? He's a heathen, that's what he is! Not long ago I went to a wedding in a nearby village. I thought it would be nice to join in on the celebrations, but that animal sent that blood-craved Bekir to ambush me. When I left, the wedding party sent their youngest son Nazim to ride with me. Only Satan himself knows how Bekir could aim so straight in the dark of that night. My horse is a treasure and she got me out of there alive, but that poor child took a bullet right in the heart. That devil shot me, too, but my horse got us away before he could kill me. The sergeant here did everything he could and he ended up saving my life. So, now, how in heaven can I trust anything about this man?"

"Who's telling you to put your trust in Hatem Agha? My belly is full up with his talk. But the first thing is to save yourself from the government. Save yourself and then we'll all be on your side with the other issue. We're all there for you—Ibrikchi's Kadir, Jenkchi's Jemal, Haciosman Agha of Talas, the Logmen's Mehmed. When he sees that we are all together with you, he'll have to give up. He won't be able to do a thing. Just say yes to this pardon. And then leave the rest to us. That would be the best thing you could do."

Osman remained silent for quite a well. While they were talking, the sergeant carried in a huge tray filled with food. There were fresh black cumin seed rolls, farmer's cheese, melon, grapes, a spicy spread, homemade hot sausages, and still-warm *bazlama* bread loaves. There was a large pitcher filled with icy water and a bottle of *raki* for the men to share. Once the glasses had been poured, Osman raised his in a toast.

"Let us drink to the honor of Mehmed Efendi, an honorable man!"

Mehmed Efendi toasted Osman in return. "And to your honor, *sherife*!"

After they had settled into eating, Osman again returned to the subject at hand. "Mehmed Efendi, I am sick and tired of this life. I want nothing more than to live like a man with my wife, my family, and my friends. I have no children of my own and my poor wife is wasting her life away waiting for me. I can't trust anybody, so I have to keep moving, always moving from one place to the next."

"It's not a life you're living, Osman. How can anyone live every day with the fear of death hanging over him? Whatever happened, happened, and you got yourself into trouble. So you got your life into trouble once, does that mean you have to spend your whole life suffering? That's why I say you should take advantage of this opportunity. An opportunity like this doesn't come everyday. We'll find some way to deal with Hatem Agha."

"And what way would that be? I know Hatem and I know him full well. Whenever there's been a robbery, he's always put the blame on me. 'That's the work of Osman,' he says. Whenever someone gets killed, it's the same story. If there's an outlaw on the road, he says it's one of my men. Who could ever be friends with a liar like that? Can the sheep lie down with the wolf? I can't believe that man. If I can believe anybody, I know I can believe you and my other friends in the city."

"Yes, believe us, Osman Agha, believe us. Look, the gendarmes are always around these parts. They are always sniffing around and, when they do, they go all over everybody's fields and vineyards, trampling the crops and beating up the people who get in their way. If you could put an end to such troubles, you would have the blessing of every single person in these parts. You and I know that you can't keep on living in the mountains forever. There has to be an end to this one day. I am telling you Osman Agha that that day has come. You should give up and save yourself and save the people."

"Giving up is easy, but what if they slip a noose around my neck? There's something fishy in all of this. Believe me, if they said I had to spend some time in prison, I would do it willingly just to be done with this. But what if they're saying that the hangman's noose is ready and that they're going to slip it over my head the second I'm caught? There's that to contend with. We're all going to die someday of course, but the truth is that I'm scared of dying in a lowly way like that."

Mehmed Efendi was feeling the effects of the *raki* and he had to push himself to sober up.

"Look Osman Agha, I swear to you on the heads of these children here; if I had even the slightest feeling that the government was up to something, I would never have come to talk to you. Are you crazy? We go back a long way; we're friends from the same neighborhood. No matter what happens, we'll never turn you over and never let anything like that happen to you. I believe the men who told me this. They're our country's leaders. You've got the word, the promise, of all the top officials. They promised."

Up to this point, Ahmed Efendi had not yet added his own thoughts to the conversation, but rather preferred to listen as he chain-smoked his cigarettes through his amber cigarette holder. He took some fruit from the tray and handed it to the young men who were sitting apart from their elders. He felt that the time had come for him to talk.

"Osman Efendi, my son," he began. "A man's best advice comes from himself. Me, Mehmed Efendi, our neighbors here, we're all talking from our own perspectives. This is your business, and I say you know best. Mehmed Efendi told you what they said at the meeting. He believes in everything they said. As Allah is my witness, I too believe in what they said. But, actually, it's hard for any of us to really understand what's driving our leaders, our government. If we're going to be fighting the Germans at the borders, then sure enough we don't want to be picking at a boil in our interior. You and I both know that they aren't offering you a pardon just because they like your looks or mine. They're just taking precautions, that's all. Just think, one man is standing up against the government and they can't catch him. The government is scared of such a thing, and that's why they want to neutralize the situation. The people are on your side. If they were to set a trap for you, they would find themselves facing a whole lot of angry people. And that's why I don't believe they would be dumb enough to do so. They can't promise to pardon you and then string you up. Listen, son, before you give your family any more sorrow, I say you take advantage of this opportunity and turn yourself in. That's what I say."

The older man's remarks were followed by a deep silence, a silence that was only broken when Osman spoke.

"What are you saying, uncle? That I'm the kind of man to shoot the army in the back? Do you think I would ever do such a thing? When the Greeks invaded Izmir, it was the resisters in the mountains who struck back at them first. And they were all men who had been mistreated by the government. I swear to you that if I had the chance, I would fight the Germans on the side of the army. Would I ever attack our army in its back?"

"Osman Efendi, you've got to remember that governing is no easy task. A lot of blood was spilled before we could claim this country, these lands. I was a prisoner of war for six years. Human life was worth nothing. Thousands of our men died. They died of lice, of the cold, or at the hands of the enemy. The dead bodies were stacked one on top of the other. War is a terrible thing. And don't forget, the Germans' tanks and weapons are all superior to ours. Our leaders know all of this and the government wants to take measures to protect the country. This is a great opportunity, Osman Efendi, and you should understand just how good a chance this is."

Chin in hand, Osman listened intensely. "All right then, Mehmed Efendi, just how are they going to do this pardon? Am I just going to come down from the mountain and walk around free as a bird? How's it going to happen?"

"I don't know that either, but they will find some way to effect it."

"They better not torture me. I wouldn't be able to endure that."

"According to the governor, you're to be treated as a guest."

"If that's the case, then I say I accept. For your sakes I will turn myself in. But I still can't believe that Hatem is going to swallow this. He's committed to having me killed."

"Let the past alone. It's better not to open those old pages. Remembering all that stuff doesn't do anybody any good. This is the government's doing and it's a great chance for you."

"Mehmed Efendi, do you think it's easy to be a fugitive? Do you think it's so easy to wander around the mountains completely alone, to be held prisoner by the fierce cold and winds,

130

to sleep and eat in places where only djinns and spirits roam? I've gone hungry and thirsty; I've been incredibly lonely. I am sick and tired of this kind of life. I'm going to surrender, no matter what the cost. But all I ask is that you give me fifteen to twenty days. I have some outstanding loans and there are other people I owe money to. I have a herd of cattle that I am having raised in Incesu. Let me settle all my accounts and then I'll send you word."

"Good for you, Osman Efendi, and may your decision be auspicious."

"What you say is correct, Mehmed Efendi, but don't forget that there's another side to the coin. If the government isn't springing a trap on me, then Hatem and I are still going to have to settle up. Listen to me now—I don't want anything bad to happen to anyone. I think the best thing is for them to send me to another province. I'll take my wife and go. It'll be hard to leave everything I know, but at least I'll be able to sleep in a soft bed and wake up without dreaming of dying all through the night."

"That's just fine then Osman Agha," continued Mehmed Efendi, supportive of Osman's decision. "That's something that can be done. So now what do you want me to say exactly to the governor and the MP?"

"Tell them that I have decided to surrender. That I don't want to be tortured or treated badly and that I don't want to stay around here, that I am going to live somewhere else. And that I don't want to be imprisoned!"

"This is very good news. Allah let it be beneficial to all of us. Does everyone here agree with me on this?" All of the men in the room voiced their agreement and then all realized that the meeting had ended. They were all pleased because they felt that something very good had been accomplished that evening.

By the time they rose, the night was just ending and there was a very pale streak of light across the horizon. Everyone was surprised to see how late it was and how quickly the time had passed. Nuhmemed and Tarik had not joined in on the conversation. They had eaten the food put before them and they had hung on to every syllable spoken. Now as they left they could make out some shadows under the trees. These were Osman's men. These were the men who never left his side and were willing to sacrifice themselves for him. Like sentries, they waited now under the trees. These were the men who had led the visitors up the hill with their whistles. Now the early morning quiet was pierced with the sounds of horses and donkeys. The men all shook each other's hands in farewell.

The men mounted their animals and began to silently wend their way home. Nuhmemed took a long look at the road stretching down before them, the vineyards and the rocks. The morning light was reflecting off the rock faces, even illuminating some of the houses below. The men were entirely alone. Uncle Ahmed put another cigarette into his amber holder and then puffed on his smoke with obvious enjoyment. The smoke was visible only momentarily before disappearing into the gray of the morning.

* * *

The next day, Mehmed Efendi rode into town tired from not having slept that night, but also excited about the turn of events. He knew he had to share this knowledge with some of the other leaders who had attended the meeting at the governor's office. He liked Rifat Agha and admired him for his intelligence, and so asked his son to call him to the shop. Rifat Agha listened as Mehmed Efendi described in detail what had transpired the night before. Rifat Agha told his friend that they must immediately inform the governor and MP. "This could not have been an easy task. The government's been searching for this man for years and has been unable to find him, even though they've had men tearing the mountains up trying to do so. And you convinced him to come down of his own accord! This is great news!"

Rifat Agha left the shoe store and headed straight for Hatem Agha's house. Hatem could tell from his friend's demeanor that something major had happened, so he immediately invited him in. Once inside, Rifat Agha started talking. "I've come with really good news: Mehmed Efendi has convinced Osman to give himself up!"

"You don't say! Now this news is really worth something, Rifat Agha. How did it happen? Tell me everything. When did you find out?"

"I don't know anything about where or how they met. I just know that they met and talked and that Mehmed Efendi convinced Osman to turn himself in. He says that you're his only fear and that he's afraid of you and what you'll do."

"For God's sake, why in hell would he be afraid of me? Allah, Allah. I don't eat people, you know that! What in the hell would I do to him? I'm doing everything I can to help him get a pardon and just look what he starts blathering about."

"He said that you're not going to leave him alone, that you'll never let him live in the city."

"Just listen to what that devil has to say! I'm doing everything I can to save his skin and then he talks trash about me."

"Mehmed Efendi said they talked for a long time. It turns out that Osman is tired of living the life of a fugitive. He wants the government's word that they won't torture him or throw him in prison. He wants them to stick to their promise. Mehmed Efendi gave his word. But Osman went on to say that you were the keystone. He told a story about how you had set a trap for him, tried to get him killed, and killed an innocent lad instead. He says that everything rests on you and what you're going to do."

"That filthy outcast! That liar! I'm just sitting here and he spins a web of lies about me. What did I ever do to anybody? And what did I ever do to him? I've closed all those old accounts. I gave up all that up when I came down to the city and started living like a man. I'm not the one to point a finger though. So, where in the hell is he coming from talking like that?"

"Well, I'm just telling you what he said to Mehmed Efendi. He said you set a trap. Actually, I heard something about it at the time, but I didn't believe the talk. Now Osman is saying the same thing. Listen to me Hatem Agha, when this man comes down from the mountain, we don't want any of the old enmities to start up again. We're just a handful of men here and we have to get along."

"Are you crazy or something, Rifat? How in the hell am I to know who set a trap? The guy's an outlaw. Who knows how many families he has torn apart, or how many girls he has defiled? An outlaw has got thousands of enemies. So how in hell could I set a trap from here, from this place?"

"Not you personally. They say your man, Bloody Bekir, did it. And that you put him up to it."

"Where in the world did they come up with Bekir? He's just a poor sap that works out at my farm. I just feed him and give him a place to sleep to keep him from starving to death. Who would want to point the finger at a guy like that? Osman was just looking for excuses and it sounds to me like he's fooled Mehmed Efendi."

"I don't know whether he fooled him or not, but that's what Osman told him."

"There's no truth to any of that, Rifat Agha. So when is Osman going to turn himself in? Did he say anything about that?"

"I guess he engages in some kind of trade or other and makes his money that way. He says he has to settle his accounts and that he'll surrender within the month."

Rifat and Hatem talked for a long time. Hatem swore that he would live in peace with Osman once he came down from the mountain and that he would even find him a job and give him some money to live on. Hatem's wife served them a fatty lamb's rib meal for lunch. They both slurped it up and then sweated profusely from the garlic she had added. The melons they ate for dessert took some of the edge off the grease. After lunch Rifat Agha went back to his lumberyard, thinking about the delicious meal as he walked.

Hatem Agha had been waiting for his friend to leave, even though he managed to conceal his impatience. No sooner had Rifat Agha turned the corner than Hatem Agha grabbed his hat and set off for the governor's office. His hat was perched on the back of his head and he walked with his head and eyes down, thinking about his next move. He only mumbled his greetings to all of his acquaintances that he passed along the way to the governor's. He passed by the club building and Kenan's Teagarden, both of which were preparing for that evening's customers. Shoeshine boys with their boxes and brushes were lined up in a long row in front of the city's only cinema. He didn't even absorb the fact that a zombie movie was playing at the Tan nor that the pavement in front of the movie house was carpeted with the shells of sunflower seeds that had been spit out by the moviegoers. Deep in thought, he kept right on walking, or rather marching, straight to the provincial building. The guard at the gate deferentially nodded him into the building. Some of Hatem Agha's anxiety dissipated when he entered the cool building that lay in deep shadow. Twirling his hat in his hand, he climbed up the broad staircase to the governor's private office. Once in the outer office, he gave his name to the *mihmandar*, the youngish man who functioned as receptionist, security guard, and general errand boy, and was then ushered into the inner office.

9.
Blue beads

Skipping down the stairs two or three at a time, the official was soon out of the provincial building and through the door of Mehmed Efendi's shoe shop. He passed on the greetings of the governor and then asked that Mehmed Efendi accompany him back to the official building. Mehmed Efendi was surprised to see how little time it had taken for the news to reach the ears of the governor, but then being called in at least spared him the trouble of making an appointment, so he wasn't much concerned.

The avenue was quiet; he noticed the sparrows lined up on the electric lines overhead and how attorney Nafiz Bey's window was smeared with dirt. Ibshircioglu was busy dusting his row of shiny bicycles while Kelemir and Ihsan Tak seemed to be in the midst of an argument. The shoeshine boys had now taken shelter in the shade cast by the citadel and were waiting for any customers that might happen by. Someone had set up three or four old bicycles near the double doors of the mosque and was trying to rent them to passing young boys.

The governor looked very pleased as he greeted Mehmed Efendi at the door to his office, formal greetings pouring from his mouth. "Welcome, welcome, Mehmed Efendi. Your coming is propitious and has brought us great happiness. I heard the auspicious news and I decided that we should meet. So welcome, welcome."

As Mehmed Efendi entered the room he came face to face with Hatem Agha and immediately registered who had brought the news to the governor. He didn't let on that he also understood that Hatem was bent on upstaging him. He sank into one of the deep Moroccan leather armchairs lined up around the governor's desk and accepted the demitasse of Turkish coffee that was smartly placed in front of him on the round glass-topped table to his right. A glass of cold water was placed next to the coffee, a secondary act of courtesy.

The governor got right to the subject. "Mehmed Bey, Hatem Agha brought me the news. He says that Osman agrees to turn himself in. God bless you, Mehmed Bey, for you have succeeded where everyone else has failed. You have done what hundreds of gendarmes, police, and even government officials have not been able to do. I hadn't gotten any word for quite some time and I was wondering what, if anything, was going on. So tell me everything now and start from the beginning."

Mehmed Efendi chose his words carefully as he described the events and talked about Osman's fears and conditions. He was still speaking when the governor interrupted him, "Did he say exactly when he would surrender?"

"Well, it turns out that he is raising animals and that he has some accounts to settle up. He wants to do this first since he will need money when he comes to the city. He said he would be able to finish up everything in one month's time and that he would send word about when he was going to surrender. He said he would trust me to work out the details."

"And he can and he should trust you. Yes, trust. And we will keep his trust. That's for sure. After all, this pardon is the personal pardon of the president himself. What else can I say? After all, we can't give him a stamped piece of paper. He's got to trust us and place himself in the merciful hands of Allah and then turn himself in. Give him every kind of guarantee. Torture? Of course we will have none of that! He will be our guest. Our guest! The important thing is that all this mess is finished."

"Well, Governor, I did the best I could. I gave him my promise. He says that he won't want to live around here anymore. He wants to start a new life in a new place."

"All right, Mehmed Efendi, all right. I'm going to pass on this information to the Secretary of the Interior and then they'll pass it on to the President. So thank you very much gentlemen, thank you."

The governor walked them as far as the staircase and then went back to his office and picked up his wireless. His voice could be heard echoing down the long corridors. He was speaking to the MP.

* * *

The Suhmbaba vineyard was nestled against the foothills of Hero's Ridge. This vast vineyard ended up joining with deeply cleft rocks that had been dug out of the rock face by the forces of ice and wind. These clefts were wonderful cold storage areas used by all of the people in the area to store their foodstuffs. The clefts were narrow openings leading to wide and spacious caves that were lined with pots of home-churned butter, pots and cakes of cheeses, salted meat, and vegetables and fruits of all kinds. Nothing was under lock or key, but no one—not even in that time of near-famine—ever thought to touch a neighbor's supplies.

The vineyard was reached via a narrow path that forked off the Hero's Ridge Road. The house itself was simple: one very basic kitchen and a sparsely furnished room. Near the house was a stable and barn. Another kitchen had been built a bit apart from the other buildings and it was here that most of the baking and cooking was done. Wheat was about the only crop that grew in abundance across the Kayseri plain and the people had, from necessity, come up with all sorts of ways to use flour in breads and pastas. *Bazlama* is the typical bread eaten at the vineyards. The sourdough loaves—the size of thick saucers—are baked in a conical oven fired by last year's dried vines and the breads seemed to absorb some of the nutty flavor of the vines as they cook. They are a treat, especially when fresh, when each person can claim a loaf; some spreading a fresh clove of garlic over its hot surface before eating. *Katmer* is a richer bread product. The baker rolls out a huge circle of unleavened dough that she then smears with melted butter and *tahin*, or thick sesame paste. The dough is rolled into a long cylinder. Long strips are cut and gathered up snail-like before being rolled out once again into plate-size cakes. These are then baked on a *sach*, a large round grill placed over an open fire. The *katmer* is a breakfast or tea food and is always served with homemade jams, preserves, or honey. *Yaglama* is lunch or dinner fare. Thin circles of unleavened dough are baked quickly on a grill and set aside. The cook then sautées hamburger and onions with a little tomato and green pepper and melts some butter. Each diner is served a thick pile of the thin breads layered with melted butter and the meat mixture and topped with a generous dollop of fresh, plain yogurt. The sergeant's wife, Ayshe, was a wonderful cook and her children and grandchildren would wait impatiently for the trays of food to be brought out from her kitchen into the *seki*.

Behind their vineyard and higher up in the tangle of rock face, punctuated by boulders both large and small that seemed to have been tossed against the hillside, was a narrow cleft, a tiny opening that led into yet another dark cave. This cave was the primary home of Osman's men: Idris the Kurd, Hadji, and young Kazim, the young bridegroom whose brother had been so coldly murdered by Bloody Bekir. These men were fed by the few families who inhabited this severe landscape. The men lived in darkness. They mostly stayed hidden in the dark cave during the day and came out only in the dark of the night to sit together under the stars, their eyes roaming over the sky curving above them and their thoughts roaming through their past lives, remembering what they once had had and once had been.

Several weeks had now passed since the night of the meeting. Osman was staying in one of the Hero Ridge vineyards, watching over the herd of horses he was keeping in one of the hidden passageways and mulling over what he had been told at the meeting. He just couldn't come to a decision. On the one hand, he was sick and tired of this outlaw life. The loneliness of his life had become an almost unbearable burden. He desperately wanted to rejoin the society of men and he knew this was his chance. But was it really? Hatem Agha was the thorn, the prickly thorn that bit into his mind as he tried to reach a decision. He thought that even if the Republic pardoned him fifty times over, there was no way on this earth that Hatem would stomach it. And how could he escape Hatem's grasp? Even if he changed his name and moved far away, he felt sure that Hatem would manage to find him, one way or another. With these thoughts plowing through his brain, he walked towards his men's cave. The stars were diamonds in the bowl of the sky, shining on the mountains and making them seem even higher against the backdrop of the sky.

Hadji, sitting on a flat rock and dreaming of his wife and sons, spotted Osman's approach. His fantasy cut off, he jumped up to tell the others. The men hurriedly put their cave into order, lit their lantern, and then stood in a straight line, military style, as Osman neared. Each of them had a string of bullets draped across his chest, a knife in his belt, and a Nagant pistol in his holster. They were loyal to Osman and would willingly die for him and with him. And he knew this.

Once in the cave, Osman sat down on one of the long stone benches and motioned for the men to sit as well. He took out the box of cigarettes he had rolled and offered one to each of the men before taking one himself. After all had lit up he began to speak.

"I've come up here because I think that we need to talk, and to talk seriously. Our lives are tied together and we have all become comrades of fate. What happens to me, happens to you. And what happens to you, happens to me."

The men nodded in assent. They had heard the discussions of that night and were curious as to what decision Osman had made. The men had talked of little else and each had his own idea of what they should do. This was why Osman had come. He told them he needed their advice.

"Agha, what can we say? You're the one with the brains and so you're the one who has to decide. But no matter what those people said that night, it's near impossible to figure out just how the government officials will act. They say one thing one day, and the exact opposite the next. They're supposed to be the people's servants, but when did they ever keep a promise? So that's why I say, I don't know what to think or what to do."

"Come on, Idris, you must be thinking something. Allah has given you a brain, so there has to be something in that mind of yours."

"Well, Agha, we did talk amongst ourselves. And we're worried that as soon as you go down to the city, those gendarmes will be on you, rope around your neck, just like that. And if and when that happens, who will there be to save you? Who can you complain to?"

If Idris had other thoughts on the matter, he chose to keep them to himself. After a brief silence, Kazim spoke. "Agha, you've always told us to act like men. We swore on our actions and our words to be men. So let's keep our promise. If we have to die, we die. What's death to us? But we shouldn't die for nothing. Let's just say the government keeps its words for once, and actually gives you a pardon. But then what about Hatem Agha? Whatever he does, we all know he'll try to get rid of you. He'll just give his men the nod, and then they'll take care of you. He's not going to want you to live a single night down there. They're all heathens. That's what they are. The government will pardon you, but Hatem won't. That's for sure. And that's why I say that believing those men about any pardon would just be a big mistake. We've chosen our life and our life is these mountains. We're not out to hurt anybody and we can put up with this misery. At least we're alive."

"I've been thinking the same things, Kazim Efendi. On the one hand, I say, 'That's enough. Let's just go and turn ourselves in,' but, on the other hand, I think that it has to be a trap, that there's a hanging tree waiting for us down there and that it would be dumb to just walk to my death."

"I'm not saying this just because Hatem and his men killed my brother. But I say that we can never trust the government. Idris Agha says the same thing. You trust Mehmed Efendi, but he was bringing us the promise of the governor, of the general. They're just civil servants themselves. And who was actually with the President when he talked about this? As for me, the only thing I want to do is clean the earth of that animal Bekir. And I'm going to do it eventually, if not today, then tomorrow. Even if it takes me fifty years. That's why I don't want to talk. I don't want to

141

talk because I think there's a lot of stink in this deal."

Kazim's words echoed off the cave walls. The pale light of the lantern wasn't strong enough to light up the men's faces, so their thoughts were veiled by the darkness of the cave. Osman also wanted to ask Hadji his thoughts, but he knew that Hadji would never speak without being urged to do so. And he knew that even if he did speak, his ideas would be up in the clouds somewhere.

"So, what have you got to say, Hadji Efendi? Have you been thinking about all of this? So, should we do this, or should we not? What do you think?"

Hadji spoke in a whisper that was hard to make out. His eyes were lifted towards the cave ceiling. "Agha, I personally just can't trust anybody anymore. It's always been those people I trust that have caused me to suffer. My wife was like a rose, and those two little kids of mine. I trusted her. I trusted her completely. And that scab was old; my wife was younger even than his daughter-in-law. If I hadn't happened to go home that day, maybe both of them would be alive. See, I trusted that wife of mine. I trusted everybody. And look where it got me? All I have to say is that you shouldn't trust anybody, Agha, cause trusting just gets you into big trouble."

"You're right, Hadji. It would be crazy to put our trust in anyone. And anyway, we're not out to hurt anybody. What difference does it make really? The mountains or the city? The best thing is to walk on firm ground. That's what I've been thinking too, gentlemen. Just like you. Why should we let them slip a noose around our necks?"

Idris had an idea. "Allah save you, Agha. What would we do without you? But it's wrong of us to just sit here and not teach that Hatem Agha a lesson. Agha, if you let us, I say we go to his farm down there in the canes. That would be something different to do. We would get to move these bones of ours and he would learn a lesson or two about who he's dealing with."

Kazim joined in. "You're right. We could set his animals free and burn his buildings. Let's pay him back for that filthy trap he set. And, Agha, there just might be no pardon after all. But there was an ambush. And I'm sick and tired of sitting around here all the time doing nothing. Come on, Agha, let's pull down everything he has on that farm. Pull it down and throw it on his head. I say we should go right now. If we leave now, we can be at his farm by dawn. For the love of Allah, just think about that. And that bloody Bekir is most likely there, too."

They were all stirred up by Kazim's proposal and the cave suddenly seemed to come alive.

"So we don't have to give anybody an answer. This'll be our answer. Let's go down and check that farm out. And if we do find that scab Bekir, it's going to be me who gets him right between his eyes. After all, I was the one who got to taste his bullet."

A short while later, there were shadows to be seen among the rocks. Like ferrets, they crept out of their hiding places and began their trek down into the valley. They took their blankets, bullets, guns, and cartridges with them. Osman went quietly into his nephew's kitchen and took whatever food he could find. He led the men down the hill until they came to Brother's Rock.

Idris the Kurd hated passing by this crag. It always seemed like a bad portend. He wasn't alone in this belief of his. All those who knew the rock believed that it was the home of a wandering spirit who came out in the early morning to say the ritual prayer. Nobody knew who the spirit was, who it was related to, or where its body's grave was located. All they knew was that the spirit came out at midnight to say its prayers before going back into the crag. It was now exactly midnight and nobody would be so brave as to pass this way at this hour. The rock itself stood like a ghost with its arms wide open. The road had to narrow to a path to get past its large frame. Osman's horse was the first to pass through that narrow passageway and disappear into darkness on the other side. Kazim was next, then Idris followed by Hadji at the rear. As always, Hadji was peering up at the sky above and letting the horse free to travel as it might. Despite all that Idris had seen and done in his life, he was still afraid of this spirit. As he neared the rock, he began to pray in the name of Allah while he pulled out his pistol just in case. He rested the gun on the horn of his saddle as he drew closer.

All at once something strange happened. Something had spooked his horse and it started moving sideways. Idris was spooked as well. He kept his eyes and ears glued on the rock, looking and listening for something. He was ready to shoot the spirit, if only it would come out in the open. But he wasn't sure if bullets could stop spirits. The hoot of an owl and the bark of a far-off dog was enough to make Idris even more wary.

Idris was right to be spooked for strange sounds could be heard from among the rocks. Suddenly a giant ghost of a figure could be seen standing in the middle of the road. The horse reared back and it was only this rearing that saved the life of the ghost. Idris had not been able to shoot before he was stopped by the shouts of Hadji.

"Hold off there, Idris. Hold off. It's Jemil. It's just Jemil." Hadji then directed his words at this huge man standing in the road. "Uncle Jemil, what are you doing out here at this time of night? For the love of Allah, what are you doing up here in these parts?"

In the darkness of the night, the shadow on the road reached out and grabbed Hadji's bridle. "With your leave, Sirs, with your leave. Blue beads, Sirs, blue beads. Blue beads are good for you. Blue beads."

As the shadow of the man held out his hand with beads, another figure appeared out of the rocks. This was a round figure that almost seemed to roll towards the road. This figure, eyes shining like an owl's, was carrying a yogurt pan full of bread loaves.

Idris was completely taken aback. Only Hadji's fast intervention had stopped him from shooting this person. He struggled to calm his horse as the man tried to thrust something at him. It was Hadji who spoke. "What's this, Uncle Jemil? What are you doing up here at midnight?"

"I've brought beads. Blue beads. Take them. For luck. You need this. You are traveling to the other side of the mountains this midnight. To a place of evil. And you, you, too, are not acting in righteousness. Those who bring death, take death. And destruction comes of evil. Take this blue bead. Take it now. For it will bring you luck."

Osman had now ridden back with Kazim and the group gathered in a dark circle around Brother's Rock.

"Osman Agha, do you know who this is? It's Jemil. Jemil and his mother. Look, they know where we're going. And they say that we are up to no-good and that taking life only begets death. That's what he says, and then he says he wants to give us some blue beads. He claims we need them to protect us."

"Allah, Allah. What hole did he pop out of at this hour of the night? If he wants to give you a blue bead then take it. How would he know what we're up to? Take the bead."

Osman rode his horse alongside the man standing in the middle of the path, his eyes peering down at him. A dirty cap was tucked low over Jemil's forehead, yet his eyes still glinted through the dark like small globes of piercing light. The eyes reflected a deep comprehension that was surprising in the stooped and dirty figure. He wore a long, oversized coat belted at this waist with a length of twine. His fingers were laced with beads, beads that he offered to the men with outstretched arm. His mother squatted in the dirt of the road next to her son. Wisps of greasy white hair poked out from under her dirty headscarf. She observed the events without speaking.

Osman was intrigued. "Jemil, do you know who I am? Do you recognize me?"

Jemil's eyes swept over the man, taking in every aspect of the figure sitting on the horse above him. "I know you are not doing good. Not the good. Fire fuels hatred and blackens the soul. Listen to me now Osman Agha, son of Ahmed Agha. Flowing blood will extinguish the flame. And the pain will be endured. But this is not a good thing you are doing now, not a good thing. There are many more lads to marry, and maids to be wives. Take them for your model, for the greatness is in that. Take these now. Take these. For the bead is good. Take the beads."

"All right, Jemil Agha, all right. But tell me now, what are you doing here at this hour? What are you doing at the Rock?"

"We are the wanderers. Tonight is a holy night; it is a Friday eve. I saw you pass and decided to give you beads. These are not just objects, not just objects."

"So you came to visit the spirit?" Osman jumped down from

145

his horse as he wanted to kiss the wanderer's hand, but he was stopped from doing so by a wall of nauseating odor. Still, Osman was surprised at what Jemil Agha had said. He grabbed the beads the man extended in his claw-like hand and gave one to each of his comrades. Osman then thrust his hand into his pocket, pulled out a ream of bills, and handed these to the man. Jemil slowly eyed the money and then picked the smallest bill out of the other's hand. This he handed to his mother who was still squatting in the dusty road. Still not uttering a sound, the old woman quickly put the money into her little coin purse without even trying to make out its denomination.

Osman urged Jemil to take more of the liras. "Come on, Jemil, take more. Don't worry about it. I take what I want from where I want and then I give it to the people who need it. That's my way."

"Money taken without permission will burn the hand of the taker. Only because you give away the money you take are you spared from burning. I don't want any money, but my mother wants money. She's the one that wants money. What's it to me? It's paper. Look at those mountains; look at these trees and rocks. You can see everything out here, everything. Open wide your spirit and you will not be empty. Look and see. See the wind and the flying bird. See them. Learn how to see. But my mother never lets me be. She always wants something. A person is only rich when they can know the truth, when they can see the truth. Then they know they are alive."

The old woman suddenly began to speak. "My son knows everything. He sees everything. But I am not like him. Look how old I am and yet he drags me everywhere, here and there. We eat stale bread. My teeth can't chew it. I don't have the strength. There's the cold and the heat; days we are sick and days we are well. But I have no power left. He takes heed of nothing."

"You will be fine, Mother. Fine. What's money to us? It only dirties the hands. And now Son of Ahmed, listen to me when I say that nothing is going to happen to you. But you are not going now to do good deeds. Come on, Mother, get up now. It's almost morning and we still have a long way to go."

The old woman slowly rose and then, without a word of farewell, she and her son began walking down the path towards the city.

Idris the Kurd was still in shock. "For God's sake, if the horse hadn't reared, I would have shot him. Thanks be to Allah that the horse got spooked. I really thought it was a djinn or something like that coming out of the crag."

"You don't know this place as well as I do," said Hadji. "Jemil and his mother are always wandering around these parts, summer and winter. But 'what surprises me is how, in all this dark, he managed to find the smallest denomination. Only Allah would understand that. But there's something to this fellow, that's for sure."

"Well, if there is," interjected Osman, "we will never be able to understand it. Let's not waste anymore time dawdling around here. He says that we're up to no good, but he doesn't have to live like we do. He doesn't have the police and gendarmes breathing down his back. And he doesn't feel the heat of that blood-crazed Hatem Agha. He thinks one way and we think another. What's good as far as he is concerned isn't necessarily good for us."

The words were scarcely out of his mouth before he urged his horse into action and the group again rode out into the dark night.

Jemil had set the men to thinking, and so as they rode they talked of life and death and debated the notions of sin and redemption amongst themselves. Kazim had been quiet up till then. "I think it's best that we not get ourselves mixed up in Allah's work. He made us the way we are and makes us do the things we do. That's our fate and that's what Allah writes for us. And now we're going to go to Hatem Agha's farm and set it alight. Do you think Allah is going to call that a sin? I don't believe so, not for a minute. That Hatem has been sinning against all of us for years. He lies and lies about us. He had my own brother killed and in the city he's got his finger into every single dirty thing that goes on down there. What we're doing tonight is bringing a tiny bit of justice to the situation, that's all. So is Allah going to blame us for doing that? Maybe our fate is to be the instruments that give Hatem the punishment that Allah wants to give him. That's what I think, that we are instruments of Allah tonight."

Idris listened closely to the words of his comrade, but he told himself that tonight he was going to change his ways. After tonight he was going to give up this life and take up a life of prayer and contemplation.

The men rode on, in silence now. They passed through White House and made their way down to Sheep Father. Here there was a well located at the spot that marked the end of the Big Snake and the beginning of Little Snake. Nobody knew who had dug this well or why, for this was an uninhabited stretch of land. According to the local legend, there was once a shepherd called Sheep Father who had prayed to God for water for his thirsty flock of sheep and as he rose to his feet after praying, water began gushing from under his staff. The mouth of the well was lined with stones, both large and small, and a small metal bucket was suspended into the water by a heavy chain. The men stopped here at the deep well and let their horses drink its icy cold water before continuing down to Robber's Creek and the reed marsh. They knew the farm lay just south of the swampland.

The men rode their horses into the river that flowed almost silently through a gorge, lined on both sides by steep rocky cliffs that rose to meet Big Snake; from there they followed the river to the neck where they crossed to the opposite side. They easily found the sheep trail that led up through the rocks and then down to the swampland. The silence of the night was broken only by the occasional strike of a hoof against stone and the darkness pierced only by the tip of Idris the Kurd's cigarette.

The dark was just on the verge of breaking and there was the early song of waking birds as they began to ride through the marsh. Suddenly the air seemed to come alive with the call of birds, mostly goslings and wild ducks. Flocks of starlings took sudden flight, wheeling and turning above their heads.

The riders paused when they came to the flat stretch of dry land. The humid air had made them hungry. Osman distributed the bread loaves he had stored in the pack at his side and each man chewed his small loaf while still mounted. Ready food was a necessity for the men, as necessary to them as their weapons and ammunition. Now was their time to prepare for action. They dismounted and checked their horses' rigging, pulling a strap tighter here or loosening another there. Everything had to be perfect.

Dawn had broken as they began to ride once again and they could now easily see their way, even though the rays of the sun were still blocked by the mountain. They cantered down the smooth road, their eyes on the horizon. The sky was a palette of pink and the sun had risen behind the purple mountains. Despite the beauty of the morning, the hatred in the souls of the riders seemed to fester and boil until it spilled out of their hearts and spread through every pore of their bodies. They urged their horses into a gallop.

The distant sounds of dogs barking and roosters crowing became more and more distinct. They quietly drew their horses to a halt under the shadow of a huge boulder. Dismounting, they led their horses to the tall bushes and hid them there. The men checked their weapons, their handguns and rifles, making sure they were loaded and ready to fire. Now ready, they walked in fast strides towards the farmhouse, the smell of blood coursing through their brains.

They were in front of the farmhouse when they came face to face with a pack of barking dogs. The five dogs advanced, saliva dripping in gobs of white foam from their mouths. The dogs barked and growled and bared their sharp teeth. They were fierce and loud, and around their necks they wore sharp nail collars to fight off wolves and foe. Their barking could wake the dead, but there was no sign of activity in the house. In time the dogs grew tired of the noise they were making and fell silent. The house, too, remained silent and no one made an appearance. Without backing from their human masters, the dogs turned tail and slunk away.

Osman and Kazim guarded the front of the house while Hadji and Idris each took a side. It was very light now and everything could be seen clearly. Osman and his men searched everywhere but found no one. The farm was empty. Once they understood that there was no threat, they slumped to the ground and held their sides as they tried to regain their breath.

What they didn't know was that the when the water in the swampland had receded, it had left an expanse of fertile soil. The farm boss, Bloody Bekir, had packed up everything at the farm, the fifty or so oxen, calves, and cows and had herded them all down to the new fields. The men wove sleeping mats from the reeds and built reed shelters. The pots and pans they took with them provided everything else they needed as they tended the new crops. They had left the farm to the care of the dogs and chickens.

The farmhands respected their boss, Hatem Agha, and his every visit was a kind of celebration. Just watching the carriage arrive was a show in itself. The springs of the one-horse carriage almost touched its wheels with Hatem's huge frame spilling over the sides of the conveyance. His driver would be squeezed onto a tiny space on the bench seat, his body almost engulfed by that of his companion. Exhausted by the bouncing trip on the dusty road, Hatem would mop his red face, sweating under the brims of his hat. Tired though he might be, he would be ready to show his men what a fine agha he really was. He would slowly descend from the carriage and then walk around his farm, hands clasped behind his back, his heavy coat thrown over his shoulders as he patted the sides of his animals, seeming to show his skills in animal husbandry. Then he would call his foreman.

"Bekir, Son. Take a look at this calf. Its got rough patches on its coat. Look here, you're not taking proper care of these animals. Look at this, right here. This. And this plate. It's not clean. Look, I don't like to stick my nose in your work, but look at that hay. Don't you take care of anything around here?"

The men would load the back of his carriage with butter, eggs, and yogurt and then came the time for him to begrudgingly hand each of the men his pay. As each man received his money, either in lesser or greater amounts, he would bend low and kiss the Agha's hand before standing in the line with the others. After completing this almost ceremonial visit, he would again slowly climb into his carriage, settle deeply into the seat, his brimmed hat perched awkwardly on his head, and leave the farm in another cloud of dust. Even though he left them half-starved, his men remained devoted to him. He gave them their pittance and then wrote their debts alongside each man's name in his thick notebook. The debts only grew larger.

Idris had discovered the henhouse. He picked up a couple of eggs and broke them raw into his mouth. The yolks were delicious, especially since he was so hungry. He then gathered up the rest of the eggs for his friends.

Kazim set a handful of straw alight and tossed the burning mass into the straw pile. The courtyard was soon filled with smoke and then the flames rose, taking the house and the barns, and rolling in a wide wave towards the swampland.

The men left without being seen, but Osman knew that the fire would cause a thick smoke that reached to the city, to the government offices. He knew that his name would spread like the flames and that soon the gendarmes would be in the countryside, pulling in villagers to question, and flogging the naked feet of those unwilling to talk. Osman had thought of this and knew it would be too dangerous for him to even go back to the mountains. The best thing was to hide in the great swampland, on Lone Grave Island, and wait for the excitement to pass.

He led his men deep into the marsh. The day was hot and the swamp was blanketed by a thick cloud of mosquitoes, sand fleas, and gnats. The insects engulfed the men and the horses, making it difficult for them to breathe. The sounds of birds and pulsating wings got louder and their nostrils were filled with the pungent smell of mud and weeds and rotting reeds. The horses' hooves first sank heavily into the mud and soon the animals were wading in knee-high water. The muddy water splashed against the horses' rumps as they rode.

Osman was very familiar with Lone Grave Island for this was his refuge when he was most in danger. Hardly anyone else knew about this island in the swampland and so it was an ideal place to hide. The horses' tracks were drowned in the mud and muddy water, so the men could not easily be followed. They rode single file deeper into the marsh, with Osman taking the lead.

10.
The Swamp

B loody Bekir's men had made camp a bullet's reach away from the mouth of the marsh. Early that morning, the farmhands were just emerging from their cots, getting ready to face another day of worrying about their next meal.

Their noise woke Bekir and, still half asleep, he reached for his shotgun and briefly ran his hands over its damp muzzle before stretching himself up onto his two feet. He called out for Irgat Fevzi and told him to bring him some fresh milk from the cow with the broken horn.

As Fevzi set out to corner the animal, Bekir headed into the thick canes to defecate. Squatting, he watched the cranes floating overhead, the morning light glinting off the blue feathers of the sandpipers, and the sudden flight of a flock made up of thousands of starlings. The morning was being welcomed in by the calls of the cranes, the noisy flight of the starlings, and the far-off honking of a flock of wild geese. While noisily emptying his bowels, he suddenly picked up the acrid whiff of smoke. He knew there was no one else in the area but themselves, and he was surprised that anyone would be burning something at this hour of the morning. When he stood up he could just peer over the top of the reeds at the farmhouse off in the distance. He saw the smoke billowing from the farm and towards the marsh and the flames shooting now high into the sky. Allah Allah. The smoke was coming from the farm. The farm was on fire. The odor of mud, reeds, oxen, and milk was being overpowered now by the stronger smell of fire. Allah Allah. How could this happen?

Bekir hurriedly finished what he was doing and ran back to the camp. He kept one eye on the fire as he hopped along trying to pull up and button his patched trousers. He grabbed his shotgun and began to howl.

"Hey Hasan! Hayri! Get over here. Up and at it. Right now! The farm's on fire. What's the Agha going say? For God's sakes, get up and get running!"

His voice was like a gunshot, resounding through the morning air and striking the farmhands like a bullet. They jumped up and didn't even bother to rub the crud from their eyes as they took off running towards Bekir, who was standing absolutely still watching the smoke and flames rising above the buildings and farmyard. He started screaming at the farmhands.

"For God's sakes, men, what in the hell are you waiting for? Don't you see what's happening? The farm is on fire! Look at that! What in the hell are we going to tell the Agha? And what's he going to say to us? Hasan, go take a look. Find out what's happened. If it was one of those renegades, I swear on all of Allah's books and on my holy religion that I will burn them and burn them good! What in the hell are you waiting for? Get moving! Now!"

Bekir stood there shouting out orders and slapping the faces and arms of any who made the mistake of trying to get near him. Hasan and a buddy took off for the farm. By the time they got there, the hay and straw piles had burned and a low cloud of smoke hung about the buildings. There was nothing left for the farmhands to do.

While Bekir was watching the fire he heard the approach of Fevzi, the farmhand who had gone off to milk the black cow.

"Hey, Bekir Agha. I saw some mounted men. I saw 'em fording in the swamp water."

"What? What mounted men? Speak up now. Where did you see them?"

"Well, Agha, I saw 'em go into the water down there at the fork. There were four of them. First I thought it must be some

153

cows or donkeys, but then I saw they were horses, mounted horses. I saw 'em real good too. I saw 'em when I was looking in the direction of the morning sun. I swear to God, they were mounted men."

At first Bloody Bekir didn't make the connection between the mounted men and the fire at the farm. He peered in the direction of the fork and wondered to himself what mounted men might be doing in these parts, but all he saw was the shining water and the reeds now hidden in a veil of mist. Still he used the opportunity to give Fevzi a resounding slap.

"You sorry idiot. You son-of-a-donkey. Why didn't you tell me when you saw those mounted men? Shouldn't you let me know? You retard you!"

Fevzi raised his arms to protect himself from Bekir's slaps and kicks.

"I swear to Allah, Agha, as soon as I saw them I came down here to tell you. That cow with the broken horn had wandered all the way to No Good Island. I went down there to bring her up and that's when I saw the men. I left her there and ran back."

"Where did they enter the water? Which way did they go? Look smart now and tell me plain."

"Agha, you know the fork? Well, that's where they went into the water. I saw them when they were half way in the water. They were pulling at the reeds. Yeah, they went that way. And I came right back to tell you."

"Listen you dunce. There's no island or land down there. So where in the hell could they be going? If there was an island or some land, then I would understand, but there's nothing down there. Nothing but swamp."

He turned in the direction that Fevzi had pointed out and squinted his eyes to look as hard as he could. Bekir stood as still as stone, but still Fevzi knew now to keep his distance. He spoke in an almost whisper.

"But, Agha, you've never been down there. None of us have been down there. They said the water was deep so we never went. But I swear to Allah, the horses went that way. They went in the water and kept going."

154

"If you're lying to me, you idiot, I swear I'll chop you to bits. And you know I will. Now tell me right."

"Okay, Agha, I saw them from No Good Island. Our cow had gone all the way down there and I went down there and got her. I was bringing her back when I saw them. They were going that way, in the direction of the Black Fortress. They were moving in a straight line, and they were pulling the reeds back as they rode."

Bekir understood that Fevzi was telling the truth. He knew, though, that there had to be a trick to it somewhere.

"Okay, I understand. I know what you're saying. So go back there now and get the cow and milk her. We're going to bring all the animals back to the farm. It'll take us till evening to do that. But I'm going to go down where you said and have a look for myself. Let's see if I can find anybody."

Bloody Bekir went back to their camp and put on the thigh-high boots he had stored there. He took a handful of bullets out of his bullet sack and thrust them in his pocket and hung the little bread bag on a branch so he could fill it with some bread and dried beef. He handled his shotgun like it was a sacred object, turning it about in his hands and peering down and around its barrel. He counted his bullets. The spinning of the cartridge gave off a metallic and icy-cold sound and gave Bekir an otherworldly sense of power.

Fevzi carefully set the copper jug of milk on the ground and broke a loaf of flat bread into two. He reached into a clay pot and pulled out a chunk of white cheese from the water. The boss's breakfast was ready.

Bekir was ready, too, with his gun at his side and his boots on his feet. He sat down in the grass, grabbed a hunk of the bread, and dipped it into the still-warm milk. He smacked his lips as he ate and licked off the drops of milk on his thick black mustache. He first looked in the direction he had to travel and then back at the burned-out hull of the farm.

"Okay, Stupid. I'm going to go and look for those men. Let's see just who they are and what they're up to. Are they hunters or outlaws? I'll find that out. Maybe they're the ones that set the farm on fire. What business have they got riding into the water anyway? I'll find that out and be back before sunset."

Before he left, he issued a storm of orders at Fevzi and then, picking up a long rod, disappeared into the reeds. Bekir had the beginning of a humpback and it gave him a strange gait. He used the rod to test the wet ground before taking each wide step. Walking in the deep mud required skill; each foot would sink into the soggy ground and he would use his other foot to pull it out. The foot would come loose with a squishy sound, finally coming free covered with a thick layer of clinging mud. It was only his physical strength and his overriding curiosity that allowed him to make headway and to follow the route of the mounted men.

He knew that the farm could not have burned on its own. There was nobody in these parts. Someone must have deliberately set it alight. It had to have been these mounted men. But who were they?

In his mind he started to make a list of Hatem Agha's enemies. And the name Osman kept popping up. It must have been Osman. Still, Osman never traveled with a gang of men. Old Stupid claimed he had seen four riders. The Osman he knew preferred to travel alone. He remembered the time he had set the trap. Osman had managed to escape that time. He was shot, but he recovered. Suddenly Bekir understood. Osman was after him! He, himself, was the target, not Hatem Agha. Osman knew he was at the farm. So he must have come out here and when he didn't find anybody, he set the farm on fire. Now the question was: who were those men traveling with him? Bekir wondered if he should be going to tell the gendarmerie. He could take care of one armed man, but four? That was something else. He felt an icy clamp in his middle.

Looking around, he saw he had come quite a long way. How would the gendarmes move in this swamp? As far as he knew, there was no island around here; it was just swamp as far as the eye could see. Maybe the riders went straight out to Black Fortress. He figured that the best thing to do at this point was to find out exactly what was going on. And if he did this right... if he could do this right... it meant a lot... a big reward at least. The original reward was still out for Osman, and this would bring him even more. There was a lot at stake here, so he decided to go as far as he could. He waded into the water with even more determination, pushing his feet into the mud and then pulling them out again with military precision. The tales of deep water turned out to be false; the water did not reach above his thighs.

It was now midmorning and the sun had long since cast its face onto Mount Erciyes. The swamp was fully alive with a cacophony of sound. Wild ducks with their bright green heads rose from their reedy nests with loud caws. The flock passed like a breeze over Bekir's head, their red and green wings flickering in the sunlight. In the distance, near Spring Lake, pelicans and sheldrakes could be heard calling back and forth to each other with cranes, too, adding their own cries.

A cool breeze started up, rustling through and flattening the reeds and bulrushes and bringing a shower of dust and sand with it onto the face of the marsh. The sun reflected off the water creating a thread-like path that stretched in fluttering light all the way to the sun's birthing place.

Bekir listened closely to the sounds in the swamp, separating each sound into a source: sheldrake, crane, wild duck, goose.

If only this had happened a short time earlier, he thought, everything would have been easier. Those who had come hunting would have ended up being easy prey themselves. Just a few weeks earlier, the gendarmes had camped at the farm and the men had fed the troops everything available; they had scraped the bottoms of the barrels of flour and bulgur to prepare food for the soldiers. On the tail of Osman, the gendarmes had gone from the farm to Snake Mountain and down to the Harami Valley. When the hunt proved unsuccessful, the powers-that-be called the troops back to their post in the city. If only he could get word to them this very minute! The gendarmes could at least guard the edges of the swamp, then they would have them trapped. So, the mounted men were cutting through the swamp to get to Black Fortress. He still couldn't understand why they would choose this difficult route.

Bloody Bekir's curiosity was piqued and he walked as far as he could. The rod he held in his hand became his map, telling him where there was a sinkhole or pit. He only took a step after he had made sure there was firm ground under the muddy surface. Now the water was below his knees, making it easier for him to walk. These boots made walking on land almost impossible, but they were perfect for this trek. At times the water had come up almost to the top of his boots and some had spilled inside, wetting his trousers and making squishing sounds inside his boots as he walked. He figured that if the men had not gone to Black Fortress, then they were going to camp somewhere near here. It was possible, after all, that they knew of some island around here that nobody else knew about. And if they did, it would make a perfect hiding spot. Bekir continually looked from side to side, trying to spot something—anything— different or unusual. Wading through the mist, the swamp had become a vast desert of water and Bekir was on the lookout for an oasis, but there was only water, water stretching for seemingly miles on all sides of him. The tiny waves wet the sheepskin cloak he wore around his shoulders and his gun's sheath, which he had slung across his chest, was almost entirely immersed in water. Clouds of insects swarmed about his head and nested in his nostrils.

Bekir kept his eyes pasted on the horizon as he waded through the water. He was trouble on water, a hunter looking for prey to kill with his bare hands. He was full of confidence. He knew the men would not be expecting anyone out here and that they would therefore be careless. They would be sitting ducks. Easy targets. He could hide among the reeds and pick them off, one by one. His body was totally alert as he pushed on with determination. He vowed to himself to keep moving, to walk with patience, and to test the ground beneath his feet before stepping down. He moved on in absolute silence, taking care not to stir the reeds.

In the far-off distance he spotted a dense stand of cane. Through the mist it seemed to Bekir that this stand was higher than the reeds around him. He walked for three more hours, without allowing himself to feel tired. Sweat coursed in streams down his forehead and neck. Now soaked through and through, the sheepskin cloak had become a heavy weight.

He was still alert and he felt that something was different about that stand of now nearby canes. As he stopped to get his breath, he had the chance to look more closely at the formation. He had been right. These canes stood higher than those around. He understood what that meant: These canes were growing on higher ground. It was difficult to see the difference, but there it was. He had seen it. It was an island. His excitement was based on a rush of fear that coursed through his body.

He became more certain of his discovery as he approached. He told himself that there was still a long time until nightfall. It was still early afternoon. He was delighted with his find, but something told him to keep back for a while. A hand seemed to be pushing at his chest, forcing him back from the island. Still, he was a man of long experience and nothing would hold him back from this challenge. He decided to go nearer and try to find out exactly where they were hiding. Then he would dig a hiding place in the mud. They would never be able to see a mud man. And not just that; he had many, many more tricks in his basket to show them—that was for sure!

A fat water snake zigzagged past Bekir as he stood still in the water. Ducks and cormorants were playing in the rushes. A blackbird with tiny raven wings and a white spotted beak struggled to take flight and then flew low over the surface of the water. A large flock of water ducks flew overhead, wings spread wide, honking noisily as it made its way.

Bekir had controlled the fear that welled up in him when he had first spotted the island and now he felt light, almost afloat, in the mud. He was a wolf who had the scent of blood in its nostrils. He crouched behind the canes, and bullrushes, and cattails, taking the slow route to the island, his path becoming more and more dense with reeds with every step he took.

* * *

Osman and his men had finished their journey for the day and had managed to reach Lone Grave Island without their horses getting mired down in the mud or sucked into the quicksand. The cane pickers from Black Fortress knew about this island, but one day one of the pickers had taken refuge here and then frozen to death. When his family finally found him, they decided there was no way they could take his body out of the swamp, so they buried him there. That's how the island got its name. For years the rounded mound of the grave lay undisturbed. No one who reached the island dared disturb the site, for they knew it would be very inauspicious to do so.

The men walked their horses through the tall canes. Finally they stopped moving and used their knives to cut a clearing for themselves and their animals. They built a tent of cane they had pulled down and tied together and then gave this makeshift shelter a floor of dry grass and reeds. Once the horses' blankets and saddles were placed in the shelter it took on an almost homey air. They placed their weapons into one corner of the tent and hung their food bags on some of the taller canes. They found spaces to safely store their canteens, cartridges, and binoculars. They were exhausted. Ignoring the clouds of bugs and insects and the daytime hour, they lay down to sleep.

Hadji, though, was curious about the grave on the other side of the island. It was a place where caravans would never pass. Who would pass by to say a prayer for the poor soul lying there? He hung his rifle over his shoulder and started walking. It was only three hundred or so strides from one side of the island to the other. The grave was easy to spot for the ground over it was rounded and smooth. Hadji raised his hands, palm-upwards towards heaven, and began reciting the Fatiha, the prayer for the dead. He believed that this kind of prayer would help God forgive him for his own sins. He prayed, he blew away his prayer, and he wiped his face with his hands.

The sky looked beautiful. He lay down on his back next to the grave to watch the sky. White, large-bodied sheldrakes, pelicans with their long red necks, wild ducks, cranes, and herons all floated above him and filled the skies with their calls. When he listened closely, he could pick out the sounds of flapping wings.

The beauty cast him back into sadness. As he stared into the sky above him, he saw again his wife's eyes, opened wide as saucers with fear. And he saw the look of pleading in her face

160

and fear in her eyes as she screamed silently. The memory of this scene was a clasp on his soul, and a dagger blow to his heart. Hadji wept blood. The rug trader with his mustache, long ago gone white, wore a brimmed hat. The chain of his pocket watch crossed his large middle. He was the answer to their prayers. That's what they both had said. He brought them the loom and the yarn, the beater comb and the rug knife. They set up the loom in their main sitting room and his beautiful wife Gulizar began to weave. The carpets she knotted and wove seemed to sing, their colors to dance. The house was alive with the rhythmic sound of the beater comb, as she beat her tiny knots into exquisite patterns. She worked with a passion and in just a month had created a large and perfect rug. The trader was generous and they were both happy to have so much money. They bought shoes and clothes for the children and the money that was left over they stashed away as savings. The trader became a frequent visitor, bringing them the carpet designs, the yarns, and the orders.

One day Hadji came home unexpectedly and found Gulizar in the trader's arms. Hadji's eyes were blinded with emotion and his world fell about his heels. That was the end of Hadji. He rarely spoke after that day. He went up to a rocky place in the mountains, in the foothills of the great Erciyes, and made that stony place his home, roaming the bare Hasan Mountain. His mustache and beard grew together and he became a hermit, cut off from all contact with other human beings. He slept in the Yellow Desert where he talked with the wind and water. In the cold months he took refuge in the narrow crevices that lined the rock face. His only companions were the wild horses that also roamed the mountains, but he envied the horses and the quails during the mating seasons.

He turned a bit in the spot where he lay and stared at the shining water, its surface alive with minute waves. Suddenly a flock of ducks rose, honking, from the marsh. Their green and white wings beat with excitement as they spread their long necks upward in flight. At first Hadji didn't register the birds' startled flight. There was no wind. Shortly after the ducks' flight, he noticed a slight movement in the reeds and the blowing of some seeds onto the water. He squinted his eyes to get a better look, but could see nothing. Still a blackbird rose hurriedly from the marsh, exposing its black body and white beak as it flew off. Hadji started to watch the spot as carefully as he could. He wondered what could be startling the birds. It was then that he spotted the man, a man moving forward and waddling like a duck. He was using a long stick for balance and the shotgun he wore over his shoulder shone in the sunlight. One glance was enough to prove to Hadji that this man was up to no good. Hadji pressed his body closer to the ground behind the grave as he watched the man approach. Something about the man's stance made him seem inhuman, almost animal or monster-like. He moved the stick very slowly and circumspectly in the water, moving like a wolf stalking its prey.

The stand of canes was only fifteen to twenty yards away and it would have been more circumspect for the man to go through them, but he was impatient and, instead, headed straight through the clearing in the marsh towards the island. He seemed to float through the water as he moved, not making even the slightest sound. When he saw the horses, he dropped his rod and grasped his shotgun with both hands, aiming them at the animals. From the corner of his eye, he sensed a movement on the island. It was Osman, stretching as he walked out of the tent. It was at that instant that Bekir perceived the tent for what it was. He slowly let his body sink into the deep mud, using his elbows and feet to prop his body out of the water. He dipped his head momentarily into the mud, making a perfect disguise for his features. He turned the barrel of the gun towards Osman, smug with the knowledge that he had caught his prey.

Finally he was going to reap the fruit of his labors and wipe that devil Osman off the face of the earth. He thought about the reward money he would get and congratulated himself on having the courage and stamina to go it alone. He hadn't needed the gendarmes after all! But there were Osman's men to consider. He couldn't just pick off Osman; he would have to take care of them, too. While turning all these thoughts around in his brain, he looked through the sight on his gun and aimed right between Osman's eyes. His finger was just about to pull back on the trigger when the marsh echoed with the noise of a gun being fired. The bullet whipped through the canes close by Bekir's side. Surprised, Bekir sunk deeper into the mud. When he raised his face, there was nothing but the breeze in the spot where Osman had been standing a few seconds earlier.

Osman had dived into the cave, grabbed his gun, and run out the cave's back. He took shelter behind a small mound. Kazim and Idris also ran out of the cave with their weapons and lay near Osman. They tried to determine from just where the shot had come. Osman had spotted the bullet traveling through the cane. Suddenly he caught sight of Hadji. Without speaking, Hadji made small hand signals pointing in the direction of the marsh. So they weren't alone after all. Who would have found them here? And how many were there? Hadji held up one finger. One person. Thank God for Hadji. He must have stopped the man in his tracks. Hadji could have shot him if he wanted to, but Hadji wouldn't. Hadji never shot anybody.

Hadji crawled over to them and then whispered the man's name in Kazim's ear. Kazim's lips curled up in a sneer, as his brow grew tight and wrinkled. He looked long and hard at his gun, just as a farmer stares long and hard at the crops blistering under the hot sun. Hearing that name was like having a pail of cool water poured over a new burn on his chest. The two men communicated with each other in blinks and winks and wrinkles of the face. They motioned for Osman and Idris to wait and then both slipped off, each quietly moving to opposite sides of the spot where they supposed Bekir to be. They couldn't see anything. There was nothing to see. They waded through the marsh and the cane and looked carefully at the open space, but there was nothing and no one. The water of the marsh lapped quietly against the mud bank and a cool breeze now gently rocked the canes. Then Kazim spotted a large lump in the mud, a lump that seemed to slightly rise and hump. The barrel of a rifle rose slightly out of the lump. The intruder must have made a nest in the mud. If Kazim had not looked so carefully, he might have missed the fact that Bekir was aiming his gun directly at Idris. He might have waited, but there was no waiting now.

Bekir was trapped. On one side he was being guarded by Hadji and on the other he had Kazim, Kazim black with desire for revenge.

Hadji waited, but Kazim did not. The young man was set on drinking Bekir's blood, the blood of the monster who had killed his little brother, for the pain of that cowardly deed was a knot wound round Kazim's throat. He had prayed to God; he had begged and entreated to be allowed to get his hands on Bekir. And now his prayers were answered. This lump of mud was Bloody Bekir. Kazim took aim, trying to make out Bekir's body parts from the shape of the mud. He took aim at what he guessed was the head and then fired his gun. One bullet was enough. Bekir reared back with the same strange rearing movement he had often seen his victims make. He reared and then dropped back. The rifle slipped from his hands and his hands reached up as if begging for pardon. It was over. He was dead.

For a while there was no movement on the island. Kazim stood as if rooted to the spot. They knew that Bekir was not only a sharpshooter, but that he was clever as well. Osman, Idris, and Hadji also stayed still. The gunfire had wakened all the wildlife in the marsh. The birds had taken noisy flight and were circling overhead. Now, with silence restored, a huge flock of starlings landed back on the island. Some also landed on the body in the mud and pecked at pieces of flesh that lay about. They only flew off again when the men rose from their hiding places and approached the body.

Osman touched the body lightly with his shoe. "This is Bloody Bekir," he said. "Kazim, this is something you have wanted to do for a long time and now you have taken your revenge."

"Thanks be to Allah, Osman Agha, for letting me see this day. And thanks to you I got my revenge. Look how the devil made a hole for himself in the mud. I only spotted him because he moved a bit. Maybe one of the worms bit him, or it was because he was trying to take aim. If he hadn't moved, I never would have seen him."

Hadji waded up from the other side. Osman was very pleased with Hadji, for it was because of this good-hearted man that they had been spared from Bekir's bullets.

"Thanks, Bekir. You did a good job. We slept, but you didn't, and it's because of you that we weren't killed. And not only were we saved, but we got the chance to get rid of this monster as well. So, let's take a deep breath, all of us. That was close. But, Bekir might have been a guide for others. They may be coming this way to look for him. Let's get busy and get him buried."

There was a brief silence and then Osman spoke again. "Maybe he wasn't alone. Maybe there are others hiding here as well. Let's take a good look around before we do anything else."

Osman's words were enough to set the men into action. They searched every direction with their binoculars and beat through the marsh and cane around the island but found nothing. They then dug a shallow grave in a muddy spot on the island and dragged Bekir's body into it. No matter how great an enemy Bekir had been to them, still Hadji had to keep with religious tradition, so he silently repeated the prayers for the dead. The poor devil had none of his people here to give him a proper burial. "Maybe my prayers will do him some good when he gets to the other side," he thought. The men finished the burial without speaking. Each had his own thoughts to mull over.

As he shoveled mud over the body, Kazim remembered his young brother. On the one hand he felt a kind of relief. The deed was done. He had revenged his brother's death. But on the other, he realized with dismay that he actually felt no relief. The pain of the loss of his brother remained as sharp as it was before, and now there was the sickening feeling of having killed. This was a new weight for him to bear. Still he hated the man who this corpse had been—Bloody Bekir, the one who spilled blood over Kazim's wedding. It was supposed to have been the happiest night of his life and Bloody Bekir had polluted that day with a horror Kazim would never forget. His wedding day and the cowardly murder of his young brother, forever intertwined, two events inseparable in his memory.

Kazim had left his nuptial bed when he heard the noise in the courtyard and went down to see his father's men bringing in his brother's body. The poor kid! There was a huge gaping hole in his brother's chest and a slight smile frozen onto his face, that sweet, open, innocent face, now so dark. That was when Kazim silently took the oath of revenge. He asked around and kicked up answers where none seemed to lie and before Osman was even out of his sick bed, Kazim had learned the truth. It was Bloody Bekir who had set the trap and pulled the trigger, Bloody Bekir acting on the orders of his boss Hatem Agha. And when he heard that Osman had recovered and gone back up to the mountain, Kazim packed his bedroll and went up to join him. He was resolute. He would find and kill the monster who had killed his brother. And now Allah had answered his prayers. Bekir had turned up in the most unimaginable way.

But the smell of death was in his nostrils and he couldn't forget the pieces of flesh that were scattered around the body. Now he worried. What if he got used to this? Used to killing? Would he be any different from Bekir, and would he, too, become a monstrous killing machine? He had set off as a seeker of revenge, but had become a murderer along the way. And would he end up like Bekir here? A killer, and killed? And just as he had taken the oath of revenge over his brother's body, now he took an oath never to be an outlaw, and he took this oath over the body of his sworn enemy. He knew where he needed to be, and that was at the side of his pretty bride. He wanted to go back to the village, back to the farm, and be the farmer he once was. No one knew where he was or what he was up to. He had said that he was going to Adana to find work. So it would be possible for him to go back and reclaim his old life. He listened to the wind whistling through the canes. The reeds danced in the breeze and he could make out the song of pelicans.

The men washed up in the water and then headed back to their shelter. Osman dug around in his bag for bread and handed a small loaf to each man, along with a large slice of dried beef sausage. Osman, too, was immersed in thought. "If we hadn't burned the farm, nobody would go out looking for Bekir. But now the farm has been burned and Bekir has disappeared. They're bound to send out a search party. There must have

166

been other farm workers with Bekir and they might have come on this search as well. He would have at least told them which way he was heading. The news is sure to reach the city by tomorrow at the latest. And then all hell is going to break loose. Now Hatem Agha has another chance to come after us and this time he won't stop. He'll put pressure on the governor and the general, too. He'll make sure that there's a whole company of gendarmes out looking for us. And they'll come this far."

"You're right, Agha, you're right," interjected Hadji. "They'll all come hunting for this devil."

"It'll be us they'll be hunting for," Osman added. "The best thing is for us to get out of here and to get out of here fast. The question is, where should we go? I think we should go up to Soysalli and, if we're cornered there, go to Everek, and then to the Copper Mountains, or maybe all the way to the Taurus Mountains. The best thing for us is to get back to the mountains."

Idris the Kurd didn't quite know how to get his words out. "Agha, how would it be if I went by myself to Plain Farm? I've got a cousin that lives up that way. I could stay with him. I'd be safe there and I wouldn't be bothering anybody."

Osman immediately replied. "I'd say that you would be doing right good, Idris, that's what I say. But be careful that you don't fall right into the gendarmes' arms when you pass through Black Fortress on your way. Look, keep riding in the water and go around Black Fortress from the top, taking the long way round to Plain Farm. You're not a kid anymore, anyway, so you'll find the village without too much trouble. Make sure you keep in the water all during the day, but travel as you want at night."

"Thanks, Agha. I guess I'll leave at first light in the morning. That's when the water is at its lowest."

"So, what's on your mind, Kazim? Do you feel better, now that this is all over? And what are your plans from this point?"

"Actually, Agha, I feel real bad. Shooting that animal upset me more than I thought it would. I want to go home, home to my wife and my mother and father. I'll leave here and head straight for Sendiremeke and then to Fine Waters and then I'll head up to the mountains and make my way down to home. Even if some of the folks back home guess what I've been up to, nobody will breathe a word. But I don't think anybody has the slightest idea of where I've been."

In this way Osman learned the wishes of his men and it was apparent that both of them had planned his own escape. Hadji, though, had not yet described his plans. It was only when Osman cast him a questioning gaze that he spoke up.

"It'll take till tomorrow for word of the fire to get to the city. They still don't know that Bekir is missing, and so it'll take the soldiers and the police at least three days to surround this place. Nothing is going to happen today. So I say that tomorrow we do whatever we're going to do. When we leave here tomorrow, Idris'll head off towards Plain Farm and Kazim towards his village. I'm not going to leave you, Agha. You can count on that. I'm with you. If you don't want me by your side, well, that's a different matter. I haven't got anybody to turn to and no place to stay. To tell you the truth, I'm sick and tired of this life and I'm sort of waiting for the day that I can meet my loved ones on the other side. I'll tell you what I'm thinking; I think I should stay here on the island and scare off anybody that happens by. It doesn't matter what happens because sooner or later they're going to pick me off anyway."

Osman was moved by Hadji's emotion-charged words, but he wasn't about to desert this comrade-at-arms. And leave him to die? Never. "Have you gone crazy, Hadji? I haven't said anything yet because I know that they have places to go. But you and me... we're in this together... from start to finish. We'll travel together to Soysalli. And then we'll play it by ear from there."

"Thanks, Agha. So I guess that means we have to leave here tomorrow at around daybreak. It's best if we break up. But, thanks be to Allah, I get to travel with my Agha."

They went back to their shelter in the canes, spread their blanket, and lay down to rest. They were exhausted, both from the long ride and from the events of the day. Hadji, though, rose from his bed, took his rifle in hand, and stepped out into the dark night. The water in the marsh slowly changed from green, to blue, to a dark black-blue until soon the marsh was blanked in a deep sorrowful shroud of night. The dark mercifully covered the signs of the murder that had just been committed. But still there was a strange silence about the place. The ducks, blackbirds, and mudhens huddled in their nests. Could it be that they sensed the violence of what had taken place? The cries of the pelicans, wild geese, and sheldrakes slowly died down and the marsh settled down into a deep quiet; the only sound to be heard was an occasional soft flapping of wings and the whistle of a cool wind through the canes. Gradually the crown of the clear night sky filled with stars. These stars had become Hadji's most loyal companions and they spoke to him now of loneliness and loss. The occasional shooting star whispered to him of his future.

There was no movement on the island or in the marsh. The stamping and snorts of the horses intermingled with the sound of the rushing wind. Standing there on the island in the night Hadji felt a keen sense of remorse and overwhelming exhaustion. Still his curiosity got the better of him. He set off towards Bekir's fresh grave. He knew there was to be plenty of action there this night. The black angels of death would come to question Bloody Bekir about his life deeds. Maybe he would hear them as they pummeled the sinner and punished him for all of the evil he had committed on this earth. Maybe if he heard them he would learn something about his own fate. He wondered what the punishment was for murder? He knew that Islam forbade killing and that it was a very grievous sin. The punishment for killing someone you love must be eternal. It had to be. That's why there was no place for him to have peace, not in this life nor in the life to come. His whole being seemed to convulse with the bitter remorse he felt. I'm not even as good as this horrible Bekir here. At least he killed people who meant nothing to him. At least he has a chance for redemption. But not Hadji. He had killed those nearest and dearest to him. He had destroyed his own treasure. With his own hands he had destroyed the most precious gifts bestowed on him by the One and Almighty.

He lay on the muddy heap on the ground, his ear against the earth. It was most likely that the devils would come after the night prayer. If only he could stay awake. This was his chance of learning what actually happened the night after death. He was very curious.

Hadji spread his thick, leather cloak down in the space between the two graves, lay down, and placed his ear over the new grave with its covering of fresh, wet dirt. The *zebani* would probably come after the evening prayer. If he could keep from sleeping, he might be able to find out what happens down there. Curiosity coursed through his body like a tingling inner massage of countless tiny fingers.

The night sky was full of stars and the deep silence of the island broken only by the croaking chorus of frogs. "What are these stars?" he wondered. "Was it true that loved ones become stars when they die?" Gazing into the sky, he saw a star shoot out of the Milky Way. Maybe that was Gulizar. But suddenly the star broke up into thousands of shiny pieces. He raised his arms to the sky in supplication, but his hands were empty. Another star slipped away, momentarily lighting up the sky.

The grave did not give up any secrets and Hadji was left alone with his own dark and solitary world. His eyes slowly closed as his body was swept with an overriding need of sleep. The breezes ruffling through the cane sang a lullaby of longing. He dreamed of Gulizar.

The tent awoke at daybreak, as did the island. The sky darkened as flocks of starlings flew to the islands in huge waves, forming a dense blanket that draped the island in black. The din was ear splitting. Hadji sat alone watching the birds as they settled on the graves, the reeds, the water, and the tent. They were sinister and he felt a cold jolt coursing down his spine.

He knew that the birds would pick at poor Bekir's brains if they could get to them. He suddenly remembered the *zebani*. He hadn't been able to hear their coming and their questioning. He was sure that they must have beat Bekir real bad with their fire-throwing canes. Hadji was angry with himself for having fallen into such a deep sleep. He watched these jinxing birds with their blue-back bodies and yellow beaks. He saw how the males chased after the females, and how the females protected their young. This while they ate whatever they could find. This reminded him of his own loneliness and loss, making him feel dejected as he angrily swept aside the reeds and rose to his feet.

His activity set off a scurry of movement and a corner of the blanket covering the island lifted as the birds nearest him took flight. The sudden flight of so many birds moved the entire blanket upward, concealing the sky from below. The birds made a loud racket as they flew above the island for a few minutes before wheeling and heading off for the great mountain. Hadji watched them as they flew, lifting and dipping towards the water and then lifting again, forming huge waves through the sky. The birds bequeathed the island to the ducks that covered a large stretch of the lake to the left.

From far off he watched a pair of sheldrakes flying towards the islands. These heavy-bodied, white-winged birds never flew alone. If one of the pair died, the other died soon after. Hunters never tried to shoot them for they knew that killing one of these birds would bring bad luck.

The men in the makeshift shelter splashed water on their faces and then straightened up their camp before squatting on their haunches. Osman opened his food sack and passed out hunks of sausage and bread. In turn each man explained his route and how he was planning to travel. The sun glimmered on the water, reflecting in broad red stripes on the water's surface. It was time for them to leave.

Before leaving the island, they made sure to cover any tracks and to cover the new grave with a thick blanket of reeds. They broke up the horse droppings and obliterated their footprints. The island looked as isolated as it had when they first reached it. They groomed their horses' manes and tails and then whispered soft endearments into their animals' ears as they saddled their horses.

Idris was the first to leave. He rode his horse out into the deep water to cover any tracks before turning towards Plain Farm.

After watching him ride away, Osman, Kazim, and Hadji also mounted their horses. Before setting off they decided just how far they would ride together and where exactly they would split up. They also entered the deep water, riding in water that licked against their horses' necks. The morning mist was rising and the marsh was being filled with the warming rays of the sun. As they rode, they were occasionally accompanied by a flock of sheldrake, geese and ducks.

Mount Erciyes loomed above them; the tall mountain seemed to be kneeling before the great expanse of sky, staring upwards with its blue eyes and white face. A trick of the eyes made it look like the twin peaks of Fortress Village were poking out of the water, now shimmering in the morning sun. The entire scene was framed by the long mountain chain.

The men were silent, each deep in his own thoughts as he rode, the surface of the marsh becoming firmer and their horses moving with more ease through the water. Their hooves sprayed water up around their sides and steam rose from their nostrils as they split a path through the water.

It seemed they had ridden forever but still had not come to the end of the marsh. The water's surface was covered with greasy clumps of dust. Tiny turquoise curlews used their red beaks to play with their chicks. Soon the riders spotted night-jars and bee-eaters. This was a good sign for the men knew that these birds flew near land. They were now in the great mountain's very shadow.

It was time to split up. None was sure that he would ever see the others again. They quickly and quietly begged and gave each other the customary forgiveness for any wrongdoing or slight: "*Hakkini helal olsun!*" with the answer, "*Helal olsun.*" There was no need for further talk as they signaled their farewells with their eyes. Kazim turned his horse east towards Everek.

Osman and Hadji watched the young man ride away and waited until he was almost out of sight before themselves setting off towards their final destination. It was dark when they got to the village of Pock-faced Mustafa, an old friend who was more than willing to give them a place to stay. Mustafa quickly made a fire in the huge fireplace and fixed a soup. The men were exhausted and happy to be able to dry out in front of the roaring fire. They thanked Allah for this comfort.

Kazim had made it home as well. Back in the village, he told only his father where he had been and what he had done. He was still smarting from the deed. Killing his enemy had had no effect on the pain he felt from the loss of his brother. He decided that revenge was an empty word, a deed without meaning.

He vowed once again never to kill another soul, never to use a gun. This vow was like the earlier one he had taken to avenge his brother's death. He was committed to it when he swore the words. He and his father discussed this and promised never to discuss it with anyone else. Kazim told his pregnant wife that going to Adana to find work had been a mistake, that he had not found anything other than occasional labor, that he had not been able to save up any money, and that he was much better off here, in the village, with her and his family.

Idris the Wolf had ridden through the water until nightfall and it was only in the wee hours of early morning that he made it back to his village. He was sopping wet when he knocked on the door of a close friend's home. The friend immediately built a fire of cane and dried dung to warm him up, and then spread mats on the attic floor for him to sleep on.

11.
Recriminations

T he farmhands were in a panic and couldn't decide what to do. Those who had gone to put out the fire found little to do and decided it would be best just to sit and wait for their boss. Fevzi had stayed with the cows and then spent the whole day looking and waiting for Bekir to appear. By nightfall his foreman had still not come back, so he gathered up all the animals—having a hard time trying to do this by himself—and drove them back to what was left of the farm. The hands all sat in a ring trying to decide what to do next. They finally came to a decision: they would go to Anbar Village and tell the gendarmes what had happened. They would also have to tell the Agha.

As soon as the military heard the news, they wound up their field telephone. When Hatem Agha finally heard what had happened, he was so distraught that he jumped to his feet, sat down again, and then jumped up once again. The last time he found himself on his feet, he took off at a trot to the governor's seat. His demands that the government immediately find and punish the rascals who had burned his farm found an ear. The governor was sympathetic and immediately began raining commands onto the military. In short order Major Ibrahim had received his orders and set off with a troop of men towards the farm.

Hatem Agha had no intention of letting the authorities take care of this job on their own. He ordered Hasan, one of his most

174

trusted men, to accompany the troops. The mounted men didn't stop until they reached the farm. Once at the scene, they combed it for any possible clues. They questioned each of the hands, over and over again, trying to find anything to go on. They asked how they had spotted the fire, where exactly Bekir had walked into the water to follow the mounted men, and how long it had been since they had seen him. They wrote everything down. They then combed the area, questioning any and every person they happened to run into. No one had anything concrete to offer, but the soldiers felt sure that it must have been the men on horseback that had set the farm alight. They thought long and hard about these men and agreed with Hatem Agha that it must surely have been Osman and his men. Osman had held to his outlaw ways and burned down this whole farm. And what was even worse was that Hatem Agha's most trusted man was missing.

This then was Osman's answer to them. He wasn't going to turn himself in. Hatem was frothing at the mouth. He kept repeating over and over again how that criminal Osman would never settle down and that his real intent was murder—the murder of none other than Hatem Agha!

Two days passed and Bekir still had not returned. The gendarmes set up a camp in the farmyard with the help of nearby villagers. The men awoke the next morning to the sounds of geese and ducks. Hatem, ever the Agha, began barking orders at his men. The cows were milked and the troops were given hot milk to drink and new bread loafs baked from flour hastily procured from the village. Hatem fed the troops whatever food he could lay his hands on. The soldiers were surprised to see so much food in this time of hunger. Hatem walked among them like a clucking hen, telling them how much he respected the troops and how he would never let a single lad go hungry.

One farmhand said that if Bekir had walked in a straight line after he entered the water, he would have exited the marsh at the Black Fortress. They decided to get word there as quickly as possible. The military took an account of what had happened at the farm, grossly exaggerating the damage.

Hatem Agha was insistent. "Let's go after the mounted men.

175

Let's follow them exactly from where they entered the water." The troop commander wasn't so sure. "I can't put my men at that kind of risk, forcing them to ride in water that could swallow them all up." Hatem was let down by this kind of talk. Especially after all he had done, all the food he had found and fed the troops. He decided to go back to the city and complain to the governor. "This officer is shirking his duty," he would say.

News of the fire exploded like a bomb in the city and talk swirled like smoke through the streets. "The farm has been burnt down to the ground," they said. "The animals have been slaughtered," they added. "The farmhands were murdered as they slept," they whispered. "Osman took his revenge," they agreed.

Mehmed Efendi was very upset by the news that reached his ears. He had to get to the bottom of this story. It was Sunday. He decided to find the Crazy Sergeant and talk to Osman's nephew. He saddled up and rode out to talk to his father and brother.

His brother Mustafa was sitting in his *seki* when he heard Mehmed's horse clapping along the path, and he immediately rose to greet his older brother. His father remained sitting cross-legged on the long bench in the *seki*, smoking with immense pleasure a hand rolled cigarette stuck tightly in his long, black amber cigarette holder. The men sat and talked of the news, while his mother, sorting through a pan of beans, sat nearby listening. Mehmed was worried that the authorities would hold him responsible. "I told them not to put pressure on Osman right now, that he was planning on giving himself up. And now look what's happened." His father tried to calm his son's fears. "Listen, Son, what's that to you? You only reported what Osman told you. You have no blame in that. You're not to blame if Osman changed his mind."

They decided to call the Crazy Sergeant to share a meal. Maybe this way they could get some better information. The day before, Mustafa had shot a rabbit and his mother, being keenly adept at preparing game, had skinned and cleaned it before leaving it to soak in her special marinade. Thus did they have both the makings of a meal and an excuse for an invitation.

His father's *seki* afforded a panoramic view of the valley. For the time being, however, a cloud of dust hanging over the lower valley hid many of the vineyards below. The road from Brother's Rock at the end of Nazmiye's Creek was clearly visible. So was the creek's other end that stopped abruptly at the sheer cliff of Filthy Rock. Eagles floated high above the rock, lighting ever so often on the face of the high rock wall before again floating over the peaks and valley.

There was a broad, stone drinking trough built into a ledge at a spot on the incline below his father's vineyard. The trough was now dry, but it still attracted all of the birds in the area, hopeful to find some water there. Mehmed Efendi went down to the trough and drew some water from the nearby well. He let his horse drink and then as he walked back up to the house watched with satisfaction as the birds chirped and clucked around the water, their wings sending up clouds of mist.

He picked up the jug he had filled with cool well water before he, his brother, and his father all began walking up from the *seki* towards his father's kiosk. The kiosk was a rough, roofed, three-sided structure built into the rocks above the vineyard. Children loved this place for here was the start of a smooth, natural slide of stone. They turned deaf ears to their mothers' protestations, for the fun of sliding down the incline on this run of smooth stone outweighed any punishment at getting caught. Trouser bottoms and underwear were the worse for wear and, though they complained, the mothers themselves realized that this temptation was just too great and not worth the battle it would take to keep the children off the slide.

When they reached the kiosk, his brother carefully put down the bottle of *raki* and his round-bellied stringed instrument, his *ud*. A cool breeze blew from the tall mountains, reaching the kiosk. Mustafa's wife soon appeared with rugs they spread out upon the stone benches and ground. A basket of grapes appeared as well. These were the grapes of the vineyard and the region. There were the delicate, thin-skinned *dirmit*, the red and sweet rose grapes, the finger grapes—the crisp grapes that were almost as long as a seven year old's fingers, and the sergeant grapes that seemed to explode in the mouth with a sweet-sour burst of flavor.

His mother's helper, Sare, climbed further up the hill to the Crazy Sergeant's vineyard to inform him of the dinner. They all called to Demircioglu and used shouts and hand signals to get him the word. These guests came as bid and were joined by Bald Mustafa, Shamirli, and Chil Agha as well. The *raki* flowed and the music echoed among the rocks. The more they drank, the more they sang, and the better it sounded. "I wander, I wander the vineyards of Gesi. I'm searching for my long lost love." And then the sad song of the soldiers who don't come home: "This is Mush. Its road is rough and rocky. Those that go down that road, never return, never return." The songs drifted through Shadow Rock and finally reached Brave Rock where they settled down into the depths of Nazmiye's Creek.

By nightfall the men were filled with the beauty and emotion of the evening and began firing their guns towards the heavens in an exuberant demonstration of joy and celebration of their lives. The sounds of the gunfire traveled even further than the music and soon other revelers answered back with their own guns, a communion of men on a summer's evening.

The men were all intoxicated, but still Mehmed Efendi took every opportunity to question the guests about Osman. He couldn't get any answer that told him anything of substance, and no one could tell him if Osman was going to keep his promise to come down from the mountain. It was late when they each set off in their own direction.

Hayriye had sat up waiting for her husband to return. "Where have you been? I've been worried sick."

"Mustafa shot a rabbit and my mother cooked it. Then we called the Sergeant and Demirci. There was no way I could get back before now."

"Well, did you find out anything then?"

"No, nothing. They don't know any more than I do. They swear they don't and I believe them."

"Forget about it then. At least you're back safe and sound. The kids are all asleep and I see now I did all this worrying for nothing."

Holding hands the couple walked up to their room, Mehmed Efendi taking care to step over the step where the snake had sunned. "You can never be too careful," he thought.

They spread their mattress on the kiosk floor, the pure white bedclothes shimmering like silver in the starlight. They threw off their clothes and climbed under the two thick comforters. It was a night for stars and lovers.

* * *

Hatem Agha's inner organs seemed to be on fire—it wasn't just the farm burning, it was also the fact that Bekir was missing. It was eating him up inside. All the while, rumors were flying around the city and all sorts of stories were being fabricated and bounced around. The people were amazed that anyone—even Osman—would have the courage, the audacity, to touch a grain of Hatem's Agha's treasures. They said that Osman had simply disappeared into thin air. He was like mercury—couldn't be held in anybody's fingers; nobody could capture him.

Hatem was even more angered by the fact that the people were making Osman into a hero. At his expense! After what all the devil had done! They said all sorts of garbage about Osman. They said that he was under the protection of no other spirit than Hizir himself. They said that he was praying when he was on horseback, and that the gendarmes had shot him, but the bullet passed right through his body.

Hatem remembered those early days. He and Osman had fought together. The empire was falling apart, attacked on all sides by enemies. He and Osman had joined forces; they were vigilantes. They had stirred up a lot of dust together. Once in Antep, they got into a firefight with the occupying French forces. The pair was famous for a while, and maybe if they hadn't started spitting in the face of the law, they might even have become heroes.

Once the War of Independence had been fought and won and a new republic formed, the new government issued a general pardon. Osman and Hatem and all those like them gave up the rebel life and the mountains. The former renegades started settling down and making a normal life for themselves. Hatem Agha was clever though. He had his nose to the ground and knew the direction to take. He entered the party, the ruling party, and he took his men with him. He had so many followers that it gave him weight in the party politics. He was smart. He understood people and so it wasn't long before he became a person that people came looking for and looking up to. He had arrived.

There was one thing Hatem couldn't stand, though, and that was competition. And Osman had always been competition. So Hatem had found ways to ruin Osman's reputation, to implicate Osman in crimes he hadn't committed, to get him sent to prison, and then even tried to have him killed. But he hadn't figured that Osman would always slip out of his grasp and that the people would make a hero of the rebel. And now Hatem was becoming scared. He knew that devil Osman was out to get revenge, one way or another. That was the start of his sleepless nights. And now Osman had burned his farm.

As these thoughts raged through his brain, Hatem paced about his house in his long nightshirt, going from room to room, opening doors and cupboards, and barking orders at anyone hapless enough to stray into his path. He was seized by fear. He had had his house doors fitted with double locks and had hired an extra guard to sleep behind the door at night. But it was all in vain. He just couldn't get a sound night's sleep. He would toss and turn under his heavy wool comforter, trying to find a way out of this mess. He kept the small lamp burning. In the dim light he would count his wife's glasses lined up in the cabinet. The sherbet glasses, the water glasses, the bowls for the compote. He counted and counted but still couldn't fall asleep. If only that outcast Osman had accepted this last pardon. But how could he? There was no way he could live in this city anymore. Hatem knew that their enmity was too strong. Hatem couldn't share this town's streets with that villain. And Osman knew that too. He knew that Hatem couldn't stomach him walking the streets like a free man, wouldn't stomach him, would have to get rid of him. One way or another.

And that fool Mehmed Efendi. He wasn't even aware of the mess he had stirred up. The stupid idiot had gone and talked to Osman, and fallen straight into Osman's trap. He'd gone and believed all that "yes sir, no sir crap" that Osman had probably spread on so thickly. And Mehmed had believed him, believed that that devil would accept the government's offer. Osman had set a trap and Mehmed Efendi and all those government bigwigs had fallen straight into it. And then Osman used the opportunity to attack.

Hatem decided he would go and talk to Mehmed Efendi first thing in the morning. Mehmed Efendi should go back to the governor, should tell him that the gendarmes alone weren't enough and that they needed to send out the police, too. What kind of government is this anyway? What kind of government can't capture one bandit that's out to get them all? And that Ibrahim. Calling himself an officer and sitting on his horse like he was somebody. Scared pansy. He was too scared to even go into the marsh. Would it have killed him to lead his men into the water? That's why they didn't catch Osman. No determination. No guts. He would go up to the governor himself tomorrow. He would talk about that major. Let them all see what kind of officer they had leading their troops. Such were the thoughts that raced through Hatem's head until he finally drifted off to sleep towards morning.

Hatem Agha had a lovely wife. Pakize was a little round woman with tiny hands and feet. She was worried about her husband. She didn't like the way he was pacing about. She knew what some people thought about her husband, but she had never seen that side of him. He had always been good to her and had never even raised his voice with her, not in all their years of marriage. She tiptoed out of the room and went quietly down the stairs to the kitchen. She started bustling about the kitchen, determined to prepare Hatem's breakfast the way he liked it. She brushed the servant girl out of the way as she heaped tiny saucers with cheeses, olives, preserves, and honey. She sliced paper-thin slices of the dried *pastirma* meat and broke a couple eggs into some butter she had melted in the small frying pan. Their man was just back from the bakery with fresh raisin rolls. She boiled some milk and poured it into a fine porcelain cup, sweetening it with a rounded teaspoon of sugar. She lined the large tray with starched white napkins she had embroidered herself and then carefully arranged the food on it. She was just on time for she heard her husband stirring in the room above and heard the grinding sound of the wire springs as he tossed in the bed.

"Girl, Pakize, where have you gone off to?"

"I'm coming Hatem Agha, I'm coming!"

"I've got to shave. It's ten o'clock already. Why didn't you wake me up? I've got to hurry up, so you'd better help."

Pakize heated a small jug of water on the stove and then she and the serving girl hurried upstairs to help the Agha get ready for the day. He was waiting for them on the back balcony. They poured the hot water into his basin and he used it to wash his face and, after brushing a frothy lather of the pure white soap on his face, to shave. He didn't have to give any orders for both women knew his needs. They brought the soft linen face cloths he would use to dry his face. After he had washed and shaved, his wife wound the broad waist scarf around his middle. The serving girl handed them the starched white shirt and his neatly brushed blue suit. His navy blue tie was also ready. He brushed and reshaped his faded brimmed hat before he placed it over his almost-bald head. His serving man had polished his black shoes to a gloss.

He ate his breakfast at the large table they also used for their evening meals. His wife and the two servants stood nearby, ready to run for anything else he should need. His demeanor signaled that this must be an important day for him for he was muttering under his breath. It sounded something like, "that idiot governor is going to get an earful today," but his wife couldn't be sure.

The way from his house to the governor's office passed through the flour market. Camels had been driven in from every corner of the province and they were scattered now around the large square, chewing their cud and dripping copious amounts of spit that scattered here and there. The horses and donkeys were tied up in a row in the shade of the old city wall ruins. The soldiers' wives, the city's poor women, and a troop of rowdy children had just finished the job of shaking the flour sacks and were using their hands to scoop whatever they had

182

found into their copper bowls. A tiny, stooped old woman and her granddaughter had placed their copper tray on the ground and were trying to fill a small cloth bag with the small heap of flour they had found. When a passerby brushed against the tray sending a tablespoon or two of flour to the ground, the old woman raised her voice, shouting stridently.

The scene upset Hatem Agha. He watched the young girl out of the corner of his eye and the sight was enough for him to momentarily forget his own problems. The little girl's bare dirty feet were clod only in wooden slippers, their leather strap about ready to give way. Her dress was a rag really and her greasy hair was matted into a brush. The child had deep circles under her eyes and her face was an unwashed mess. Despite this, the child had beautiful eyes and a face that verged on being beautiful. They had fought and fought hard, but it hadn't been enough to save this country and save these people. And now there was another war to bring them down even more.

The pathos of the scene had stirred something in Hatem Agha so that he did something quite uncharacteristic. He dropped a fifty kurush piece in front of the girl. The girl didn't understand that the money was for her. "Uncle, you dropped your money." "No, daughter, that's for you." The words were scarcely out of his mouth before the old grandmother had scooped up the coin and stuffed it into her pocket. As Hatem Agha walked away, he heard their prayers of thanks issuing from behind him.

He walked now like a true agha, hands clutched behind his back and his head held high, his shiny black shoes squeaking his authority. He exchanged his selams with everyone he met, but still he was aware of the stares at his back and he could almost feel the whispers, how Osman had burned his farm and how his best man Bekir had disappeared. He walked like this all the way to the Republic Square, passing among the line of shoe shine boys lined up around the cinema before turning left into the main shopping district.

Mehmed Efendi was sitting in his shoe shop, thumbing through his *Ulus* newspaper like always, supposedly reading, but today not making sense of the words. His thoughts were elsewhere and he turned them over and over in his brain. The Sergeant and Demircioglu really didn't know anything, and neither did Shamirli or Chil Agha. Whatever Osman was up to, he hadn't shared his thoughts with any of his friends. What could he be thinking? First he says he is going to turn himself in and then the next thing he does is burn a place and cause somebody else to disappear. After this, who would ever believe anything he said; who would ever try to help him after this? Mehmed Efendi's thoughts were broken off when the light in the door was extinguished by the huge body of Hatem Agha. Mehmed Efendi rose to greet his guest.

Hatem Agha answered the greetings. "Hello, Mehmed Efendi, hello. I was just walking by and decided to pop in. We're comrades after all, brothers really. Brothers, and I thought we could console each other some."

"Of course, we are brothers Agha. And you know that this place is as much yours as it is mine. May you live a long life. It is enough that you just remember who we are."

"No, no Mehmed Efendi, that's not enough. There are some things that can be solved only by talking, by discussion. I thought that I would talk with you. Look, I know you must have heard the news. Someone's burned my farm. And you know I had a hot-blooded young man working for me out there, a man named Bekir. And he's lost. Just disappeared. We haven't heard anything from or about him. And who could do something like this? Who? You and I both know who this has to be. It has to be Osman. Who but Osman would do something like this? That troublemaker just will not keep his word. He has no word to keep. And now he's burned my farm."

"Now, listen Agha, you just keep calm now. Just keep calm for a bit," said Mehmet Efendi before turning to address his son. "Ahmed, go run and order us two coffees-just a little sugar in both."

"There's no keeping calm, Mehmed Efendi. Not right now. Didn't that low devil tell you he would turn himself in? Didn't he? First he gives his word and then he goes and burns down a farm! That's what upsets me the most. And what have I ever done to deserve this? Did I touch anything of his? Did I ever try to put my hands on his woman? Whenever anybody does anything against him, he immediately puts the blame on me. Is that fair? So if he wasn't going to turn himself in, then why did he ever make such a promise? And if he did decide to go back on his word, why would he think of burning my farm or doing away with one of my men? And now look at this town! There are even people who are celebrating the fact that he burned down my farm!"

Mehmed Efendi found truth in what Hatem Agha was saying but didn't know how to respond.

"Remember the old saying, Agha? You know the one: 'Never place your trust in an outlaw.' Now I have gone and talked to his friends and, truth of the matter, they don't know anything either. Nobody knows what's happened. All they know is that he filled his bags with food and feed and rode off. And nobody knows where he went."

"They came down from The Big Snake along the valley bed. They followed the track alongside the swampland until they came to the farm. And that they burned and tore down. But they were seen; four horsemen were seen riding into the waters of the swamp. That's when my man Bekir followed them, him on foot and them on horses. The fool! Why didn't he go to the gendarmes instead? No, the fool had to go after him by himself! Alone! And now he's gone. Just disappeared into nowhere. If he were alive, he would have come back by now "

Their coffee arrived and the two men slurped it down as they pondered on the events. As they drank their coffee and smoked their unfiltered cigarettes, Hatem Agha employed all his arts of persuasion until he was able to convince Mehmed Efendi to come with him to the governor's office. There, he argued, they could ask the governor to send the troops into the swamp.

They rose and left the shop, the smaller Mehmed Efendi walking in the shadow of the much larger Hatem Agha, trodding on cobblestones that had been worn down through centuries of use, and staying out of the already-hot morning sun by walking along the ancient fortress walls. Hatem Agha looked far more presentable than he had a day earlier; he was clean-shaven and was wearing a clean shirt and tie. Perspiration had started, though, to course down his body. He mopped at his forehead with his handkerchief as he talked. "The nosy people of this town, watching every move I make. Everybody waiting to see what I'm going to do. The government can't muster up enough courage to take that devil out of the mountain, so what do they expect from me? I'm just one person. They're all like hawks, just waiting for me to cry and raise a fuss. Well, that's just not going to happen. Actually, I don't really care. All I lost was the building's four main posts. That's it. Let 'em burn. I do not care. I've seen too much in this life of mine to care about something like that."

"Don't talk like that, Agha. Of course it's sad that you lost your farmhouse like that. Just bide your time. Allah willing, he's sure to turn up somewhere. And forget about what people say. Just let it go in one ear and out the other."

The two men walked slowly through the downtown area, talking as they went. The further they walked, the louder Hatem Agha's black leather shoes seemed to squeak. They passed the clock tower in the main square before finally reaching the provincial headquarters. The building, the "residence," as it was called, was a squat, compact building with a nice feel to it. Crafted in local cut stone blocks, it was the kind of structure that conveys a sense of propriety and trust. They climbed the wide curving staircase up to the second floor and gave their names to the lackey waiting outside the governor's office. Each man took off his wide brimmed hat—the hat forcibly introduced to Turkey with the westernization reforms of the 1930s—and hung it on the rack before entering the governor's inner office.

Befitting the traditions of the Near East, the office was huge, with the desk at one end and numbers of armchairs grouped around the other. The governor stood to greet them and ushered them into the leather chairs. First came the small talk, and then the miniscule cups of Turkish coffee served with a glass of cold water to rinse away any dregs from the heavy liquid. It was only after these rituals were completed that they could get down to serious talk.

Hatem Agha jumped in first. He told the governor all of the details of the events before grumbling, "What kind of government can't even catch a single outlaw?"

186

The government took this thinly veiled put-down and turned it towards Mehmed Efendi: "I know, I know, we've talked about this all before. But what happened, Mehmed Efendi, we promised him a pardon and then you told us that he was turning himself in."

Mehmed Efendi was ready, "Yes, governor, for he promised me that he was turning himself in. He said he was sick and tired of living that life up in the mountains and that he wanted to live a normal life, like any normal man. That's what he said and he said it over and over again. Something must have happened or somebody must have talked to him to get him to go back on his words."

He was suddenly interrupted by Hatem Agha, "But Mehmed Efendi, you said he was going to give himself up in one month's time. And that news traveled all the way to the President. And now we're all in a sorry state. This bandit pulled us out of a pile of filth and then pushed us back into it again. You shouldn't have said anything, not until you knew for sure what you were talking about. Now see how badly he has tricked you. And you, in turn, have tricked us."

This sudden shift in Hatem Agha and his laying the blame squarely on Mehmed Efendi's shoulders changed the atmosphere in the room and drove Mehmed Efendi to the offensive: "Listen to me, Hatem Agha, you have something to do with the reason why Osman has not turned himself in. He kept saying over and over again how he thought you would do something if he came down from the mountain. I swore, swore on my wife and children, that you wouldn't touch him, that you'd live like brothers. But his words were clear. It's not the government he's scared of; it's you."

"Why just listen to that devil! Why in the hell would he be scared of me? Did I ever do anything to him? Does he think that I sent that fool Bekir to bring him down? I sent Bekir that day as a guide to the gendarmes and then the fool got it in his head to get the reward for himself. That's not my fault. And if the government had acted like a real government and brought Osman in, well then none of this would have happened."

These last words got the governor stirred up as he interjected, "Well then that Bekir, or whoever he is, that real bellyache, then he should have done his job and acted like a guide and then maybe our men could have brought Osman in. When you stuck that Bekir into our business, you messed it up. That's what you did, Hatem Agha, you messed it up."

The crown of Hatem Agha's head turned a bright pink and even more perspiration began to flow out of the pores of his greasy body. He was so angry that his eyeballs seemed to pop out. His anger was evident, but he tried to mask it. "The people's mouths have turned into a huge wad of gum. Talk about me is being bantered around the city. I lost my farm and I lost a farmhand and now I am being told that I am to blame! Governor, I am not looking for persecution, I am looking for justice. Justice. If the government isn't strong enough to bring in just one man, then what kind of strength does it have? If you can't do it, then I will pay men that can. The man is hiding in the marsh. He can't get away from there. That's when you should surround the swamp and send soldiers in after him. Then you'll see what'll happen."

The governor decided to dispel the tension that had been steadily building. "Nobody is saying anything against you, Hatem Agha. I represent the government, and of course I'll do everything I can to find a solution to the problems. Maybe we can come up with a new plan. I was thinking to myself that we should come up with a very big operation. Let's see what our MP thinks about this."

The governor rose to signal that the meeting was over and he walked his guests to the door. As they took their hats the two men did not speak with one another. It was obvious that each was angry with the other. Mehmed Efendi turned back towards the clock tower while Hatem Agha walked in the opposite direction, his body swaying side to side as he moved along the long avenue.

The governor called a meeting of his gendarmerie officers. The men grouped around a topographical map as they constructed their detailed plan of action. They decided that the Kayseri gendarmes would enter the water with boats and follow the direction of the mounted men. A company would also be called in from neighboring Yozgat and they would be charged with surrounding the immediate area. Another company would be brought in from the Cappadocian city of Nigde and they would be sent to the opposite side of the swamp, to monitor the exit area. They also decided to call in the gendarmes from as far away as Adana in Turkey's southeastern region. In this case, the more the better, they decided. They worked until the late hours of the night, detailing every road, every crossing and every bridge and deciding who would be stationed where. Major Ibrahim was given the task of briefing the coming gendarmerie officers.

The next day the men began arriving by train, as did the ten rubber boats. The boats were loaded onto a truck and driven up to what remained of Hatem Agha's farm. The soldiers were pleased with the diversionary activities. They were happy to quarter their horses and ride on a boat instead.

Hatem again got his way when he convinced the governor that one of his own men should ride in the first boat with the major. This Hasan knew a lot about the swamp and immediately declared the oars unworkable in the shallow swamp water. The men scouted around the farm for long, thin poles that they then used to support the work of the rowers.

The water stretched out to the horizon. It would be easy, they thought, to spot anything unusual in this wide flat space. They fastened the boats together with long ropes and for each boat they chose a commander, a strong man to use the pole, and three soldiers. All were heavily armed. The major would lead the way and the men would communicate with each other by whistles.

It was midnight when they pushed their boats out into the marsh waters. The major was dismayed to see Hatem Agha climb into his boat, settling his heavy frame in its very center. Ibrahim's head immediately began to hurt as he tried to blot out the man's incessantly repeated orders.

In the meantime, the gendarmerie companies from the neighboring provinces were also on the move, taking their stations and covering everywhere possible in the area. The Adana gendarmes came as far as Pock-faced Mustafa's village but failed to find any hints indicating that Osman and Hadji were there. After all, Mustafa was a successful leather merchant, successful because he knew his trade and traded honestly, with seller and buyer alike. The villagers respected and trusted him and no one would think about questioning his motives in bringing Osman and Hadji to their village.

It wasn't long before the gendarmes got the knack of using the pole to propel their boat through the shallow waters of the swamp. With the help of the rowers, the boats moved quickly over the surface of the water. As the men sped through the night, they began to lose all sense of where the water ended and the sky began. They had the sensation of being one with the night and the stars twinkling on the water around them. The only sound came from the oars as they swooped through the water, hitting against the bullrushes, reeds, and canes and sending flocks of ducks into startled flight.

Major Ibrahim was on the alert trying to make out anything he could see in the night. His body trembled for he knew that the night and the place were fraught with dangers. They were moving targets. He felt, rather than saw, the tension of the ropes between the boats as the ropes grew taut at times and slacked into the water at others.

The night was long. Sounds popped out occasionally from among the canes; these were the sounds of the swamp, the swamp's intake of breath. They were surrounded by shadows and each shadow was pregnant with an uneasy silence. The swamp was alive in the darkness and the silence. Shadow and life merged and filled the air. The men knew no fear as they moved, only their commander perspired in dread of the night.

Gradually the curtains of the night begin to lift. The utter blackness gave way to a lead gray color, and with the first strains of light the vast desert of water began to bubble and perk. The sky was covered with the sounds of birds. The men tried to ignore the pelicans, the wild geese, and the ducks as they searched the horizon for any sign of the enemy.

They moved their boats towards any stand of canes searching for land, but were disappointed to see that the canes all stood in water. The major kept his eyes on his compass, making sure they continued to move westerly. Hours passed and the sun now beat on his back. The sun had first peeked over the peak of Erciyes and then had slowly spread down through the canes and across the expanse of water.

Suddenly the patch of canes before them seemed thicker than the others they had explored. Major Ibrahim used his binoculars to get a better look. He ordered the men in his boat to move towards that wide clump of cane as he signaled for complete silence. The men hunched down into the boat to hide their approach. Each man had grabbed his rifle, holding his finger just over the trigger. It was an island. They silently poled their boats to its edge.

Although he searched with his binoculars, the major could see nothing to cause alarm. He ordered one of the corporals out of the boat and onto the island. The corporal first crawled across the land but, sensing no danger, finally stood up and began to search in earnest. He signaled that it was all clear for the other soldiers to join him.

The men searched everywhere. They found the horse droppings under their covering of cane. They found the makeshift shelter. A private found the mound of fresh dirt and the men used their bayonets as digging tools. First they found Bloody Bekir's rifle, then his smelly boots, and finally his body.

His head had been opened by the blast and was covered with blood and mud. The huge man's face seemed to have shrunk, his features melted into one another. His body was alive with insects and worms. The men neither wept nor rained curses on the murderers. They coldly went about their labors and loaded the body onto one of the boats. They even found the traces of where the men had ridden their horses into the water. The major used his field phone to notify headquarters and asked that a security unit be sent to the shore.

There was nothing left for them to do on the island. They left the island as they had come. Hatem Agha kept up a steady stream of complaints, raining insults upon them for not having searched earlier. He said they would have found the outlaws if they had been men enough to go after them when there was still time.

The major had had enough of this talk. "Listen, Agha, these men are entrusted to me. I am responsible for them and to their mothers and I am not about to send them off on some foolhardy adventure just because you might want me to. Even you had no idea there was an island here. On that open water those outlaws could have cut us down like sitting ducks. In those boats there is absolutely no place to take cover. I am not about to place my men in danger just for your sake. I want to catch him as much as you do. I have sworn to do so. But the man knows where to hide. If we had come here at night, we never would have found this place. It was only because we arrived at daylight that we spotted it. Look, Agha, I am trying to do everything you ask. And I don't want anymore of your talk."

Hatem Agha finally fell silent.

The outlaws had managed to escape capture once again. After riding around the countryside for three or four days, the companies of gendarmes from the neighboring regions were sent to their home bases.

12.
Autumn Approaches

Nothing much had changed in the vineyards. The only really new thing was Tarik's sudden interest in the daughter of the neighboring vineyard, a girl called Elmas, "Diamond." When had she suddenly grown up, he wondered. She had dimples, raven black hair, and large, chestnut colored eyes. She wore the traditional woven shoes, perfect envelopes for her tiny feet. Her large breasts seemed ready to pop out from behind her tightly buttoned knitted vest. She was sixteen, beautiful, and had a smooth white throat. Whenever Tarik caught sight of her, his heart would leap to his mouth and his eyes would rivet onto the girl, the girl that occupied his dreams at night.

The days at the vineyards were passing by quickly and soon it would be time for the families to migrate back to their houses in the city. This was the busiest time of the year at the vineyards. The grapes were picked and readied for the making of grape molasses. The dry vines were cut and stacked. They would be used next year as fuel in the open-air ovens. The gilaboru berries were boiled down into syrup and strained into clay jugs. They would be used as a medicine for anyone having urinary problems and would also be reconstituted with water and a bit of sugar as a fruit drink during the winter months. The dried mulberries, apricots, green beans, peppers, eggplants, and sheets of sweet fruit pulp were all stored in separate, clean white muslin sacks. The men began transporting these to their city homes in the morning as they set off for work. It was almost time to make the molasses, a time when whole families came together to perfom this weekend long task that was a combination of both work and celebration.

Tarik felt that his time was running out. On that particular day his father ordered him to stay home and cut down the gum tragacanth bushes. He, however, spent most of the morning watching Elmas' house and then decided that today was a perfect opportunity to go hunting. Luck was with him, and about an hour later he was on his way back home dragging a large rabbit he had skillfully shot.

It was indeed his lucky day for as he returned down to the vineyard settlement, he saw Elmas who was standing near their vineyard wall, eating a bunch of grapes. Actually, unseen by anyone, she had watched him climbing up the mountain path, heard the explosion of his gun, and knew that he would be returning soon. She told her mother she was going to gather some grapes. She chose to gather grapes from the lowest vineyard at a spot out of sight of the house and the neighbors, near the wall adjacent to the path. That's how she managed to come face to face with Tarik as he walked home while congratulating himself on his luck.

She was the first to speak. "Mashallah! Mashallah! You've caught a rabbit as big as a lamb. I knew you would catch something. Oh, look how pretty the poor thing is. Can I touch it?"

As Tarik handed the animal towards her, their hands touched ever so briefly. This was enough for our hunter. His hands were all over the girl as he clumsily kissed her hair, her hands, her shoulders. She rather limply turned her face away from him and murmured quite unconvincing protests, but did nothing to stop his hands or his face. It was at that very instant that the unthinkable happened. They were caught by the gendarmes!

Major Ibrahim, decked out in his shiny boots and creased uniform, and accompanied by one of his most trusted sergeants, appeared suddenly from among the trees. He was on another mission, sent by the governor, the governor who was quite angry. The gendarmes had let Osman slip away from them in the swamps and the governor was now raining even more

194

orders down on the major and his men. They were ordered up to these very vineyards and told to search every inch of Mehmed Efendi's fields and house. The men had left the barracks that morning and had taken the back roads to the vineyards, as they did not want to be seen. And now they had stumbled on this young couple.

Elmas noticed the approach of the men, pushed Tarik away from her, and took off running like a scared rabbit, abandoning her full basket of grapes as she ran.

Tarik was first startled, but then quickly regained his composure. He walked up to the men as if nothing had happened, and they reacted accordingly. The major questioned Tarik about his rifle, congratulated him on his rabbit, and then started getting down to business. "Okay now lad, tell me, which one of these houses belongs to Mehmed Efendi? We're going to search it. We're looking for that outlaw who hangs out in these parts."

Tarik was quick to defend his uncle. "You mean Osman? We're looking for him, too. But he's not that easy to find. He never comes down this way anyway."

"We know he's hard to find, but we heard that he does indeed come this way and that you people are feeding him, especially Mehmed Efendi. That's why we're here looking for him."

"Commander, I don't mean to disagree with you, but why would we, of all people, harbor a man like him? We did everything we could to get him to turn himself in. He promised us and then went back on his word. He made us look like fools. After he did something like that, do you think we would ever want to help him?"

The major didn't answer the young man, but gave him credit for his words. Still an order was an order and there would be no going back to the city until they had carried out the governor's wishes. He called for the rest of the men on his field telephone and then surrounded the neighborhood of vineyards. What was the governor thinking? Even if Osman had been here, he would never be found at daylight. And he would never stay here when all the men were away.

Though it left a bad taste in his mouth, the major ordered all the women and children to leave their houses and gather in the

195

large empty square. Once they had assembled, he left some men to guard the crowd while, accompanied by others, they searched each and every house. They overturned crates in the kitchens, peered down the wells, and flattened the piles of straw and hay.

It was noon by the time they had finished their unproductive search. The men were hungry and so had started shaking the ripe fruit out of the branches of the mulberry trees. They gazed longingly at the grapes hanging in bunches from the vines, but the major ordered them not to touch them.

Although she had not appreciated the way she and her children had been ordered out of her home and the way the soldiers had so brazenly touched her belongings, still Hayriye knew they were only boys like her sons, that they were following orders, and that they were hungry. Once they were allowed to go back into their houses, the women gathered together and begin to prepare trays of food. They warmed the small loaves and cut wide triangles of cheeses, hunks of fresh tomatoes and cucumbers, and slices of cold melon and heaped bunches and bunches of grapes, which they piled high on trays. They used their whisks to beat yogurt with cold water into a refreshing and thirst-quenching beverage. They had their sons carry these out to the resting troops.

Abashed but very grateful, the men devoured the food. When the men were ready to leave, the major went back up to the house, thanked Hayriye and her neighbors for the kindness, and apologized profusely for having had to search the property. "We are under orders, Ma'am, and I have to obey my orders. Give my greetings to Mehmed Efendi and tell him that I won't be bothering him again, even if I get another order."

The major had carefully questioned Tarik and was now determined to go up to Big Snake himself and see if he could find Osman's shelter there. The gendarmerie cavalry formed a long line as they wound their way up the mountain. There were dappled horses and spotted ones, white, black, and gray; but the further away they rode, the more they looked like a line of ants. From the *seki*'s, the kiosks, the vineyards, the fields, and orchards, the people below watched their ascent.

Tarik had told the major to follow Brother-in-law's Creek till they got to the huge rock. From there, he had said, they would be able to see the arched shelter. The major led the men as Tarik had described. They found the well and then went through the walnut grove until they came out at the goat path that led up Little Snake. They found the huge rock just as Tarik had said they would, and there was the shelter. The major drew his Thompson, and drew in his breath, as he and his corporal stepped into the shelter.

The major found the same signs of occupancy that Tarik had described: horse droppings, cigarette butts, some eggshells and melon rinds, and a pile of straw. Standing in front of the shelter, the major could see why it was a perfect hiding place. It afforded a view of the entire valley, but was completely out of sight from below. Using binoculars, the city below drew near and life in the city could be completely monitored from this vantage point. Even without binoculars, the approach of any cavalry would be immediately evident.

This place also provided multiple means of escape. One path led down to the city. Someone cornered on the northern end of the gully could easily slip to the southern end and escape from there to the villages below. The major had passed the lower path countless times but never once had suspected or seen this shelter above. When Osman was here, anyone below would make easy prey.

Finding Osman was never going to be an easy task. The major understood this even better now. If Osman had this cunning shelter, he must also have many more—other shelters that no lad could or would tell them about. The major also knew that, unlike the young man who was so willing to talk, most of the people here liked Osman and would never give him up. After all, he was always ready to help the poor whenever they most needed it. Times were hard and the people were at a loss to meet the demands of the government for new and higher taxes and more and more young men to feed the armies. The officials were stern with the little folk and resentment was always there, seething through the society. It seemed that the only people who were getting by were those who could worm their way into the inner circles of power and influence. The people were grateful for a hero like Osman, for someone who could outwit the government, and who was always ready to help them out.

The major started mulling over possible plans. Maybe he could send two units. One could ride from White House and close off the northern mouth, while the second could approach from the lower villages and shut off the southern. That way they might be able to corner Osman.

As he was thinking these things through, his eyes suddenly lit on the mass of Big Snake rising to the west. A goat trail wound up to the top of the mountain, but here was no escape for the south gave way to the stone sea and the north to Harami Valley. If someone were driven up the trail, they would be caught, for there was no possible way out. But how could they go about driving Osman up that path? That would be the trick of it.

He took his cavalry back down the steep path and they rested at a flat area near the gully ridge. They set off again down to the village of Seygalan below and then found their way back. The evening prayer was being called from the minaret as they rode into their barracks.

The city was still abuzz with talk of the burning of the farm and how Osman had again managed to elude the government forces. The government, in turn, was trying to regain face among the populace.

The chief of police, Eshref Bey, was a person who knew how to squeeze every gram of personal benefit out of his office. He was cruel to those who ranked beneath him, and never caused a bit of trouble for those over him. The governor knew the man inside and out and knew how to use him to his own best advantage.

The governor signed an order that Mehmed Efendi be brought in for questioning. He also told the police chief how this was to be carried out. Mehmed Efendi received an invitation to come in and was questioned politely. His responses were recorded and then Mehmed Efendi was asked to sign the document before being given permission to leave.

That night, Mehmed Efendi and some of his friends arranged

to meet at the club. They sent their sons home and spent the evening drinking and talking. It was quite late by the time Mehmed Efendi set off for his vineyard. It was a dark night, with the moon only offering a sliver of light to guide him as he rode. He was alone as he rode up the sand hill, and then up Salli until he came to Hero's Rock. Suddenly the silence of the night was pierced by a whistle, a whistle through taut fingers at the mouth. Mehmed Efendi slowed his horse to listen more closely. This was the same kind of sound he had heard the night they rode up to meet with Osman. He released the reins as he slid a bullet into his pistol. The horse kept walking, picking its way along the hilly track. Mehmed Efendi could see the lights of the city below, but could see nothing in front or around him.

When he reached flat ground at the top of the hill, he urged his horse into a canter, but still kept his ears and his eyes wide open, trying to figure out if anyone were near. Just as he had gotten over his fear, he heard another whistle coming from some unknown direction. This sound again set him upright on his horse. "Hey! Who's out there? Who's whistling? Hey! Why don't you answer?"

The words were no sooner out of his mouth then he heard a popping noise. There was a sudden burst of light as a shotgun was fired and the sound began echoing off the rock faces. He felt the bullet whiz by his ear.

Mehmed Efendi threw himself to the ground and then took whatever refuge he could behind his horse's heavy body. He began shooting his pistol in the direction of the light he had seen. The sound of his tiny gun being fired was like a drop of water next to a waterfall. He shouted into the night as he shot. "You yellow-bellied bandit! Come out where I can see you. Whoever you are, come out."

There was no response, in words or in bullets. Mehmed Efendi knew that whoever it was could have easily shot his horse and then shot him. The bullet had been close, very close. Taking a deep breath, he climbed back on his horse's back and set off for home as quickly as his horse could gallop, holding the reins with one hand and his gun with the other.

When Hayriye heard her husband ride in, she slipped down

to the lower *seki* to help him unharness. There was something strange about his demeanor. As soon as she got a better look in the lantern light, she saw that his clothes were covered with dirt. "What happened? You didn't fall, did you?"

Mehmed Efendi decided not to keep the events secret from his wife. "Somebody took a shot at me. It was just outside of White House. The bullet went right past my head."

"Allah, Allah. Who would have done something like that? Maybe it wasn't you they were after. It was dark and maybe they mistook you for somebody else. Allah, Allah. Allah have pity on our children. Who would do something like that?"

"They didn't do it for nothing. They were trying to scare me. That's for sure. That's what I guess, at least. They could have shot me if they had wanted to, could have got me when I was on horseback, or when I was lying in the road. They didn't shoot me, so it means they were just out to give me a scare."

They hurriedly stabled and fed the horse before heading up to the *seki*. Hayriye clucked like a mother hen as she went into action. They woke up the children and then quickly prodded them up the stairs and into the relative safety of the kiosk. Mattresses were carelessly thrown down near the back wall and the younger children put back to sleep.

Mehmed Efendi sat with his rifle in his lap and Hayriye at his side. Nuhmehmed, meanwhile, ran off to his uncle's house. When he heard what his nephew breathlessly related, the older man quickly unpacked his Smith-Wesson and began assembling it. Both families spent the night waiting and watching in the dark, ready to jump to action at the slightest noise.

They spent several succeeding nights doing the same, jumping out of their beds at the slightest rustle in the dark and grabbing at their shotguns. In the mornings, they looked at the dirt floor of the *seki*, searching for footprints. But their fears were unfounded. Nobody had approached their houses in the dark and no one had walked through their fields or yards.

* * *

Autumn was fast approaching and Mehmed Efendi and many of his neighbors began leaving the city earlier and earlier. There was a lot of work to be done at the vineyards before the families could move back to the city. It was time to pick the grapes, and soon everyone on hand was busy in the vineyards picking the many varieties and carefully placing them in baskets that were loaded on donkeys and carried up to the houses. Here the grapes had to be picked over and separated. Some were sent to the city where they would be carefully hung to dry into raisins.

The family separated all the grapes to be used for molasses and then washed them carefully before packing them into clean sacks. Hayriye monitored the washing of the serving girl Resmine's feet. She stood over her watching as Resmine washed, rinsed, and dried her feet, over and over again, until even the meticulous Hayriye was satisfied with the result. The boys carried the sacks and then neatly stacked one into the low stone trough so that Resmine could stomp on it, stomp and dance to her heart's content, as she beat out all the juices locked within those tender skins. The juice was poured into a huge, tin-lined copper pot and placed on a fire fueled by whatever dry weeds and branches the children had found and carried up to the house.

When the mass of juice was boiling away, Hayriye added a complementary flavor to the pot, first a quince, saving the eggplant and zucchini for later batches. Once the juice had boiled to syrup of just the right consistency, it was poured into large jugs. Throughout the long winter the grape molasses *pekmez* was to serve as a sweetener for most of the pastries baked in kitchens too poor to afford refined sugar. The work continued, batch after batch.

While most of the grapes were boiled down into syrup, some was also used for other treats. The children loved to make the sweet sausage, the *sucuk*. Hayriye had put aside most of the walnuts from their tree just for this confection. They broke the walnuts and separated them into halves. The halves were strung on thick strings and then the children dunked the strings into the boiling *pekmez*, dipping it in and out until it had formed a thick sausage. These "sausages" were hung to dry and then, all

201

through the winter, sliced and eaten as candy. Some of the molasses was also boiled down to a thick paste-like confection to spread on bread.

Although this spread was a standard item on breakfast trays, the children's favorite winter spread was when their mother poured some sesame seed paste into a small bowl and then poured a little of the *pekmez* over it. They dipped their warm homemade bread into this tasty spread that was like a kind of peanut butter and jelly; sweet and filling, this food would stave off hunger pangs until the child could get home from school and into his or her mother's kitchen for a snack.

After the vineyard had been stripped of all its bounty, and its fruits and vegetables either eaten or preserved in one way or another for the upcoming winter, the family made their arrangements to "migrate" back to the city. On the appointed day, a string of donkeys appeared at the lower *seki*. The family's belongings, the few clothes and bedding wrapped and tied in large bundles, the cooking pots, and the laundry tub, all were loaded onto the donkeys' backs. There was also a spare donkey for each family member to ride, even though Mehmed Efendi rode his horse and Nuhmemed his own short donkey.

And so the family, and the other families in the vineyard neighborhood, all set off for the city. The only ones to stay behind were some of the retired couples, as they did not have to worry about getting back in time for the children's school. These elderly couples would stay on in the quiet and deserted settlements until the bitter cold forced them to leave for the city and before the snow blocked their roads.

It was on such a quiet day, with the wind blowing cold from over Big Snake and scattering the leaves about, just as it would soon scatter the heavy snow, that a solitary figure stood in the nest of rocks at Hero's Rock. His cheeks were hollow and his blond mustache drooped around his sad mouth. His dark eyes swept over the valley below. It was deserted now. Everyone had gone. The residents of the vineyards below were all in their own houses in the city, warming themselves as they sat around the *kursu*, the stout, heavy table that had been placed over an iron pot holding glowing embers buried in ash. The table was covered with a thick comforter that stretched to the floor and the family sat on benches around the table, the comforter pulled up to their chests, cozy and warm, an entire family warmed with a mere handful of charcoal. The families snacked on the dry grape roll-ups they had made at the vineyards.

Loneliness stuck to Osman's soul, a cloying glue that burned into his spirit. The wind, bitter cold, only fueled the fire of his isolation. He talked to the partridges, the rocks, and the bare trees, but they offered him sorry companionship. His only solace was that he was free. Free to stand and gaze over the valley, free to shout as loud as he wished, free to sing, free to ride among the deserted houses and in the empty streets. But the price of this freedom was a high one, a price that dragged him down, that made his cheeks cave in, and that robbed the sparkle from his eyes.

He was happy, though, happy for Hadji, happy that that lonely and dispirited person had found a reason to go on living. Osman had been the first to notice the long and meaningful looks that pock-faced Mustafa's daughter was sending in Hadji's direction. The girl had stayed out of the men's way, only appearing to carry in a tray of pilaf or a jug of yogurt drink, but when she did enter the room, her eyes darted about until they could rest on Hadji. She too was lonely, a solitary female figure in her father's world, a world apart from society. Osman saw all that and so began whispering to Hadji about the girl's good traits, about the thick, clean braid hanging down her back, about her tiny waist, her tasty food, and her sweet smile.

Hadji suddenly came to life. His eyes cleared and he seemed to stand straighter. And his clear eyes now searched out the girl's. He saw her thick braid, her round pretty face, her light skin, and her soft character. Some little spark took hold in the heart of his being, took hold and burst into flame. The looks were finally exchanged, and the conversation held with the father. Osman said the words: "In obedience to the command of Allah and with the accord of the Prophet, we have come to ask you for the hand of your daughter Hanife in marriage." Mustafa did not resist the plea. He accepted the rather large sum of money they placed on the table as the bride's price, but he did that more out of tradition than avarice. He would never sell his daughter and he was happy that she had met her kismet. Mustafa used the money to buy the couple several acres of land that had a small hut on it. Osman provided more money for the purchase of thirty sheep and a couple of cows.

When the two riders had left the swamp and ridden into Mustafa's village, Mustafa had explained their presence to his neighbors by saying that Osman was a sheep buyer from Adana and Hadji was his helper. The villagers accepted this at face value, especially as Osman really did buy many sheep from them. Two days after the men arrived, the gendarmes swept into the village to search for Osman. No one was at all suspicious of the sheep-buyer and they were never brought in for questioning. Now fate had twisted and turned once again and Osman was leaving Hadji in the village with his pretty wife and the sheep Osman had purchased. Osman, though, knew it was time for him to leave.

Osman was alone once again. He knew that winter was fast approaching and he had to find shelter for these cold months. The winds blowing off the mountain were a portent of the fierce winter to come.

13.
Keeping a Woman

Veli, son of Hadji Dabak, Swamp Hasan, and Amir Efe were a gang of three. They fought as one, and this gained them a certain respect. Amir Efe was their leader and the others did his bidding. The kind of respect they commanded in the town did not come easily though. They had to prove that they were truly of a "crazy blood."

Young toughs joined in gun and knife fights, all to be recognized as a "crazy blood," and these three had managed to fight their way to the top of the pile. Amir Efe had a body perfectly suited to street fighting for he was tall, broad shouldered, and muscular in build. His punch always found its aim, and when it landed, it brought sound with it. He knew who sided with him and was smart enough never to attack those who might prove to be useful friends. He carried a Parabellum pistol in a holster around his waist, and a long knife in another strapped under his arm. Amir Efe would sit for hours in his favorite coffeehouse smoking a water pipe and considered it only natural that the young boy of the house would run to place a cushion under him before he took his seat.

Gaining a foothold into any profession in Turkey traditionally demanded the passing of various tests of strength, skill, and character. And the position of town tough was no exception. To be recognized as a true macho in Kayseri society, the young man not only had to gain fame at fighting, he also had to be known for "keeping a woman." So Amir Efe kept a woman. He was famous for his Fadime, and she was famous for her relationship with Amir Efe.

Keeping a woman was a difficult task in this time of poverty and famine. It was expensive, but it was a prerequisite to being identified as a "crazy blood." Amir Efe, like others in the same position, received help from his friends when it came to Fadime's keeping. They took turns bringing her to their houses and giving her a place to sleep and food to eat. But no matter at whose house she was staying, she was Amir Efe's kept woman. Everyone knew that.

Fadime was a member of the Afshar tribe. She married into a Kayseri family, but her husband was called to the military. When news of his drowning in the Izmir Bay reached the family months after the fact, her in-laws—old and barely getting by on their meagre savings—asked her to leave. Times were hard all over and her own family also greeted her attempted return with a closed door. So she moved in with Amir Efe, and out of necessity became a kept woman.

She moved among the homes of Amir Efe and his friends and, depending on the economic situation in the particular home, sometimes stayed only for days and sometimes for months. The man whose turn it was would personally come to collect the young woman. She was fed the best food the household had to offer and presents would be given to her, bolts of cloths and little dainties.

Sometimes men of importance would ask a favor and she would be brought to receptions and parties. Fadime was beautiful. Her skin was light and her hair black, as were her eyes. She had a sweet mole on one of her cheeks, so she was generally referred to as "Fadime with the Mole." On party nights she would arrive before the men to hand roll cigarettes from smuggled tobacco. These she would later pass out to the men as she served them their *raki*. Having a woman at an all men's party only slightly changed the way the event was held; her attendance added a certain mystique and excitement. A music group consisting of tambourine, clarinet, and *saz* players would play favorite folk songs and some of the men would dance, raising their arms and legs in slow motions that communicated the dancer's unspoken emotions.

One day Hatem Agha sent word to Amir Efe that an important dinner party was to be held and he asked that Fadime with the Mole be present to serve the guests. Hatem had thought at great length about the guest list, a list that included the chief prosecutor and the chief of police. There would be music, of course, and a great deal of food and drink.

Hatem Agha, though, true to his character, was planning more than just entertaining the powerful of the province. His plan was to introduce the more staid members of the community to this "crazy blood." He would find a way to get the authorities to agree to send Amir Efe out after Osman. That was why he opened his pockets for this party. That's why he brought in the best *raki* the country had to offer, why he had all sorts of dishes both hot and cold prepared, and why he found quail to grill and chickens to make into a casserole.

Amir Efe chose the night to show off his standing in the macho community. He borrowed Arap Hadji's carriage and made sure Fadime arrived in style, with the carriage curtains tightly closed to keep her out of sight of the street ruffians who tried to peer through the windows. She was wrapped in an all-enveloping black veil as she stepped out of the house and into the carriage, but the sway in her walk was enough to make the on-lookers swoon.

Amir Efe accompanied her with a stylish flair of his own. His gray jacket hung from his shoulders, giving all the opportunity to see his pistol and his knife. Veli and Hasan sat across from the couple, weapons on their laps, keeping a lookout for anyone who might try to kidnap the woman.

The carriage moved down the narrow, snow-lined streets, bells ringing, attracting the attention of all. It was winter and had been snowing, but had not snowed as much as was usual, so the streets were not closed off. The mud roofs had to be quickly cleared of any snow accumulation, as there was always a chance of a dangerous cave-in. After heavy storms, men would walk through the streets with their wooden snow pushers, offering to clear roofs in exchange for a small sum. This snow would be pushed into the narrow streets, which would fill so high that they were sometimes even difficult to walk through.

The party was held at the home of another notable, Muzaffer, and he was waiting for them at the door as they arrived. He ushered them into the large sitting room. The men took their places on the *sedir* benches lining the walls of the room. Fadime was led upstairs to sit with Muzaffer's wife.

The guests quietly slipped into the room, having taken their muddy shoes off in the stone entry way and entered wearing their thick, knitted wool socks. Each newcomer shook the hand of everyone in the room before taking his own place. Amir Efe had stood at the door to greet each man and only took his own seat after everyone else had arrived. Once he sat down, the greeting ceremony could begin. Each man greeted the other and asked brief and very stylized questions to prove his friendship. "And you are fine and your wife, Ayshe, my cousin, is she fine as well?" "Yes, thanks be to Allah, we are all well." And on and on, about the room, each man asking and each man answering in this timeless ceremony of kinship and propriety.

Once the men were all seated and the greetings completed, two young men carried in a huge try that was placed on a drum-like ring in the middle of the room. Cushions and mats were arranged around the tray. The crystal in the built-in wall cabinets sparkled in the light and the table looked rich indeed. The sweet perfume of the grapes and melons hanging in the indoor bower wafted into the room.

Hatem Agha began to speak: "My friends, we all know of the valor of our good friend, Amir Efe. We know he is brave and we know he is a true gentleman. I wanted all of you to have the opportunity to meet him face to face. I thought we might be able to spend a pleasant evening together. We all know what a find musician our friend Ismail is. So, I wish you all an entertaining evening, with the willingness of Allah."

Amir Efe felt he had to answer these compliments. "I thank you, Hatem Agha, for those kind words. We all know what a gentleman you are. We all like you and respect you. We all know that Hatem Agha always extends a helping hand to anyone in the city who has a problem. And we thank Allah for him and for his kindness."

"What are you saying, my friend? What are you saying? Today we have the world and tomorrow we have eternity. Whatever happens, we are transients here in this life. And after we have gone, what is left of us? Only the acts of kindness we have done, only friendship. But let us not think of that now. Let us eat and drink. And so, to the table, my friends, to the table!"

So saying, he smoothed the cushions and pointed out a place for all the guests to sit. The men were seated according to their rank, with the chief of police called first and then each man in turn according to his age and his status in the city. Hatem Agha had outdone himself. The table was literally groaning with all of the local delights. There was dried meat, soft in the new season and cut from the filet of the beef. There were homemade sausages, spicy and spitting in butter, the fresh thick cream spread produced by ever so slowly cooking down rich milk, honey brought down from the mountain, soft cheese packed into jugs and dotted with black cumin, pickled melon and pickled peppers, boiled lamb brain, cold roasted meats, and tender meat-stuffed grape leaves from leaves that came from the vineyards at Erkilet. All of these were accompanied by loaves of warm bread, fresh from the oven. The glasses were half-filled with *raki* and then topped with cold water. As soon as the water hit the clear *raki* it turned cloudy, becoming "lion's milk," the drink that makes the drinker a lion. The men drank the *raki* slowly, sipping as they ate. Emptied glasses were immediately refilled.

There were only a few people in the city who could possibly entertain their friends with such extravagance in these hard times. When the men had finished off the table, the main meal was served: the soup and the quail. And then each man, as he finished eating, rose, thanked Hatem Agha and took his seat on the *sedir*.

Once all the men were back in their seats, the music began. The room was filled with the mysterious voice of the *saz* as Ismail strummed and plucked the strings of this ancient instrument.

Ismail seemed to be in a trance, traveling to another planet as he created his musical world and presented it to the guests.

When Hatem Agha and Emir Efe exchanged knowing glances, Hatem gave a sign to Muzaffer who tapped on the side door. Fadime with the Mole, her eyes lined with kohl and the natural blush of her cheeks highlighted with rouge, walked in with fluid motions, keeping time to the music with her brass finger cymbals. She stopped in front of Amir Efe, knelt before him and then kissed his hand. Ismail gave a nod of his head and then the tempo of the music gradually increased, filling the room with the coquettish airs of "Flower Mountain." Fadime began to move her body in time to the faster beat, stamping out the rhythm on the wood floor with her patent leather shoes, shoes now visible as her red skirt swayed around her calves. Her cymbals beat out a hazel nut-cracking sound, those snaps accompanying the tiny beat of her shoes. She began to swirl around the room, her body and her skirt twirling with the rhythm, as her fingers and feet kept the beat. Her red skirt swirled wider and wider, revealing a sudden glimpse of garter and white bloomers that extended almost to the knee.

None of the men looked at the woman's face for the guests knew the tradition and the rules. No one could look at this beauty. They had to keep their eyes down or turned away from her, even as they drained their *raki* glasses. Amir Efe's chair was slightly higher than those of the others present and he kept his eyes darting about, trying to spot any man who would dishonor him by glancing at his woman's face.

The chief prosecutor was not from these parts and didn't know the tradition, so he made the mistake of looking directly at the woman's face. In truth, he could scarcely take his eyes off of her as his needs for a woman were great. He was a bachelor and, even though he had a position of power within the town, understood full well that he was an outsider and that no family would ever agree to his marrying one of their daughters. He suddenly felt the sharp eyes of Amir Efe piercing him. When he looked around and saw that all of the other guests were keeping their eyes to the floor, he immediately understood that he had committed trespass of a sort and so cast his eyes down as well.

Amir Efe understood the prosecutor's dilemma and was relieved when the young man finally looked away, saving all from an embarrassing impasse. Fadime with the Mole kept up the dance, moving this way and that, her little tummy now beating time with the rhythm and her breasts delightfully bobbing up and down. The room was filled with smoke and dust as Fadime danced for the men until she was too exhausted to go on. Ismail was tired as well and glad when she stopped. He stole a look and saw that the kohl and rouge were flowing down her face in rivulets of perspiration. She skipped to the door and made her escape.

The room exploded into a sudden and overwhelming silence. The guests took the opportunity to raise their heads, uncross their numbed legs, and light up some of the cigarettes laid out on the tobacco trays.

Hatem Agha rose and walked over to Amir Efe's side, finding a place next to him. When he started speaking, his voice was low but could still be heard by all in the room. "Amir Efe, you and I have been friends for years and I know you have a gift for reading people's thoughts. You know what I've been up against. That bandit Osman has put me through a wringer. And I've tried to stop him. The police have tried. The gendarmerie has tried. We even tried to stop him with a pardon. But nothing worked. Nothing. And now he's burned down my farm. What did I ever do to him that he has it out for me? He's not going to stop until he sees me dead."

As he poured out all his woes, he watched the reaction of the room out of the corner of his eyes.

Amir Efe was quick to agree. "I know what you're saying. I know Osman. He does whatever he has a mind to, that one. What I'm going to say next is not directed to you, Hatem Agha, but they're not telling the whole truth about Osman. The Osman I know would never kill anybody if he didn't have to. He'd never set a trap. Maybe if he were in a tight corner, then it would be a different matter. I think you should just let him be. Don't put any pressure on him."

"We tried that, too. We tried just to let him alone and then what did he do? He attacked the farm and killed Bekir. When you give him an inch, he takes a mile. He climbs on top of us and spreads filth on our heads. That's what he does."

"No, no. Come on now. Osman is an old friend of mine, and an old friend of yours, too. It wouldn't be right for me to talk in front of all these gentlemen here, but you brought it up, so I I'll put in my own two cents worth. Osman has never shot another man in the back. And he has never stolen from the poor. What I hear is that he helps the needy. He even provides dowries for girls who haven't got fathers to do it for them. So what's so bad about all that?"

Hatem Agha shook his head back and forth. "I guess you don't know him. You don't really know him. He's so slippery that you never know what he'll do next. He killed two men at the Black Fortress. And he killed Bloody Bekir. We know that for sure. And there must be many, many more that we haven't heard about."

"Those two men were trying to kill him. They had set a trap. That's why he shot them. And your Bloody Bekir also had set a trap for Osman. He was trying to get that award. There's a reason behind everything that Osman has done. He doesn't do anything without a good reason."

"Listen Efe Agha, whatever you say, whether you say it happened like this, or it happened like that, whatever the case is, the government, and us, and the whole city have decided that this man is up to no good. They've put out a wanted order for him, dead or alive. And they've issued a reward. Amir Efe, these gentlemen here may not know what kind of person you are, but there are many that do know. You're the kind who will find the rascal, but you will protect the weak. All you have to do is put your mind to it. Decide on it. Track this man. Find him, and I swear on my mother's head that the government will give you an award of ten thousand liras. And we'll give you whatever you want or need. Right now. This minute."

Amir Efe sat as still as a statue. The only sound he made came from the soft slap of his worry beads as he slipped them threw his fingers. His cheekbones were even more pronounced in the soft light and his eyes shot out arrows into the empty space into which he gazed. His lips were closed tightly. It seemed strange that any man could sit so still with not even the slightest hint of a muscle moving in his face. He acted as if he had not heard a word of what Hatem Agha had just said.

Taking their cue from Amir Efe's stillness, the room also fell into a deep silence. The only sound came from the rustling noises made by Veli and Hasan who squirmed about in their seats. Once they heard the mention of ten thousand liras, they began to cast long looks at their leader as if pleading with him to accept the job.

Hatem Agha again broke the silence, nodding his head in the direction of the prosecutor and police chief. "Look at our guests here. These are government men. And they're on my side in this matter. On your side. They're willing to go ahead with this. All they're waiting for is to hear that you are ready. We need you. I need you to save me and they need you to save the country. That devil Osman. We offered him everything. We offered him a pardon. He knows the country is in trouble with the Germans, but he doesn't care. You have your ear to the ground, Amir Efe. You know everything that's going on. You will be able to find Osman. That's for sure. You do it and I promise you here and now in front of all of these people that I'll give you my mother and my wife if you do this job. Come on now, just say you'll do it."

Amir Efe was still silent. The only sound in the room came from the light snoring of Ismail, the *saz* player, who had nodded off, his chin sunk low into his chest.

"Look Hatem Agha," said Amir Efe, finally breaking the silence. I am sitting on your cushions and I am eating your food. I understand now why you invited us all here tonight. Thanks be to Allah, but I am not destitute. I like money as much as any other man, but Allah has smiled on me and I at least don't have to do dirty work just to earn my keep. This job you're talking about, that's the responsibility of the government, of the state. Let me think about it. I'll talk to Veli and Hasan about it and then I'll get back with you."

That said, he picked up a cigarette off of the tobacco tray, pressed it into his amber cigarette holder, and lit it with a decisive click of his lighter. It was obvious that he had closed the subject.

Hatem Agha spoke up, "Muzaffer, wake up this rascal Ismail. He's snoring so loud that I can't hear myself think. And tell those lads to bring in the *ara ashi*."

Ara ashi, "interval soup," is a spicy chicken soup known only in Kayseri. The soup is accompanied with a large platter of boiled dough. Spoonfuls of the dough are dropped into the soup and then swallowed whole along with the bits of chicken and vegetables. It is usually drunk after a night of drinking and is supposed to prevent a hangover the next morning.

The men all began to dip their spoons into the dough and then into the soup, slurping it all down and being careful not to chew into the dough for they knew that doing so would leave a bitter taste in their mouths. The young prosecutor felt that this was one new tradition he could pass up, so he made do with the soup without the lumps of dough.

The chief of police had been very quiet that evening, preferring just to listen and watch. Now he spoke. "Amir Efe, this is the first time I have had the honor of meeting you in person. In this life we lead, I have learned that one man always needs another. One day I may need you and another day you may need me. Take my advice, and do what Hatem asks. That Osman is an enemy of the state, an enemy of the people. We are doing everything we can to bring him in, but we have failed. We sent in the police and then we sent in the gendarmes, but he has always slipped away from us. The devil has holes in every corner of the city. I think, though, that you have what it takes. I have the feeling that you could do the job."

"Thank you, Sir, for the compliments, but those words are hard for me to swallow. I am not at all sure that I am the man for the job. You sound as if this kind of thing is a snap to do. This isn't the kind of thing one does for money or influence. Anyway, give me time to think about it and to talk to Veli and Hasan.

14.
Morning Music

W inter's arrival was belated but harsh. Snow blanketed the
city and closed off the narrow lanes. Icicles began to
pose a threat to passers-by. It was the kind of winter that drove
everyone indoors, including Osman. Osman had to live a fugitive life, moving from one house and one village to another,
never staying in one place long enough to draw suspicion, and
covering his tracks when he moved. Finally, though, he decided to chance a visit with his wife.

In the late autumn his wife Hurmet also migrated to the city,
to the house she and Osman owned there. The house was next
door to the city house of Ahmed Kirishchi, the Crazy Sergeant.

The houses of Kayseri are usually two story structures made
of huge blocks of stone. The houses are built into courtyards
and are surrounded by high stone walls. Unbeknownst to anyone else, Osman and the Sergeant's house and the house on the
other side of Hurmet's, a house belonging to an Armenian
named Vahap Jamjiyan, were connected to each other via
underground tunnels that ran from one basement to another.
This system of tunnels allowed Osman an occasional visit home.
On his rare visits home, he would steal into the Sergeant's home
during the late evening and pass underground to his own home.
In the morning, he would again pass to the sergeant's side and
then spend the day hidden in the pile of sheepskins the sergeant kept in a small outbuilding.

Hurmet had received a whispered message that Osman would be arriving, so she had prepared his favorite foods and made sure that the already spotless house was waxed to a high shine.

The Crazy Sergeant was going through another of his hard times. He was a newly wedded young man when he was first called up to the Army to fight in the Balkan Wars. From there he was sent to other battles and other fronts. After the war in North Africa and the Middle East was fought and lost, he fought in Gallipoli, in Galicia, Sakarya, and at Dumlu Pinar. He was taken captive in Romania, sterilized by a Greek soldier's bayonet in Sakarya, and received massive head and ear injuries from a grenade thrown by an English soldier in Canakkale.

When he returned to his wife and mother after twelve years of fighting, they found him badly injured in body and spirit. Occasionally he would retreat into a cloudy depression, and then would try to find solace in a bottle of *raki*. His family and friends understood the depression and the binges and would wait patiently for him to "snap out of it," meanwhile trying to humor him through the bout.

This was one of those times. The sergeant was depressed and was drinking. Driven low by the memories of his fallen comrades and the flashbacks of events he wanted to stamp out of his brain for good, he turned to *raki*. He believed that this was the only medicine that could take the edge off the memories and, if he drank enough, put him into a stupor that was almost like the sleep he longed for.

That night he led Osman to the tiny door in the basement that connected the two houses and then went back to his drinking. His thoughts were racing though and he began to hear the voices of his old friends and the sounds of the cannons and battlefield cries. The worst thing was that all of his friends had died, while he had been spared. His joy of being alive was marred by this guilt of having abandoned his friends.

Two years earlier the city had decided that they needed a larger cemetery. Land was purchased and then the population was ordered to collect the bones of their relatives from the old cemetery and transport them to the new. This gruesome task was carried out with patience and understanding for this is not an unusual request in these parts. The bones that no one had claimed were all piled into a large ossuary. The whole town turned out on the cemetery move day. While taking a rest after the hard job of digging new graves and replacing the bones of their relatives, the townspeople watched with interest as the huge pile of bones was placed in the ossuary vault.

That night the Sergeant sank into another one of his depressions. The sight of those bones had reminded him of his friends, forgotten and unclaimed. He convinced himself that some of those bones must belong to his comrades, so he took a huge sack, went to the new cemetery and gently took fifteen skulls from the common vault. He took these home and hid them in a corner of his basement.

Now when he needed to visit with his friends he would take the skulls up to the sitting room and line them up on the *sedir*. As he looked at these bare bones they would flesh out and take on a shadowy image in the almost dark room and then, one by one, all of his old friends would appear, sitting on his *sedir* and staring at him with their bloody faces.

Tonight they looked angry with him. He wondered if they were upset because he was drinking and not serving them, his guests. He took glasses out of the built-in cabinet and set one next to each of the apparitions. He poured a bit into each glass.

It was too quiet, though, too quiet to be a party for him and his guests. A party needed music and these old friends of his deserved the best, he thought—they deserved to listen to good music as they drank his *raki*.

The Sergeant slipped out of the house, making sure to shut the door very softly so as not to waken his wife or mother. He walked in the dark, deserted streets until he came to Jemal's house. The house was dark, but he knew his friend would help him out when he asked. He picked up a small pebble and threw it lightly at Jemal's bedroom window. Then he threw another and yet another. Soon Jemal's head appeared.

A blast of cold air immediately filled the room as soon as Jemal opened the window. He noticed that his wife, still asleep, crept lower under their thick wool comforter. Looking out, he saw his friend the Crazy Sergeant sitting on a stone, gazing up at

217

the window. Jemal understood that his friend must need him, so he slipped into his clothes and headed downstairs. Cemal stepped out into the narrow street and whispered to the Sergeant, "What's up now, at this hour? Are you all right?"

"Oh, I'm all right, but I have a lot of guests and they want to listen to music, so I came to get you."

"Friends? At this hour of the night?" Jemal wondered what was up with the Sergeant, but the odor of *raki* was thick on his friend's body and Jemal realized that the Sergeant must be on another of his binges. Jemal was a loyal friend, so without further talk went into his house, picked up his *ud,* and quietly accompanied the Sergeant back to his house.

The two men tiptoed up the stone stairs into the second floor guest room. Jemal was shocked to see about fifteen skulls lined up on the *sedir*, each had a half-filled glass sitting beside it. "Those are my friends sitting there, my fallen friends. They didn't make it back, but I did. I want to cheer them up a little, make a little party for them, for old times sake, you know? I gave them all a drink, but I figure they need some music, too. Be a good friend, now, and try to cheer up these chaps."

Jemal was not really surprised at the skulls and the Sergeant's insistence that his dead comrades were in the room. He knew that there was a reason why the Sergeant was called the "Crazy Sergeant," but Jemal also knew that the Sergeant was actually a very good person, honest and loyal to a fault. The Sergeant had done many favors for Jemal when he needed help, and Jemal figured it wouldn't do any harm to humor the man now. Besides, there wasn't much left of the night and he might as well greet the morning with some pleasant melodies.

"I'll be happy to play for you and your friends, Sergeant, if you say that they are there. But who else is in the house? I don't want to wake anybody up but the dead."

"My mother and wife are sleeping downstairs, but I really don't care if they hear the music or not. I have the right to have my friends in sometimes, too. But we are liable to get another visitor as well. Osman came to visit his wife and he'll slip in here in the early morning hours, so don't have a fright when you see him. He's just visiting his wife, that's all. He'll be on his way out of here by evening fall."

Jemal was surprised to hear that Osman would be so brash as to come to the city, under the very noses of the authorities and, truth to tell, he was suddenly frightened at the thought of being in close quarters with one who was hunted by all and sundry, but his loyalty to the Sergeant won out and he simply nodded his head, picked up his *ud*, and began to play.

Soon the room was filled with the lovely strains of Turkish folk songs. Jemal sang songs of love and longing, of valor on the battlefield, of friendship, of family, and of untimely death. "This is Mush. Its road is rough and rocky. Those that go down that road, never return, never return."

Downstairs Ayshe and her mother-in-law woke to the sounds of music. They were used to Ahmed's "different" ways. They knew that once he started brooding about his war days, he would bring home bottles wrapped in brown paper and then close himself in the upstairs room. Sometimes he would demand a huge table be prepared and then would sit there alone, speaking to no one they could see, and only picking at at bits of all the food he had wanted cooked. Sometimes they would find him curled up in a ball in a heavy comforter in a corner. The women would care for him during these hard times, care for him as lovingly as they wished they could have when he was away for all those years being battered and harassed and wounded. They heard the music and realized he must have brought Jemal home to play.

They knew Osman had come home to visit Hurmet, so were not surprised when he came up the steps from the basement and poked his head into their kitchen. "Who's playing the *ud*?"

"Oh, it's just Jemal and Ahmed. Ahmed's been a little down lately and has been spending a lot of time in the upstairs room. He must have brought Jemal in during the night to keep him company. Sometimes he does stuff like that."

"Music at this hour? Well, I'll pop in and have a look. By the way, Hurmet sends her love. She says she's going to make a big batch of *manti* dough today and she'll bring it over so you can all stuff it together. She says you can all share it at dinner tonight."

"Now won't that be nice? She's such a good girl that Hurmet. That she is. Thank you as well, Osman Bey."

Osman withdrew his pistol before he walked into the court-yard. He looked at the upper window where he could see the shadow of a man playing an instrument. He climbed the stairs and opened the door. He was surprised by the scene before him. Jemal was hunched over his *ud*, strumming the strings and singing a folk song. The sergeant sat with his back to the cabinet, his eyes staring before him and his lips moving faintly to the words of the song. Around the *sedir* were skulls, some with cigarette butts that seemed clenched between jagged bones of teeth and each with a half glass of *raki* standing before it.

"What in the hell is this?"

"Don't worry, Osman, these are my buddies. They're my guests. They won't hurt you. They're just taking this opportunity to enjoy themselves a bit. That's all. They're just enjoying themselves a bit."

"My God, Sarge, you really are a crazy one. You know that, don't you? Why are you messing around with God's business? He kills the one he wants and leaves the others be. Your friends are dead and that was God's doing. Now you need to let them rest in peace."

"And if I let them just lie there, who will remember them? That's what I'm asking you: Who will remember them? Who they were and what they did? Well, I remember them and this is a way of remembering and a way of thanking. So, if you don't like it, you can just leave by the door you came in. But, you're my friend, too. And this is our party, so I suggest you just sit yourself down there and join us."

Osman and Jemal stared at this friend. They could see he was upset. His eyes were round and bloody in his anger and sweat poured down his face. Osman decided that the best thing to do was to humor the older man. "All right, then, I'll sit down right here. And Jemal Bey, why don't you start playing again?" There was no place for him on the *sedir*, so he threw a cushion on the floor and sat on it. Soon the room filled with the strains of Jemal's *ud* and his song.

* * *

It was still dark with just a slight hint of light in the early morning as the handful of the very faithful left their houses to attend Morning Prayer at the mosque. The baker, Ali, was not very religious, but he had to get up early to heat up his oven anyway, so he had made a habit of first going to the morning prayer before heading off to his bakery shop. He was also aware of the fact that going to the mosque was a plus as far as his reputation in the town was concerned.

The handful of people who passed by the sergeant's house on this day were surprised by the sounds of music coming from the second story room. Ali was an especially curious type; some said he was just plain nosy. They said that if a housefly took flight in the neighborhood, Ali was sure to know about it. And Ali had to know what was going on behind those high walls and closed gates to his neighbors' houses, for when his curiosity got the better of him, he would go to almost any ends to satisfy it.

The music emanating from the upper floor of the Crazy Sergeant's house was enough to trigger his curiosity. What could be going on at this hour of the morning, he wondered. He looked over his shoulder to make sure he wasn't being watched before walking to the back of the Sergeant's house where a pile of debris was heaped against the wall. He climbed up the heap with a surprising agility and then leapt up to the Sergeant's flat roof. He tiptoed across the roof until he was standing directly above the Sergeant's "star window," a round window cut into the upper section of the wall designed to catch the morning light and send it filtering into the room. Ali lay down on the roof so that he could look directly through this small "light catcher" window.

In the very first rays of light his eyes tried to make sense of what he could see. In the pale lantern light of the room he saw a large man with a blond drooping mustache sitting on a mat on the floor and then he spotted the *ud* player Jemal Agha. Jemal was hunched over his *ud*, lightly picking the strings and singing softly. The Sergeant was also sitting on the floor with his back leaning against the cabinet. His eyes were closed and he appeared to be asleep. Then Ali noticed some white objects lined up along the *sedir*. Ali scrunched up his eyes to get a better look. "Oh my God," he thought, "they're skulls, human skulls on the Sergeant's *sedir*, skulls with cigarettes clamped into their teeth and a row of *raki* glasses in front of them, one for each skull." Ali quickly stood up. Fear seemed to wash over him as his body began to tremble almost violently. He tried to calm himself with prayer. "Bismillah! Bismillah!"

Ali jumped off the roof and hurried to his shop. As he slipped on his apron he tried to make sense of what he had seen. His actions were automatic as he lit the oven. The first stalks were stubborn, but then the pile of dry branches took light, illuminating the inside of his small shop and gradually heating up the huge oven.

Times were hard in the city, so most people made their own bread. Most homes did not have ovens, though, so the dough would be brought to the neighborhood bakery shop and the baker, for a very small sum, would bake the bread that would be fetched by a family member while still warm. Soon pans of dough began to appear and Ali's helper numbered them in the order they would bake. The dough loaves were lined up on the long, flat wooden paddle and then Ali expertly stretched it into the oven and deposited each loaf inside in the same order it had been in on the board. Each woman had her own request and each batch of dough and the kinds of breads to be made from it had to be kept separate.

Ali formed some of the dough into small rolls and then gave each lump a light sprinkling of sesame or black cumin seeds; other batches of dough he shaped into rather thick, flat bread that he lightly scored on top before sliding it into the oven.

Skillful and experienced, Ali didn't have to concentrate much on what he did. He didn't confuse the orders or the breads as they baked or when he removed them from the oven and set them aside for their rightful owners. While he worked, he kept thinking about what he had seen, trying to make sense of what was going on in the Crazy Sergeant's house that morning. He was also deliberating what he should do next. He could go to the police and tell them about the music and the skulls, but that Sergeant was really and truly crazy and Allah knows what kind of revenge he might seek if he found out that it had been Ali who reported him.

The Sergeant was crazy and he always had a dagger stuck deep into the sash he wrapped around his waist as a belt. Could he have killed that many men and then kept their skulls as trophies? But why the cigarettes? And the *raki*? And who was the tall man with the drooping blond mustache? Ali's thoughts spun around and around in his head as he baked loaf after loaf in his now-hot oven.

A scant two and half hours later he pulled the last morning loaf out of his oven. He took off his apron, washed his face and hands with the water his helper poured from the copper pitcher, and left. He quickly walked back to the sergeant's house. Luckily enough, the sounds of music could still be heard coming from the upper floor. Ali waited until there was no one on the narrow street before climbing up to the sergeant's roof once again. It was daylight now, so he had to be more circumspect as he lowered the upper half of his body down over the flat roof to get a look through the star window. His eyes first took in the *sedir* and the skulls, still lined up on the bench with cigarettes stuck between their teeth and the row of still-full glasses of *raki* in front of them. The Sergeant had moved to a new spot and was still listening to the music, although his eyelids often dropped shut. Ali next stared long and hard at the tall man with the blond mustache. Suddenly everything fell into place and when it did, Ali got so excited that he, too, almost fell from the roof.

"That's it, by God, that's it! The tall man is none other than the outlaw Osman. Osman, here, in the city, in this room, in this house!" Ali quickly pulled himself up, jumped down off the roof, and quickly walked away from this God-forsaken house. As if it weren't enough that the room was filled with dead men's skulls, he thought, but Osman was there as well. "So he's come down from the mountains and is staying with the Sergeant. Who would have guessed?" Then Ali remembered that Osman's house was next door to the Crazy Sergeant's. It was as though

Ali had found the key piece to a difficult puzzle and when one piece fits, all the others seem to fall into place. The fear that had seized him—both mind and body— at first now seemed to gradually fade away. He collected himself, and his thoughts, as he walked.

He still couldn't understand the meaning of the skulls, though. Were they Osman's trophies and not those of the Sergeant? As he walked, another light coursed through his brain. The reward! There was money to be had from Osman's capture! Big money, if he remembered correctly. Enough money to change Ali's life. When he got to the flour market, he was so engrossed in his thoughts that he didn't even register the donkeys and camels with their loads, and the women and bare-footed children carrying their bags and ready to pounce on any empty sack they found. Ali had walked as far as the square and now, with decisive steps, turned and headed for the governor's office. In his mind, he planned on what he would say to the governor. How he would say, "Give me the reward and I'll take you to Osman." But would they let him see the governor? How could he get by the governor's doormen and guards without giving the secret away? And then how would the governor react? Would he believe what Ali had to say and hand him the reward money, or would he withhold it while he told his men, "Lock this man up. Beat him with a cane until he tells us where Osman is"? Would it be better to go straight to the police? No, that would not do. If two police went out to catch Osman and then he got away, it would end up being Ali's fault. And then Ali would be a goner; Osman would take care of him.

Ali sifted all of these possibilities through his mind until he made his decision. He would go to the gendarmes. He would find Major Ibrahim, because everyone knew how honest that man was. The gendarmerie command was quartered in the same building that housed the governor's office. It had not yet turned 9 AM when Ali arrived at the building, so the junior officials were not at their desks. Ali waited in a corner outside, making himself as inconspicuous as possible as he watched the civil servants arrive. First came the *hademi*. These were the men of the lowest administrative rungs. It was their jobs to clean the offices, make and bring the tea, and carry messages from one office to another. As far as the general public was concerned, they were fierce guards blocking entry to their supervisors' doors, guards who had to be placated with a coin to the palm if the door were to be opened. Next came the *kâtip*. These were the clerks, the men who recorded all official happenings in ink in large ledgers that they filed away in dark closets, the men who made the appointments and whispered messages into their supervisors' ears. Finally, the officials themselves arrived, from the petty civil servants to the ones whose crossed eyebrows caused all to quake with fear. The last to arrive were the major, the head of the provincial gendarmerie, and the governor himself.

Ali buttoned his jacket and smoothed his hair with his fingers, all the while rehearsing what he would say. Gathering up all his courage, he entered the government building. The Office of Deeds and Registers was on the left, as was the tax office. On the right there were several courtrooms and the military offices. To the far right was the hall leading to the office of the Gendarmerie Commander, Ibrahim Bey. His door at the end of the hall was blocked by a corporal who immediately began barking at Ali as the latter approached. "Hey, neighbor, where do you think you're going? Deeds and Registers are the other way. Get out of here now."

Ali responded timidly, "I don't have any work to do there. I need to see the commander, Ibrahim Bey. I've got something important to talk to him about."

The corporal was not impressed. "You tell me what's so important that you've got to see the commander. I can't let anybody into his office right now. Not just anybody can waltz in here and see the major. So, speak up, what have you come to see him about?"

"I know that. But what I've got to say is very important. Very important. And I have to see him myself and right away!"

The corporal was steadfast in his disapproval, but Ali continued to press him as politely as he possibly could. Finally, the corporal was convinced. He looked Ali over one more time, from head to toe, before turning around and lightly tapping on the major's door. When he heard the deep, "Come in," from the other side of the door, he softly pushed it open, entered, and, at attention, barked: "Major, there's a civilian at the door. He wants to see you. I told him to leave, but he insists that he has to talk to you. He says it's important, very important."

The major had unbuttoned his jacket and was busy looking at a magazine full of political cartoons. His coffee was only half-drunk and he never liked to be disturbed until he had finished his coffee.

"Didn't I tell you not to bother me? Who is it? What's his name? For God's sake, haven't I taught you anything! You can't just let anybody waltz in here and ask me for a favor that I can't do. Oh for God's sake! Tell him to come in and let's see what this is about."

Having said his piece, the major buttoned up his jacket and swiped his mustache with the back of his hand. He put on his sternest expression as a defense against the kinds of pleas that common people flooded him with. The corporal entered and was followed by a tall, thin man with an eagle beak nose and eyes that darted about like that of a vulture. The visitor turned his cap around in his hands as the gaze of his eyes slid politely toward the floor.

"So what is it you want? This early in the morning? So, what is so important that you had to come and see me?"

The major's loud and stern voice seemed to have no effect. "It's important, what I have to tell you, Major."

"What can be that important? And who are you anyway? What's your name?"

"Ali, they call me Ali the Baker, Commander. I've got a bak-ery shop near the flour market.

"All right then, and what is it that's so important?"

Before he answered, Ali turned his gaze from the floor up to that of the corporal and then directly to the major. "It's secret, Major. What I've got to say is very secret."

This made the major angry. "Just spit it out, whatever it is."

"I'm afraid I can't. I have to talk to you in private and then you'll understand how important it is."

The major felt he had been backed into a corner. He looked at Ali carefully, noting his serious demeanor and assured stance.

"All right then, Corporal, you go out and close the door and wait outside." Now turning towards Ali, he asked, "All right then, now tell me what it is you have to say."

Ali knew how to get the major's attention. "I've heard that you're looking for Sariahmed's Osman. Well I have news about him."

The very word "Osman" was enough to propel the major out of his seat and in front of Ali. "What do you know about Osman?"

"I know where he is, that's what I know. And I am going to tell you and then you can go and arrest him."

The tables had turned and now the power was in Ali's hands. Recognizing his new status, Ali took a seat without being bid. He continued talking. "Of course I will tell you where he is. I will tell you, but when I do, I will also be putting my own life at risk. I know the government has issued a reward. And I want to make sure I get it."

"Of course you'll get your reward. If you give us the right information and we catch him, then you'll get your reward. But if you give us wrong information, well, then that'll get you into hot water."

"So, Commander, I want to know first how much the reward will be. I want to know all about that before I tell you anything."

"For God's sakes man, we're losing time here. I said you will get your reward. I don't carry the money around in my pockets that I can just reach in and hand it over to you. We'll catch the man and when we do, the Governor will issue an order for you to be paid. And that'll be it. There's no way we can hand over that money before the man has been caught."

"You know, Major, I trust you and that's why I came here to you. I want to get the money and then leave immediately. I have to get away because that gang will never let me stay alive. And nobody should know that it was me. If word gets out, that'll be the end of me. That's for sure."

"I can't guarantee that you'll be safe. That's the risk you have to take. But if you want to get the reward, you have to give a spoken statement and then sign it. How else will the government know who is going to get the reward?"

"Hay Allah! If this gets out, I'm a goner for sure. For the love of Allah, let this just be between the two of us. Nobody should know but you and me."

"How will that work? You both want the reward, but you don't want anybody to know! That won't do."

"Then I won't tell."

"What in the hell does that mean? 'I won't tell.' I'll have you on the ground and whipped till you turn purple. I can make you talk. You know that. But you came of your own accord. Make your statement. Get your reward and then leave. Now tell me, what did you see? Where are they?"

"All right, I'll tell you, but you're going to have a hard time believing it. So did I. There are three men. One is serving. And one is playing the *ud*. Osman is lying on the floor. Seems to be asleep."

"Go on."

"I will, but there is something else. I don't know how to say this. But there are also about twenty heads."

"What do you mean? Heads? Twenty? Now they've turned into an army. You said there were only three of them. How did they become twenty?"

"That's what's strange about it. Three of them are alive, but the rest are dead. Dead. The heads are skulls. Dead people's heads, you know?"

As Ali talked, the major became more and more confused. Music and drinking and skulls with cigarettes.

"And where was this all taking place?"

"There's a man we call the Crazy Sergeant. Served in the Army for sixteen years and came back crazy as a loon. But he's not the type to kill anybody. Not that I would guess anyway. I'm thinking that maybe the skulls belong to men that Osman has killed."

"Anyway, no harm can come from skulls, so let's not worry about them. Let's worry about catching Osman. I want you to come with me now. You'll give your statement and sign it and then we can go and see if it really is Osman in that house. And if it is, then you will get your reward."

228

Ali was now caught in a web of his own making. He watched as the major called for the clerk and the typewriter. Soon the clerk, meticulous in dress and demeanor, walked in carrying a heavy Remington typewriter. He placed it carefully on the desk, sat down before it, and with expert movements inserted a clean sheet of paper into the machine.

The major began to speak. "Start writing, Son. First put today's date. All right then. Let's start: 'While working in my office I, Gendarmerie Commander Ibrahim Acar, was visited by a person named Ali Alkanat who claims to live in the district of the flour market and says he works as a baker." The commander continued to dictate, giving all of the names, addresses, and times that Ali had told him. He also dictated the events as they had been told to him, but he did not include the description of the skulls as he thought that would rob the account of some of its veracity. He then handed the statement over to the baker for his signature.

Once the statement was signed, he turned to Ali. "It wouldn't be right for us to leave you here like this. When the whole thing is over and done with, you'll get your money and you can go whereever you want. But for the time being, we're going to host you in one of our cells here."

When he heard the word "cell" Ali's skin color turned an ashy gray color. He jumped up and began to plead. "Commander, I've changed my mind. I don't want a reward either. I haven't done anything wrong that you would want to lock me up. I kiss your hands and feet, but please let me go. If this gets out, they'll never let me stay alive. Just let me go."

"Don't be afraid, Son. Nothing is going to happen to you. We're not going to let you go until this is all done. Once we've captured Osman, you'll be free to go. All we're going to do with you now is make sure you are safe and sound."

So saying the major called his corporal and ordered him to take Ali to a cell. He then straightened his mustache and tie before picking up the statement and heading to the governor's office.

The governor listened carefully, read the statement, and asked the major a myriad of questions. He next called his chief of police so that the three of them could come up with a quick plan of action. First they sent a couple of plain clothes policeman—one dressed as a garbage man, the other as a street sweeper—to have a look around the sergeant's house. A squad of policemen were sent to block all access to the neighborhood. Each policeman was accompanied by three gendarmes to ensure that they had enough force to back them up. The calvary was ordered out of their barracks and into alert. Sharpshooters were brought out with their Thompson machine guns. Other sharpshooters with lighter weapons were positioned on neighboring roofs. To forestall a possible escape, the major also ordered troops to guard the main roads leading into the city. He had his men stationed at spots near the well, the cemetary, Forked Road, and Lower Citadel.

15.
Surrounded!

O sman was wide awake and staring at the clouds in the sky through the star window. He noticed a brief flash of a shadow across the window. He was on his feet in an instant.

"There's somebody on the roof!"

Osman and the Sergeant drew their guns while Jemal quietly lay down his *ud*. Peeking through the window, Osman spotted the gendarmes and police. He saw that they were positioned on all of the neighboring roofs, some lying down with guns in position. Jemal also withdrew a tiny pistol he had stashed in his waist band and, proving himself utterly fearless, began firing randomly through the star window. His fire opened a barrage from outside and soon bullets were lodging into the stone walls and piercing the windows. The neighborhood was in an absolute panic. Mothers grabbed their children and threw them to the floor as they tried to protect them with their own bodies.

Osman was fast. He was out the door and down the steps of the courtyard in seconds. He grabbed Ayshe's long street veil from its nail and slipped down to the basement. From there he fled through the secret door, first to his own basement, and then across and into the basement of their Armenian neighbor. No one saw him as he slipped into the neighbor's courtyard and then, veiled, into the street.

The street was filled with police and gendarmes, all firing at the Sergeant's house. It was a hellish scene. Osman was behind the soldiers and he moved through the chaos quickly down the street and into an alley. He knew his way through the warren of streets and soon was on the edge of the neighborhood. A barricade had been set up, but because everyone was so enraptured by the fire fight, nobody noticed the seemingly old, veiled woman who passed out of the neighborhood.

Osman knew enough to stay away from the major streets. He kept turning and turning through the twisted narrow streets until he had come to a spot behind the main square. He planned to leave the city, but he realized that they would probably have all the roads blocked. He turned back into the warren of narrow roads and found himself a corner to hide in.

"Cease fire! Cease fire! I'm ordering you fools to stop shooting. Cease fire!" Major Ibrahim's deep voice finally made itself heard and gradually the sounds of shooting died down. The major and Eshref Bey slowly rose from their positions and looked towards the Sergeant's house. The firing from inside had also stopped.

The two men very carefully made their way up to the house as the major shouted, "Hey, Osman, give yourself up! We've got you surrounded. The house is surrounded by police and soldiers. So come out now, slowly, and with your hands in the air. If you don't, we're going to come in after you. Come out now, before you are killed. I'm telling you this for your own good."

They expected Osman to appear, but when he did not, the major repeated his call. When there was still no response, he assumed that all the men must have been shot. Just then, Jemal Bey called out in his thin voice, "We're giving ourselves up! We give up! Don't shoot! For God's sake, Ahmed, wave that white handkerchief out the window there! Let 'em see it!"

The Sergeant was still lying face down on the floor and had no intention of standing up and making himself a decoy. Besides, he wasn't the kind of person to surrender. "I'm not waving no flag out no window. I didn't turn tail to the English and not to the Greeks neither. If they want me, they can come and get me. If you're so keen, you wave your hanky out that window!"

"Ahmed, but these ain't English or Greeks. These are government men. And they're not looking for us; they're after Osman. Where is Osman anyway? Ahmed, Osman's not here."

"He just disappeared into thin air."

"How can that be? I didn't even hear the door close after him. He'll get into trouble downstairs, they'll shoot him."

"Don't worry. He'll be just fine, he must already have found himself a safe spot."

Jemal Agha, now covered in sweat, mopped at his brow with a white handkerchief before getting up in the smoke and dust filled room. Through the heavy fog he leaned towards the window and started waving his handkerchief.

"It's us, it's us! Don't shoot, we're surrendering!"

The commander and the chief of police were grinning with happiness.

"Now that's better," said the commander. "Anyway, even if you'd been birds, you couldn't have flown away! Throw your guns from the window! Come on now, be quick about it!"

"Okay, Okay. Just a minute. Hey Ahmed, you got a gun? Gimme your gun."

Jemal drew his tiny five-shot Browning from his belt, getting ready to throw it from the window holding it by its barrel.

"I don't carry no gun," said Sergeant Ahmed. "Here, all I have is a butcher's knife, take it and give it to those devils. God knows, even a measly knife is probably enough to frighten those fellas."

While saying this he thrust his butcher's knife in Jemal's hand. Jemal looked longingly at his gun for the last time and after a final silent farewell threw it out of the window. The gun was followed by the knife. Finally the two men appeared at the window.

"You ignoramuses, you shameless ignoramuses!" muttered Sergeant Ahmed. "Is this the way to shoot! Have you got no conscience? Even the English didn't carry on like this. First you should knock on the door and then start shooting. That's the way these things are done."

Sergeant Ahmed was muttering, but was not keen on leaving the relative safety of the window. The shooting had stopped, but all the guns were still aimed at the windows, ready to start shooting at the slightest misstep. The relative calm was belied by the smoke and dust still in the air. The sharp and cloying smell of aniseed from the broken *raki* jug mixed and mingled with the acrid gunpowder smell.

Jemal Agha and Sergeant Ahmed were at the window trying to justify themselves.

"Major, we haven't done anything wrong. We were playing our *ud* and drinking. You won't believe it, but we also had other guests. We weren't breaking any laws. You could have killed us. What need was there to shoot like that: Look at all the dust and the holes in the walls and floors. There is nothing left undamaged in the room. Even my *ud*."

"You can thank God I didn't have hand grenades thrown and killed you all. What's your name? Both of you, tell me your names!"

"I am Jemal, Jemal Gezer, and this is Sergeant Ahmed, Ahmed Kirishchi."

The major looked extremely annoyed.

"And where are your other guests? The other man, where is he? Mind what you do, because all I have to do is say the word and this house will be blown up instantly! Tell him to come forward!"

"Major, I swear there is nobody but us. Actually there are, but they don't count. They are already dead. Come and see for yourself the company we were keeping."

"Hey look here, stop making fun of me or you'll be really sorry. Osman is supposed to be there. Tell him to show his face, or I'll have the house demolished, with you inside. Tell that miserable dog to come out!"

"Osman ran away. I swear; I really swear that he is not here. Look, there is nobody in the room but me and Sergeant Kirishchi. And the only runaways we got here are the escapees from the cemetery."

The major ordered a handful of men to search the house. They went to the door, all guns at the ready. The stout courtyard door did not budge at first, but with all the kicks of Sergeant Muharrem and the shoulder blows of the gendarmes, it finally caved in. The police and gendarmes stormed the court-yard. After a quick observation of the scene, they took positions around each door opening towards the courtyard. Once up the stairs, they kicked upon the door to the upstairs room and stormed in. They saw that Jemal and the Sergeant were still at the window with their hands raised. The dust and the smell of aniseed were so strong that breathing was difficult. The men glanced at the low bench along the wall and saw the skulls star-ing at them. In the grip of fear and shock they ran back out of the room, stepping on the pieces of the broken *ud*, the bones, and the shards of pottery. It was up to Sergeant Muharrem to stop the panicky escape, but he, too, was already half way down the staircase when he came to his senses. He led his men back into the room. A short while later, the major entered the room trying not to step on the bones. The major was curious more than anything else.

"Who among you is Osman of Sariahmed, out with it!" he barked. In response the two men looked at each other. Jemal Agha said, "Osman's not here. He ran away as soon the shoot-ing started. Gone in a flash he was."

The major was not amused. Not at all. "What? You miserable skunks, there were three of you at this orgy or whatever if was. Where is that dog? Where has he gone? I swear I'll shoot both of you, I really will, out with it! Where has he gone?"

Overcome with rage, the major was gesticulating wildly with his pistol, yet all the while still managing to keep the weapon pointed directly at the faces of the two heedless friends.

Sergeant Ahmed pushed aside Jemal and stepped forward.

"What are you saying, commander?" he asked in a show of bravery. "If the artillery and rifles of the English couldn't stop me, tell me why I should be afraid of those bullets of yours? Come on, shoot me. What are you waiting for, shoot me!"

While saying this Sergeant Ahmed had opened his shirtfront and was advancing towards the major. The major was in a sweat and his hand was shaking. He took a few steps back while the Sergeant advanced towards him, but he kept his pistol pointied at the face of the Sergeant. At that point Jemal Agha intervened:

"Major, never you mind him. My friend the Sergeant here

served in the army for exactly sixteen years. He actually likes and respects military men, but the only thing this devil had was his house of his and now look at it. And look at my poor *ud*. This instrument has been my friend and company for the past forty years and look what you've gone and done to it!"

"What do I care if he served? I am a soldier myself. We all are."

"Major, I swear that if someone is to blame, it's me. I saw someone looking into the window and fired at the window. You understand; I fired towards the window, not at the soldiers or the police. If I had known it was the military, would I have fired? Anyway, I didn't shoot to hit. Was anyone among your men wounded? The bullets just broke the glass. If you had made your presence known, we would have surrendered immediately."

"Yes, very smart. We should give advance notice of our arrival so that the skunk called Osman can slip away in peace. Cut out this nonsense and give me Osman. That's the only way you'll walk from here as free men. If not, you will be convicted of aiding and abetting a criminal. Oh, and by the way, what are all these skulls? Have you been collecting the skulls of your victims? What, for goodness sake, are they?"

"We didn't kill nobody. This was the Sergeant's idea. He remembered his dead friends from the army and was sorry that they couldn't eat, drink, and be merry with us. But what can we do, after all, they're dead. So, he came to my house around midnight saying that he had some important guests and then brought me here. We thought that it wasn't fair that only living people should have fun and so we decided to have them as guests."

"I can't believe what I'm hearing. Have you all gone crazy? This place stinks of aniseed. Idiots, do dead men drink? You weren't by any chance doing some sorcery, were you?"

This remark was a blow to Sergeant Ahmed's pride.

"What sorcery? We are no sorcerers. The poor chaps were just lying in their graves with nobody ever praying for them. So we thought we might as well raise their spirits a bit. Is it just the living who have the right to amuse themselves? Hundreds of my friends were killed while serving. Nobody even remembers them. All of them were strong, young men and now their bones have turned into dust. Major, after all this, do you really think that this small feast was something they didn't deserve?"

"Oh my God, you really are crazy as a loon! You idiot, do you really think that this is the best way to commemorate our martyrs? They are dead. Normal people say prayers at their graves or organize readings of the Holy Quran to commemorate them. What you did is unheard of. Anyway, I couldn't care less about this nonsense so long as you tell me about Osman. Where did you hide him? Where is he now?"

"Commander, Osman is like a snake. The moment he saw the shadow on the window he disappeared. Since he didn't go out of the door, he must have gone to his house through the cellar and from there he must have reached the house of the Armenian. And that's the truth, for I don't lie."

"Let me find him in this house and you'll see. First we're going to search this place and search it good. Sergeant! Take your men and search the house! Come on! If you encounter any resistance, don't hesitate, just shoot them. Just be sure that not a single corner of this house is left unsearched!" Turning back towards Jemal and Sergeant Ahmed, who were both waiting at attention, he said: "Come on, you tomb looters, get a move on. Do you know the nature of your crime? It's a hanging offence! Do you understand me? You are accomplices of Osman. Whatever he has done, you'll be punished with him. Come on now!"

The soldiers ran down the staircase together and kicked open the door of the inner room. Once their eyes got used to the low light, they could make out the doors leading to the cellar and to the kitchen. Along the opposite wall there was the usual low divan typical of Turkish homes. Sergeant Muharrem reached it with a single bound and stripped back its cover. The heads of two scared people appeared. One was extremely elderly with gray hair and a face deeply lined with wrinkles. The younger woman also had gray hair that she clumsily and nervously tried to cover with her headscarf. The men were taken aback by the sight of the two gray haired heads and wrinkled faces. Through half sobs the women protested their innocence and wept at the state of their ruined house. Sergeant Muharrem began to bombard the women with questions about Osman.

"We didn't hide anybody. His house is next door. You can reach it through the cellar. When we heard the shooting, we saw him go down the cellar door. Who knows, he may have even reached the street and got away."

The women were terrified, as the soldiers did not turn their weapons aside. When demanded to do so by the officer in command, the Sergeant's wife covered her hair closely with her scarf and, trembling with fear, got up. Lighting her way with a match, she opened the door of the stairs leading to the cellar and, muttering to herself, started descending, careful not to omit the formula, *bismillahirahmanirrahim* (in the name of God, the Compassionate, the Merciful). She was followed closely by a policeman holding both his pistol and a torch. They in turn were followed by the rest of the men.

Food stocks were stored in a pile on one side of the cellar and wood and coal on the other. Just in front of them was a small door, slightly open. Sergeant Muharrem carefully inspected the food in the earthenware jars. They were packed with pickles, carrots, and *geliboru* berries. This inspection was followed by an equally careful inspection of the burning material.

"What's in these jars? Why are these jars half buried? Why has the wood been stacked like this?"

Ayshe was shocked at the ignorance of the sergeant.

"What do you think? We need all this for the winter," she said. "The half-buried jars are used to store cheese. Do you think Osman is crazy? Do you think he would be here waiting for you? He must have fled long ago."

The NCO pushed open the small door. Keeping his gun toting hand well ahead, he crouched slightly and passed through the door. He saw another stair ending with a door, through which someone had clearly passed in a hurry. In this half crouching position, the group reached the cellar of the neighbor's house. Unlike the cellar that they had just left behind, the floor of this cellar was covered with wooden pallets; all the food had been neatly stacked and the room was completely full. Dried onions, potatoes, melons, apples, pears were visible in the light of the torch and looked very appetizing. The room got slightly larger towards the right side. Bunches of grapes and melons hung on strings from the ceiling.

As in the cellar they had left behind, all along the wall were half buried earthenware jars. Passing near the bunches of grapes, Sergeant Muharrem could not resist the temptation to eat one of them. In this he was followed by all the other policemen and gendarmes, who took what they could reach. There was a stone staircase leading up from the cellar and at the end of it there was another open door. At the head of the stairs they entered a well-lit entrance hall. They crossed a paved courtyard and reached the kitchen. From within there came the sounds of talking and of pots and pans being used. Sergeant Muharrem looked inside and just as quickly turned his head away, for the kitchen exposed a gory scene. People with blood-soaked hands and clothing were busily cutting meat. Having recovered, the sergeant, gun in hand, barged into the kitchen.

"Nobody move or I shoot!" he shouted. "Drop those knives! What's all this meat?"

The kitchen was occupied by two men and two women. They cowered in a corner, looking in terror at the soldiers and policemen who had suddenly rushed into their kitchen. One of them, with a trembling voice said:

"Sir, we slaughtered an animal and we were cutting its meat to make sausages and dry meat *pastirma*."

"And you think this is a good time for making *pastirma?* All hell has broken loose outside and all you think about is sitting here and making sausages and *pastirma?* Does this seem normal to you?"

"Sir, this morning we slaughtered a heifer. If we don't treat its meat quickly, it will be spoiled. We did actually hear all the shooting. It sounded as if a war had broken out."

"Never mind the shooting and all that! Don't try being smart with me or you'll be sorry for it! And especially, don't pretend not to know! Where is he? Where have you hidden him?"

"We didn't hide anybody."

"Look at him! You know what you bloody well are? Accomplices! You are all accomplices! And you know in what? Murder, highway robbery! Whatever Osman of Sariahmed has done, you are his accomplices! Don't dare to deny or I swear I'll have all of you shot! Where is Osman? Where have you hidden him? Speak up, immediately!"

Jamjiyan was cleaning his hands on his apron and at the same time trying to approach the sergeant. With a feeble voice he added:

"Sir, I swear we didn't hide anybody. Every time Osman is in trouble, he runs away through here. We are neighbors; we have never harmed each other. We know that the government is looking for him and that he is known as a bandit, but he has never harmed us. Every time his family cooks something, they offer us some. We do the same. If the government is looking for him, let it catch him. Why should we ruin our relations with our nice neighbor."

"Shut up! What neighbor? Do you think that neighborliness is what you should worry about right now? You'll very soon see the government representatives and then we'll see how important neighborliness is. Where is he? Speak up quickly, or I'll not be answering for my actions here!"

Jamjiyan's brother Artin, who up to that moment had not interfered in the conversation and had been content with following the unfolding of the scene, could not resist any longer and blurted out:

"Osman passed through here while all the shooting was still going on. He must have gone out to the street. He had his pistol. How were we supposed to catch him and hand him over to the government, if you, with all the gendarmes at your disposal, weren't able to? You tell us that."

"What is that supposed to mean?" the sergeant objected. "The culprit passes under your nose and you can't do a thing? This is a plain case of aiding and abetting a criminal and as such you are good for the noose. Come on, be sensible and show me where you have hidden him and let's close the matter. It's in your interest. Show me where he is hiding, help me to lead him away from here all tied up and you may even be forgiven."

While repeating himself over and over again, the sergeant kicked helplessly at the stones lining the kitchen floor, being careful all the while not to step in the blood.

He was convinced that the situation was fishy.

It was at that moment that the idea of searching the whole house occurred to him. The house was a stately old mansion. Once it had been the property of the chief of the Tashnak Armenian Nationalist Party. This Jamjiyan became involved with people who were working for the establishment of an Armenian state in Cilicia and as such had collaborated with enemies of the Ottoman State. He had ended up being caught, tried, and convicted. This had been his residence and its present occupiers were his grandchildren.

Sergeant Muharrem went on ignoring the women, but took Artin and Vahap with him and started looking in every nook and cranny of the house. They first went into the hall. On the two sides of the hall there were the usual divans. The shelves in the built-in cabinets on the opposite wall were full of precious crystals, glasses, and French porcelain. Various plates and glasses were being displayed on embroidered napkins. In a corner stood the folding table used for meals, with mother-of-pearl-encrusted chairs around it, while the floor was covered with carpets decorated with floral patterns. The low seats were covered with precious carpets from the Kayseri town of Yahyali. From here a wooden staircase led to the upper stories of the building.

The sergeant started a very thorough search, careful to check even the wooden base of the staircase and the insides of the benches. Later, under the guidance of the owners of the house, they went upstairs. The first room they entered was the master bedroom. The centerpiece of this room was a big, brass bedstead with woolen covers and a richly decorated bedspread, underneath which were glimpses of clean white linen. Over the bed hung an antique rifle with a hammer mechanism. On one side of this carpeted room there was an enormous covered brazier with a brass pedestal emanating a mysterious and somber light. The walls had niches in them, the doors of which were firmly closed. The sergeant and his men literally overturned all that was in the room. Rifles at the ready, as if they were about to be attacked, they looked into and under the bed and into the cupboards, leaving nothing unturned. Following this frenzied search, they all went on into the adjacent small room. This room

had two windowa, one facing the street and the other the courtyard. In it were largish divans. Once again there were many
splendid Yahyali carpets, in this case covering the divans. The
same frantic search was repeated in this room. The sergeant
even searched the crystal water pipes and their multicolored
tubes. The sergeant suddenly noticed the grand piano in a corner of the room. This was the first piano the sergeant had seen
in his life, so he approached it warily. He did not enquire as to
the nature of the mechanism, but having discovered the presence of a lid, he asked the landlord to open it. The white and
black keys of the piano appeared. The sergeant, not daring to
lower his pistol, went on to examine the chords in the back of
the piano.

The piano was unlike anything the sergeant had seen in his
life, so he was not about to underestimate it and was trying to
understand if it might, by any chance, be a newfangled weapon
that he had not yet heard about. Finally, not having been able
to discover its use, he very bravely touched one of the keys. To
the consternation of the poor sergeant, the ensuing "la" note
reverberated throughout the room. Making a brave attempt at
hiding his fright, he asked:

"What, for goodness sake, is this?"

Jamciyan courteously tried to explain:

"Sir, this is a piano, a musical instrument, we play it from
time to time for our enjoyment."

"You play it? I mean for music, or what?"

"Yes, yes. We use it to accompany songs. You should hear
it. It produces beautiful sounds."

"Oh my God, but who can play such a thing?"

"My daughter, but now she is in Istanbul, so these days it is
mostly my wife who plays it."

"Isn't that immoral? Having your women entertain people
with music?"

"Why not, sir? I mean, many women play the *ud* or the man-
dolin, so why shouldn't my women play the piano?"

"All right, all right. We haven't come here to talk about
music. Come on boys, let's go downstairs. What a house, full of
all sorts of marvelous objects, not to mention all the food. Plus

242

they also have this enormous monster just for the sake of playing music. Meanwhile, God knows that our people can't find a
morsel of food. Whoever has such a mansion with eight or ten
rooms? In our hovels, people die because of the cold. What is
your business by the way?"

"Me? I am in the textile business. I have relations in Istanbul.
They import stuff and I sell it around here. You know, calico,
flannel, printed cloth, that kind of stuff..."

The sergeant had taken on a supercilious air and looking
around once more he added:

"Good, good. May God help you to preserve all this loot.
Most of us haven't got a thing, but I see you and your family are
richly endowed.

Jamjiyan felt it best not to reply.

"Anyway, I only pray to God that He may preserve your
stuff. Back to Osman, God knows where you hid him. Since you
must have served in the army and of course pay taxes, you are
one of us. So you are duty bound to help us. That's why I am
asking about Osman. Things are not like they once were. If I
catch you lying, you'll find yourself in front of a judge, just like
any common criminal."

The two men both went down to the hall, and then from
there out to the paved courtyard. They had just gone out when
Major Ibrahim, the soldiers, and the policemen appeared from
the cellar door,

The sergeant sprang to attention. "Major, we've searched
everywhere, in every nook and cranny. It looks as though he
got away. The only clue we have is this person's statement that
Osman passed through the courtyard and that he was armed."

"So that's it! Take them all and bring them to headquarters.
Take these two, that retired sergeant Ahmed and Jemal, and the
two women from the first house. Those two women know a lot.
I want you also to arrest Hurmet, Osman's wife. We are going
to question them all."

"At your orders Major, sir!" said the sergeant and, having
smartly turned back, he barked an order to the two men to follow him.

That day all the suspects that could be found in the district

243

were rounded up. The major immediately started the questioning of the presumed witnesses, beginning with the Sergeant and Jemal Agha. Fingerprints, signatures, documents stamped with all sorts of stamps—nothing was omitted. The minutes of each statement were prepared and sent to the relevant court via the prosecutor's office. Some of the people were detained, while all the women were let go. The Crazy Sergeant, Jemal, the two Armenian brothers, and a few other inhabitants of the district were among those detained.

Thus was the operation completed and the mystery of the skulls and the songs solved. A new place was added to the list of Osman's probable hideouts. That day, despite having blocked all roads leading to Demirci Yazisi and organized ambushes, the gendarmes once again failed to catch the bandit Osman.

16.
Veiled and Running

O sman spent the rest of the day hiding in an ice-pit on a narrow side street. This pit was squeezed between mud brick houses and was not very large. Osman was exhausted; he had both the gendarmes and the police breathing down his neck. He was particularly afraid of Major Ibrahim, who was both bright and brave. Just as sure as my name is Osman, he thought, they've got all roads leading out of the city under surveillance. The moment he ventured in that direction, he would be trapped. He had to keep cool and not act in a rush.

Since Osman knew those parts so well he was confident he could guess on which roads the gendarmes would have set up ambushes. He knew that he could venture out from his hiding place only after sundown when everybody had retired. With his pistol at the ready, he lay swathed under Ayshe's chequered veil, waiting for nightfall. The day slowly ended, the ice pit getting dark before the rest of his surroundings. The muezzin of the nearby mosque chanted the call for sunset prayers. Osman decided to wait until the next set of prayers—the evening prayers—were also completed. He listened closely as all those coming out of the mosque went to their homes until in a short time, the whole area had become silent and deserted. It was at that point that Osman finally got up. It was pitch dark and not a soul was to be seen in the streets.

He had come to a conclusion concerning the problem of where to go. He decided to take the road passing the cemetery and proceed from there to Mount Hasan. If he could then go on to White Rock from there, he would also be able to reach Mahrumlar and from there his friend Chitoglu. He had entrusted both his horse and his rifle to this friend before he made his way down to the city to visit his wife. Now he was in desperate need of both in order to make a successful escape. He was sure that many check points and ambushes must have been set between the town and the district where the farm was located, making it impossible for him to follow the usual route. Most probably, though, they would not have put lookouts at the cemetery. Even if they had, it would be relatively easy to hide among the tombstones. Having made this detailed plan and thought through, as far as was possible, all the contingencies, he listened intently to the sounds of the night, trying to catch any suspect sound, and observed the few lights at the windows.

It was time to move. He jumped into the narrow alleyway and, following the shadows, reached the mosque courtyard. There was no one around. The sky was clear and starry, but a cold wind chilled Osman, who had nothing but the woolen shawl to cover him, to his bones.

He took shelter in the cover of the shadows as he made his way to the end of the road. He had come to the half ruined walls of the cemetery. In the distance, he could hear the whistles of the night guards. He waited a while near the walls, peering through the spaces between the tombstones, trying to discern any sound or movement.

Notwithstanding the freezing cold, Osman was perspiring heavily. He wiped at the sweat with the veil he had taken with him, got up, and with tentative steps proceeded among the tombstones. At first he assumed that the small shiny, point-like lights were the eyes of foxes, but all the same something did not look quite right. Suddenly it dawned upon him that they were lit cigarettes. He froze in place. He had discovered an ambush in the nick of time. From the shadow of a sarcophagus he observed the men who were lying in wait. There were around eight or ten of them and their rifles shone even in the dark. Clearly they were guarding the road along the cemetery walls, but were not aware that he was so near them, even though he was so close that he could hear their voices. There was no time to lose. Osman made a detour towards the center of the cemetery.

He climbed over the plastered wall at the end of the cemetery. Careful not to jostle even the smallest pebble, he left the cemetery and proceeded through the higher ground behind it, until he was in sight of the imposing Mount Hasan. He put his ear to the ground, looked at the horizon as far as he could see it in the dark, and smelled the air to see if the wind was carrying any unusual smell. Having ascertained that the coast was clear, he continued moving and after some time reached White Rock.

White Rock was a big rock formation that in ancient times had housed people in its caves. Osman entered one of the abandoned and damp caves. Completely out of breath and soaked in perspiration, he was forced to take a respite. He used Ayshe's veil once more as a towel to dry his perspiration.

Once he had caught his breath, he turned towards the face of White Rock so he might observe the dark plain. He was looking for any suspect movement or any other sign that would alert him against impending peril, but all was calm and silent, except for the dry branches of the trees rustling in the wind. He had to move quickly if he wanted to reach the farm before sunrise. His horse, rifle, and felt greatcoat were all there. With the same careful steps Osman went down the rock and across the vineyards. It was the end of winter and the vineyards were deserted. He proceeded very quickly in the dark. Shortly afterwards, he heard dogs barking and then the whitewashed walls of the farmhouse came into view. The farmhouse was surrounded by a natural fence made of oleaster bushes. As he approached the fence, the guard dogs came forward. Their leader, Karabash, recognized Osman and stopped barking, with the other dogs following suit. Surrounded by the dogs, Osman entered the farmyard. In the east the first faint glimmerings of dawn were visible. He walked towards the stable and, opening the door, saw his beloved horse behind the cows and the oxen. Recognizing his master, the horse raised his head from the fodder and whinnied. Osman kissed and affectionately stroked his horse. Exhausted by his exertions, he lay down on the sacks and immediately fell asleep.

A stable hand of around seventeen years of age worked and lived at the farm. His job was to herd the cattle, look after the poultry and the pigeons, and in general make himself useful doing odd jobs. This boy, Hussein, was not very bright and sometimes would do things that left his master puzzled, and sometimes even enraged. One day, for God knows what reason, he cut the tails of the donkey, the colt, the two cows, and the heifer. Ignoring the strenuous resistance of the animals, he used a knife he had sharpened on the millstone and accomplished the insane job. The animals brayed pitifully and the stable was a gory mess. Chitoglu, upon seeing what had happened, could not believe his eyes.

"Hussein," he asked, "what's happened to their tails? Who cut them?"

Hussein looked proud of what he had done and answered, "I did, sir."

"Why? You idiot!"

'To make the animals look better. I cut them."

At that moment all hell broke lose. Chitoglu picked up a flat shovel that was leaning against the stable wall and began to beat Hussein ferociously on the back and legs.

In the following days and months, Chitoglu was contrite for he knew he had overreacted. He tried to make Hussein forgive him by showering him with small kindnesses, but the boy never forgot what had happened that day. The boy's devotion to his master was transformed into a kindling hatred and he dreamed of the day when he could avenge the beating and pay back Chitoglu for what he had done. Hussein feared his master as he feared God Himself, so he was very careful not to let his feelings show.

That day, when Hussein woke up he noticed that someone was sleeping in the stable. Full of curiosity, he approached the sleeping man. As soon as he was near him and saw his blond mustache and his dirty and perspired face, he recognised him: This was Osman Agha, the bandit Osman Agha, acquaintance of Chitoglu. So, Osman Agha had returned. This was the owner of that splendid horse without equals, the horse that Hussein loved to look after, as if it were the dearest thing in his life. Hussein relished the times he could groom the great beast, take him out to the paddocks and exercise him. When the horse galloped it was with the smoothest of movements and it looked as if his feet never touched the ground. So now the owner of the horse had returned. He went to tell the news to his master.

Chitoglu Mehmed Efendi had a striking and very unusual appearance, with a sparse red beard, a long, bald head, and bright blue eyes. He could be very tender hearted when he wished, but could also lose his temper very easily. He was a man of the world, who had enjoyed himself for part of his life in Istanbul and was now living in semi-seclusion on this farm. His father, Hadji Mustafa Efendi, had been a notable of the town, famous for his honesty and affability. He was also one of the few Moslem cloth merchants in the shopping district of the town. He was respected and well received wherever he went.

In those days, most of his neighbors were Armenian, plus a few Greeks. Hadji Mustafa Efendi was also respected and counted as a friend by most of the non-Moslems. Unfortunately, this peaceful state of affairs did not last. Under the prodding of Russia and England, the Armenians were instilled with the idea of carving their own country out of Ottoman territory. Not only did they fail in this armed uprising, but also the Ottoman State, which was at the time fighting for its own survival, decided to eliminate the threat by banishing them from their own lands.

Demirciyan Efendi, who owned the shop next to Hadji Mustafa Efendi's, found his name on the list of those to be exiled. The day when he and his family were going to be sent to Adana was fast approaching and most preparations were complete. Chief among Demirciyan Efendi's worries was what to do with his lifelong savings made up of gold coins. He did not have the faintest idea of what to do with them. There were many people in his position and many had decided to bury their gold in safe places with the hope of one day coming back and recovering it. Demirciyan Efendi had taken into consideration the same option, but could not find a place he deemed sufficiently secure.

After pondering the alternatives at length, Demirciyan Efendi reached the conclusion that the best thing would be to leave his coins with a trusted friend. He reasoned that the person best fitting that description was the God-fearing Hadji Mustafa Efendi, a man who had a clear idea concerning the difference between sin and pious acts. Demirciyan Efendi was sure that his friend would not stray from the path of virtue and honesty. He knew that if God's will so ordered and one day he could come back, he could recover his hoard of gold.

Demirciyan went to see Hadji Mustafa Efendi a few days before his departure, carrying with him the earthenware jar full of gold, its top closed with a thick piece of leather. Mustafa Efendi had just returned from noon prayers and was sitting in his shop.

Mustafa Efendi was distressed because of the banishment of so many people, and his powerlessness to prevent it. Why had some of them run after such impossible dreams? Hadn't they been comfortable with the situation as it was? Many of Kayseri's Armenians had already been sent to Adana and they had even received word from some of these. With their departure, though, the shopping district had lost much of its former appeal.

He greeted his neighbor Demirciyan at the door of his shop. The poor man was extremely depressed and tired looking. He put his heavy saddlebag near the chair on which he had sat, exhausted. After the usual greetings, he immediately broached the subject that was worrying him:

"Hadji Mustafendi, may God bless you. For so many years we have been neighbors and never once did we hurt each other with words or acts. We always loved and respected each other. Unfortunately, fate has willed an end to our stay here. There is no longer water for us to drink nor food for us to eat here. The government has decided to banish us from these lands. There is nothing we can do about it. This, apparently, is our destiny."

Hadji Mustafa Efendi was deeply moved by the sadness of his neighbor. "Demirciyan Efendi," he said with a deep sigh, "it's not the end of the world after all. We must bow to our destiny. How nice it would be if we could do something and try to prevent it, but this operation has begun and can't be stopped."

"We were happy here. We had influence and a good place within society. It was this war with Russia that ruined us. In particular it was Jamjiyan that ruined us. He started with the so-called Armenian Union and we helped him. He asked for money and we contributed. He asked for volunteers and we gave him those, too. Unfortunately he organized those men into guerilla bands. That, of course, was the last straw. How the government possibly be unaware of all this? Of course they *were* aware, and that's why we find ourselves in such a situation today. This apparently was our destiny."

"Demirciyan Efendi, which country in the world will permit a new state to be established within its borders? Which country will give up its lands? None, of course. Armenians already were very influential and controlled much of the local administration and commerce—what more did you want? Your people worked as doctors, lawyers, as architects, as government leaders. Forgive me for saying this, but you were stupid to throw all that away. Instead of supporting the Ottoman State that provided you with all of this, you worked to overthrow it. That's why I am angry, but also extremely sad."

"You are right; our Armenian community didn't think their actions through well enough. But before the Turkish Nationalist Reformists came to power in 1908, we didn't have such problems. Their nationalism led our people to found our own nationalist parties like the Tashnak and the Hinchak. It was those people that got us in this mess."

"Demirciyan, it was the Allies who organized all this. They promised the Armenians that they would support them in the creation of an Armenian state on Ottoman lands and people like Jamjiyan believed them. It was their stupidity that landed my dear neighbors into trouble. Think of the massacres of Turkish villagers around Tomarza just outside of Kayseri that were carried out by the Tashnak and the Hinchak. And then the retaliations! May God forbid that we ever see such days again!"

The two neighbors slowly sipped their coffees and continued with their conversation. Hadji Mustafa Efendi was not indifferent to the troubled state of mind of Demirciyan Efendi and he was wondering if there weren't some way in which he could help him. It was at that point that Demirciyan Efendi broached the subject of his gold coins:

251

"Look, we were very comfortable in this place. But what's done is done and now they are making us pay for it. If God wills it, we shall soon be on our way to Adana. What fate awaits us, especially during the journey, I don't know. In the same way that lack of money is a problem during a trip, an excess of it is also a dire problem. I have money saved thanks to my business and I don't have the slightest idea where to hide it. As I said before, carrying it with me could land me into trouble; somebody could get ideas. On the other hand, I don't know where I could bury such a big jar."

At this point of the conversation he opened his saddlebag and used both hands to take out the heavy jar. The shop in which they were sitting was narrow and long. At the back of the shop was a star-shaped window. Below the window stood a glass case, a set of wooden drawers, a rather heavy safe, prayer rugs, and a wooden desk set parallel to the wall. Under the desk were a pair of old wooden clogs and a small ewer used during ablutions. This is where the two men sat as they drank their coffee and at the moment when Demirciyan Efendi removed the jar, the only people in the shop full of colorful printed cloth and white calico were the two old friends. Mustafa Efendi looked on with uncomprehending eyes.

"Look Mustafendi, this jar is full of gold coins. You might not be aware of it, but I own a number of fields and orchards around here. I have entrusted these to the villagers who work on them. I have sold everything I had in my house. I will have some money hidden on me as we travel, but I could never manage to carry this big jar. A lot of us have been hiding money thinking that someday we may return. I hope we do return someday, but I am far from sure that they'll let us come back to these places. Even if the Ottoman Empire loses the war it will be very difficult for us to return. Look at all the gold. I could never hope to put together the same amount anywhere else. You are a good Moslem, that's why I am entrusting this jar to you!"

Hadji Mustafa Efendi looked at the jar sealed with a leather piece. It was a big, round jar. With a surprised look on his face he said, "Demirciyan Efendi, I would never begrudge you your wealth, may God provide you with even more. We don't know who is going to die and who is going to survive. Only God knows. You have decided to entrust me with your jar because you have faith in me, but what if it is stolen or some other disaster befalls it? If something like that happened, how could I justify myself in the other world? Better that you should entrust it to somebody else or do as the others have done and bury it some place. Forget about me. If I should fail your trust, I would have committed a grave sin."

"Hadji Mustafendi, in such a case I wouldn't claim anything, nor would you have committed a sin. Why are you worried? Don't I know you? If you manage to keep it safely, so much the better. If not, you won't owe me anything, just as you owe nothing to your mother for the milk she let you suck."

"Allah! Allah! You're right that this much gold would cause you trouble during the trip. Even your best friend could be tempted. In this you are right. But what if something happens to you? If your children or even your grandchildren come and claim the gold, it would be all right. But what if nobody comes and I am left with the jar? I would pay dearly for it in the afterlife."

Demirciyan Efendi, moved by the honesty of his friend, replied, "Didn't you hear what I said? Only you, me, and God knows about this. If I can come back, so much the better. If it still exists by then, I would take back the jar. If I can't come back, the jar is yours. God is my witness that I am stating that you would be the rightful owner of the gold. I have thought at length before making this decision. If you don't do what I am asking you to do, you'll put me in a difficult situation. In a way it's your duty towards me as a neighbor. Let's open it, so you can see for yourself."

Upon saying this, Demirciyan Efendi opened the jar and started removing some of the gold coins. Full of hesitance, Hadji Mustafa Efendi finally screwed up the courage to look at the gold coins. The glitter of the gold dazzled their eyes and seemed to illuminate the dark atmosphere of the shop. Nevertheless, the two friends still felt the weight of not being able to do more for each other. Both were very pessimistic about the future. A little while later, with quick movements,

Demirciyan Efendi closed the jar, took his tobacco pouch, and without adding a single word walked towards the door.

Hadji Mustafa Efendi ran after his friend and the two embraced, trying to hide their tears and cursing their fate. After this last embrace among old friends, one went away and the other took his usual place in the shop.

The same day that Demirciyan Efendi left, his friend took the jar to his own home and at a moment when there wasn't anybody around, buried it in the ground under the trellis behind the empty earthenware water storage tank. Demirciyan Efendi was able to send greetings from Adana, but that was the last news Hadji Mustafa Efendi had from his old friend. For years Hadji Mustafa Efendi waited anxiously for news.

Not even his wife and children knew anything about the jar. Not once did Hadji Mustafa Efendi go and look at the gold pieces.

One day Mustafa Efendi fell ill. Cobwebs were applied, Mustafa Efendi was cauterised, lead was melted and poured on cold water over his head, amulets were prepared, prayers were said, propitiatory blowings of air were done, cupping glasses were applied... All to no avail. Feeling that he was nearing his end, he tried to impart all his last wishes to his sons. One day, he called them both and told them about Demirciyan Efendi and his pot of gold buried in the garden. Thus did the two sons learn about the jar.

'This jar must end up in the hands of its rightful owner," he said. "If anything should happen to the jar, it would weigh on your consciences and I would pursue you in the afterlife. If you can't find him, find his children or his grandchildren, but be sure to return the gold. This is the main request I leave with you." In peace with himself, Hadji Mustafa Efendi passed away a few days later.

The two brothers, Chitoglu Mehmed Efendi and Ahmed Efendi, did not talk about this matter during the forty days of mourning following their father's death. On the fortieth day the family hosted the traditional chanting of the Mevlûd poem at the local mosque. Prayers were said for the departed soul and the Sacred Quran was recited in its entirety.

Upon their return from the mosque, the two brothers took a lantern and went to the trellis in the garden where the water tank stood half buried in the ground. They dug up the jar full of gold and opened it. The leather cover had dried up, but the gold coins were still shiny. The two brothers sat there for some time in silence, just handling the gold pieces. A little while later, they put everything back as they had found it.

After that day the two brothers pursued their mission of finding the Demirciyan family. They asked everywhere; they wrote letters; they asked the assistance of various embassies, consulates, and refugee agencies. They even asked the assistance of the Turkish government. Then, finally, one day they were able to trace the family to Beirut. Via the Turkish Embassy at Beirut they wrote to Demirciyan's son, Agop. After the fall of the Ottoman State following the disastrous consequences of uprisings and the defeat of the First World War, this former province of the empire had become foreign land. At first the Demirciyans were suspicious when they were approached, but later they received a letter from the Ahmed and Mehmed Efendis. The letter, worded with great insistence, invited Agop Efendi, son of their former neighbor, to Turkey for what was claimed to be "an auspicious reason." After receiving several letters reiterating the invitation, Agop Efendi was overcome by curiosity and decided to make the trip.

He was received with great joy by the Ahmed and Mehmed Efendis. The three men exchanged their childhood memories. Agop Efendi had not forgotten that long trip he had undertaken then, together with his family. He remembered, even if a bit hazily, the heartrending separation from the land of his birth. Once it was established, with no ground for the slightest doubt, that Agop was really Demirciyan Efendi's son, Mehmed Efendi brought the jar and placed it in front of Agop Efendi. At first Agop Efendi could not understand why the container had been put in front of him, and when he opened it, he was shocked beyond belief. He was left speechless. It was only later that he recovered enough to be able to embrace and kiss the two brothers repeatedly.

Agop managed somehow to smuggle this money to Beirut where he invested it in commerce, becoming a person of some influence in Lebanese society. Each year he sent presents to the two brothers and never failed to keep up correspondence with them.

Now upon hearing that his friend Osman had arrived and was in desperate need of an escape route, it occurred to Chitoglu Mehmet Efendi that he could send Osman to Beirut to Agop. While he was going down the stairs he smelled the delicious aroma of flat bread being baked on a heated iron grille by his wife, Ayshe.

Entering the stable he saw Osman, who had just got up, near his horse. For a while he stood there watching Osman affectionately stroking his horse. It was as if Osman were talking to his horse, even listening to him, consulting with him. That is why at first he did not hear the landlord approaching. As soon as he saw him he tried to kiss his hand, but Mehmed Efendi did not let him and they embraced.

The two men squatted on their haunches on the wooden platform. They dipped into their tobacco pouches and rolled their cigarettes. It was Mehmed Efendi who began the conversation.

"Osman, what would you say if I advised you to disappear from around here for a while? I have an acquaintance in Beirut called Agop. Let me write him a letter so that he can help you. You can't wander around these mountains all your life."

This unexpected but very welcome suggestion gave Osman a glimmer of hope for his future. The two men continued their conversation as they began making plans about how Osman could get to the Lebanon. A tray arrived with the warm and fresh flat bread, which the two men ate with bowls of creamy yogurt and fresh garlic. Once Mehmed Efendi left for the house, the now relaxed Osman could again stretch out on the sacks near his beloved horse.

Mehmed Efendi went up to his room, wrote Agop's name and address on an envelope, and then began penning a letter to his friend...

* * *

While all this was happening, the stable boy was mulling over the fact that his moment of revenge had finally arrived. He could not forget the way he had been beaten by his master and the presence of Osman had put an idea in his mind. He was going to be avenged and also make some money. From the conversation he had overheard, he had understood that the gendarmes were everywhere in the valley and that they were looking for Osman. He decided to leave the farm with the excuse of looking after the cattle and instead go to the gendarmes. He knew that a money reward had been put on Osman's head. If Osman were caught, he reasoned, his master would also be put in prison. There was also the possibility that the police would punish him with the *falaka*, that is, that they would beat him with a stinging rod to the soles of the feet. Oh, how he wished that such a thing would happen and that his master would be beaten, just like the master had dared to beat him. He certainly wasn't going to feel sorry for him. He still couldn't understand the reason for his master's fury. If cutting the tail of a dog or braiding the tail of a horse was such a fancy thing to do, why was it that cutting the tail of a calf was such an offence?

Hussein left the farmhouse, driving the cattle in front of him, and headed towards town. His master Chitoglu had told him to signal home if he saw any gendarmes or police, but Hussein was certainly not going to do that; quite the contrary, he was going to look for the gendarmes and tell them everything. He was going to make his master really sorry for what he had done.

At a little distance from the farm, he left the animals in the common pasture and proceeded in the direction of the Chained Well, where a squad of gendarmes led by Sergeant Muharrem and the police had set up an ambush for Osman.

Sergeant Muharrem was sitting, blinking back his sleep, and listening to his stomach grumble. Just as he was thinking of how annoying it was to be sitting there in the wind in his sleepy state, he suddenly saw a figure approaching. It was a frail looking lad who, judging by the fluff of hair under his nose, couldn't be yet twenty. The tattered hat was too large for the young man's head and came down to his ears. His trousers barely covered his knees and he was barefoot. He looked over the men lying around and, having ascertained the fact that Sergeant Muharrem was their commander, proceeded towards him.

"Sirs," he said, "I am busy tending my animals, but I figure

257

you must be looking for Osman, Sariahmed's Osman."

Upon hearing the name Osman, the sergeant's ears pricked up. "What do you know about Osman? What makes you think that we're looking for him?"

Hussein exhaled heavily before answering, "I know where he is; I was with him a little while ago."

The sergeant jumped up all excited and shook the lad by his arm. The youngster was scared by this and for a moment was sorry that he had come, but there was no turning back at this point. He realized perfectly well what would happen to him if he did not tell them all he knew.

"Hey, let go of my arm, you're hurting me," he squealed. "I'll tell you everything. I heard my master talking with him. It seems you have been chasing him since his escape in the town. Do you know my master? He is with him. You can't even imagine what a scoundrel my master is."

"Who is your master? Speak up, or it will mean trouble for you."

"No, no. It's not that simple. What do I get in exchange? Wasn't there a prize on his head? I want that money, plus I want something else."

The gendarmes and the policemen were by then all aroused from their slumber and had gathered around the boy and the sergeant. They were all extremely excited and were trying to remember if they had ever seen Hussein before. Meanwhile, putting on the most grown-up of airs, the boy went on with what he had to say:

"You know my master? He is one of Osman's accomplices. He beat me till I was half-dead just because I cut the tails of the cows and the donkeys. I still haven't forgotten what happened. That's why I want to see my master tied to the *falaka*, in addition to receiving my reward."

"You just tell me where your master is now and I'll skin him alive. Just tell me who he is and watch how I tie him to the *falaka*! Beating children is also a crime. What's your name?"

"Hussein. My master brought me here from the village and raised me, but you couldn't even imagine how badly he beats me when he is in a temper. When I cut the tails of the animals, he beat me real bad. If he knew I was here talking to you in this way, he would skin me alive. I swear that he would skin me alive."

"Don't you be afraid. Just tell us the name of your master. And tell us exactly where Osman is."

"What about the money? I've got to know about that, too. I want both my money and to see my master tied to the *falaka*. You're just a sergeant. I want to talk to an officer."

The sergeant was stung.

"What! You devil you! You know what I could do to you? Do you know who I am? Do you see my chevron? It wasn't your mother that pinned it on me. Let me beat you up like you deserve and we shall get all the information we need."

While saying this, the sergeant had already started to rough up the boy. It was at this point that the police chief Eshref Efendi intervened and saved the lad from the clutches of the sergeant.

"Cut it out sergeant," he said, "the boy is going to tell us all that he knows. There's no need to get violent." Then he turned to the boy: "It's all right, Hussein my boy, we've agreed. You just tell us where Osman is and you'll get your money. Do you also wish to see your master tied to the *falaka*? Well just leave that to us. You'll hear your master braying like an ox."

Hussein didn't trust these men one bit, but he was in their clutches, so he decided to tell them everything.

"Look, I am the shepherd of that farm over there and my master is Chitoglu Mehmed Efendi. I heard the dogs barking this morning and thought somebody must be coming. Then I saw that someone had spent the night on the wooden platform in the barn. Later, I saw that that someone was Osman. I know him real good, because he is a close friend of my master. Whenever he doesn't have a place to spend the night, he sleeps in the barn. He keeps a horse there, which he grooms personally. This morning I saw him sleeping on the sacks."

Eshref Efendi, the chief of police, tried to sooth the boy. "Look, Hussein my boy," he said, "the money is as good as in your pocket already. Let's catch your master; let's tie him to the *falaka*, and you can do the beating till he screams his head off. But you have to tell us the truth. Which farm did you say it was?"

"I never lie. Not me. Osman has a pistol, grenades, and binoculars hanging from his neck. Once he's on horseback, he moves like the wind. God knows that even the swiftest bullet couldn't reach him. Even if it did, his horse is such that he would change direction just when the bullet was about to strike. That's the kind of horse it is. At this very moment it's in the stables at the farm. Its coat is so shiny that it looks like its on fire. Its tail's so long that it trails on the ground."

The men were sure now that the boy was not lying. Sergeant Muharrem was impatient and got the lad to give him all the details about the farm's location and layout. Once he had the information he needed, the sergeant grabbed one of the horses tied nearby. He told the men to keep an eye on the farm, but without arousing any suspicion, and, having put Hussein on the hindquarters of his horse, galloped towards the town. In their pursuit, they literally flew through its narrow, paved alleyways. Sergeant Muharrem, all flustered and hot, with his rifle crosswise, was riding like a madman, while Hussein was hanging for dear life, trying not to slip from the round hind quarters of the well-fed horse. They finally reached the main square where the sergeant secured the horse to the venerable plane tree standing in its middle.

Never once loosening his grip, the sergeant took the boy up the stairs of the government building. Noon recess had just ended and the inside of the building was dimly lit. Sergeant Muharrem walked along the corridor where the regimental headquarters were stationed.

Ibrahim Bey had just finished eating and, with eyes bloodshot from a lack of sleep, was trying to concentrate on the documents in front of him. There was something puzzling concerning the question of Osman. He had gotten away, literally slipped right through their fingers. The major had filled the streets with policemen and soldiers, had all the roads leading to town under surveillance, had set ambushes all over the place, but it was all for nought. If the man had been misbehaving towards the population, he would have been long since caught and at this moment he would be below the noose that had been specially prepared just for him. But that was not how things had turned out. Clearly he had the support of the populace. As a matter of fact, it was far from obvious that Osman was even a bandit. There was no really grave incident that could be attributed directly to him. If something happened as far away as Marash, someone would claim that it was Osman who did it. If the very same day something also happened in Adana, the culprit would again be Osman. Clearly it could not always be Osman. If they eventually ever did catch him, they would have the chance to shed some light on this mystery.

While Major Ibrahim was immersed in such thoughts, there was a knock on the door. To this he promptly responded with the imperative: "Enter!"

The door opened revealing Sergeant Muharrem with a flushed face covered in perspiration. His clothes were smeared with dust and he looked absolutely miserable, but nevertheless he sprang to attention smartly.

"Sir, I have established the whereabouts of the bandit. I am waiting for your orders, in which case I'll proceed to apprehend him."

With this the sergeant related all that he knew. The commander, who at the beginning was rather incredulous, suddenly saw that the sergeant was serious. The major looked carefully at the stable boy standing next to the sergeant. He was moved by his obvious fear and sorry appearance.

"Hello my boy," he said, "don't be afraid, straighten up, like a man. That's better! We won't harm you. Now, tell us, at whose farm do you work? What's your name?"

The shepherd was still not completely at ease.

"My name is Hussein," he said. "I work at Chitoglu's farm."

"What do you do there?"

"I look after the horses and the cows. I'm the stable boy."

"Who's your master?

"He's called Mehmed Efendi, Mehmed Efendi of Chitoglu."

The lad had relaxed and started to talk. "My master told me to cut off farm dogs' tails and so I did. But at the same time, I decided to cut the tails of the donkey and of the cows, too. They also smartened up. But my master was furious; he beat me blue. With the shovel."

"What sort of a master is he to do this? Anyway, apparently you said that Osman is hiding out at the farm where you work. How do you know it's Osman? What if it's somebody else?"

"Don't I know Osman? Osman has blue eyes and a blond mustache. He carries a big pistol; he has grenades. Don't you think I'd recognize such a man! Sometimes he comes and sleeps in the stable. Once he's gotten his rest and filled his belly, he leaves again. He had his horse in the farm stable. Yesterday night he suddenly came during the night. I noticed it because the dogs barked. In the morning I went to see and, sure enough, there he was, sleeping. I heard them talking later and he said he was in trouble and that he'd had difficulty reaching the farm.

"I'm only telling you all this because I don't think my master should have beat me like that. There's a reward, isn't there? If he's caught, I want to get that reward. Plus, like I said to the sergeant here, I want to see my master tied to the *falaka*. Whatever else happens, I want to see him beaten."

"Okay, Okay. You'll get your money. So you want to see your master bound and thrashed? Don't worry, if he's been hiding a fugitive in his farm, that's the least that will happen to him. You start by describing where exactly this farm is."

Major Ibrahim was convinced that the trail he described would indeed lead them to the farm. He knew the farm very well and also Mehmed Efendi of Chitoglu. He remembered that the man had a red beard, blue eyes, and a flat head. More than once the major had the horses of his unit watered there and on occasion Mehmed Efendi had even fed his troops. He was well known for his kindliness and benevolence, but he was also feared for his bad temper. So Osman was hiding there. Regardless of what the boy thought, Mehmet Efendi must have keeping Osman there because he was afraid of him since he wasn't the type to otherwise cooperate with a criminal. Now was the time to keep a cool head and move intelligently; he wasn't about to squander this opportunity.

17.
Pursuit and Treachery

The major did not go to the governor. At this point, he did not trust anybody and preferred instead to work with the utmost secrecy. He went directly to the barracks where he had a fully equipped platoon of gendarmes readied and put under the command of Sergeant Muharrem. He and Sergeant Muharrem discussed, down to the last detail, the position his platoon was to take.

By the time the platoon of mounted gendarmes had left the barracks it was almost sundown and the horizon was turning red. The fact that the gendarmes were galloping in double file at that hour of the day did not fail to arouse the curiosity of the populace. Upon seeing them many feared that the troops had been mobilized against the German infidels and were on their way to the border. Only a few surmised that the mounted gendarmes could have been on the trail of Osman at this hour of the day. And even if this did occur to some of them, they were not saying so.

The greatcoats of the troopers, expertly riding their mounts, were buttoned up to their necks, the hoofs of the horses beat rhythmically on the pavement, and the rifles glistened in the evening sun.

A short while later, part of the mounted troops separated and proceeded towards Inecik Pass, while the rest reached the vicinity of the farm. They took up position in the Mahrumlar vineyards before nightfall. The sergeant explained individually to each trooper his duties and the watch began. The horses had been stabled in empty outbuildings in the vineyard, while the gendarmes huddled inside their greatcoats and prepared to spend the night in the open.

Major Ibrahim Bey ordered the remaining mounted gendarmes and two hundred foot gendarmes to assemble. He reviewed the squads and their materiel. Like the sergeant had done before him, he ordered, with the greatest detail, their individual duties and how they were to proceed. He had the foot troops move before the mounted troops, which were to go to the plain after sundown. The two units would assemble at Chain Well, where they would wait for further instructions. There were various platoons of foot gendarmes, each under the command of a sergeant. It was late at night when the troops took their predetermined positions.

The operation was to continue throughout the night, with the troops approaching the farmhouse. At sunrise the raid would begin.

They rested at the assembly point, drank from the well, and filled their water flasks. With the first glimmerings of light visible on the horizon, the major gave the order for the raid to begin. The troops moved forward enthusiastically. Most of the soldiers were sent in the direction of Erciyes with the aim of encircling the southern flank of the farmhouse.

The foot soldiers moved cautiously, rifles at the ready, with the utmost silence and careful not to be distanced. They moved until the whitewashed walls of the farmhouse became visible. Once they were near enough, they stopped and took up their positions. They observed the farmhouse in silence.

* * *

In those days many rumors were circulating through the town. According to some, Osman had been shot, while some others thought that he had been caught. Finally it became clear that nobody had been shot, but that Jemal Agha and Sergeant Ahmed had been detained. What business Jemal had with Osman was not clear. Also, to the consternation and fear of the

264

people, news spread that the raided house was full of skulls. Hatem Agha, who went to see the governor to learn just what exactly had happened, was quite astonished.

Hatem Agha was on the balcony with his friends when they watched the passage of the mounted gendarmes and foot soldiers. They had been having a conversation and watching the goings-on at the flour market when they suddenly saw a platoon of mounted gendarmes riding through the square in double file on their bay, gray, and chestnut horses. The troopers had their rifles on their shoulders crosswise. Their blankets had been rolled up and placed on the hindquarters of the horses. The mounted troops were followed by the foot gendarmes. It was as if all the gendarmes in the garrison were being sent out on this mission. Fully equipped, they marched on smartly.

An hour later another unit of mounted gendarmes passed through the square, the shoes of the horses striking sparks on the cobblestones. These were under the command of Ibrahim Bey, majestically riding a bay horse, the collar of his greatcoat raised and the crescent and star visible on his cap. The stars denoting his rank were shining; his boots had just been polished, and his pistol belt was over his greatcoat. Thus was Major Ibrahim leading his mounted troops.

Hatem Agha was the first to comment. "I wonder what's up. Where are they going? There can't be a single gendarme left in the town. They are all on the move, but where to?"

Puffing on a water pipe, Amir Efe did not even bother to take the tube of the pipe out of his mouth before speaking. "It's obvious that they mean business," he said. "Yesterday they let Osman slip through their fingers. Today maybe they'll catch him. They must have got their orders from some high place."

Upon hearing the name of Osman, Hatem Agha got up from where he was sitting and, leaning out of the balcony as much as he dared to, looked towards the point on the horizon where the gendarmes had disappeared. "You're right. A crowd of soldiers this big could only be after Osman. On the other hand, they must know that Osman won't be hanging around waiting to be caught. Once he is on the run, they won't be able to catch him, even if they could fly. Major Ibrahim would be the first to know this, so why is he riding off with all this crowd?"

Amir Efe's mate, Hadji Dabak, was hanging around anxiously waiting for an order from Hatem Agha. He offered to go have a look. .

As soon as he had the Agha's permission, he was on his horse and off like lightning. Once he had ridden out of town, he saw that the mounted and foot troops had assembled at Chained Well and then separated into three groups. It was already late by then and the sun was at the same height as the summit of Mount Erciyes.

There was intense activity at Chained Well. Some of the soldiers were leaving to ride towards the vineyards to the north, while most were heading south towards the great mountain. They swarmed all over the plain like ants. Both groups proceeded for a while before those going southwards turned north and those going northwards turned south. Hadji Dabak noticed this and all the other maneuvers and positions of the troops. It dawned upon him that they were encircling the Chitoglu farm in the center of the plain. In addition to the troops in the north and in the south, some remained at Chained Well. So it was the Chitoglu farm!

He looked at the position of the sun; it was about to disappear behind the mountains and darkness was quickly enveloping the whole plain. Nevertheless, Hadji Dabak had enough time to get all the information he needed. It was clear at this point that they would need the assistance of Amir Efe. If only Hatem Agha would keep his word. He had promised ten thousand violet banknotes. That was an amount that not even Amir Efe had ever seen, despite his reputation as the city henchman. Actually, his reputation was just about all he had, for Amir had neither bread nor vittles to speak off. Why should he turn his back on the ten thousand? Hadji Dabak figured they should take the money and at least try to catch Osman, and if couldn't succeed, well then that would just be tough luck. That would be understandable, for nobody else had ever managed to catch him. But still again Amir Efe might even manage what so many had failed to do. He really was tough after all, and smart, too. He always kept his promises and he was a man of his word.

266

Why didn't he go after Osman? That money would certainly come in handy.

As he spun these thoughts around in his head, Hadji Dabak returned to town with the same lightning speed with which he had left. The plain was wrapped in total silence. All those troops seemed to be buried in the dark.

As soon as he reached the Agha's town house, Hadji Dabak was up the stairs and in the presence of the gentlemen. The dinner table had just been set and the men sat around a table groaning with local delicacies, food almost impossible to find in any other house in the city during these trying times. As they ate they listened to Hadji Dabak's report, all the while trying to interpret the meaning of the events.

"Gentlemen! As just as sure as my name is Hadji Dabak, that Osman is now at Chitoglu's farm and the soldiers have got it surrounded," Hadji Dabak said at the conclusion of their discussion. "They're probably planning to raid the place during the night. I am also just as sure that the mounted gendarmes are in the west. Osman must be trapped, with no escape route."

"Hmm, but I don't think that they'll raid the farmhouse during the night,"Amir Efe intervened, "because that would be the best way to let Osman escape. In the darkness he could just cross their lines and they wouldn't even notice it. I am sure that Major Ibrahim is aware of this and that he'll wait for sunrise."

Hatem Agha did not want to let this chance slip away. "But Amir Efe, let's not underestimate Osman and his sixth sense. He could sense the presence of the soldiers and act accordingly. He has eyes that see in the dark like those of a cat. He will notice the soldiers and make his getaway without waiting for sunrise. Amir Efe, you'll never again find such an opportunity. Show everybody what kind of a man you are. Finish this business. Come on, I beseech you."

Having thus spoken, Hatem Agha went into the small side room and opened the door on the opposite wall. He locked it behind him. After lighting the lamp, he opened the deep cupboard and emptied it of all the bedclothes that had been stored in it for the day. Once it was completely empty, a wooden lid covering a small metal safe became visible. Hatem Agha opened it with one of the keys he had in his pocket. The safe contained land deeds and other important documents and certificates. The top two shelves were full of bundles of thousand lira banknotes. He took two bundles of the violet banknotes, put them in his pocket and closed the safe. When he was back in the dining room, he dropped them into Amir Efe's lap. The silence was broken by Hatem Agha's voice.

"Amir Efe," he said, "the gendarmes and the police are sure to make a mess of it all again this time. They can't cope with Osman; they'll let him slip through their fingers. You'll see. You're the only one that stands any chance against him. You show me that dog Osman's dead body and I'll give you a bundle of these. For you or for your friends."

Amir Efe, sitting cross-legged surreptitiously looked at the bundle of banknotes on his lap. His imposing physique had tensed up and the expression on his face in no way revealed what he was thinking or feeling at that moment. The room was silent as everyone waited for the indecisive Efe to speak up, which after a short while, he finally did.

"Look, Hatem Agha," he said. "A man has to be rich first of all in spirit. Praise be to the Lord, I don't need anything. I don't have many horses, carriages, big fields or anything of the kind, but I live and support my family without help from anybody. Money doesn't mean anything. It's dirt. It's here today, gone tomorrow. At least that's how I see it, but my friends don't agree. For years we have supported each other. We have been a very tight knit group. Now they are angry with me and they may even be right, because they can't feed their families properly. This hurts me. I would like them to be happy. I don't want your money, but if you wish, you can give it to them. If you do so, then we could take part in the hunt for Osman and see what God's will is. Whatever it is; it will be just."

"That's what I call talking. Without you, this will never end. Take the money or give it away. It's not for me to say what you should do. Just show me the dead body of Osman. That's all I ask of you."

"Okay, okay," said Amir Efe as he handed half of the banknotes over to Hadji Dabak and the other to Batagin Hamdi. They grabbed the money enthusiastically and couldn't resist the temptation of handling the banknotes even after they had put them in their pockets. Amir Efe once more started talking:

"Osman is bound to take the road to Inecik. He will try to go through the Inecik Pass and from there reach the marshes below. That's the only way of escape he has. If he attempted to go through the lower vineyards, he'd be ambushed. Osman has a fast horse. As long as he is on the plain, nobody can catch him, that's why he will try to reach Inecik. If the major has already thought of blocking the pass, we can organize an ambush somewhere else. For example, we could take a position in the flats between Mount Hasan and White Rock. If he can pass through the lines of troops encircling him, he will inevitably have to pass in front of us.

Hatem Agha was delighted that Amir Efe had finally decided to act. They quickly ate their food. Rifles appeared from secret compartments and ammunition was distributed. When these preparations were done with, the men mounted their horses and then they were gone.

While all this was happening, Chitoglu was busy writing a letter to Agop Efendi. He wrote, sparing no detail, that Osman was an unfortunate man to whom destiny had not been kind, that it had become impossible for him to go on living in these parts, and that whatever kindness or help was offered to him would be considered as having been offered to Chitoglu himself. He put the letter in an envelope. Once he was through with this, he started to look outside with a dreamy expression in his face. Pigeons were flying over the roof, their black wings reflecting the last lights of the sun. He let his gaze turn in the direction towards town. He noticed his animals grazing along the slopes. They were more spread out than usual and some were gradually returning to the farm by themselves. Chitoglu sensed that something was amiss. This was the hour when the stable boy Hussein led the cattle back to the farmhouse, but he was nowhere to be seen.

It was at this moment that he noticed a movement, far in the distance, around Chained Well. Some dark human shapes were running to and fro and many more people were swarming around like ants. He took his field binoculars from the cupboard and pointed them at Chained Well where he could pick out figures of mounted and foot troops. Even though it was almost sundown, the single soldiers and even their rifles were clearly visible. Chitoglu looked at them with interest. It was only when he noticed that some had stationed themselves at the well that he understood. They were surrounding the farmhouse!

Considering that Hussein was nowhere to be seen, it was easy to conclude that he must have told the gendarmes about Osman's presence at the farm. The gendarmes had already blocked the escape routes towards the town and were now busy completely encircling the farmhouse. He went up to the roof to better see the overall situation, especially the sides not visible from that room. On the roof, hundreds of pigeons were running around, with the males swaggering boldly after the females. From his vantage point on the roof he gazed for a long time towards the lower vineyards. There were gendarmes there as well. This meant that the farm was completely surrounded. Suddenly he realized, though, that even if they moved immediately, the gendarmes could never hope to complete their operation before sundown and after dark there was always the possibility of finding a suitable place to pass through the lines of troops. He was sure that the commander of the gendarmes, too, had reached the same conclusion and that he was going to move towards the farmhouse after sunrise. This train of thought made Chitoglu relax a bit before he rushed down to see Osman.

Osman was asleep among the sacks, while the horse, which perhaps had sensed the danger, was whinnying softly.

"Hey, Osman!" Chitoglu called to him. "Osman Efendi, wake up!"

Osman was instantly up and awake.

"Mehmed Efendi, what's happening?"

"Nothing, nothing. Don't be alarmed, but get up, because we've got a lot of work to do now."

"The Lord and you be praised. I slept very well and am completely rested. I want to leave tonight. You mentioned Beirut. Have you written the letter?"

"Yes. You are to go directly to Beirut, find Agop and convey him my greetings. I'm sure he'll find you a job, a place to live, and everything else you'll need. I'll help send Hurmet later when I receive word from you. The only thing is, we have a problem. The stablehand has run away and seems to have told the gendarmes about you."

"What? The gendarmes?

"Now keep calm. He seems to have gone to the gendarmes. At this very moment they're busy surrounding the farmhouse. They're moving very slowly though. Clearly they have not yet been able to surround the farm, so they'll raid us after sunrise. My advice to you is that you act quickly and cross their lines now before they get settled in completely. I figure you should make a dash in the direction of Erciyes. They can't catch you. Even if they should shoot, they wouldn't be able to hit you in the dark."

"Let me think a moment. Give me my rifle."

The moment he heard the word "rifle" Chitoglu moved a nail in one of the boards of the wood paneling and a secret compartment opened. In it was a shiny and very well kept rifle covered with cloth. There was also a box of ammunition, which Chitoglu took down with great difficulty, using both hands."

Osman was very relieved to have his rifle back and started to clean it with great care. He put as many bullets as he could in his saddlebag. He finished dressing, an operation that included putting a pistol and hand grenades in his belt and his binoculars around his neck. He took great care not to forget anything. He wrapped his head with his covering and approached his horse, stroking the animal and talking to him. He put the blanket and the saddle on the horse, readied the stirrups, and attached the saddlebag. Everything was ready.

They went out to the yard. Osman took Hussein's felt cape from where it was hanging on the wall and proceeded to cut it into several pieces. He tied the thick strips of felt around the hoofs of the horse, ensuring complete silence at every kind of gait. During all these operations, the horse never lost its docility and moved as though it was doing its utmost to help its master.

As Osman loaded his rifle, the points of the bullets shone like little stars in the dark. More than once, almost as a reflex, Osman raised his rifle as if he were aiming to shoot.

"Here's the letter, Osman Efendi," said Chitoglu. "I have written all the necessary information. You also have the name and address of the man. The important thing is that you reach Beirut safe and sound. Once there, he and his family will look after you. What worries me is how you'll pass through the lines of gendarmes. If they catch you, I'll also be in trouble. In that case, try to destroy the letter. But if you can't manage to do that, it's all right. I value our friendship and I'm willing to accept whatever happens."

"Thank you Mehmed Efendi. Many people have helped me in the past, but only out of fear, because they were afraid of me. You're not one of those. I promise that my days wandering in the mountains as a fugitive are over. With God's help I'll get through this alive. If by chance I'm caught, don't worry, I'll die rather than let them get hold of your letter."

Chitoglu had faith in Osman, but was worried about how he would be able to escape. "Osman Efendi, we have made a plan and we'll stick to it. There's no getting away from one's destiny. I am not afraid of all this, but it's best for all concerned if you disappear a while from these parts. You'll finally leave these inhospitable mountains, the government won't be able to reach you, and you'll be able to live in a more civilized way, with at least some hot food in your stomach."

"I can never thank you enough. God will not forget what you're doing for me. Helping someone like me who has lost everything is really very noble on your part. Now let's get ready, but first let me see if the coast is clear."

"I've already looked; they've got us completely surrounded. Your only hope is the southern side, towards Erciyes. You may be able to pass from there, even if there are troops. Immediately after the lines there is the vast plain; in the dark they wouldn't be able to establish in which direction you were going. They could ride all over the place shooting and they still wouldn't be able to get you. Your horse is fleet of foot, so I think that if you go towards Erciyes, you should be able to get away."

"You're right. If I reach the plain, they can't catch me. I've covered the hoofs of the horse, so I should be able to move without being heard. All the same, they'll follow me. Let them.

I'll go down to Inecik and from there to the marshes. Once the situation has calmed down a bit, I'll proceed to Adana first and then to Aleppo. From there, reaching Beirut will be easy."

Suddenly Mehmed Efendi realized something. "Osman Efendi, what about the Inecik Pass, won't it be guarded as well?" he asked. "I would guess that the gendarmes will have it under their control."

Osman was taken aback as if he had just thought about that possibility. "You're right," he said. "The major isn't stupid; he would have thought about that, but there's no other way for me, except for that other narrow trail. That path would take me straight to Seygalan and from there it would be easy riding. The only problem is finding that narrow trail in the midst of all that confusion, and in the dark to boot. If I'm not able to find it, that means the end of me. Mehmed Efendi, please pray that I get through this."

"Osman, I'll start praying the moment you set off. We must put our faith in Allah for only He can ensure a safe passage. But while we place our trust in Allah, we also have to do everything we can and use the brains He gave us. One shouldn't be fool-hardy when it's something to do with the gendarmes. Let me scare the animals so that they stampede towards town. In the dark that'll confuse them and you can use that moment to pass through their lines and gallop on the plain towards Erciyes. Once you're through their lines, nobody can catch you."

"I wouldn't want you to get into trouble because of me, but it would be a great help to me if you'd do that."

It was totally dark. The locust and oleaster trees on both sides of the country road looked as if they were waiting, branches outstretched towards the sky. The two men felt as though they were surrounded by a mysterious emptiness.

They were careful not to make the slightest noise, because they knew that the darkness stretching out in front of them was not, contrary to appearances, empty. Looking into the darkness Osman involuntarily shivered, because he knew that it was full of deathly dangers.

Osman kissed the hand of Mehmed Efendi and took his leave. He put the letter in his breast pocket. Once all preparations were finished, Mehmed Efendi turned to his wife who had brought a bundle of food to be placed on Osman's horse.

"Woman, open the gate," he said. "I'll let the cattle loose. You start shouting that a wolf has entered into the yard."

The husband and his wife were in complete agreement. They pushed both the stable and farm yard gates wide open. Mehmed Efendi entered the stable with a big stick and started to drive out the cattle, first into the yard and from there into the country road leading to town. The two shouted loudly to increase the panic of the poor animals.

Animal and human sounds reverberated through the night. At first the troops didn't understand what was happening, but Major Ibrahim quickly sensed that something was amiss. The major alerted the sergeant and the two of them mounted their horses and galloped down the road leading to the farm.

When they reached the farmhouse they saw that the cattle were running through the fields. It was at that point that they heard the angry voice of a man swearing and shouting. He was hitting every single animal he came across and shouting that the wolf was in their midst. The cattle were running to and fro. The major rode up to Chitoglu and the two, one on horseback and the other on foot, tried to make out the identity of the other. Chitoglu noticed the glitter of the the major's pistol.

"Who are you? What's happening? What's all this noise?" asked the major.

The other man seemed to be taken aback. "It's the animals; they've taken fright. Where have you come from at this time of the night? What's going on?"

"You should know better than me what's going on. Where's that scoundrel? Or was all this confusion a diversion to let him escape? I hope you're aware that what you have done is a criminal act."

"Do you really think midnight is a good time to be talking about such matters? The animals have taken fright and have stampeded. It was a wolf. A wolf spooked them and now I am trying to herd them back together again."

"Do you call this herding? You are scaring them and dispersing them even worse! Are these your animals? And is this your farm?"

"That's right. I'm the owner, and both the animals and the farm are mine. And who are you?"

"I'm Ibrahim, commander of the gendarmes, and this is my sergeant. So you're Chitoglu. You'll have to account for what you've done."

"What? Account for what? And in the middle of the night nonetheless! I've got no business with you. Where have you come from at this hour of the night?"

"Stop fooling with me! Where have you hidden that bandit? Quick, confess, before I tear down the whole farm! Sergeant, take your men and search every single corner of the farm until you find that scoundrel!"

"Yes, sir!" snapped the sergeant, and he was about to do as he had been told when there was a sudden commotion from below. The gendarmes were shouting, the horses whinnying, rifles were being fired, and bullets were flying in all directions. The commander was obliged to forget about Chitoglu and rush towards the center of the confusion.

* * *

The mounted and foot troops had assembled; some had been lying on the ground while others were sitting around secretly smoking, taking care to hide the lighted ends in their palms. All were in pleasant conversation with each other. The horses had been left at the back of the lines.

It was then that a sudden din of beasts' braying and people shouting broke out. The men jumped to their feet, but suddenly a swift shadow passed through and by them. Not a one of them could react, because nobody had heard it arriving. The mounted fugitive had suddenly appeared like a creature of the night and had literally flown away. They all understood that what had passed them was nothing other than the bandit they were looking for, but by then it was too late.

They ran to their rifles. The confusion was immense and the plain had suddenly become a scene from hell. At that moment, the major arrived and started shouting commands. He managed to establish some sort of order and instructed the troops to mount. They rode at a breakneck gallop in the direction towards which Osman had gone. Without slowing and without stopping their shooting, they finally reached the huge plain. The troops hadn't the faintest idea where Osman was, but were nevertheless galloping in the general direction towards which he had run.

The troops were taken by the excitement of the chase and were shouting for no apparent reason and shooting towards nothing in particular. In any case, the darkness was such that rational aiming and shooting were out of the question. The sounds of the commotion reached Hatem Agha and his friends, who had taken up a position near Mount Hasan to ambush Osman. The galloping and the shouting, similar to distant thunder, alerted them to the fact that something was happening.

So Osman had been able to get away and the great chase had begun. Amir Efe's guess that Osman would escape and head straight for the Inecik Pass would turn out to be correct. Unfortunately, thought Amir Efe, Osman was galloping straight towards his own death. Efe did not relish the prospect of having to kill his old friend. It was he who had established the place of ambush and who had organized everything, but he knew that none of his men would be able to shoot Osman, who would be galloping like mad and in the darkness to boot. Amir Efe himself would have to do the firing. This was worrying him immensely.

Hatem Agha was exhilarated. Osman, he reckoned, had no chance now; he was rushing straight to his own end. A chase that had been going on for years would finally end on that night. They were going to kill that godless dog Osman right there and he would be able to spit on his dead body. Hatem Agha knew that Amir Efe was waiting at a point a little lower than his, like a beast of prey. There was no denying it; Amir Efe had chosen his position very well, for the valley became narrower at that point, and anybody who wanted to proceed towards Erciyes by means of the Inecik pass, had to go from there. With all of these thoughts in his head Hatem Agha stared into the darkness and, just like old times, waited for his prey, rifle at the ready.

Amir Efe leaned with his back on the dead apricot tree. He was still undecided on what he was going to do, even though, with Osman being chased by the gendarmes, the moment of reckoning was fast approaching. It looked like Osman would escape from the wolves only to be massacred by a pack of jackals.

For years they had shared their food. They had survived countless clashes with enemy bands; they had braved all sorts of dangers together. They were brothers in blood, but look at what had happened now. He, Amir Efe, was going to ambush his old friend Osman in the dark and kill him. It was a shame— all because of those two, Hadji Dabak and Hasan, who had been complaining for so long. He had been obliged to accept this job so that they could be paid a miserable sum. He had accepted, but he was far from being convinced. He had not even readied his rifle. It was as if his arms did not want to obey his will. The strong and brave man could do nothing but sit listlessly, brooding. Any moment now Osman would be passing through here. Amir Efe did not even need to make a special effort. No! Amir Efe finally made his decision: He was not going to do it. He was not going to ambush his friend.

"Blast that Hasan, and Hadji Dabak, too. For years they've sponged on me. I don't have to behave in this dastardly way. If they insist, I'll find the money somehow and pay them myself. I'm not going to shoot him like this in an ambush, after he has been able to evade a whole regiment. That's not the way I do things."

He came to a conclusion: He was not going to shoot Osman; even if he did shoot, he would be careful to miss. He was not a Godless infidel after all. With this decision, a load as heavy as Erciyes Mountain was lifted from his shoulders. He could finally relax. Even the dead tree on which he was leaning felt more comfortable. He realized that he was soaked with perspiration.

It was at that moment that the shouts of the gendarmes and the sound of rifle shots grew nearer. They were preceded by a shadow. At first, nobody but Amir Efe saw it. It was like a ball of darkness galloping through the night.

When Hatem Agha saw it, he started shooting like a madman, but the shadow did not even swerve; it just went on, passing near him. Once the ammunition in his rifle finished, he started firing his pistol, but it was all to no avail.

It was only after Osman had passed that Amir Efe from Enduruk fired. He fired continuously, and it sounded as if his rifle were a machine-gun. He also emptied his second drum of ammunition into the pitch darkness. Hadji Dabak and Swamp Hasan, too, shot in the general direction of Osman. They only stopped when they realized that more firing was useless. All this had occurred in the space of a few minutes.

Hatem Agha had seen Amir Efe shoot and, knowing what a good marksman he was, was very hopeful. He knew that his own shots had been for naught, but that chap from Enduruk, he usually hit what he was aiming at. He was so curious that he started running down the hill. Unfortunately, this placed him straight in the line of the shooting gendarmes' fire. During the ensuing panic, compounded by the darkness, he fell and landed on top of a blackberry bush. Among the many interesting botanical characteristics of the blackberry, the most relevant at that moment were its pointed and hard thorns. Poor Hatem Agha felt them everywhere in his body. Swearing and cursing, he freed himself from the thorns that were torturing him, got up, found his rifle, and reached Amir Efe. "Did you get him Amir? You fired a lot. Did you hit him?"

From his position under the dead tree, Amir Efe replied: "I don't know; your fire misled me. I shot at him, but you were on the same line. I shot at him minding you, but he didn't even slow down. Maybe I got him all the same. We'll be able to better assess the situation once it's daylight."

Hatem Agha sounded crestfallen. "So it seems we couldn't hit that dog," he said. "It sounds incredible, but I didn't even hear his hoofs beating on the ground. He just went by in complete silence. I was looking into the darkness when suddenly this ball came rolling towards me, or no, not rolling, *flying*. A dark ball that clearly was a galloping horse. He just appeared and was gone before I fully realized what was happening. I still can't believe it."

"You fired well, Hatem Agha. He was nearer to you. Your bullets were flying over me; maybe some hit him. Anyway, let's wait for sunrise, then we can look for him."

Amir Efe was satisfied; he took his tobacco pouch and was just getting ready to roll a cigarette when Hadji Dabak and Hasan arrived. "He passed like a wind, not a human being!" said Hadji. "Don't worry, we'll find his dead body in the morning. Amir Efe was wonderful, made his rifle sing. He recharged it five times for every time we were able to recharge our own. I'm sure he got him, you'll see."

Hasan was also talking in a similar vein. "He was here one moment and gone the next, he said. "The moment he appeared, he also disappeared. I just saw something indefinite rushing past in the dark. I fired after him, oh yes I did. But did I hit him? That I don't know. He was like a cloud, a black cloud. He came and went like the wind. God willing, somebody will have hit him."

Amir Efe lit his cigarette with a tinder lighter. "He was riding flat on his horse. It was as if the horse was riderless. I shot both towards the horse and towards where I supposed the rider would be. In the morning we'll see if I got him. I also had the additional problem of trying not to hit Hatem Agha. And the darkness. I mean, it was all very difficult."

Amir Efe from Enduruk inhaled deeply on his cigarette. In the morning he would try to understand something from the footprints of the horse. Hatem Agha had not been able to hit him, that was for sure. He himself would have realized it if he had hit something. He was sure that Osman had passed unscathed.

"Gentlemen, if we hit him, so much the better. If not, we'll follow his trail and get him in any case. Let's assume that not one shot got him. There remains the fact that he wasn't flying. He must have left some sort of footmarks. We'll follow them and catch him in his den."

"Yes, yes, you're right. In the morning it'll be a new day and we'll see then how things will go. But how he just passed through us, I still can't believe it. The most incredible thing was the silence of the horse. I mean, a horse snorts, it breathes, its hoofs beat on the ground. But there was no sound, nothing, complete silence. He was here one instant and then suddenly he wasn't. He galloped at bounds of ten feet. Incredible, absolutely incredible." While he was saying this, Hatem Agha was at the same time observing the advancing gendarmes.

Amir Efe's men collected around him. They were all trying to see through the darkness. The first to appear was Major Ibrahim on his bay horse. When he saw the assembled company, he pulled on the reins, stopping the horse. The major had been surprised when he had heard Amir Efe's shots, because he hadn't been expecting anybody there. Who could have been there at that hour of the night, in the middle of nowhere? He could see them sitting on the hillside, their rifles shining.

When the major began to question Hatem Agha as to what they were doing up there at that hour of the night, Hatem, like always, was ready with an answer. "We were returning from the orchards."

"Returning from the orchards, at this hour? Why pass from these parts? Hatem, you seem to creep up and appear whenever there's something amiss."

"We put snow in the wells in the orchards; that's why we are so late. We heard shots from the distance and then suddenly a rider and his mount appeared. As soon as he saw us, he started shooting at us. Major, I would like to enter an official complaint about this affair. Thanks be to Allah that we weren't shot in this confusion. We did fire after whomever it was you were chasing. We might have hit him, but in the darkness we can't be sure. We'll have to wait till morning to see."

"So you were busy putting snow into the wells were you? Now, now, now. How very interesting. And these are your helpers I presume. What a coincidence that you all came with your rifles, as if you all knew what was going to happen. Hatem Agha, were you able to hit him at least? That would be nice, for it would mean we had finally rid ourselves of Sariahmed Osman, an enemy of the state."

"Osman, you say? Well, he suddenly appeared out of nowhere like a bat. The sparks of your rifles were visible from up here. We immediately understood that there was something amiss and we were curious to know what it was exactly. It was at that moment that he suddenly appeared. When he saw us he started shooting. We heard the bullets passing all around us, so at that point we had no alternative but to shoot back. And we did, oh yes we did, all of us. Maybe our shots were for naught, but maybe Amir Efe hit him. If not, we would like to complain officially."

"Never mind the legal nonsense now; let's try and catch him. We almost had him in town. We surrounded the building where he was, but he managed to slip through all the same. How he managed it I don't know, but he was somehow able to get by all our checkpoints and reach the farm. And do you know whose farm it is? Chitoglu's. Osman took refuge there. If the errand boy of the farm hadn't alerted us, we never would've known. That Chitoglu, daring to help Osman. I'll have that red bearded devil on the *falaka* yet."

"Anyway, our problem isn't Chitoglu, it is Osman, But the fact remains that we lost Osman because of Chitoglu. He organized that diversion; he let loose all that cattle to distract the soldiers attention. It was thanks to him that Osman managed to escape. It was a clear case of aiding a criminal, but I'll show him."

"Major, first rest a little. Smoke a cigarette. Don't forget that Amir Efe is a very good shot; he may have hit him. While we were busy recharging, he had already fired five times. His rifle was going like a machine-gun. Amir Efe generally hits what he's aiming at."

The major looked hard Amir Efe. In the half darkness he seemed more like a statue than a man. He was sitting and smoking. His bony face structure was invisible in the darkness of the night. Nevertheless, there was something imposing about his posture. He looked like the type that meant business.

"I hope so. Even if you didn't hit him, he has nowhere to go. The only place he can pass through is the Inecik Pass, from where he can hope to reach the marshes. What he doesn't know is that the gendarmes have prepared an ambush for him at the pass. Once he enters the pass, he's finished, he has nowhere else to go. If he tried to go through the Sakar Farm on the slopes of Erciyes, he would get lost and then we would just pick him off."

The major's talk cheered Hatem Agha up even more. Amir Efe, on the other hand, sat silently listening to their conversation. He had his rifle on his shoulder and when he finished one cigarette, he immediately lit up a new one.

The first glimmer of daylight was visible on the horizon. After sunrise they would be able to follow the trail taken by Osman and then everything would become clearer. There was no point in trying to follow Osman in the dark. It would not only be useless, but the confusion could mess up the situation even more. In the morning they would see. The major ordered his soldiers to take up resting positions for the night. Some of the gendarmes wiped down their horses, while others rested.

18.
Morning Breaks

A t sunrise the first thing to become visible was the imposing Erciyes Mountain. Its snow-capped summit glittered in
the morning sun and looked as if it were guarding the plain. On
the eastern side of the plain, Mount Hasan, with its treeless
round summit, looked much more modest. Big Snake Mountain,
with its rocks and small bushes, also came into view. A glacial
wind was blowing and the troops had already begun saddling
their horses in the twilight. Hatem Agha and his friends had also
got up and watched the soldiers getting ready.

The troops assembled and the major ordered them to proceed in single file. The major and Hatem Agha followed
Osman's trail. Later they let Amir Efe be the scout.

By looking at the tracks the horse had left, Amir Efe understood how Osman had been able to appear suddenly in complete silence. Osman had tied pieces of felt around the horse's
hoofs. Looking at the footmarks, everything had become clear.

So Osman had been able to pass through the troops, but it
ultimately would not do him a bit of good, because the moment
he entered the Inecik Pass, he was a dead man. Amir Efe did
not really think that Osman would be that stupid. Efe surmised
that Osman would try to find the narrow trail leading to
Seygalan. If he hadn't been able to find the trail in the dark,
Osman was finished. At that point, his friendship for Osman
would not mean anything; even he could not help him. Amir
followed the horse's tracks and imagined how it must have gal-

loped through the night with jumps and bounds over the obstacles before it.

By now the sun was high and its rays were brightening the glittering summit of Erciyes. Gradually, even the lower valleys became bathed in sunlight. The scenery unfolding in front of the soldiers was a wide sweep of dried-up vineyards, solitary, forlorn looking houses, wells with upturned lids, walls made up of piles of stones and the water elder trees with their thick trunks. The air was dry, but cold. The mounted gendarmes huddled inside their thick greatcoats. Cold misery had taken the place of the previous night's enthusiasm and excitement.

Amir Efe entered the road towards Inecik. By then they were approaching the Big Snake's Seygalan thicket. Further on, Seygalan Fortress's few remaining walls were visible on a hill that looked as if it would be impervious to the efforts of any who dare try to scale it. The trail that Osman might have looked for branched out of the main road a little further on. It was at this moment, when Amir Efe was deep in thought, that a group of gendarmes approached. Until a short while ago, they had been freezing in the cold night wind and they were hungry, having had to make do with no more than a few dry crackers. Before midnight they had heard the rifle shots, the shouts, and the hoofs beating on the ground. Notwithstanding all the commotion, not a soul had left his post. They were positioned in ambush at the top of the ravine ending at the glen. They had waited, huddled around the rocks, without giving in to slumber, and without letting their attention waver for even a minute. By dawn, not only were they hungry and cold, they were exhausted as well. When the major saw the bedraggled troops, he immediately understood that they did not have good news for him. The sergeant in command ran to the major and reported the events of the night, shouting as he had been taught. The gist of the report was that nothing had happened, which of course was bad news. The major nevertheless asked all sorts of questions, like where they had set up the ambush, when, what had they eaten and drunk, and so on and so forth.

The gendarmes had not seen anybody, but Osman's tracks were leading them to him. Ibrahim Bey hailed Amir Efe, who was proceeding further on. "Scout!" he yelled. "The tracks don't lead to the pass! He must have turned off the road. There must be a trail leading off the road somewhere here. Keep a sharp lookout!"

Amir Efe signaled that he had understood the major's instructions, but went on going forward as if nothing had happened. Actually, he himself had noticed how Osman's tracks led away from the road towards a barely visible trail. Amir Efe mumbled to himself, "Osman, you blessed man, how on earth were you able to find that trail in the dark and, what's more, in the midst of all that confusion, with all those men on your tail pursuing you?"

When Amir Efe started going up the narrow trail, he was followed by the whole group that was snaking up the hill in single file. Efe watched the ground and followed the tracks. The terrain being very steep and difficult, he gave his horse its head and the horse proceeded carefully, following the curves of the trail and minding his step. The entire mounted group went forward up the steep and rocky hillside. Major Ibrahim was just behind Amir Efe. The major observed the scene and the slopes covered with thorny bushes and squat oaks. There was absolutely no chance that Osman could have remained around these parts. The narrow trail went even higher and started following the slopes of the Seygalan Valley. The troops were now proceeding along the valley and observing the opposite slopes. The valley echoed with the sound of the horses' hooves.

* * *

Osman sensed that he was out of danger. He had had great difficulty passing along White Rock. It was his horse that had saved his life and seen him through the danger. The rifle shots in general had not scared him, but there had been a single rifle on his left that had fired as if it were a machine-gun. The fact that not even one of all those bullets had hit him was truly a miracle. He knew of only one person who could shoot and recharge so quickly. They had been close friends and fought together against the enemy. They had shared everything and faced all sorts of dangers together. This friend was the only man who could possible fire that way. Osman felt his heart sadden enormously. If even Amir Efe were pursuing him, things were really serious. If that hero of his, Amir Efe, to whom he had entrusted his safety, was pursuing him, the world had got to a sorry state, make no mistake about that. On the other hand, wouldn't Amir Efe have hit him? This thought seemed to console Osman. Amir Efe must have been the mysterious shooter, but he also must have missed him on purpose for it was unheard of for Amir Efe to miss someone who passed just in front of his nose. This could mean only that he had spared both his and his horse's life. Amir, Amir! Blessed Amir! All the same, he was still not completely out of danger. He must on no account try to pass through the Inecik Pass. As he thought of what must be waiting for him in the pass, he was gripped by fear.

On one side there was the dark ravine like the mouth of a monster, and on the other, steep rocks that constituted an unbridgeable wall. It looked as if there was no other way but the road leading to the pass. He kept remembering Chitoglu's advice not to enter the Inecik Pass. A single armed soldier in the pass could have blocked the passage of a whole army. The soldiers at ambush could shoot and kill at will, leaving no chance to fight back nor to escape. He did not want to venture into the pass, but on the other hand, there was no other way to go behind the Erciyes Mountain, not even if he had been a crow.

The horse was soaked in perspiration and was covered with white foam. Even Osman was perspiring in anxiety. Nevertheless, he entered the road leading towards the pass. His only hope rested in the narrow trail that he was, somehow, supposed to find in the complete darkness. Once the rocks on the summit of the pass became visible, Osman stopped his horse. He frantically tried to peer through the darkness, hoping to find that elusive and faint opening in the north side. The trail's beginning must be somewhere near. Osman searched his memory trying to recollect a sign, a rock, a stone, a small bush, anything that could signal him the trail.

The horse somehow seemed to sense what Osman was trying to do. It moved cautiously forward until it suddenly veered off the main road. Osman dismounted and felt the ground with his hands. It was a trail! The trail! The horse once again had saved its master's life.

Osman felt enormously relieved and breathed easily once more. Had he not found this trail, he would have gone on into the Inecik Pass and that, most probably, would have meant his death. In the throes of an indescribable emotion he hugged the neck of his horse and stroked its mane lovingly for a long while. The horse had been able to find the narrow trail through which they had only passed a few times before.

The horse and its rider continued to pick their way up the path. The narrow trail got steeper and the terrain surrounding it became rockier. Further on lay the Seygalan Valley. That valley would end at the Brother's-in-Law Valley from where he could reach Sheep Father. From there he could follow through the Harami valley, which would lead him to the marshes. The horse proceeded according to his own will. The pieces of felt which Osman had attached to the hoofs of the horse were tiring him more than necessary, so at the first favorable point he dismounted and got rid of them, making sure to hide them among the rocks.

Osman was trying to surmise who the other ambushers were. There was only one person who would be accepted by the gendarmes and that person was Hatem Agha. The men who shot at him must have been Hatem's band, but what was Amir Efe doing in his company? It was very strange that Amir Efe should be cooperating with Hatem's men and shooting at him. There were other men also down below. He had seen the flames of rifles in two separate places. He could, more or less, guess who they were though.

Osman felt much relieved for he was once more among these shady valleys, with the morning breeze, the smell of earth, the clouds in the sky. Being free amidst all this beauty compensated partially for the hardships of being a fugitive from the law. The snowdrop flowers that had appeared here and there were harbingers of the approaching spring. To Osman the flowers seemed to have broken the darkness and grief that had been enveloping him of late. He took in the entire scene joyfully. Of course, this rebirth, the possibility of being able to look freely at the mountains and valleys, to smell the breeze and rain, had a cost. The cost Osman had to pay to be able to taste this boundless freedom in the prairies and hills was that of being a fugitive. How dearly he wished, at that moment, to be living in a house surrounded by a garden full of roses, in the company of a lot of people. But alas, that had not been included in his fate.

After a short rest he dismounted and put his ear to the ground to check if there was anybody approaching. Yes, he could hear riders and they were not even too far away. Clearly they were not going to let him go so easily. Thank God there was nobody blocking his path and as long as he had his horse, nobody could catch him. Once more he tenderly approached his horse, stroking him everywhere. He checked his equipment and almost apologetically mounted his horse. Osman went forward following the winding trail and looking at the valley, the squat oaks, the blackberry bushes, the rocks that seemed on the verge of rolling down the valley, and the flocks of geese high up. Osman knew these parts very well. He knew every nook and cranny, what kind of bushes there were under each rock, and what kind of grasses were under each bush. The fact that he had both his mount and his rifle and that he was going through places he knew so well renewed his strength. He felt as if these were secret places that nobody else but he himself could reach.

Even if it were broad daylight, he would go down to White House from where he could reach the valley and the road leading to the marshes. He left the decision of which of the two islands to go to till the last minute for he knew they could never follow his trail in the water and among the reeds of the marshes.

He tried not to needlessly tire his horse and whispered to the animal that there were no more roads to be climbed, that from then on it would always be downhill.

It was then that the thought of having a look with his binoculars occurred to him. He looked first towards the north, which was the direction towards which he was proceeding. But for empty valleys and rocks there was nothing. Then he turned back and looked at the snow-capped mountains and the slopes of Big Snake Mountain. The narrow trail leading to it began at its slopes and wound its way upwards. It was while he was observing this mountain that he saw the advance party of scouts approaching from the south. They were following the narrow trail along the valley and they were being led by Amir Efe. Amir Efe also knew these parts very well and he was certainly able to guess that Osman would try to reach the marshes.

Osman, aware of the approaching danger and that there was no more time to lose, spurred his horse down towards the valley. The horse had also sensed the danger and they shortly reached the riverbed and proceeded towards White House. They galloped on, heedless to the fact that the road to White House was very stony. Soon the cliffs on the sides of the valley got lower and Osman could see the morning sun in the east. The horse seemed more bird than beast as it proceeded to fly over all obstacles. The road had become more passable, when Osman noticed a detachment of mounted gendarmes climbing the road towards him. The gendarmes had given their horses their heads and were galloping briskly. The end of the detachment had not yet reached the slope.

If they had chanced to look upwards, they certainly would have seen Osman, but it was his lucky day and he saw them before they could notice him. He quickly turned back, for the previous rosy plans had turned out to be impracticable. With his way blocked, Osman felt trapped and started to tremble with fear. Both ends of the valley were blocked. Gendarmes were approaching from all directions. His survival depended on his finding an alternative road, but both sides were steep and Osman was not hopeful that he could find a way out of the valley. He decided to resist. That would mean his end, but he was going to take more than one person with him.

While prey to such somber thoughts and desperately trying to find a way out, he decided that the upper parts of the valley were bound to be safer. He turned his horse and started climbing the narrow trail winding up to the Big Snake. The horse climbed with a desperate energy. With an enormous effort, foaming at its mouth and snorting, the animal made its way towards the ridge.

Its strong legs were literally pulling the weight of both of them, with the forward feet gripping the earth and his hindquarters pushing up. Osman lay flat over his mount. He hoped to get over the ridge as soon as possible so as to be out of shooting range. The gendarmes were not yet aware of his position, but were sure to start shooting like madmen the moment they saw him, in which case neither Osman nor his horse would have the slightest chance of survival. The horse climbed the steep cliff with bounds and jumps as if it, too, were aware of the danger.

Osman kept looking over his back as he spurred on his horse with kind words. They finally reached the top and the flat plateau appeared in front of them. Osman had a sudden inspiration. The trail ended there, so that was the point at which he should make his last stand. From there he could block the way and prevent anybody from approaching him. It was an impregnable position. Shots fired from there would be deadly. The advancing parties would have nothing but a few blades of grass to use for cover.

The only doubt in Osman's mind arose from the fact that, apart from Hatem Agha, he did not want to harm anybody. Amir Efe could have hit him, even in the dark of the previous night, if he had wanted to. On the other hand, there was also the fact that he had followed his trail and led the gendarmes to him. Clearly Amir Efe had got into a vicious circle from which he could not free himself so easily.

He tied his horse to one of the poplar trees at the end of the plain overlooking the steep valley. He went back to the edge with his ammunition and food-laden saddlebag.

Amir Efe followed Osman's exact footsteps. The tracks, which at first were not very clear, had become more visible after the point where Osman had taken off the pieces of felt covering his horse's hooves. From that point on the scouts had been able to proceed with great speed in their pursuit of Osman. They reached the point where Osman had set his ambush. Using his binoculars, Amir Efe saw what he could of the area and in particular the road leading to White House. It was Amir Efe who saw the detachment of gendarmes coming from the direction of the valley. This surprised him because he could not imagine how they had not seen Osman. Both ends of the valley were blocked. Where had Osman gone? He must have hid somewhere. Amir Efe looked up towards the opposite slope, where the winding trail led to the Big Snake and it was then that he saw Osman on his horse approaching the ridge. The horse was leaping along the winding trail. The commander, following Amir Efe's gaze, saw the rider at the same moment as Amir.

"He can't go anywhere from there. We've got him!" he exulted. Seeing the detachment coming from the opposite direction, the major had understood why Osman had decided to climb the ridge. The detachment coming from White House along the valley had blocked Osman's way, leaving him no other route apart from climbing towards Big Snake.

Seeing their excitement, Hatem Agha approached them to ask what they had seen.

"We've found Osman. We've got him trapped. Do you see him? There, look at the slopes of Big Snake, at the end of the narrow trail. Osman is there. He hasn't been able to reach Harami Valley thanks to the detachment of Sergeant Muharrem and, knowing that we were following him, he's gone and climbed those slopes."

"The dog! Where does he hope to hide up there?" exclaimed Hatem Agha. "He is surrounded by precipices. I have never heard of anybody going down those ravines. He seems to have walked straight into a trap. He's finished. We'll be able to spit on his dead body after all."

Hatem could not contain his joy. By then the troops had also seen Osman and were busy pointing out his position to one another. So Osman was a mortal after all and could be caught like any other common criminal. Some of the gendarmes took aim, but the major told them to hold their fire until he ordered them. Osman was too far away and the only way to approach him was to follow him up the same trail. From his position Osman could only continue to climb up towards the summits of Big Snake and Big Cedar. From there, the ravines were so steep and the terrain was so forbidding that no living creature, not even a bird, could proceed. The major went down to the riverbed with his men and joined up with the detachment under the command of Sergeant Muharrem.

He decided to forestall action until the troops had rested a bit and had had something to eat. It was imperative to end the standoff before sundown, though, because once it was dark, Osman could easily slip away again.

The major prayed that nothing unfavorable should happen during the ascent that would start in a little while. He smoked incessantly. He ate the same rations of hard biscuits as his troops.

Hatem Agha remained at a distance, intently watching the major. He was terrified at the thought that the major might have given up on the chase, but at the same time he consoled himself with the thought that having come so far, the major would hardly have desisted at this point. He was sure to want to catch that bandit.

The major ordered his troops to get ready. The thought that Osman might resist had not even occurred to him. All his plans were based on the premise that Osman would attempt an escape. In any case, he ensured the safety of himself and of his troops by letting Amir and his band go first.

Finally the ascent began. Amir Efe led the way on foot, having entrusted his horse to Swamp Hasan. He was followed by Hatem Agha and his men, who were on foot leading their horses. The trail was bordered by thick clusters of blackberry bushes and was extremely steep. At parts it was almost blocked by the bushes and rocks. Among the blackberry bushes were stones and dry grass. Amir Efe climbed without once taking his eyes away from the top of the ridge. He was conscious of each step he took. He was very closely followed by Hatem Agha and the rest of his company. The major had let his attendant lead his horse. The gendarmes followed their commander in a long, snaking line. Seen from above, the detachment looked like a centipede of monstrous dimensions. The monster was treading carefully, without losing sight of the top, but was advancing nevertheless. The air was tense with expectation. The sense of expectation was soon broken. At first it was a head-sized stone that rolled down the slope.

The stone's speed increased every time it hit the ground. As it spun down the steep slope, it made a noise out of all proportion to its size. It soon started to carry with it other pebbles and loose pieces of earth until it had become a formidable landslide. The men froze in their tracks when they saw what was happening. The single rock hit the ground once more at a point near their line and then was thrown to the opposite slope of the valley, where it broke into innumerable pieces. It was soon followed by a rumbling mass of pebbles and loose earth. Both going forward and going back were equally dangerous. The major did not know what to do, because at that point an order to retreat would only create panic. He realized that attempting the ascent with the horses had been a mistake. He had to make a decision without any further delay. He ordered the greater part of the group to wait where it was, while the group at the head was to proceed. The men at the back were to turn back, if possible.

Escape was out of the question. Osman concentrated on holding his ground while he continued to send stones volleying down the slope. The centipede was at its most vulnerable. Osman was delighted that the idea of rolling stones had occurred to him. He let loose a medium sized rock that started slowly, but then gained speed as it went hurtling down and bounding every time it hit the ground. It finally broke into thousands of pieces, but by then it had let loose all sorts of other stones, pebbles, and loose earth that rolled down on the soldiers, multiplying themselves along the way. The horses were shying and rearing, with the gendarmes having great difficulty in keeping them in their place.

Osman suddenly spotted Amir Efe, who was climbing alone and with great care, without losing sight of the top for a single moment. Yesterday night not one of Amir Efe's bullets had hit Osman, but now in a reversal of roles, it was Osman who was aiming his rifle at Efe's chest. Amir Efe was a big man, but a single bullet was all that was needed to fell him. Could a person do that to an old friend? On the other hand, there remained the troubling thought that Amir Efe had joined the gendarmes pursuing him and had helped them to find the trail. The gendarmes could never have found it by themselves.

Osman looked through his binoculars and picked out Swamp Hasan and Hadji Dabak. He also saw Hatem Agha, the

293

cowardly scoundrel, lying on the earth, desperately trying to dig himself a hole in which to hide. Without the binoculars Hatem Agha was not visible, but all the same Osman took aim towards where he thought Hatem was lying and fired. The bullets missed him by the smallest of margins, upon which, swearing and cursing, Hatem redoubled his energies, literally trying to disappear in the earth. If Osman was firing directly towards him, this could mean only one thing—he had recognized him. The more Hatem Agha thought such thoughts, the more he scraped away the stones and the earth, with his—by then extremely bloody—hands.

The shots of Osman's rifle echoed for a long time along the valley and upon hearing them, the troops also started firing. Almost all the gendarmes were firing, creating an infernal din and showering the immediate vicinity of Osman with bullets. The noise of the shots and of the shying horses was nothing in comparison to the enormous landslides being created by the rumble of the mass of stones and earth let loose down the slope by Osman. One of the large rocks hit a horse on the head causing it to crash down the slope towards a horrible death. Its death cries reverberated in the valley, increasing the fear of the other horses. By then the group of men and beasts was in utter confusion.

The horses were rearing, those that had managed to break loose were trying to run, some were rolling down the slope, some slipping on the loose earth, while others were kicking and thereby increasing the confusion on the narrow trail. Most of the gendarmes had not let go of their mounts and were rolling with their horses in an attempt to save them. A few rocks cunningly let loose down the slope had been enough to throw the detachment of gendarmes into a state of utter confusion. The horses and their riders desperately tried to reach the bottom of the valley. Major Ibrahim Bey watched in helpless horror as his unit disintegrated in panic. He began to shout orders: "Stay where you are! Control your horses! Don't move!"

No matter how much he shouted, though, the major could not prevent the catastrophe, and so the imposing centipede simply evaporated.

Even the corporal holding the major's horse had slipped down to the bottom of the valley with no thought but to save his own skin. It was only much later that the poor commander realized that he was alone. In anger, he drew his pistol and slipping and cursing started to climb once more, all the while shouting: "Osman! You devil! If you call yourself a man, come out and fight like one! You scoundrel. Come out from where you're hiding!" His once proud mustache was drooping. Soaked in perspiration, he continued his ascent.

Osman was extremely satisfied with what he had accomplished and at the same time admired the major's bravery and tenacity. For all his bravery, however, there was not much the major could accomplish. His unit had just melted away with everybody running for dear life. All the same, nothing could stop the major, and so having fallen prey to a great wave of emotion, he climbed higher, shouting like a madman all along the way. The horse rolling down to his death had been watched with horror by all, including Osman himself, because, even more horribly, the horse had dragged with it its rider, who had not been able to dismount in time.

Without losing his control, Osman fired a single shot. The bullet passed near the major's ear, who, swearing, threw himself on the ground. Osman could have shot the major if he had wanted to, but he had never shot a soldier and did not want to break this tradition. The major was not to be discouraged by such a trifle and stood up to proceed climbing. He was blindly firing off his Smith & Wesson, swearing incessantly, and trying to find a grappling point among the grass and stones. Osman fired once more, this time aiming at a point near the major's hand. The bullet hit the earth at a point almost exactly where the desperate major's hand had taken hold of a stone. This shot had the desired effect—the major finally understood. Osman could have shot him if he had wanted, but had not, and this could only mean that he just wanted to warn the major, so he stopped.

A short while later all the firing stopped. The gendarmes had not obeyed their major and had all rushed to the bottom of the valley to save their mounts. All the same, the major could not bring himself to scold his troops, much less to discipline them. Finally, a semblance of order was established almost spontaneously. The tail part of the column descended, followed by the rest. Two privates and four horses had fallen down the ravine, while ten horses were hurt. Two privates had broken feet and some had hurt their backs. There was no counting the gendarmes who had been kicked by horses or hit by flying stones.

Only Amir Efe had been able to remain in his position. He had understood perfectly well that Osman had not really wanted to shoot the major and that his real target had been Hatem Agha, who had not been able to do anything except try to disappear under the stones like a worm. Amir Efe had noticed a gap to the north of the ridge. He realized that if he could pass from there, he would find himself at a point behind Osman.

Amir Efe had not shot Osman, but now he had an opportunity to catch him. He had been a fugitive for so many years with hundreds of soldiers pursuing him. The government had decreed an amnesty, but he had not believed it and for such a long time he had enjoyed a complete freedom. Amir Efe wanted to talk about all this with Osman. If they could only sit down calmly and talk, there was a chance that they could find a solution.

Slithering among the grass and the bushes like a snake, Amir Efe approached the gap. He wanted to come out at a distance of about five hundred feet. He could not help but appreciate what Osman had managed to do. Single-handedly, Osman had blocked the way of a detachment that must have been the equivalent of a regiment, by holding on to the most strategic point of the narrow trail. The gendarmes' only way out had been to retreat to the bottom of the valley, whence they had come. After this, Osman would become even more famous. The legend that he had defeated an entire regiment would live on through the ages.

Osman was still perched on top of the ridge, watching the events unfold. Just to let everybody know of his presence, from time to time he let loose a volley of shots in the direction of Hatem Agha. At first, every one of his shots provoked hundreds of others from the troops down below. All in all, Osman was enjoying himself immensely. He congratulated himself for putting up resistance at that very point. There were still horses running around in panic at the bottom of the valley and shouts echoing throughout the valley.

Osman happened to glance towards the point where he had previously seen Amir Efe, but he was no longer there. That was strange. Amir Efe had been lying among those dried up thornbushes just a short while ago. Now he had gone, but where to? He was not the kind to give up. It was simply impossible that he could have run away like all the others. Osman did not like this sudden disappearance. It looked fishy. Amir Efe must be planning something.

The major, who just a short while ago had been attacking and swearing, had straightened up his uniform a bit and was descending. Osman could see the major, but Amir Efe was nowhere to be seen. The binoculars in Osman's possession were very strong field binoculars. He adjusted the lenses so that he could see much farther out. After observing the area for some time, he noticed the gap at an approximate distance of five hundred feet and it suddenly dawned upon him that Amir Efe must have also noticed it, too, and must, at that very moment, be approaching him from there. By then Osman had lost all faith in humankind. It was true that his old friend had not shot him the previous night and that he himself had in a way paid him back by not shooting him a short while ago, but here now was Amir Efe from Enduruk trying to surprise him from the rear. Osman shot a few more times in the general direction of Hatem Agha and then started slithering through the grass like a snake.

Osman was also keen on conversing with Amir Efe. It was Amir Efe who had been scouting on behalf of the gendarmes, who had brought them up there, and who had set up an ambush on the instructions of Hatem Agha. The time had now come for him to account for all of this.

After he had reached a position from which he could observe the gap, he stopped, checked his ammunition and rifle, and then resumed his advance as carefully as before. He reached the mouth of the gap. All was silent for the time being;

nobody had yet reached that point. He saw a slight mound from which he decided to watch the surrounding area. He lay down among the blackberry bushes where nobody could see him. The area was covered with thorn bushes. A little further up one could see also oak trees. Further up, on the southern side, among the rocks, there was a forest of poplar trees with white trunks and leafless branches. Suddenly a group of red legged partridges, with their red beaks, black breasts, and gray white wings, who had been hopping around, took fright and flew away among a chorus of chirps. The partridges flew in front of Osman, passing so near him that even their eyes were visible amidst their colored feathers. Osman understood perfectly well what had scared them and redoubled the attention with which he was observing his vicinity.

At first he did not notice anything untoward, even though he was using his binoculars, but then suddenly a head appeared among the dry grass. It moved like the head of a wolf stalking its prey, listening, smelling the air, and watching carefully, on the lookout for the slightest sign. After a while it started to move carefully, this time as if it had been attached to a slithering snake advancing among the tall grasses. The big and muscular body of Amir Efe, for it was his head that was visible among the grass, with his rifle on his shoulders, was slowly emerging sky-wards with the lightness of a butterfly. Osman aimed straight at the barely visible forehead. At that moment a single bullet would have been enough to extinguish the life in that muscular body, but Osman could not bring himself to pull the trigger. He just could not bear the thought of killing his old friend. Many memories that he had shared with the same friend who was advancing towards him now came back to him. Once the two friends had been outnumbered by a large gang of toughs, but the combined strength of Amir and Osman had been enough to send the crowd running. Oh yes, they had had many strange adventures together. Like the time they had played dice in the cemetery. Or the night when they had waited freezing, crouched near a rock, leaning on each other's shoulders. These thoughts, however, did not prevent him from keeping his rifle pointed directly at Amir Efe's forehead.

Amir Efe had managed to get over the gap and was looking for a safe spot. He had perspired profusely, but he was nevertheless looking all around him, careful not to miss anything. He had climbed from what he hope was an unexpected angle. He planned to first rest in the shade of a huge boulder he had noticed and from there proceed in the direction of town, in which case he could hope to approach Osman from the back and thus surprise him. The sides of the rivulet along which he was advancing were covered with blackberry bushes, while the upper parts were full of white poplar trees. There were also oak trees with their rounded shapes, which still had green leaves. These sites brought back memories of Amir Efe's childhood. He had known these parts very well in those days. Down to the tiniest rock. He also knew that Osman was not as familiar with these parts as he was. He could not have found the way leading north to the Harami Valley among the excessively steep ravines and precipices. The trail he had followed up here had been blocked by the gendarmes. But there was a third route. There was a trail leading towards the Inecik Pass in the south that ended up in one of the vast vineyards of the area. It was a route that Amir Efe alone was aware of.

Nobody but he knew that road. Nobody was able to go further than Stone Sea, through which neither man nor beast could travel. A very long time ago Amir Efe had discovered that narrow trail used only by partridges and goats, and had traveled along it to the vineyards. From there it was possible to reach the reed marshes to the west of Inecik Pass without further difficulties. On horseback, however, the road was impassable. Once he had tried to lead sheep through it and he had had great difficulty. That had been his last attempt of that kind.

The muscular Amir Efe, deep in such thoughts, advancing in bear fashion, on his hands and knees and naturally enough all covered with dust after so many exertions, reached the massive boulder which he had targeted a little while ago. He stopped in its shade to rest a bit. From his vantage point he observed every single blade of grass, the bushes, the round oaks. It was as if he were even able to see behind the mound as he vividly imagined all that was happening in that area. Suddenly, he was gripped by an indescribable emotion, as if his heart had been pierced by red-hot spears, as if lightning were flashing just in front of his eyes. He barely saw, sensed would be more correct, the presence behind the bushes. He raised his rifle taking aim. Osman also had his rifle at the ready and was completely immobile. Amir Efe pushed back his dust-covered cap revealing his broad and sweaty forehead. His eyes burned, but at the same time, he could feel the ice-cold breath of death. Nevertheless, he did not lose his calm even though he realized that he had been ambushed. He aimed his rifle very carefully. Thirty seconds later, he took his tobacco pouch from his pocket and started rolling a cigarette. After having lit it with his tinder lighter he inhaled deeply a couple of times. Blowing the smoke in the general direction of Osman's hiding place, he called to him: "What are you waiting for Osman? Press the trigger and let's get it over with. The position is as good as it can get. Shoot me now."

Not only did no answer come back from the bushes, but also there was absolutely no movement. Amir Efe inhaled again on his cigarette: "What are you waiting for Osman? I am the one who brought your tormentors here. I am the one who found your trail and trapped you up here like a wild animal. There's nowhere you can go from here. You can't escape and since I'm the one that put you in this situation, shoot me—don't hesitate, just finish me off and get it over with."

After another short silence, he finally heard the answer he had been waiting for. "Amir Agha, I would have expected this from everybody, but not from you. I can't say that you were bought off, because you're not the kind with a soft spot for money. And you're not the kind to do this so that you could boast about it later. So why did you do it? Why did you bring them up here?"

"Osman, my intention was to approach you from the back and shoot you, but you were quicker than me. So you're perfectly entitled to shoot me. God would not condemn you. Shoot and take your revenge!"

Amir Efe was not imploring, far from it in fact; his voice was the voice of someone challenging his adversary, daring him to do something difficult.

"Do you think it would be as simple as that for me, to shoot you? Twice today I had your forehead in the sights of my rifle, twice your life was in my hands to dispose of as I felt fit. On both occasions, I did not forget our blood brotherhood, our friendship, nor your bravery and honesty. But you? You must never even have thought of such things if you were able to bring yourself to track me with those people."

"Look Osman, you're entitled to do as you please with me. If I had been the one to catch you, I would have cut off your head and brought it to the major. Instead, though, you caught me, so you can do the same to me. Osman you're a scoundrel, a dog. What more can I say? Shoot me; my honor will be safe-guarded. My family has been an honorable family for at least seven generations. If I'd had the chance, I would've shot you. So you see, you have all the right in the world to shoot me. Finish me off and let's get it over with!"

Osman was all tensed up and kept looking at Amir Efe through the sights of his rifle, which he kept unwaveringly trained on his adversary's forehead. It was as if Amir Efe were challenging death, daring Osman to kill him. It was with this purpose that he spoke these insulting, unrepeatable words. If Osman had not known Amir Efe so well, he most probably would have responded to all those insults and challenges by killing him instantly, but he did know him and understood per-fectly well that Amir was abashed at having been ambushed and considered it a blemish on his reputation. He was not the type to implore upon another to spare his life. Osman could not keep himself from responding in the same way.

"Amir Efe, don't challenge me too much," he said, "because I'm already thinking seriously of pressing the trigger and leaving you lying there so that wolves and birds can feast on your carcass. What are you up to? You are guilty as all get-out and yet you lie there blabbering and insulting me. I know very well that you would never implore anyone to have your life spared, but please don't be angry if I don't behave like you did towards me by spar-ing your life! As if I didn't know you. You still play the tough guy even though it would be so easy for me to shoot you right now, shoot you like a dog . So, tell me—what's going on here?"

By then, Osman had begun to find the situation faintly amusing. So he had managed to ruffle the feathers of that big bear of a man after all! He was also absolutely sure that on the night before, when Amir Efe opened fire at him, he had not really intended to hit him. Efe could use his rifle with the deadly speed and efficiency with which lesser mortals used a machine-gun. Shooting both him and his mount would have been child's play. Nevertheless, he had not done so, and now the fact of having been ambushed was deeply wounding his pride. This explained his reaction, for it certainly was not caused by the fear of death, which Amir would have considered a blessing. Anyway, there was no longer any need to hide and so Osman got up as if nothing were amiss. Holding his rifle like a shepherd would hold his stick, he stood up near the mound.

"Amir Efe, you've changed a lot since I last saw you. Once you wouldn't have told so many lies. If you were going to shoot me, then why didn't you do so last night when I on the soldiers passed just in front of you? You thought I hadn't noticed it? I rode through your band of men and like everybody else, you also fired. You were the only one among those present that could've got me, but you didn't. Why? Because you couldn't square it with our friendship, that's why. Now you lie there gibbering about hitting me from the back, cutting off my head, and I don't know what else. You shameless lying scoundrel, then why didn't you? If that's the case, then you've got another occasion. Look, I've put down my rifle. So you take yours and shoot me. Since you were ready to do it in any case, shoot me."

As he was saying this, Osman took his rifle by its barrel and stood there. Waiting. Amir Efe was astounded; he pretended to draw his weapon, but still Osman did not budge. It was then that the big and tough man was overcome by emotion; he collapsed on the ground in a kneeling position, covering his face with his hands. For a while both stood there without uttering a single word. Then Osman got down from the mound and took his water flask. He gently helped Amir Efe to his feet and they both sat down in the shade of the big rock. The dry stream bed, with all its yellow, dry grasses, was just in front of them. Two white eagles flew overhead in circles, their great immobile wings similar to spread out fans, looking for prey. Further up the hill the leaves of the poplars were rustling as were those of the still green oaks.

They drank from Osman's water flask until they had both quenched their thirst. Amir Efe took out his tobacco pouch and rolled cigarettes for both of them, which they proceeded to smoke without saying a word. They did not talk about what had happened to them in the years since they had last seen each other. They both concentrated on the here and now, on the practical results. It was much later that Amir Efe, his eyes fixed on nothing in particular, asked, "Well, how do you intend to get out of here?"

Osman could not answer immediately. "I really don't know," he said. "I have the Joplan Valley at the back, the Harami Valley on my side and my front side is blocked by the gendarmes. That leaves only the side towards Erciyes, but that route is also blocked by the Stone Sea that cannot be crossed by man nor beast. Even you couldn't survive there, so what I say is that you should just leave me to my fate and get out of here. What I most want at the moment is to kill that scoundrel Hatem Agha. If I could just kill him, then I would be able to contemplate death with absolute serenity."

"That's one piece of business that you could finish some other time. Now you listen to me. I'll lead you out of here. God knows that I couldn't bring myself to push the trigger yesterday. I didn't come here to save you or anything of that kind. I was just curious, wanted to talk to you."

Osman sighed,"I have no intention of staying around here. I'm sick and tired of this life. Moving from one mountain to the other—there's no end to it. I can't even sleep, in my overworked and nervous imagination even tree trunks and rabbits become men lying in ambush. The wind makes me nervous. I spend hours observing mountains, empty roads. So, I say, enough of this torture I've been inflicting on myself. The moment I can get rid of my pursuers, I intend to go far away. To Aleppo and from there to Beirut. I am planning on living in Beirut for a spell."

"Now, listen carefully—there is a way out."

"How?"

"From here we'll go directly to Stone Sea. There's a trail that goes around Stone Sea. Nobody has ever been able to go from there with a horse, but we'll try. I'll pull the horse while you hold its tail. If the horse doesn't shy, we can follow the trail, even if it is as narrow as a string. The trail will lead us directly to some vineyards. From there you can get to the reed marshes. After all you've been through, it'll be like a promenade."

"May Allah bless and keep you! Whatever else happens, let's not let our friendship die off."

"Don't worry. It was Hadji Dabak and Swamp Hasan who convinced me to do this. Hatem Agha corrupted them; he gave them money yesterday. I didn't take any money, but I admit that I did agree to catch you. Those people don't understand a thing about friendship or anything else like that. The only thing they're concerned about is being able to get their hands on some money. If I hadn't agreed to come hunting for you, they wouldn't have got the money that it seems they needed for their families. That's the only reason I did what I did. So isn't it ironic in a way that now I'm trying to save you?"

'Thank God that you came after me." Osman observed the environs once more with a thoughtful expression on his face. "All right, if it's true that this narrow trail of yours will lead me to the reed marshes, let's not lose any more time and let's get going while we still can."

"All right, let's go. We have a long way to travel. It was lucky that you didn't attempt to go through the Inecik pass. There was a detachment of gendarmes waiting for you there. If you had decided to go from there, they would be busy carrying your dead body to the town this very moment. The sergeant waited and waited and left his position only in the morning. Now you'll be able to go to the reed marshes without going through the pass."

It was already late afternoon, with the sun losing, slowly but inexorably, its brightness. The two friends got up and crossed the mound, then Osman fetched the horse and Amir Efe guided them towards the trail. Before leaving, Osman looked back at the valley with his binoculars. Not much had changed. There were still people and horses moving about the valley. A wounded horse was braying pitifully, with a trooper, miserable in his helplessness, trying to assist him.

Osman looked a little further up and saw that Hatem Agha and his friends were still lying in the grass. It was almost as if they had burrowed holes for themselves and become one with the earth. He fired a few shots and let loose a few more rocks and stones. Since the bulk of the troops had assembled on the south side of the valley, they weren't affected. The few gendarmes in harm's way hid behind big rocks. As before, the rocks broke into splinters after having rumbled noisily down the ravine.

Hearing the shots, Hatem Agha and his friends who, encouraged by the long silence, had decided that all danger had passed and were preparing to descend, flattened themselves even tighter against the ground. "Now it's you who has the upper hand, but if I'm still alive by nightfall, I'll teach you a thing or two," Hatem Agha was shouting.

Osman and Amir did not lose any more time. Osman put all his belongings in his woven saddlebag. He let his horse drink the last drops of water in his flask. By then the horse had rested and was once again his usual lively self. The two friends proceeded on foot leading the horse. Amir Efe was in front of the animal, while Osman was at the back. They climbed the narrow trail used only by partridges and goats. The trail was surrounded by fist sized stones green with moss, boulders big as houses, squat oaks the leaves of which were still green, and poplar trees with leaves rustling in the wind. They stepped on dry grasses and thorn bushes as they walked. In the springtime, when the oleasters were in bloom, these same places would be infested with black snakes. Now, with the snow almost completely gone, the snowdrop flowers were in bloom among the yellow grasses and in the shade of the rocks, enlivening the scenery.

They quickly reached the highest point of the trail. How many places were visible from there, each of them with their countless stories! The summit afforded a beautiful view of mountain plains and deep valleys. The whole region of this very center of Anatolia could be seen from this vantage point. From there the two men proceeded towards Erciyes in the south. The sun was quickly setting and the plain darkening, but the few waterways magnificently reflected the last rays of the sun. The air was misting over the town of Incesu. The sounds of the pelicans and wild geese on the Yay Lake, in the far distance, could be heard from there.

It had been years since Amir Efe had last been here, but he still remembered which rock, which bush, which group of blackberry plants he would see after the next turn. His hat on his head, his rifle on his shoulder, slightly stooped, he went forward along the trail with big and slightly nervous steps. Osman had difficulty keeping the same pace. The misty plain on their right had already gotten dark. The narrow goat trail passed along imposingly gigantic rock formations. It dipped and climbed along the terrain, but was always full of stones, which made passage extremely difficult and dangerous. They passed around smaller hills until they finally saw Stone Sea in front of them.

The Stone Sea stretched before them, a terrain that was impossible for either man or beast to transverse. One step on the stones would send the walker careening forward or under, swallowed by the sea of stones that sent the hapless person under an avalanche. Many of the stones along the trail that led along the edge of this death trap were also extremely precariously balanced and it was these that created the biggest danger for the tiny caravan, since an unguarded step could easily overturn these stones and hurt man and beast alike. If someone should happen to break a foot or a leg and if that someone, in the greatest of misfortunes, chanced to be alone, it was extremely unlikely that he would come out of that place alive, for he would have no hope of being able to crawl such a rocky trail. Such was this place that only partridges nested in its rocks and only animals ventured along it.

On the northern face of the Stone Sea there were still remnants of winter snow. Deep holes in the ground full of snow were even more of a danger. Amir Efe was conscious of all these dangers and approached Stone Sea with great care. Before proceeding, he studied the area carefully and pointed out their destination to Osman. An immense rock formation was visible further on, before the plain. It looked as if it had been standing there since the beginning of time. It was on the edge of a precipice and appeared to afford no passage of any kind. Gum and blackberry bushes and lichens had grown over it. The rock clearly had a past of millions of years. Amir Efe went forward with careful steps, checking the position and stability of each stone before stepping on it.

At first it looked as if the narrow trail were leading them towards the very center of Stone Sea, but later it turned in the direction of the plain, leading straight towards the massive rock formation. Once he had ascertained that everything was safe, Amir told Osman not to let the horse step anywhere but where he had just stepped himself.

Osman and the horse proceeded with the greatest care. So long as they stepped where Amir Efe had just stepped, there was no danger of stones overturning. God knows who had walked first along this route towards the majestic rock formation, inaugurating in a way what was to become the goat trail that the two friends and the horse were following. Its presence was barely visible and all it served was to avoid going through the pass.

Under the guidance of Amir Efe they traversed the area safe and sound. Amir Efe studied from a distance the remaining part of the trail and, not having noticed anything untoward, went on, beginning the descent. Osman, firmly gripping the bridle of the horse, gazed into the black emptiness below him and proceeding warily.

The sun had by then completely disappeared and Osman was following, step by step, Amir Efe's descent.

The trail was still extremely dangerous. Osman held fast to his horse and whispered endearments into his ear as if he were trying to explain the dangers they would encounter and how he was to proceed if they had to reach safety. The horse showed signs of restlessness, but did not panic. Like its master, it kept an eye on the precipice.

Parts of the trail were slippery and presented life threatening dangers. The slightest carelessness would have meant a dreadful death at the bottom of the precipice. Nevertheless, Osman went on, calculating each step while trying to see the road further on with his binoculars. Black crows wheeled and turned overhead, as if astonished by the presence of humans in such a God for-saken place.

Amir Efe, who had gone scouting, returned, stating that the trail was clear and that they would be able to follow it, provid-ed they were very careful. They removed all the packs on the horse, leaving only its bridle and bit. Amir Efe told Osman to hold the horse's tail to ensure his balance, while he himself took firm hold of the bridle. To the sound of many Bismillahs they went forward.

The trail they were following was barely large enough for the foot of a person and in many places even that narrow surface sloped towards the precipice. The horse displayed a quasi-human care in watching where it stepped, careful to walk along a straight line with all four hooves. At one point the trail got so narrow that the poor horse had to scrape through the rocks, bruising and cutting its skin. Never once did the poor sweat-soaked Osman let go of the horse's tail, nor did Amir Efe loosen his grip on the animal's bit, taking care to cover the eye of the horse on the side where the precipice loomed dangerously. Osman continuously talked to the horse to keep it from shying, but it looked as if the animal was giving the instructions.

Finally, after great exertions and nerve shattering trials, they found themselves in a field of stubbles. They had left behind the Stone Sea, which continued towards the west. The trail on the other side went on a little more among fields, until it melted in the vineyards visible further on.

The travelers were enormously relieved and stood in the midst of the stubble embracing the horse and congratulating it on its performance. The sense of relief they filled simply could not be put into words. They dried the horse, which looked as relieved and happy as its master. The two men once more took out their tobacco and rolled cigarettes, which they lit with their tinder lighters. Having caught their breath, Amir Efe was the first to get up as he headed back up among the rocks to retrieve the equipment they had left behind.

Osman looked towards the snow-capped summit of Erciyes among the clouds further south. They were very near the mountain it and it looked as if it had grown in size. He had once more been able to escape his pursuers, but the only place that would afford him safety now were foreign lands. After resting a bit in the reed marshes, he would proceed to Adana, and from there to Aleppo.

While reflecting happily on his escape, he was also busy planning his route from there on out. They had been able to reach the other side of the Inecik Pass. From the vineyards where they were at that moment, it would be very easy to reach the reed marshes. After hiding for a bit there, he would proceed to the Gap of the Arabs, from where he would reach Chamardi and the Taurus mountain range. On those mountains he would be in perfect safety. From there it would be Adana, Aintab, and Aleppo.

He thought of Major Ibrahim, whom he knew very well, and of Hatem Agha. His friends would look for him and, unable to find him, would conclude that once again he had mysteriously disappeared. Hatem Agha was even capable of claiming that he had eliminated him, but he couldn't care less what people said. What was important was that he would go to Beirut, find Agop, get Mehmet to send Hurmet, and findly achieve a little peace of mind. The existence of the letter in his breast pocket gave him confidence in the future.

It was at that moment that Amir Efe returned from the dangerous trail. He was carrying the woven saddlebag, the saddle, and the felt greatcoat. He had retrieved everything. Osman turning to him said, "May God reward you for what you did today Amir Efe. If it hadn't been for you, I wouldn't have been able to get out of that place. I couldn't have rid myself of Hatem Agha, nor of his scheming friends."

"Look," said Amir Efe, "the Inecik Pass is on our left, just behind those rocks you see over there. If you follow this narrow trail, you'll reach the lower vineyards. From there you can go either to Everek or to the Gap of the Arabs, but I think it would be best for you if you first went to the marsh islands where you could rest for a few days."

"I agree with you Amir Efe. I'll rest a little on one of the islands, wait for everything to settle down a bit, and then Allah will provide me with a further plan. Hatem Agha and the major will go on looking up there where we met. They must be convinced that nobody but a bird could go through Stone Sea. So when they can't find me, they'll really be very surprised. They'll say, 'Osman turned into a bird and flew away.' That's the only way they'll be able to explain my disappearance."

While Osman talked, he was also busy saddling the horse for the next part of the trip. He fixed the saddlebag onto the saddle and put on his felt greatcoat. Now he was completely ready. It was at that moment that he realized how hungry he was. He decided to share his bread with his friend. He took out from the saddlebag the biggest among the flat breads prepared by Chitoglu's wife and gave it to Amir Efe. At first Amir Efe did not want to take it. "Osman, never mind, there won't be any food where you're going, you should be more careful how you consume your bread and your water."

Nevertheless, he could not risk offending his friend by refusing the bread and so took it and swallowed it almost immediately.

"Yes," said Osman. "I really think that the moment for the last farewell has arrived. Forgive me if I have wronged you in any way."

"You've no debt of any kind Osman; don't worry."

The two friends embraced. Amir Efe stroked Osman's back, while Osman solemnly kissed both of Amir's cheeks.

Osman left his friend and turned towards his horse. For one last time he turned and looked back at Amir Efe, who was looking at him from under his hat, with shiny eyes. He mounted, and with a wave of his hand galloped down the slope.

For a long time, the sound of the horse's hoofs on the rocky path echoed in the stillness of the night.

Amir Efe had been left there with his rifle in his hands. He saw again the shadow of the galloping horse in the distant glen and that was it. He looked towards the marshes where he imagined seeing the very last glimmer of the sun. With a sigh he said, "Allah willing, he will become a more sensible person over there and I hope he will also finally sleep in a normal bed."

From that day on, no one heard anything about Osman. Some claimed that he had been killed, while others claimed more simply that he had just flown away. Some noticed that Hurmet also disappeared a few months later, but decided not to voice their suspicions. The families of White Horse were happy that peace was restored to their vineyards and that they were finally free from the raids of the gendarmes, but in their hearts, everyone missed the presence of the shadow that embraced the mountains.

For some reason, though, that spring the rose colored starlings did not come to the vineyards. The partridges did not sing at the Brave Rock nor on the Barley Mountain. The glens and the shadows of the rocks remained empty. That summer the vineyard owners faced a dry, rainless season. Families broke the silence of the night with stories, stories about the rider, his bravery, and their dreams.

1996-1998
Süleyman Sağlam

Stories from the Sandgate

Jaklin Çelik

In her first book of short stories, Jaklin Çelik brings the panorama that is Istanbul's "Kumkapı", its "Sandgate", to life. Whether it's the young woman passing out cigarettes at the women's ward or the transvestite prostitute infuriating her neighbor; the middle-aged Onnik going on a long-awaited date or fisherman Mıgırdıç arguing with his senile wife; the old man Kirkor in search of a young bride or the tough Kurdish mama Hazal on her first trip to Istanbul, these brief glimpses into the lives of Armenians, Kurds, and Turks who are pushed and pulled by the energy of the cosmopolitan neighborhood is certain to draw you in...

Stories from the Sandgate
Jaklin Çelik - 121 pages,
Isbn: 975-6663-12-X
Price: 10.000.000 TL

Çitlembik Publications
Tel: 0 212 292 30 32 / 252 31 63
Fax: 0 212 293 34 66
www.citlembik.com.tr
kitap@citlembik.com.tr

Nettleberry, LLC
44030 123rd Street
Eden, South Dakota 57232
www.nettleberry.com

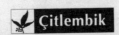
Çitlembik